Vanessa Alexander lives in Essex with her family. She is a keen historian and a full-time writer. She is also the author of THE LOVE KNOT – 'a richly evocative novel . . . Completely immersed in the colours, scents, sounds and ambience of medieval life' *Historical Novel Review*

OF LOVE
AND WAR

Vanessa Alexander

HEADLINE

First published in Great Britain in 2000
by HEADLINE BOOK PUBLISHING
First published in paperback in 2001 by
HEADLINE BOOK PUBLISHING

10 9 8 7 6 5 4 3 2 1

ISBN 0 7472 6464 3

Typeset by Palimpsest Book Production Limited,
Polmont, Stirlingshire
Printed and bound in Great Britain by
Mackays of Chatham plc, Chatham, Kent

HEADLINE BOOK PUBLISHING
A division of Hodder Headline
338 Euston Road
London NW1 3BH

www.headline.co.uk
www.hodderheadline.com

Chapter 1

Major Oscar Fairfax drew deeply on his cigarette. He stared through the half-lowered carriage window as if admiring the different greens of the countryside.

The businessman, sitting in the opposite corner, studied the officer closely: the thin face, the furrows around the mouth, the perfectly stencilled moustache along the upper lip, the long nose and those large but seemingly dead dark eyes. A soldier, the businessman concluded, who had definitely fought in the Great War. Very much the officer, with his gleaming boots, light khaki trousers and dark-brown jacket. The shirt and tie matched the trousers; the flat cap and the heavy coat piled beside the officer showed the silver flashes of a major. Similar emblems studded the shiny leather tanned belts across his shoulder and round his waist.

Fairfax glanced across at the businessman, a bored, supercilious stare. The businessman refused to hold his gaze and looked out of the window. The countryside was beginning to give way to outlying farms, the criss-crossed rusting tracks used by the mines and, on a distant hill, the black skeletal scaffolding of a disused pithead. The businessman knew little about the army but concluded the officer was not from one of the Durham regiments, certainly not the Glorious 68th. Fairfax opened his silver cigarette case. He was about to take one out then smiled thinly at the red-faced businessman studying him from head to toe.

'Do you want one?'

The cigarette case was not within the businessman's reach.

'What were you in the war?' Fairfax asked.

'In iron and steel,' the businessman huffed. 'Supplying our boys with tanks, rifles and bullets.' The businessman's fat neck strained like a chicken against his high, white collar. He was about to stretch out his hand and take a cigarette when the case was snapped shut and summarily withdrawn.

Fairfax turned away as if he had already forgotten his companion's existence. The businessman's face turned puce at the insult. Out of the corner of his eye he studied the red flashes on Fairfax's sleeves. They indicated he was part of the military police, an officer from the Provost Marshal's Office. What on earth was he doing in Durham? Hunting out deserters, men who'd fled the ranks? The businessman had read about such cases in the *Northern Echo*. The British Army never forgot. The Great War had finished three years ago but the Crown was still hunting down culprits. If only the arrogant bastard would talk! The businessman would love to collect a bit of scandal. Tell his colleagues in Newcastle how he had been the confidant of this enigmatic officer. He took out a blue-dotted handkerchief and blew his nose noisily, a gesture of contempt.

Major Fairfax had taken out a cigarette and was beating it on the silver embossed lid. He put it between his lips and stared out of the window. He played absent-mindedly with the thick leather strap which drew the window up and down. Smoke from the engine billowed out, rolling down the train. Fairfax watched it rise and disappear against the blue August sky. He remembered the shell bursts above the Somme, columns of white, drifting smoke. He'd often wondered if they were the souls of those killed being wafted up to heaven. An idle thought; the truth was so different. Fairfax closed his eyes. No matter how long he stared at any rural scene, painted or real, the landscape of hell always came back: lacerated, bullet-stricken trees, shell craters, trench holes. Bombs, muffled or shrieking, falling like an iron rain, columns of earth whooshing up and crashing down in a screed of dust and stones. Trenches knee deep in red-coloured mud, smoke-wreathed skies, the mad tap-tap of the machine guns, blazing sheets of orange or deep red, spouts of flame, poisoned gas like liquid mustard drifting across. The only protection for his mouth, nose and eyes had been a rag soaked in his own urine.

Even here, in this carriage, reeking of leather upholstery and cigarette smoke, the stench of war came curling back. That terrible odour of disembowelled, fetid, blackening, swollen, blood-soaked corpses. What time was it? The unlit cigarette slipped from Fairfax's mouth. What did it matter? In the war, day had slipped into night without his even noticing it. Attack and counter-attack. Barbed wire tearing at face and hands. The dead lying around. A headless corpse, the serene, smiling face of one young man sitting in the trench where he had fallen back, as if preparing for a picnic. And the others! Those who had died lashed to a post, waiting for the order, the grim drill of the firing squad. Fairfax opened his eyes. He no longer saw the greenery but black, barren stumps of trees, stretching up against the sky like the topsails of a sunken ship.

'I wish you'd stop that!'

Fairfax broke from his reverie. He glanced sharply at the businessman who was pointing at Fairfax's boot. He'd been hitting it hard against the carriage door. Fairfax picked up the cigarette and lit it even as the shrill blast of the whistle informed him that they would soon be in Caundon. He got up, took his briefcase and traveller's bag from the luggage net above him, put on his coat and hat, sat down and finished the cigarette. The train slowed down in a screech of iron and steel. Caundon station with its hard stone platform, fretted wooden roof, fly-blown windows and fading posters came into view. Every piece of wood, Fairfax grimly noted, had been painted a dull green, just like an army post. The train creaked to a stop, shuddering backwards and forwards. Fairfax waited, lowered the window further and opened the door.

'And what did you do in the war, Daddy?' the businessman asked spitefully.

Fairfax climbed down. He turned to collect his luggage. 'What did you do, dear?'

The businessman was glaring at him. He knew he was safe, the train would be pulling out soon. Fairfax lifted his head. The businessman wished he had kept his mouth shut as those sombre eyes studied him closely. Fairfax seemed unaware of the train's imminent departure. He was staring at the businessman, remembering his face.

'I wouldn't ask that question again,' Fairfax declared.

He pulled his baggage out, put it on the platform and made to close the door. He pulled it open again.

'If you want to know, I shot cowards.' He smiled, swinging

4

the door backwards and forwards. 'But the war ended before I could get to bastards like you!'

He slammed the door shut, picked up his luggage and walked down the platform. Stationmaster Thompson came striding up, his untidy white hair clamped by a neat cap, his black waistcoat heavily stained with pipe ash. He paused, pulled out his fob watch, nodded to himself, lifted the green flag and blew hard on the whistle. The train's pistons screeched, puffs of smoke billowed up as it pulled slowly out. Fairfax stood as if uncertain where to go. Thompson waddled up.

'Business or pleasure?' he chortled. It was his standard question to all strangers.

'Justice,' Fairfax replied. He opened his warrant card and handed the rail ticket to Thompson.

The stationmaster was perplexed. 'What do you mean, man, justice?'

'A joke,' Fairfax said. 'For now, the Beaumont Arms.'

'Ah, the Allertons' place.'

'Yes, the Allertons' place,' Fairfax echoed. 'Where is it?'

'Down the street,' Thompson replied. 'This is Caundon. One high street.' His voice faltered. 'We are not used to the likes of you. Mind you,' he added wistfully, 'we used to be.' Thompson put the whistle into his trouser pocket, his popping eyes stared down the platform.

'This is where they used to gather,' he said. 'All the lads, the boys going off to the front. Not many of them came back. On a morning like this, such memories surface. You half close your eyes and you can see them all: a sea of khaki, the women all tearful, the children running around. Poor buggers thought they were going on a holiday. Full of stories about France,

5

the mademoiselles and what they'd do. Those who returned didn't talk like that. They wandered back like ghosts. You'd ask them about France; they'd just shake their heads and push by you. You never dared ask: "How's Tommy? How's Bill?" If they weren't there, they were dead. Eventually my turn came. Lost a lad, I did.'

'Where?' Fairfax asked. But he knew the answer before it was given.

'Where do you think?' Thompson glanced at him. 'He's with the legion of dead on the Somme. Couldn't even find his body. One soldier told me if all the dead came back to life, they'd stand like a field of corn along the Somme. Were you there, sir?'

But Fairfax had picked up his luggage and was already walking down the platform. He didn't want to talk about the Somme or Ypres, any of those places filled with mounds of ash-grey dead, of corpses swimming in mortar-made pools, unless it was connected with his business, the task in hand. Fairfax never discussed the war. Even his fellow officers left him alone. Fairfax was a man with a mission, that's why he was here in Caundon.

He went out of the station and realised it stood on the gently sloping brow of a hill. Caundon lay below him. Fairfax looked through the thick, smoke-blackened window of the station-master's office. The large, round clock on the wall showed eleven thirty. Beside it the calendar should have proclaimed the day's date, 21 August 1921; instead it displayed 8 July 1916 as if Thompson's life had ended then. Fairfax shifted his gaze and looked down the high street. Two facing rows of terraced houses. Doors opened and slammed. A few children played with a broken pram. Chimneys coughed smoke. At the far end Fairfax glimpsed the pithead with its double arch of pulling wheels, the rusting stanchions, girders and steel ropes. The breeze smelt of grime and coal. A pit lorry, battered and noisy, swung out from the station's coal yard and clattered back along the street towards the pithead.

'Mister!'

Fairfax glanced to his left. The station children had been watching this new arrival from their usual vantage point. Three in all. Mary, Michael and Joan Ashcroft. Good Catholic names, their father had boasted, but he was now gone; went to France and didn't return. Their mother had been left to scrub her steps, wash their clothes and do what anyone else wanted to earn a few pennies. The Ashcroft children spent their time around the station, waiting for arrivals, hoping to beg a penny or two. This one certainly looked rich, his boots were so shiny, everything spick-and-span.

'Mister, do you have a penny?' Mary was the eldest; her face was thin and white as any waif, a tattered dress, two sizes too big for her, hung down just above her bare feet. She pulled back her hair from her grimy face and tried to look enticing. Sometimes this worked. People felt sorry.

Fairfax studied her and glanced away. He dropped the cigarette, lifted his luggage and walked into Caundon. Behind him the children fought for the cigarette. Fairfax kept to the middle of the street. He was aware of tawdry curtains and blinds being pulled back, doors opening and shutting. The children playing with the pram had disappeared up an alleyway. He passed the large corner shop, posters in its windows and fruit packed in boxes outside. The large red sign above the door proclaimed 'Grant's: Family Grocer'.

'Edmund Grant,' Fairfax murmured. 'The father of Stephen

7

Grant, shot for desertion at La Boiselle, spring nineteen seventeen. I'll be paying you a visit, Master Grant.'

A door was flung open. A tousled, red-haired man stepped out, dressed in shirt, trousers and battered shoes. He was young with a florid face. He knelt down on the flagstoned pavement and, with a piece of chalk, began to draw frantically whilst talking to some invisible presence. Fairfax gripped his luggage tightly and watched the scene. Ah yes, he thought: Robert Daventry, known to his friends as Bob. Corporal Bob Daventry of the Durham Light Infantry. He walked across.

'What's the matter?' Fairfax asked.

The man lifted his head: dirty face, wild staring eyes. He patted his side frantically and pointed at the door as if Fairfax could see whoever was standing on the step.

'I'm having my cup of beef tea!' he shouted. 'Having a cup of beef tea on a Saturday morning. Just sitting there by the table. Old Millsey comes in! Shot through the left hip, Millsey was. Pierced his bowels. He got tangled on a wire, along with the rest, like dead flies on flypaper. "Millsey", I said, "what the hell are you doing here? I buried you." I did, you know. Grabbed his corpse from the wire, him and the rest. Put them in a ditch, one of those great mortar holes. I shovelled the mud over. Now he's returned, like the others come back, just when I'm having my beef tea. So I bring him out here. I'm drawing a map.'

Fairfax stared down at the haphazard drawing on the pavement.

'That's why I carry plenty of chalk,' Daventry chattered. 'Buy it at Grant's. I always show them where they are buried. Then they leave me alone. If they don't, I've got a shovel. I take them out to the woods and I—'

'Attention!' Fairfax barked.

Daventry shot to his feet, stiff as a ramrod, heels together, arms slightly out, hands down to his side, head slightly up.

'At ease, Corporal Daventry!'

'You heard the officer,' Daventry shouted at the invisible presence. 'At ease!' Daventry spread his feet and put his hands behind his back.

'Who are you talking to, Corporal?' Fairfax asked.

'Old Millsey here. We were in a fire trench. Captain George, he's the one that got his head blown off, well, that was a week later. He says, "Millsey, go over there towards the wire, see what's happening." Old Millsey leaves, crawls on his belly, he does. He has to have a good look, hasn't he? Up he gets. That's when the sniper got him.' Daventry's face became puzzled. 'Captain George was really upset. He said that there were at least three snipers. Anyway, sir, as I have said, Millsey took it in the bowels and, of course, he got stuck on the wire and none of us dared move. Terribly hot, sir. All we had was some old brandy and that made our thirst worse. Millsey took hours to die. We got drunk on brandy, roaring with thirst, till some Australians came and relieved us.' Daventry abruptly recollected where he was, his face and body fell slack. He glanced fearfully at Fairfax. 'What's the matter, sir? Why am I here?'

And, before Fairfax could stop him, he flung himself at the door and disappeared inside. Fairfax let him go. He was about to continue his walk when a door further up the street opened and a priest stepped out. He wore a battered trilby, his black suit was rather shiny. He carried a shabby Gladstone bag. He paused, took off his hat and came forward, hand extended.

'We don't often have strangers here. I'm Father Tom

Headon, parish priest of St Bede's. Caundon,' he added proudly, 'has its own Catholic church and school.'

The priest was small, thickset with a florid face and bushy white hair. It was a friendly, open approach but the light-blue eyes were guarded as if he was trying to stifle his suspicions.

Fairfax grasped the priest's hand slowly as if he had been debating the matter. He shook it coldly. 'Why didn't you ask me, Father, who I was? You know my insignia. You've served in the army yourself, haven't you? As a young chaplain. Weren't you at Spion Kop in South Africa?'

'You seem to know all about me.' The priest put his hat back on and switched the Gladstone bag from one hand to the other. 'Do you have the gift of second sight, Major Fairfax? Major Oscar Fairfax, isn't it, from the Provost Marshal's Office in London?' The priest's face and tone had turned chilly.

Fairfax was enjoying himself. He tapped the briefcase against his knee then put it down on the pavement. He was about to take his cigarette case out but thought again.

'At a guess, Father, you've been visiting Widow Kavanagh. Sixty years old, isn't she? With rotting lungs? You've taken her the Sacrament?'

The priest's face was now hard set. He took a step closer and stared up at the impassive officer. 'I've met you before, Major Fairfax.'

'I don't think I've had the pleasure, Father.'

'I mean I've met your type before,' the priest said. He scratched his unshaven cheek. 'Yes, I've been to see Widow Kavanagh. I've given her the Eucharist and, before four o'clock this evening, I hope to have visited all the sick in Caundon. A good number of them are Catholics. They come from Scotland, Ireland or Northumberland to work in the mines. They are decent, hard-working people. They would like to have a proper wage and good houses. Most of the men fought for King and country, many of them did not come home.'

'So, you know why I am here, Father?'

'I can guess why you are here. Colonel Morrison . . .'

'Ah yes, Colonel Morrison. I must go and have a chat with him as well.'

'He hinted at why you have come. Sniffing out sin, Major? Searching out defaulters?'

Fairfax studied the priest's rubicund face, the hard eyes, the firm set of lips and jaw.

'Are you going to denounce me, Father, from the pulpit? I am the King's officer. I carry his commission. In fact, I am fulfilling one of Christ's commandments: "To bear witness to the truth".'

'Do you read the Gospels, Major? Even Satan can quote Scripture.'

Fairfax laughed, his eyes twinkling in amusement. 'So, that's who you think I am, Father, Old Nick himself.'

'No, I don't.' The priest was about to turn away but then, gripping the bag, tilted the rim of his hat back as he searched for words. 'Colonel Morrison has a great library.' He glanced up at Fairfax. 'He always lets me borrow a book or two. Have you ever heard of Matthew Hopkins, Major?'

'The Witch-Finder General?'

'Yes, Major Fairfax, the Witch-Finder General. During the seventeenth century he used to prowl the Essex villages and accuse this person or that of witchcraft, stir up hysteria,

11

release pent-up wrongs and hurts, shatter communities before he went hunting somewhere else.'

Fairfax decided to take out a cigarette. He lit it slowly.

'Are you a witch-finder, Fairfax?'

'No, Father, but something like it. I come to search out hidden, serious sin.'

'Sin? So you believe in God, Major Fairfax?'

'I used to – before he was killed on the Somme.'

'It's August now.' Kitty Allerton sat on the edge of the bed and made herself comfortable. 'The weather's remained fine but rather cloudy. Mother's well but dreamy-eyed, a little weepy at times. Jack's fine. He won't help out here. He says he was born a miner.' She laughed. 'He insists he will die as one. We have a good life. The pay in the mines has not yet improved but there are rumours. Jack told me about a man called Sankey who's recommended that the mines be taken over by the government once and for all. Jack and the lads still play football. They meet every Saturday with the Dead Hand Club in the snug of the far corner of the bar.' She shifted her gaze. 'Sometimes I stand and watch them. I feel you very close. School's going well and the papers are talking of great changes there. Father Headon says that, later on in the year, after the harvest is in, he will call a meeting. The schoolroom's not much, still in the parish hall. The same desks with the same faded blackboard, crumbling chalk and cracked globe. Some of the children come in without shoes. In winter it takes some time to get the boiler going. Silly, isn't it? In a mining village you'd think there'd be no lack of coal.' Kitty Allerton paused and re-arranged the folds of her thick grey dress. 'One of the women found an old catalogue from London, one of those big stores. The fashions have all changed. Look at my dress just above the ankles!' Kitty stretched out a foot and waggled one brown polished shoe. 'And the hairstyles! Eeh, we did have a good laugh! I tried to copy them. I think you'd like it.'

Kitty turned and stared at the faded mirror on the dresser. You do look like a schoolmarm, she thought. Her jet-black hair was parted down the middle and rolled into bobs round her ears, the white collar of the dress especially starched by her mother.

'If you were here you'd ask me why I am dressed like this. Well, it's Saturday and we have a visitor. Ten days ago a letter came from the War Office about a Major Oscar Fairfax. No one knows why he is coming here. I asked Father Headon but he just shook his head, said it was none of his business. Jack looks a little worried. Mind you, you know the way he is. Furrowing his brows and screwing up his eyes. When I mentioned Oscar Fairfax's name he just scratched his head, muttered something and turned away. Everyone else is fine,' Kitty chattered on. 'Jim Cunningham makes everyone laugh. He says Karl Marx – do you know who he is?' Anyway, Jim was saying in the bar last Saturday night that Marx is the new Holy Ghost. He still insists on blaspheming outside church. Bob Daventry, poor man, is still seeing visions. Every so often he goes out in the countryside and digs. Dr Martin says if he doesn't improve he may have to go to a hospital near Sedgefield. And the German, Ernst Kurtz – he has settled down here! Rather sweet on our Betty, he is. She's the girl who helps in the bar. She was only knee high to a buttercup when you left. Tom O'Neill is the same as ever and Len Evans is a policeman.'

Kitty stopped and listened to the sounds of the small hotel her mother managed. Clanking from the cobbled yard below. The splash of someone using the water pump followed by the shrill blast from the minehead.

'Jack will be coming home soon, Billy.'

'Kitty!'

The battered door opened. Her mother came through. She looked as anxious as ever. Kitty noticed how pale her face was, wiry grey hair turning to white. Her mother just stared at her.

'Have you forgotten?' Kitty asked.

'Have I forgotten what?'

'You came to see me.' Kitty laughed. 'What is it you want, Mother?'

Her mother looked at the faded, gilt-edged photograph on the dresser, laced with a piece of black ribbon.

'I see you're talking again.'

'I always talk to Billy.'

'You shouldn't really. I'd like your help downstairs.'

Kitty nodded but the door was already closing, wafting in the smell of the dish they called Cousin Jim, which Mother was cooking in the kitchen below.

'Liver and onions,' Kitty murmured. 'You'd like that, wouldn't you, Billy? I have a poem. I saw it in the book Father Tom brought. It's by a Jesuit: "Elected silence sing to me and beat upon my whorled ear—"'

'Kitty!' Her mother's voice was now strident. 'Kitty, if you are ready.'

Her daughter got up and moved across to the photograph on the dresser. She had bought the frame specially three years ago at a miners' gala. The gilt edge was becoming a little faded

14

and her mother had told her to keep the photograph out of the sunlight. She stared at the youthful face it contained: the gentle eyes, the humorous mouth and the black hair, smartly combed back, parting down one side.

'You hated photographs,' Kitty murmured. 'I wish you hadn't been wearing a uniform.'

She picked the photograph up, kissed it then held it away to study it more carefully.

'Mother says I shouldn't talk to you but that's foolish. I've been talking to you for years. You, me and Jack.'

'Kitty!'

She opened the top drawer of the dresser and slipped the photograph in along with her best gloves, worsted stockings, the ribbon choker Billy had bought her at the fair. She closed the drawer and looked round the room. Jack had done well here. He was a good hand at plastering and had put up a ceiling to cover the beams. The wardrobe had been scraped down and re-polished. The fire grate was empty; the cold weather hadn't come in yet.

'Kitty!'

She sighed, opened the door, went along the landing and down the narrow, winding stairs built close to the wall. The Beaumont Arms had once been a coaching house, the stairs led directly into the porch. She turned left and went into the small office. From there she could see into the bar. Edmund Grant the grocer, fat-faced and well-dressed, sat drinking his customary bottle of stout. Nearby, lost in his own thoughts, was the tall, dark-haired Ernst Kurtz. She heard harsh footsteps and looked over the counter. The passageway down to the small lounge and parlour was always dark, even in summer. She glimpsed a tall figure, brass buttons on his

15

coat, and noticed the briefcase and bag leaning against the far wall. Her mother came out of the bar, all flustered.

'Kitty, this is Major Oscar Fairfax.'

The officer stepped into the light streaming through the door. Kitty was immediately struck by his eyes: pieces of hard glass. A very handsome face but like that of a picture she had seen or one of the statues going up on the village war memorial, cleanly chiselled, rather harsh. 'Hard of face, hard of heart.' Kitty recalled the old proverb.

Fairfax remembered his manners and took off his hat. He put it on the counter and peeled off his leather gloves. Kitty shook his hand; the grip was strong though the skin was soft and warm. She caught a whiff of fine soap and tobacco.

'Major Oscar Fairfax. You must be Kitty Allerton.'

'How long are you staying?' She didn't mean to be so abrupt but the man unnerved her, standing and staring at her like that.

'I don't really know. Possibly a week.'

Kitty pulled across the inkpot and turned the ledger round. 'You have to fill it in,' she declared. 'During the war the police were very strict.'

'Of course.'

'There's a room on the second floor,' Kitty said quickly. 'I am afraid we haven't got a porter. Old John pretends to be one but he likes his drink and isn't usually around till the afternoon. My mother will take you up.'

Fairfax grasped the pen, dipped it into the inkpot and wrote his name alongside the date. In the column marked 'Reason for visit', he entered 'Official'. He put the pen back, turned the ledger round and pushed it towards Kitty.

'I've travelled far,' he said.

Kitty gestured towards the bar. 'We are cooking. A bottle of stout, some ale?'

'I would prefer tea. Is it possible for me to have tea?'

Kitty couldn't understand why she felt so frightened of this tall, dark-haired officer, his hair carefully groomed back, that fine moustache, the gentle voice with a tinge of harshness. A man completely sure of himself. He didn't move away or look around.

'You can come to the kitchen,' Kitty offered.

Fairfax smiled; his face became boyish. 'I thought you'd never ask.'

And, taking his bag, he followed Kitty's mother up the stairs to his room. Kitty fiddled with a small bell on the counter. Betty, red-faced, came bustling out of the bar, her hair all awry, her apron drenched in a dark-brown liquid. Her bright button eyes glared at Kitty.

'I've spilt some bloody ale. I'm always spilling the bloody ale!' Betty bustled down the passageway to change.

Kitty stood waiting. She heard her mother's voice. Fairfax followed her downstairs.

'You like the room?' Kitty asked.

Fairfax lit a cigarette and pulled on it. 'It's a good room. Clean and . . .' He chose his words carefully. 'Most appropriate.'

'Appropriate? And you think a cup of tea is also appropriate?'

Fairfax smiled.

Kitty asked her mother to look after the ledger. She raised the flap and led Fairfax down to the kitchen at the back of the hotel. She felt slightly embarrassed, her face was flushed.

17

Fairfax made her feel rather scruffy with his immaculate clothes and polished boots.

Kitty, however, was proud of their kitchen: spacious, stone-flagged, with a long scrubbed pine table, polished oak benches on either side, and a huge open dresser in the corner for cups and crockery; a soaring fireplace with pelmet and ornaments – clay pipes and figurines bought at fairs. Kitty had always been in awe of the range, with its huge iron hotplates and ovens on either side. Forks and skillets hung from hooks above it. The fire of log and peat had been allowed to burn low. She grasped a cloth and placed the kettle on the iron grille above the fire, and, taking down two cups, placed them on the table.

'What's that smell?' Fairfax sat down on a corner of the bench.

Kitty pushed a large metal tray her father had used when smoking his pipe in front of him. He thanked her with his eyes.

'It's Cousin Jim.' Kitty pointed to a pot bubbling on the stove. 'Liver, bacon, potatoes. We then thicken the gravy. Would you like to try some when it's ready?'

'I did say I would have my meals here.'

Kitty felt uncomfortable. She ladled hot water into the pot to warm it before going to the side door to throw the water out. She wondered how Major Fairfax's wife made tea. China pots, she supposed. Both Billy and Jack had talked about army officers. 'Talk like ladies, fight like wild cats,' Kitty remembered. 'Very posh.'

'Are you married?' she asked. The question was out before she could stop it.

'I once was. She died in the great influenza epidemic.'

Kitty glanced up. 'I'm sorry.'

'She was always frail,' Fairfax replied. 'Like a lily.' He shook his head. 'Then she was gone. Death is a constant companion, isn't it, Mrs Allerton? Your father's dead?'

'He volunteered as soon as the war began. Killed in the first few weeks . . .'

'Along with the rest,' Fairfax finished the sentence. 'People don't realise, Mrs Allerton, that an entire British army was wiped out in months.'

'You can call me Kitty,' she said over her shoulder. 'Mrs Allerton sounds so formal. Everyone calls me Kitty.'

'You've had many names, haven't you?'

Kitty blushed. She turned and stared at this officer.

'I didn't mean to be uncouth,' he apologised.

'I was born Courtney,' she declared.

'And then you married Billy Hammond.'

'Billy died.' Kitty felt her famous temper beginning to boil. 'He was killed and I married Jack.'

'I am sorry.' Fairfax took out his cigarette case. 'Do you smoke?'

'No, I don't, I'm not from London!' Kitty turned her back on him and finished making the tea. She poured it out and hurried to the buttery, pleased to be away from this inquisitive officer. She took the cloth off the milk jug and took it into the kitchen. Fairfax was now standing up. He came across holding both cups. Kitty wished he hadn't. She noticed one of the cups was cracked and tried to keep her hands steady as she poured in the milk.

'I have no sugar,' she said.

'It doesn't matter.'

Fairfax took the cups back to the table, placed one down for Kitty and then sat opposite her. Kitty was very flustered and she sensed Fairfax was enjoying this. She took a deep breath and remembered a group of rowdy school children she had had to confront. She fought to stay calm and stared across at him. I'll study you as closely as you are studying me, she thought: the dark eyebrows, the straight nose, thin lips, the slight pucker in the chin, the well-groomed moustache, the hair with the short sideburns, finally his hands. She noticed the mark where his wedding ring had been and the thick leather watch strap beneath the cuff. He sipped his tea.

'Very nice,' he murmured. 'One thing I can't stand about stations is the tea they make. Or should I say brew? Well.' He rubbed his brow. 'I'm tired. Perhaps I shall sleep well tonight.' He looked round the kitchen as if fascinated by the hooks embedded in the beam, the raised clothes rail. 'Tell me about the Beaumont Arms. How do you call it in the north-east? A grand place?'

'It's big enough,' Kitty replied. 'Caundon was once on the main stagecoach route; that's why we have the yard and stables. A coaching house they called it. My father's people held it for generations. It's falling into disrepair now and is partly owned by the brewery, but we have tenants' rights. My mother manages it.'

'Do you have many visitors?'

'Salesmen passing through. It hasn't the luxuries of a London hotel.' She laughed. 'In fact Caundon hasn't yet got gas, electricity and running water, not like you'll find in Durham or Newcastle.'

'Tell me,' Fairfax pushed his cup away, 'what sort of place is Caundon?'

'It's a mining village fallen on hard times. Once it was a great staging post; the farmers used to bring their produce in. The steam engine came and life changed. Now it's coal. Most of the men work down the mines. They are, like other miners, fighting the owners for better pay, better conditions. They are good people.' Kitty held Fairfax's gaze. 'Most of them are immigrants.'

Fairfax studied the olive-skinned woman with her clear grey eyes. He noticed how fine her hair was, well kept, the spotless grey dress, its crisp white collar. In a ballgown, he thought, walking into the Ritz, she'd certainly make heads turn.

'Are you the daughter of an immigrant?'

'Oh, Mother said there are Italians in the family tree. People came here looking for work. A good number of them are Catholics – Irish, Italians. We even have a German.'

'Ah, Ernst Kurtz.'

Kitty sipped her tea. 'He's a strange one. He was captured during the first few months of the war. One of those Germans shipped across the Channel. He tried to escape a number of times but, when the war ended, he didn't go home. He's a good carpenter and an even better butcher. He owns a small shop at the far end of the town. He buys small livestock, slaughters it and sells the meat fresh.'

'Why didn't he go home?'

Kitty lifted her head, her beautiful butterfly eyes dancing with mischief. You think you're the clever one, Major Fairfax, Kitty thought. You walk into Caundon as if visitors like you are an everyday occurrence. You're here for a reason. You probably know all there is to know about us.

Fairfax, however, remained unabashed. 'The German?' he insisted. 'Why does he stay here?'

'Why don't you ask him yourself? It's his business.'

Fairfax smiled and undid the top button of his jacket.

21

'Come on, Major Fairfax.' Kitty batted her eyelids. 'You probably know more about Kurtz than I do. My Jack says that Kurtz is a deserter, that he deliberately wandered into the British lines with his hands up, and his attempts at escape were only to fool the others.'

Fairfax didn't reply. He lifted his cup and seemed engrossed by the large fireplace. Oh yes, the woman was right. He knew a lot about Kurtz – deserter, traitor. Reports from Berlin talked of the Frei Korps patrolling the streets of the city, organised bands of soldiers, searching for those responsible for Germany's defeat. Kurtz would never go home to face the wrath of his comrades, perhaps even a court-martial.

'We were talking about Caundon,' he declared. 'I'll deal with Kurtz.' He lifted the cup.

'Why should you deal with Kurtz?' Kitty asked sharply. 'What are you really here for, Major Fairfax?'

'I am making inquiries.'

'About what?'

'Oh, this and that. But you were telling me about Caundon.'

'I've told you what there is. It's built in a T shape: one high street, the main road cuts across. We have shops, we have mines, oil lamps in the streets. Some of us are very poor, none of us are rich, except Grant the grocer.'

'And the war?' Fairfax said. 'The war changed everything, didn't it?'

Chapter 2

Bob Daventry was in Nightshade Woods near Neville's Oak. According to local lore, during a great battle many years ago Roger de Neville had been caught by his enemies and hanged from one of its branches. Locals claimed his ghost still haunted the windswept fields and lonely glades.

Bob Daventry didn't care. He was used to ghosts. They sat round his table, followed him down the streets, said hello and raised their hands. They were all dressed in khaki, of course, friends and acquaintances, comrades in arms. They'd known him since they'd left Caundon, going by train to Darlington or Bishop Auckland when the Great War had broken out. Daventry had gone with them, singing the songs of the music halls. All a great adventure! The train hurtling south, the shared companionship, the boiling, milkless tea, the cigarette smoke thick and heavy, uniforms rough on the skin, boots which pinched. The sea crossing – everyone was sick – followed by the long slog up those strange French country lanes. Bob Daventry paused, leaning on his shovel. And so it began. Who was first to go? Ah yes, Charlie Ashcroft who'd bought it from a sniper within a month of landing in France.

Bob always remembered that morning. They were waiting by a canteen, in the distance the crump of guns and the snap of rifle fire. Headquarters had warned them to be careful but Charlie was always curious.

'I told you not to go up the road,' Bob said crossly. 'But not you, Charlie, always curious. That's why we called you Curious Charlie.'

Daventry stared at the deep hole he had dug. He had come to re-bury Charlie again. Charlie was the first he had ever buried. Gone up that French road, he had, holding his mug of tea. A volley of shots rang out, men running and Charlie lying near a ditch, a great pool of blood seeping out of his head. The sniper had taken him straight through the eye.

Daventry kept digging. Sometimes he'd pause and wonder what he was doing here. He'd come back to Caundon after the war. He'd realised his old mother was dead and that he couldn't go back down the mines. He had tried that but they had turned him away. Sometimes old Dr Martin came down to see him, a gentle, cheery-faced old man who did it for kindness – Bob paid no subscription. Sometimes Dr Martin would bring a young woman to clean the kitchen. So, Daventry reflected, what had upset him this morning? Oh aye, that officer! It had been years since Daventry had met an officer. What was he here for? What did he intend to do? Daventry peered through the trees. He glimpsed the hay, cut and gathered into windrows to dry. This was just like the weather when he had first marched away. Daventry dug his spade into the soil and sat down.

'You'll have to wait, Charlie boy,' he muttered to the ghost. 'Old Bob's got things on his mind.'

In a tree not too far away a bird began to sing. Bob grasped those notes like he would the rail of a stair or a stick to lean on. Birdsong meant he must be back in Caundon, away from the landscape of hell where no birds ever sang. Bob stared down at the freshly dug pit. Charlie was no longer around. Like all the ghosts, he had an irritating habit of disappearing. Now what was he trying to remember? Daventry closed his eyes and concentrated. The officer with the flashes on his sleeves. He was not a field officer.

'Oh no, no,' Daventry muttered. 'He's from headquarters: the military police, the Redcaps. So, what was he doing in Caundon?' Daventry shivered. 'You started it.' He pointed across at Charlie who had now reappeared.

At the beginning of the fighting the officers always took care of the dead but within a few months no one really cared. They'd even shared their trenches with the dead. Corpses were used to reinforce the walls. Sometimes they were buried deep in the mud but rose back up, all rotting and stinking. It wasn't like that in the beginning. An officer had told him to bury Charlie; from that day onwards, Daventry had been the official stretcher-bearer, leader of every burial detail. His mates joked, called him the "undertaker" but regarded him as lucky. Daventry was never wounded. Never once in all that flying rain of shells, red-hot metal, screaming bullets or dropping bombs. He stared down at the deep hole. So, why had that officer arrived in Caundon this morning? Had he found out? Had they discovered that he had made mistakes, buried men alive? Not checked they were truly dead? Or was it something else? Something he had forgotten?

Daventry leaned back against a tree trunk. He recalled the battle where Billy, Kitty's man, had been killed. They had all moved forward, shells whistling overhead. One or two landed fairly close. Daventry had really seen nothing except the sides of the trench, the chalk underlay poking through the mud. What other memories? A row of steel helmets, the lifting, swaying shoulders of the men. The trees all black and stark. There was little light but, under the brims of helmets, Daventry had glimpsed living eyes, shifting restlessly in blank faces. Daventry licked his lips. There'd been a battle and, yes, they had taken refuge in that trench but the Germans had found out where they were and the shelling began again. Young Russell, the runner of the regiment, he had been thrown up into the air. A young lieutenant got himself shot by a sniper. And then what had happened? Ah yes, they had sheltered there all that night. The colonel had asked two of them to go on a reconnaissance patrol. Billy and Jack had volunteered.

'Go on!' Colonel Morrison had urged. 'Get forward, lads, and see what's happening.'

The colonel trusted Jack and Billy because they were the best of mates. They would look after each other. Both men had crawled out like worms through the mud, flat on their bellies, faces down, creeping into the night. Above them stardust, flares, and the swirling, pungent acrid smoke from the shells. They had all sheltered, waiting for Jack and Billy to return. The silence was shattered by the clatter of a machine gun. The colonel had got onto the firing platform, peering through his periscope, hoping the flashes of light would show him something. He'd said others were out there, scouts from the Berkshires further down the line. Jack and Billy should have come back. It wasn't a night raid, not one of those daring attempts to go out and pick up a German prisoner, just what the lads called a 'peek-a-boo', a quick look round and back.

The night wore on and still the missing soldiers didn't return. At dawn the colonel had tried to send a couple more lads out but the German machine-gunners forced them to retreat. The waiting had been tense. At last, just when they were giving up hope, they heard a cry and Jack, covered in mud, slipped into the trench. He sat gasping for a while.

'Where's Billy?' the colonel had asked.

'I don't know,' Jack had replied. 'We got separated in the darkness.'

Later in the morning an officer from divisional headquarters had come down. Reinforcements were moving up. They had fixed bayonets and gone over the top. Men running against the sky. Now and again some would drop quietly. Others would do a strange dance as the hail of bullets caught them. They'd been forced back but Daventry went searching for Billy. He had been crawling on his hands and knees like a wounded dog. Suddenly the ground had collapsed beneath him and he'd found himself in one of those yawning crater holes with Billy sprawled against the side; his stomach was gashed and there was a bullet wound in the side of his head.

'What are you doing here, Billy?' Daventry had asked.

Then he realised his comrade was dead and, by his boot – yes, that was it – by his boot was Jack's helmet. Daventry blinked and stared across at Neville's Oak. But that couldn't be because Jack had said he and Billy had become separated. Daventry suddenly felt cold. He got up and searched around. He gathered kindling and heaped it up, struck a match and let the flames catch the dry twigs and leaves. He stretched out his hands to warm them.

'Strange, you know,' he murmured to himself. Of all the ghosts who came to visit him, Billy never did. He had picked up Billy's corpse and carried it back to the trench. A hospital station was nearby. Daventry had handed the corpse over to an orderly who had looked at him kindly.

'I come from Manchester,' the man had said. 'I know how to bandage a wound but I can't bring the dead back to life, lad.'

They had taken Billy's corpse and laid it on the ground beneath a sheet. It was only hours later that Daventry realised he had still got Jack's helmet with the tag inside, hooked to his belt. Colonel Morrison saw it.

'What's that, lad?' he asked. 'Do you have two heads?'

Daventry handed the helmet over. Morrison inspected it curiously.

'Why,' he said, 'this is Jack's. Where did you find it?'

Daventry told him. Morrison listened, nodding carefully. The colonel stared up at the sky, muttered something and, taking the helmet, had flung it down the trench.

That was the last Daventry had heard of the matter. Sometimes he just wondered. On one occasion, before the mist fogged his brain and the ghosts began to gather, he'd told Jack what he had seen. Jack had just blinked, opened his mouth as if to reply but said he knew nothing about it and walked away.

The fire sent a small column of smoke up to the outstretched branches of the trees. Charlie's ghost had disappeared, there was no need to be here but Daventry wondered once again why that officer had come. Nor could he forget Jack's helmet being sent spinning by the colonel.

For a while Daventry dozed. He vaguely knew it was Saturday, and the shrill whistle from the pithead informed him the men would soon be up from the mines, walking through the villages, bait boxes under their arms, helmets and lamps in their hands.

He heard a sound and whirled round. Evans the policeman stood there gripping the handles of his push-bike.

Daventry shuffled to his feet. He liked Len, he was always kind.

'What are you doing here, Bob?' The policeman leaned his bike against a tree and came forward, great black boots crunching the twigs. He pointed to the fire. 'What are you trying to do? Set Nightshade Woods alight?'

He took off his bicycle clips, undid the straps of his helmet and, grasping Daventry's arm, made him sit down beside him on a log.

'I saw the smoke rising,' Evans told him. 'Thought I'd come along the lane and catch some fresh air. What on earth are you doing, Bob? Why aren't you home?' He kicked at the loose earth. 'Still burying ghosts, are you?' Evans mopped his lean, sallow face with a rag kept up his cuff. 'You're quite ill, aren't you, lad?' he continued. 'If you go on like this you're going to have to go away.' He studied Daventry's dirty, unshaven face. 'And perhaps it will be for the best.'

'I've been thinking,' Daventry replied. 'I came out here because of Charlie Ashcroft.'

'Ah yes, old Curious.' Evans narrowed his eyes. 'Took a bullet in the head, didn't he, outside Arras in the early days of the war? When the news came back to Caundon, did you hear what happened? One of those do-gooders went and knocked on Charlie's door. "Does Widow Ashcroft live here?" she asked. "No," the poor woman replied. "I'm married to Charlie." "Well, not any longer," came the reply.' Evans laughed deep in his throat. 'But that's how it was, wasn't it? After the Somme they knocked at every door in this village and every village around: Johnnie's dead! Mike's dead! Brian's dead! Everyone's dead!'

'We are not,' Daventry declared.

'You might as well be,' Evans responded. 'I understand why you see ghosts, Bob, me old son. I pass through the village, I see this kid or that and I recognise the likeness. Do you know how many men left Caundon?' He stretched his fingers out to the flame. 'Over a hundred. Do you know how many came back? Forty, and some of them are bloody useless. What was it all about, eh? Look at us, me a policeman on a push-bike and you lighting fires out in Nightshade Woods!' He sniffed. 'Everything's changed. God, the church, the squire, the colonel. No wonder old Cunningham stands outside Mass and blasphemes. I'm half tempted to join him!'

'What about the officer?' Daventry asked.

'What officer?'

In halting phrases Daventry described what he had seen that morning. Evans heard him out.

'Describe him again. No, don't go wandering off, Bob. Just tell me what you saw. If you do, I'll help you bury old Ashcroft myself.'

Daventry did so. Evans mopped the sweat from his cheeks. He'd heard about this. Kitty had said something when he was in the bar but he hadn't thought anything of it. He also regularly visited the colonel but he had said nothing so Evans had dismissed it. Perhaps he was just an officer passing through. All Kitty had said was that an officer, Oscar Fairfax, was staying at the Beaumont Arms. However, if Daventry was correct, this was a high-ranker from the Provost Marshal's Office. He wasn't just passing through. He was coming to investigate.

Despite the thick serge uniform and tight-collared shirt, Evans felt a cold prickle of fear. Won't the war ever go away? Evans knew all about the Provost Marshal's Office. At the end of the war he'd served there for a while, as a clerk: that's how he had been allowed into the police force. The Provost Marshal's unit was staffed with officers who had done valiant service at the front: hard-bitten, keen-eyed. The war with Germany might be over but the British Army had its own secret war against the deserters, the defaulters, the thieves, the cowards, those who pretended to be ill, even murderers. Evans's throat went dry. Murder! And hadn't he a lot to hide?

Evans closed his eyes. He was back in that trench. There had been a group of them, some Australians, even a few Belgians, the flotsam and jetsam of broken lives and shattered regiments. An officer had come along, slipping into the trench, a gun in one hand, riding crop in the other. He had yelled how they were a bunch of cowards. All Evans could remember was the smoke billowing about and a young soldier who had taken a piece of shrapnel in his buttocks. He was lying screaming on the floor of the trench, his hair white with dust, face muscles leaping in pain. The officer had ignored him, ordering the rest to get up and back over the top.

'Over the top?' one of the Australians shouted. 'You stupid bastard!'

The officer threatened them with his gun so they had no choice but to obey.

They were halfway out of the trench, there was the crack of rifle shot and the young captain fell. Evans knew he had been shot in the back by his own men but everyone kept silent. They buried him with the young soldier, who'd stopped his shrieking. They'd covered both in mud and settled down to be relieved.

'I'm going back.' Daventry shot to his feet and stamped on the fire. 'I can't see Ashcroft here so I'm going back.'

'Aye,' Evans nodded. 'And, worse luck, so am I.'

He slipped his bicycle clips on and re-strapped his helmet, his mind full of dark, dreary images. He stared up at the sky and wondered if justice had caught up with him at last.

'The war changed everything, didn't it?' Fairfax asked again, breaking into Kitty's reverie.

Kitty nodded and sipped from her tea. It had gone cold. 'Everything, Major Fairfax. Before nineteen fourteen it was the dream time. I was born here. I went to school. I had my friends. We attended galas and fairs, holidayed at the seaside where I collected different coloured shells. We had picnics out in Nightshade Woods. I have a favourite tree there, Neville's Oak. Everywhere I went, Jack and Billy followed. Father Headon called us the Shamrock.' She smiled. 'Three leaves in one. Do you remember your summers, Major Fairfax?'

He watched the cigarette smoke curl away, did not reply.

'When you are a child,' Kitty continued, 'every day seems summer. When it grows cold you think of Christmas, the holly and the ivy, preparing the crib in the church.'

'And the war?' Fairfax asked.

'Oh, we heard all the news about Austria and Serbia. People travelled to Bishop Auckland and Sedgefield to collect newspapers and proclamations. The war posters went up. Everyone flocked round. It was like one of those galas. The men would leave; they'd teach the Kaiser a lesson and all be home by the end of the year.' Kitty pushed the cup away.

Fairfax watched her intently. 'And you?' he asked.

'Billy and I were married in the spring of nineteen thirteen. A lovely service. Dad took me to Newcastle to buy my dress. A beautiful day,' she whispered. 'Jack was best man and we danced and we sang, everyone did music hall turns.'

'And then came war,' Fairfax said.

'Billy, Jack and all the lads left. My father also volunteered although he was really too old. Events came like the carriages of a train whirling by. Terrible stories about entire regiments being lost. Companies of friends wiped out in a day. The men started coming home. I'd watched them leave, marching down to the station. When they came back, they'd changed.'

'In what way?'

'Foreigners. That's what they called themselves: foreigners from a different country. I remember the first time Billy came home on leave. He sat upstairs on the bed and just gazed at the wall. I put my arms round him and asked him, "What's the matter?" He began to laugh. "Kitty," he whispered, "the world's gone mad. We are all going back to the slaughter fields." I asked him what he meant but he stared blankly at me. I inquired about this person or that. It was like a litany in church: "Dead, dead, missing, possibly a prisoner," as if a plague had come to the village; that's what happened here, in every home throughout Caundon. The men would come down to the Beaumont Arms to drink. It was like a party of the dead. They never talked about each other, the old times or the good times. Oh, sometimes, when they had drunk enough, they'd start singing songs. One would even do a dance. Afterwards they'd slope out like ghosts into the night. When I was a child,' Kitty continued, 'a blacksmith came here. He used the yard near the old stables to shoe horses. I would hear his hammer beat upon the anvil. That's what the war was like, Major Fairfax: every time the hammer fell, more bad news. Fathers killed, brothers, sons, sweethearts and husbands.'

'And Billy?'

'Killed in nineteen seventeen, when a shell hit the trench he was in.'

'And Jack?'

'Jack came home. The war ended. He picked up the pieces, the loose threads, and tried to start again.'

Fairfax was about to continue, he was fascinated by this young woman. She was so calm, composed, and those sea-grey eyes were so serene. He had this irresistible urge to try and shatter her serenity but experience told him to pause, to go no further.

He took a cigarette out and again offered one. Kitty shook her head. Fairfax noticed how the light coming through the window glistened on her hair. For the first time since the death of Eleanora he felt a thrill of excitement, that keenness of interest when his attention was aroused by a beautiful, attractive woman. Yet Kitty Allerton was so unaware of it. You are a dreamer, Fairfax reflected, no coquetry or flirtation, no attempt to please or flatter. She was talking and describing things as they were and wistfully implying she wished they were different. Fairfax would concentrate on that. Was there regret? Recrimination? How could this young woman marry one man, hear about his death in hideous circumstances, then marry his best friend? Fairfax raised the cigarette to hide his smile. Such occurrences were common in England. Yet this was different. Caundon was a small place. Kitty, Jack and Billy had been the Shamrock, three leaves in one. Kitty was staring down at the table. Fairfax decided to push the boat a little further up the stream.

'And now?' he asked.

'And now what?'

Fairfax tapped the silver cigarette case on the table. Kitty noticed the initials engraved on the side: "M.F." Fairfax followed her gaze.

'It was my brother's,' he remarked. 'Maurice. He wasn't a soldier.' He played with the cup. 'Not one for the trenches, was Maurice. Mad about aeroplanes. If anyone was born with wings, Maurice was. "To fly is to live," he'd say.' Fairfax pulled a face. 'He was only nineteen when he was shot down.'

'Was he married?'

'Oh, goodness no. I called Maurice the Sultan.'

Kitty laughed.

'At a party or a dance, I'd look for the crowd of girls and the sounds of laughter, and Maurice would be at the centre of it.'

'Do you miss him?' Kitty asked.

'Do you miss Billy?' Fairfax regretted the question.

Kitty flinched, pulling away.

'I'm sorry,' he apologised. 'The answer's obvious. Every day I miss Maurice. Every single day. He had flown on numerous occasions. One day his squadron received information that a large enemy formation was up to strafe our lads in the trenches. Maurice was ill, some type of stomach trouble. He had also been wounded in the left shoulder. The young fool was told to stay but he insisted on flying. He wasn't brave or playing the hero. That boy just had no nerves. When we were young he'd deliberately swim out into the middle of a fast-running river and hold his hands up. "Look, Oscar, I'm drowning!"' Fairfax rubbed his forehead. 'Anyway, he went up and the Germans fell on them like wolves on a sheepfold. They were out-numbered, out-gunned. Maurice took a burst of fire. He tried to reach the base, was almost there but the plane crashed. He'd used up all his fuel so the fire was small and they managed to pull him out but he was dead. My parents were rather ancient. They adored Maurice. Our drawing room became like a shrine to him. Neither survived the year.' Fairfax paused. This was a strategy he often used, to share his own experiences, but this time it was different. He could feel the sadness and rage bubbling within him. Sadness at the profound loss, rage that a brave man had died whilst so many cowards walked away.

'And you?' Kitty asked, curious about this stone-faced officer, speaking in such measured tones.

'Royal Worcestershire Regiment,' he replied. 'I was at all the great killings when the dead were piled high and the mud seemed to be a shifting carpet of corpses. In the second year of the war, an acquaintance of mine invited me to join the Provost Marshal's Office.' He smiled. 'So, here I am.'

'Aye, and I wish to God you were elsewhere!'

Kitty whirled round. Jack stood in the doorway; black grime covered his old shirt, waistcoat and trousers tied with string. He had taken his boots off, so they hadn't heard him. He hardly ever came in here before he had bathed and changed. Jack stood leaning on the door handle, eyes gleaming in his dark face, his shock of red hair sweat-soaked.

'Ah, Jack, this is Major—'

'I know who he is.' Jack raised his hand and let it fall. 'I'd shake yours but we don't want to dirty the officer, do we?'

Fairfax got to his feet, picking up his silver cigarette case. He walked forward and extended his hand. 'I never say no to a fellow soldier.'

Jack stared at Kitty. She glared back. Jack could be so stubborn. She often called him a pit pony, so resolute in his ways. Jack took the proffered hand and shook it. Fairfax didn't even bother to wipe his hands. Jack studied the flashes on the cuff and epaulettes of Fairfax's jacket.

'And what's an officer from the Provost Marshal's Office doing here in Caundon? The war has been over for three years. You're not still chasing deserters?'

'Business, Mr Allerton, War Office business. I am here to see Colonel Morrison.'

Jack wiped his brow with the back of his wrist. 'Well, you are welcome to do that if you can get sense from him. He gets up, goes out to shoots and, from what I can gather, spends most of his time staring out of the window. Kitty, I'm dying of thirst!'

Kitty went across and filled an enamel mug from the pitcher and brought it over. She found it hard to stop her hands shaking. Jack was usually so diffident, now he stood threateningly, aggressive. No kiss, no teasing, eyes only for the officer. He grasped the mug and drank.

'And how long are you staying, Major Fairfax?'

'Until my business is done.'

'Spoken like an officer and a gentleman.' Jack drained the mug and handed it back to Kitty. 'I'd best be going. I need a bath.'

'No, no, I'll go.' Fairfax turned, nodded at Kitty and brushed by Jack out into the passageway.

'There was no need for that,' Kitty protested.

'No need for what? I come home to find my wife entertaining an officer in the kitchen.' He grinned. 'The news will be all over Caundon. Kitty Allerton at home—'

'Stop it, Jack!' She went to punch him on the shoulder but he moved sideways.

'I'd hug you, Kitty Allerton, but I'm all dirty and it would only make the tongues wag. They'd be saying we'd had a fight. Come on, woman!' he teased.

They went out, across the kitchen and through the back door into the weed-filled yard. Helped by Kitty, Jack took the galvanised bath off the hook in one of the outhouses and used the pump to fill it.

'Why don't you let me heat the water?' Kitty asked. 'I know the weather's warm but . . .'

Jack was already stripping off. On the bench nearby he had placed his helmet and lamp, the box which held his bait, and underneath the bench were his steel-capped, hobnailed boots. Jack reminded Kitty of a priest, following the same ritual every day except Sunday. He'd come straight in, fill the bath, strip and wash himself. She would bring out his collarless shirt, trousers, the woollen socks Mother knitted as often as she could, and what Jack called his "drinking" shoes, as he always wore them when he was in the bar. Kitty liked to watch him bathe. Jack was thickset and muscular. Grimed with coal dust, he reminded her of a picture she had seen of the Greek god Vulcan. The coal dust got everywhere.

'You'd think you'd swum in the stuff,' she murmured.

'You always say that.' Jack grasped a thick bar of carbolic soap, a flannel cloth and began to rub himself down.

Kitty watched the transformation: the black flesh turning to white, the slight sunburn which tinged his shoulders and back. Jack had said how, in the war, one of the things he always felt was not so much the cold but the searing heat, the acrid gunpowder, the cordite which would sting his nose and dry his throat and give him a terrible thirst. Then there was the mustard gas, though, by the time the war was through, they had proper masks.

'I used to sit in the trench, mud up to my knees,' Jack remarked. 'I'd think of standing under a waterfall for day after day, letting the cool water brush away the dirt and drink and drink until I had my fill.'

'Will you be going down to watch the football game?'

'No, I think it's time for the garden.' He glanced at her. 'Another memory of the war, eh? Just like that officer. Do you know, Kitty, I rarely saw a flower, green grass or a tree. One day we were pulled back. There was a field of marigolds. I don't know what season it was but I went and lay down amongst them.' He grinned. 'It was almost as lovely as lying beside you.'

Kitty took the jug and threw the contents over him. She refilled the jug and came back. Jack had stepped out of the bath and poured the water over his head to clear away the suds. He dried himself slowly with a thick, coarse rope-towel. Kitty had offered a softer one but again the 'pit pony' refused.

'That's the way a man should feel,' he insisted. 'As if he's had a real good bath and dry.'

'Well?' she asked. 'How did the shift go?'

'I'll tell you when I'm dressed, woman. I don't want Betty coming out and saying I exposed myself.'

Kitty's fingers flew to her lips. Fairfax's arrival had broken her routine. She hurried back to the house and brought out Jack's clothes and shoes. The bar was already beginning to fill, the air thick with cigarette and pipe smoke. The golden rule in Caundon was that no man was allowed in until he had washed and changed. However, as Father Headon had pointedly declared, that rule, like Scripture, could be generously interpreted. Men, the sides of their faces still grimed with coal dust, were already at the bar demanding pints. Betty and old John were busy and Kitty's mother bustled past her with a grim look in her eyes.

'Come on!' she urged. 'We need to get into the kitchen!'

'Where's Major Fairfax?' Kitty asked.

'Gone up to his room. Said he'd like to sleep. He'll have lunch.' Kitty's mother smiled at the posh word. 'Said he'd have lunch when he came down.'

Kitty brought Jack his clothes. Usually he'd be hopping from foot to foot but now he just stood staring at the ground, the towel round him. He took the clothes from her like a dream-walker and dressed.

'Well,' she said. 'How was the mine?'

'Dirty, dark and sweaty,' he replied absent-mindedly. 'The new shaft's good, the disaster at Stanley is having some effect. Proper beams and loadings, ropes and chains are checked, more boys being used to look for danger. We had a good laugh. Stories from a nearby village of a man who told his wife to cook something special because the vicar was coming to dinner. The silly hinny killed his prize pigeon.' Jack dropped the towel and grasped her by the waist. 'But never mind about that. What did Fairfax want?'

Chapter 3

'I don't like the military police.' Jack rammed the crust round the plate and popped it into his mouth.

The Beaumont Arms had now fallen quiet, the men and boys drifting off to watch the football match. Fairfax had still not re-appeared. Kitty's mother had gone for her usual lie-down. Jack felt annoyed, a slight pang of jealousy at his wife's interest in that elegant, cold-faced officer. Fairfax's arrival also stirred fears of his own.

'Do you remember Tommy Randall?' he asked.

'Ah yes, the carter's son. Tall, gangly fellow,' Kitty replied. 'He had a pet raven.'

'That's right, till Father Headon's cat ate it. In the trenches once we were in a tight corner, me, Tommy and a few others. It was chaos, everything got mixed up. One regiment with another. Companies which had lost their officers were looking for someone in charge. All we had was a line of men going backwards and forwards across a sea of mud. Well, Tommy and I dropped into a German trench. It was a great place, beautifully made.' Jack pushed the plate away. 'White sandbagged, back and front. The trench floor was littered with German dead. Inside we found a real comfortable little hole fitted with seats and shelves, bottles of beer and tinned meat.' Jack grinned. 'More joined us, about fifteen in all – we were like children released into a chocolate factory. We drank the beer, ate the meat and put their helmets on. We settled down and thought we'd wait the war out, until along comes this officer. He was all right, he just jumped into the trench and helped himself to some beer. Two military policemen also arrived. I hadn't had much to do with them. They usually brought in stragglers or looked after prisoners. One of them, a big bugger, a real Cockney, he accused us of being cowards. The officer got onto the parapet to have a look. He took a bullet in his lungs. He could still walk so the Redcaps ordered two of our lads to take him to the orderly station. They were hardly out of the trench when a sniper shot them, pop, pop, like knocking bottles off a wall. We put our own helmets back on and fixed bayonets. Tommy just shook his head and said he wouldn't. Anyway, the policeman blew his whistle and over the top he went. As usual, we ran ten paces, fell flat on our faces, the bullets whistling over us. Everything went quiet. I could hear Tommy shouting, arguing with the other military policeman back in the trench. A pistol cracked and that was the end of Tommy.'

'He was shot!' Kitty exclaimed. 'By his own side!'

'He wasn't the only one. I could tell you stories you wouldn't believe, lass. Men being shot in trenches, deserters left out in no-man's-land on the barbed wire. So-called cowards marched off to be executed.'

Kitty stretched her hand out and clasped his. 'But that's all over, pet.' She rubbed her thumb along his knuckles. Jack's face was pale, the worry lines under his eyes had deepened. Kitty experienced a chill of fear. Why was Fairfax here? Why had he come striding into Caundon? Hadn't these men suffered enough?

'You'd think they'd leave it alone.'

'What do you mean, leave it alone?' Jack's head came up. 'Leave what alone? Shall I tell you what we talk about down the mine? People think we hate the Germans. Oh, we talk about the reparations mentioned in the newspapers. In truth, there's not a man Jack amongst us,' he laughed at the pun, 'that doesn't hate the British Army even more. Stories are circling in the working men's clubs and trade unions. The Redcaps were bastards and haven't changed. They've set up a special investigation office to look at crimes committed by our lads at the front.'

Kitty felt his hand, ice-cold. She was aware of a shadow shifting across their lives.

'You don't know what the army was like!' Jack was glaring at her as if she was an enemy rather than a loving wife. 'The army never, ever gives up on you. They argue that many good men died, so why should the cowards, the deserters, the murderers get away?'

Kitty recalled Fairfax talking about his brother Maurice.

'It's not just a job,' Jack continued. He lifted the mug of steaming tea and sipped. 'The army views it as a personal insult if one soldier didn't do his duty. To a certain extent you can understand it. Why should one man fight and die and another one run away?' He shook his head. 'But they act like judge, jury and executioner.'

'You mentioned murderers.' Kitty withdrew her hand.

'Aye, that's the laugh of it,' Jack replied. 'I've seen trenches full of dead men, Kitty, blood pouring out like water from a barrel. The things that happened! Men wounding themselves so as to get a ticket to Blighty. Men shooting their officers in the back. Soldiers crammed up in trenches, losing their temper with each other. People pretending to be dead and crawling away or absconding from hospital. It's all the same. The army collects it all up.' Jack spread his hands as if he was scooping up leaves. 'They take up all the rubbish and debris of war, and carefully sift it.'

'And here?' Kitty tapped the table. 'Our lads didn't do anything wrong.'

Jack stared at the floor. 'Can I have some more bread?'

Kitty walked across, took the dark-brown loaf out of the bin and grasped the knife. She cut two slices and glanced quickly over her shoulder. Jack sat with his face in his hands. She opened a small butter dish and skimmed the top of the bread lightly, put it on a plate and brought it back. Jack had taken his hands away.

'Did you do anything, Jack?'

He munched the bread slowly.

'Did you do anything wrong?'

Jack pushed the rest of the bread into his mouth like a child making an excuse not to reply.

'We all did things,' he said thickly. 'We attacked a German trench once, shaped in the form of a 'V', what the officers called a redoubt. They held machine-gun posts which had done dreadful damage to our lads. We managed to get behind it. The Germans had the cheek to put their hands up, shouting, "Comrade! Comrade!" We just bayoneted them. According to the rules of war they were surrendering. However, thirty-four of our men left the trench, only sixteen returned. The redoubt held three young Germans. One had blond hair, he was crying for his mother.'

Kitty shivered and stared at her husband's lined face. Is this you, Jack? she thought. I've never questioned you about the war and you've never told me.

'Did we do wrong, Kitty? It's easy to say we did but you weren't there. Oh, I know it was bad for you at home but no one knows what it was really like in the trenches. The world had stopped. We were in a different place, no trees, no pubs, no picnics, no church, just a sea of mud with big holes in the ground. A dead man became as common as a leaf on a path. The awful smells. It was like being in a nightmare for four years,' he added.

Kitty recalled Jack waking up, sweat-soaked, wild-eyed, hands flailing. In the last few months such nightmares had faded. She now wished she had listened more to the Dead Hand Club when they gathered on a Saturday night: Jack and the rest sitting, talking quietly. Now and again she'd hear them laugh or glimpse one of them silently weep.

'Did Billy do anything wrong?'

'We all did wrong things. There wasn't any right or wrong. Just surviving while your friends and mates died around you.'

'But the army knows that,' Kitty insisted. 'I am sure Major Fairfax has his memories. He would show little mercy to the enemy.' She watched her husband eating the second slice of bread. 'And I suppose neither would I.'

Jack leaned across and touched her cheek with his finger. 'You'd look pretty in a helmet. You'd look pretty in anything, Kitty.'

'Why don't you speak about it more? Why don't you tell me?'

'Oh, in time. But people aren't going to be interested. Start talking and, within a few years, you'd be regarded as the village bore. What's happened, Kitty, is that the trenches have changed us. You lived for the moment, not yesterday, or tomorrow, or even the next hour. You ate and you drank. You went to the netty. You tried to keep yourself safe. When Ashcroft was killed, the first man to die in our platoon, we all sat round and wept. It was a real ceremony. A year later, when someone was killed, all we were bothered about was who could have his rations.'

'And Billy?' Kitty insisted. 'Did he do anything?'

Jack shook his head. 'Billy wouldn't hurt a fly. He didn't like soldiering, he didn't like war. You know that. Do you remember when we used to go chasing rabbits?'

Kitty smiled and nodded.

'And Billy made that catapult? He was such a good shot he actually knocked one over. Well, Billy became a sniper.' He noticed Kitty's surprise. 'Didn't you know that? Oh yes, every platoon had its marksman. Billy was ours. One Sunday morning we were in a trench. Colonel Morrison will confirm the story. He said: "Eh, Billy lad, there's a German, you've got a good shot at him." Billy took his rifle, got onto the firing platform and sighted his rifle. Then he said, "Ah no!" and sat down. "What's the matter?" the colonel asked. "Oh," Billy replied, "the poor bugger's de-lousing himself, he's got enough problems without me killing him." Morrison laughed. He clapped Billy on the shoulder and that was it.'

Kitty couldn't stop the tears brimming in her eyes: Fairfax's arrival, Jack's talk. It seemed as if Billy was here with his gentle eyes and kind face; the unruly hair which always spilled down over his forehead and the collar of his shirt, the trousers and the heavy braces given to him by his father, of which Billy had been ever so proud. Jack was staring at her curiously. Image followed image. Billy and herself on their wedding night, hands slipping down her bodice, soft fingers touching her back. They way they would go out to the fields: Billy's teasing, eyes crinkled up in amusement. How he talked about the future and being the best miner in Caundon. He'd organise a union, bring the Co-operative Society into town to bait Grant's as well as create genuine competition. Kitty tried to stop the tears.

'What's the matter, pet?' Jack came round, sat on the bench and put his arm round her. For the first time ever Kitty didn't want him there. She leaned her head on his shoulder but wished she could go out into the garden, anywhere, alone with her memories of Billy.

'I'm sorry,' Jack whispered. 'Perhaps I shouldn't have mentioned it.'

'It's nothing. It's nothing.' Kitty felt foolish and embarrassed, as if she was sitting with a stranger and Billy might come through the door and find them together. Yet this was Jack! In all her memories there were always the three of them, even when they were only knee high to a buttercup; Jack, Billy and Kitty. She wanted to get up and run out. She preferred to be with Fairfax rather than Jack right now. She bit back her sob.

'What is the matter?' Jack stood up. 'Billy didn't do anything wrong. Nobody did anything wrong.'

Kitty looked up. 'Do you love me, Jack?'

'That's a daft question.'

'No, do you really love me?'

'I have always loved you.'

'And when I married Billy, what did you think?'

Jack eased himself down on the bench opposite. 'I still loved you. I felt happy and I felt sad all at the same time.'

'And on our wedding night?' Kitty persisted.

'Ah, it was a grand—' Jack stopped in horror. Kitty was no longer smiling but glaring at him. His heart skipped a beat. He realised the word "our" did not refer to his wedding night with Kitty but to Billy's.

'You came back here with the lads that night. What did you think?'

'I didn't think anything.' Jack's mouth had gone dry. He deeply regretted ever beginning this conversation and remembered the whispered advice of Father Tom in confession. 'There's an old phrase, Jack,' the old priest had murmured through the grille. 'The Romans used it: "Let sleeping dogs lie." Don't open your memories. The past is the past.' Jack realised the wisdom of such advice. A coldness had sprung up between himself and Kitty, the first time in two years, like an icy draught through a warm room.

'I'd best go.'

Kitty leaned across. She dug her nails into the back of his hand. 'Do you truly love me, Jack? Or was it because I was Billy's?'

Jack found himself floundering. Kitty could be sharp. She had what her mother called 'a fearful temper'. Jack was always wary of it.

'Look, pet, I love you, I loved Billy. I married you because I loved you and I loved Billy. You know that. You know what happened. I have always loved you and I always will. Why, Kitty, do you still love me?'

'Yes.'

The answer was curt. Kitty blinked and stared around. What was happening here? Why today, 21 August 1921? She had been married to this man for two years and had never thought to ask such questions, not until Major Oscar Fairfax had arrived. It was true what she had said the way she'd described her life, like standing on a railway station and watching the carriages clatter by one after the other. Now it was all slowing down. But why?

Jack sighed and got to his feet. 'I'll be in the garden.'

He stopped by her, grasped her shoulder and kissed her on the top of her head. Kitty didn't move. She heard the back door open and close. She stared at the empty plate. What had happened? She pulled the plate over, turning it with her fingers. Why now? She got to her feet, left the kitchen and walked upstairs. She paused at the stairwell and looked up at the door to Fairfax's room. You are the cause, she thought. You've come to the Beaumont Arms for a reason. You are here because of some of the stories Jack won't tell me.

She went into their bedroom. Jack had opened the window; it had turned slightly chilly so she closed it. She opened the top drawer of the dresser. A knock on the door made her jump. She went across and opened it. Fairfax stood holding a large, brown manila envelope. He had a hard, knowing look. He realised what was happening might change, even shatter, her life. He offered the envelope.

'This is your property.'

Kitty took it. Fairfax stepped forward as if to follow her into the room. Kitty grasped the door. Fairfax shrugged and stepped back.

'My property?' Kitty turned the manila envelope over.

'Billy's journal,' he said. 'It was found on him.'

'Why now? Four years later?'

'Fortunes of war,' Fairfax replied. 'It probably got separated from the rest. You know how it is.'

'No, Major Fairfax, I don't know how it is. Have you read it?'

'Of course. It's interesting . . .'

'You know all about us, don't you, Major Fairfax? You are like a hawk which surveys the ground. I am beginning to wonder whether you know more about me than I do.'

Fairfax turned away. 'Accept my apologies and that of the army for the tardy return, Miss Kitty, but now you have it.' He walked slowly back up the stairs.

Kitty closed the door and grasped the envelope, folding her arms across her chest.

So much, she thought. So much is happening. It's almost like the day they told me Billy was dead. All the wounds are re-opening. She weighed the package in her hands. She'd often wondered where this had gone. She felt a spurt of anger that someone like Fairfax should have read it. But at least she had it now; it was some form of contact with Billy. What else had Fairfax said? Ah yes, he had called her "Miss Kitty". Strange, she mused, that's what that dreadful Edmund Grant always called her.

Kitty fingered the brown manila envelope with its big black official letters in one corner. The journal felt more like cardboard than paper. She undid the little metal clasp and, hands shaking, pulled the exercise book out. Her heart leapt. She caught the sob in her throat. Billy must have reinforced the dark-blue covers with strips of cardboard and glue. The pages looked as if they had been soaked, thickened and expanded. Yet the staples held them firm. A piece of paper stuck on the front gave its simple title in black pencil: 'BILLY'S BOOK – March 1917'. Kitty couldn't stop crying; the tears rolled hot and fast down her cheeks. She lifted the book to her face. It smelt of dust. She sniffed again and caught a whiff of oil and a strange soapy smell. She opened the pages. Billy's writing, small and neat, in thick black pencil. 'Write a book, Billy,' she had said, thrusting the exercise book into his hands, together with a box of pencils. 'They are specially made for the trenches.'

Kitty got up and walked to the window. When had she said that? Ah yes, the last time Billy had been home. Not this time of year, later, the leaves had turned red-gold and Neville's Oak had looked like something from fairy land. They had walked hand in hand after Mass one Sunday morning, laughing and talking. She had brought this along, it was the only present she could think of. Billy had taken it, put it inside his jacket, the pencils with it, and pulled her towards him.

'I could think of better gifts,' he teased, his gentle eyes gleaming. He'd never mentioned the book again. Never once. When his effects were sent home, they had been so meagre: a pen an old aunt had given him, a ribbon from her wedding dress. They were all in the metal box in the top drawer. She had put them there with her other memories. She thought the exercise book had been destroyed, along with his watch, her gift to him on their wedding day. Billy had told her many a time: 'In the trenches everything rots. Nothing remains. Your boots, your belt and, if you are not careful, even your rifle. What doesn't decay and the rats miss, the shells and bullets destroy.'

Kitty opened the exercise book. Billy had written poetry and attended the Evening Institute to improve his writing. He'd borrowed books from Father Headon, particularly the novels of H.G. Wells and the detective stories of Conan Doyle.

'Don't tell anyone I have given you them,' the priest had warned. 'The Catholic Church is fond of neither author. I don't want the Bishop of Newcastle threatening me with hellfire for distributing suspect literature.'

Kitty took Billy's photograph out and put it on the dresser.

'You were always a great reader, weren't you, Billy, and a great dreamer.'

Kitty had heard of the war poets. She had seen one of Wilfred Owen's poems printed in the *Northern Echo*. Last year she had nearly gone to Bishop Auckland to hear a university lecturer talk about the growing influence of the war poets. Jack had stopped her.

'There's no poetry in war,' he'd murmured.

'But these were soldiers,' she'd protested. 'They fought like you, Jack.'

In the end she hadn't gone and bitterly regretted it.

She sat on the bed and stared at the picture. 'You would have been a great poet, Billy. Wouldn't it have been grand? A northern lad like you, with an outside netty and a job in the pits, being acclaimed a poet!'

Kitty heard a sound from downstairs.

'I don't want Jack here, Billy.' The words were out before she could stop them. 'At least not for the moment.'

She opened the exercise book again. It was like a present at Christmas, a rare treasure but so precious she wanted to revel in the moment of discovery, of unwrapping it. Once she began to read, her life would change. Billy had sent her letters but they had been censored by the military and Billy had hated that.

'I can't stand it!' he had protested. 'Writing to you and knowing that someone else is reading it. It's a bit like kissing you whilst someone plays peeping Tom. I wouldn't mind Jack but not some bloody clerk or, worse, some officer whose daddy used influence to keep him away from the mud and blood!'

Kitty heard soft footsteps on the stairs. Fairfax had left his room and had paused outside her door. She glanced towards it and whispered the words, "Thank you." Of course he wouldn't hear.

She heard the boards creak as Fairfax moved away. Kitty got up and, struggling hard, pushed the bolt at the top of the door across. She wouldn't go down and if her mother or Jack knocked, she wouldn't answer. This was her moment, her time. She returned and made herself comfortable and read the first page.

The date was February 1917.

The last week has not been so bad. The sun has warmed the earth and the air's soft. When night falls, the stars are clear. There's no fighting at the moment. The colonel says it has shifted somewhere to the west. An aeroplane is drifting overhead and the clouds are like a white flock of sheep. The countryside here is drab. A trackway winds its way past the village. I can see chimney stacks and tall trees. Now and again a covered farm cart makes its way out. The officers say we should enjoy the sight, it won't last long.

Bad news has come in. Toby Stephenson has died of wounds, he was knocked over by a shell last night. I felt sad. Toby was a good man. He always reminded me of a robin with his red nose and cheeks, his little head and bright eyes: always perky, ready for a laugh. They said he went looking for water. He and the shell just seemed to meet. The Germans haven't started firing here yet. They are still getting ready. No one knows what's going to happen.

I think of Kitty often. Every time I close my eyes she's there. How lucky I am! I wish she was here and I wish she wasn't. I would like to share what I have seen and heard. Above all, I want to tell her how much I love her. Other men talk of their girls and sweethearts, their wives or even the French lasses they have met in the villages but all I do is think about Kitty. Isn't it strange? My earliest memory is of Kitty, looking across at her in church, or as an altar boy holding the paten beneath her chin when she made her first Communion. I'll never forget that, her head back, her eyes closed, her mouth open, her little pink tongue poking out. She looked beautiful in her white dress. Boys aren't supposed to have such thoughts but that's when I decided to marry her. I immediately informed Jack as we took our cassocks off in the sacristy.

'I'm going to marry Kitty,' I proclaimed. 'And we'll buy a farm!'

'You can marry Kitty,' Jack replied, 'but it won't be a farm, it will be the pit for you and me.'

How time went! Memories like puffs of smoke. The life that I had, and the love that I felt, were one and the same. Kitty was me and I was Kitty. Never a doubt, never a moment's hesitation. I know that people used to laugh at me. Granddad gave me a penny once. I told him I'd save it to buy the farm. Everyone laughed and said I'd need more than a penny.

Jack asks me what I'm writing. I've told him I'm keeping a journal. He asks to see it but I shake my head. I have managed to find a waterproof pouch and I'll keep it in there. I'll write my thoughts and, when I take it home, if I take it home, I'll show it all to Kitty so she'll know what it was like. Now there's a thought that keeps me happy.

The entry ended. Kitty found her hands couldn't stop trembling. The next entry was a week later.

Sorry I haven't written before. Things have turned bad. The Germans have brought up their big guns. I went out last night on a raid. Jack, me and thirty others. Our faces blackened. We were given hatchets and bombs and waited in the dug-out. Colonel Morrison led us. Most of the other officers have been killed, we are still awaiting replacements. Shells droned across, falling with an awful smack and crash. Flare lights glowed, more whizz-bangs came and went. It gets so confusing, you can't tell which is ours and which is theirs. I am sure the Hun thinks the same.

The first men went over, Jack was one of them. He came back a few minutes later, said it was bloody useless, the wire-cutters didn't work and the bombs had to be lit by matches. Both them and the fuses were soaking. Jack was no sooner in the trench than the bullets began to whizz. We started throwing bombs, anything we could lay our hands on. It was a nightmare. Men cursing and swearing, stumbling figures as others got back to the trench. Someone said only eleven returned. Morgan's missing. Colonel Morrison told our group that we would be next.

I got out and crawled through the mud. The enemy was still throwing bombs at us. Bullets smacked in the water, little showers of earth. I scurried to my left and dropped into a crater. Two of our lads were already there. Stubbins was dead, head blown off. I couldn't find it. Morgan was moaning, his right arm was a complete mess, just flesh and bone. I dragged him by the collar. I could hear the men shouting 'Gas!' but it wasn't, just clouds of cordite, making us all hot. I dragged Morgan back. We fell into the trench together. Jack came up to help. I thought I had saved Morgan but he died. Even as I write, he's propped in the mud next to me, his face all grey and dirty, eyes half closed, his chin soaked in blood. He'll stay there till Daventry takes him. Poor Bob, I worry about him. He's talking to himself more and more. He keeps digging holes when they are not needed.

It's morning now. Beautiful blue sky. No clouds at all. I've been onto the platform and looked over quickly. The grass and trees have gone and so has the farm, the cart and the trackway. Everything has turned a dark brown. The barbed wire has sprung up as if it is some sort of grim harvest. The fruit it carries are corpses. I see a few tangled there. One or two Germans, grey-uniformed. God knows who'll collect the poor buggers.

Colonel Morrison got some rum and has given us

two tots each. He says it's the best breakfast he can provide. For the first time in days I feel warm. We've got to watch the skies. The enemy like nothing better than to put a few planes up to come and strafe. Daventry is running up and down the trenches asking 'Have all my corpses gone?' Jack says the soil round here will be fertile for centuries, it holds so many dead. Cunningham is blaspheming again. Strange, isn't it, one of Father Tom's most faithful altar boys. He's daring God to kill him. Colonel Morrison let him go on for a while then he told him to shut up. Most of the men think the joke is wearing thin. Cunningham is a good lad. He's brave, seems to show no fear. When we are short of water, he'll always go and get some.

I dreamt of Kitty last night. She was naked, lying in my arms, not in bed but out near Neville's Oak. It was a beautiful night. There were carpets beneath us, thick and soft, like those in the London hotels. We drank some wine, strong and fruity. Kitty was laughing. She was leaning over me, head propped on her hand, staring down at me, tickling my nose with a piece of grass. She was asking when I was going to buy the farm. I held her body, soft and cool. I felt as if she was both within and outside of me, like taking the Sacrament. I'm glad Father Tom can't read this. I wish I'd died then. I wish I could stay in that dream and never wake up. I wish I could go home and forget the horrors. I want to sit beneath Neville's Oak with Kitty and look at green things.

I have one regret. I wish, before I left, I had told her how deeply I loved her. No, really told her. What she means to me. She is my life and my meaning. She is my happiness. My sorrow is not being with her.

For the life that I have is the life that she gave me.
And the life that she gave me is the love that I have.
And the love that I have is the meaning of all.
And the meaning of all is my life with her.

I read the lines again. Somebody would say it was a riddle, the type we lads make up to pass the time. It's the best I can do. Here in France, in this God-forsaken field, I can love deeper, truer, than I have ever done before. I find that strange. Perhaps that's what absence does, or is it just the war? With corpses stacked around you and death falling like rain, you soon find out what's important. I know it's not a dirty trench, unburied corpses and whizzing bullets. I wonder if there's a German, sitting only a few yards away, writing the same about his sweetheart. I bet if we met, if we were the only two left, we'd shake hands and agree to go home. That's what frightens me. Not the bullets, not death, more that I won't see Kitty again. I won't enter her world. I'll never see her glance sideways at me, or hide myself to watch her walk, or catch her face all screwed up in puzzlement as she reads a book and comes across a passage she doesn't understand. She'll make a great teacher. That's the world I want to be in!

Jack has just been up. He brought me a pannikin of water. We sat and chattered about Caundon. I talked to him about being killed. He just looked gravely at me.

'You'll go home, Billy. I promised Kitty that.'

'What!' I exclaimed. 'First I know of it. I thought we shared everything?'

I made him confess. He looked a bit sheepish but I got it out of him. It made me love Kitty even more.

'It happened the night before we left,' Jack said. 'Kitty caught me in the yard as I was leaving with the other lads. She pulled me by the jacket and made me promise that, whatever happened, I'd bring you back. I swore great oaths I would.'

I wish Jack hadn't done that. I told him so. Only God knows which poor devil will be killed, who will be given life and health. I don't think many. What's that phrase from the Bible, the one written above the sacristy door? 'We are like flowers of the field, here today and gone tomorrow.' Such thoughts don't do you a lot of good. Before Jack left I reminded him of our promise. The solemn oath I made him take that, if I don't go back and he does, he'll look after my Kitty. He'll marry her, they'll remember me. At first Kitty thought that was strange. She lost her temper and became angry at my dark thoughts. I begged her. 'If I'm dead, Kitty, you know Jack loves you and you love Jack.' 'Not the way I love you,' she replied. I persisted and Kitty agreed. So there it is.

The day is drawing on. Provisions have arrived, some tinned meat. Colonel Morrison says he's going to check it first. The last batch smelt worse than the corpses. I think of the meals I've had before: ale or beer, good and strong, and Kitty's mother making me Durham hotpots. Oh, the savoury smells! I'd sit at the kitchen table, look at Kitty, the luckiest man in God's creation! How I love my life because of her. If I close my eyes now and think hard, pencil in one hand, book in the other, I know she'll come to me, like she did along the lane when I came up from the pit. I'd see her waiting on the corner. Dreams are all I have. My dreams, her dreams . . .

The entry broke off.

Kitty closed the book and, putting her face in her hands, sobbed softly to herself.

Chapter 4

Jack crouched in the middle of the vegetable patch and dug at the earth with a dusty trowel. He heard the crunch of hobnailed boots and wondered who it was.

'Don't be so skittish, Jack,' he murmured to himself.

He didn't really know what he was doing. He had never seen Kitty like that before. When he was troubled, Jack always came out and dug up the soil, clearing the weeds which seemed to have a life of their own. It helped him think, calm down. The other lads, members of the Dead Hand Club, had heard about Fairfax's arrival. Few matters remained secret in a village like Caundon.

Jack put the trowel in the earth and sat staring at the red brick wall which separated the garden from the alleyway beyond. He really should go back and talk to Kitty. He felt almost sick with love for her but what could he say? Himself, Billy and Kitty, 'three peas from the same pod' was how his mother had described them. Only one divide, one yawning gap. The day Kitty told him in hushed whispers how Billy had proposed to her and how excited she was that they were to be married. She had taken the silence as approval,

consent, happiness. In fact Jack went off work for a week
complaining of an infection in his lungs, but old Dr Martin
hadn't found anything wrong. Jack had just sat in his small
cot room and bleakly faced a life without the woman he'd
always loved. 'Face as hard as a brick wall,' his father had
described Jack.

Old Miss Martindale, their teacher, had confided to his
parents that she never knew what he was thinking. It was
the same in the trenches. Some men cried or laughed. Bob
Daventry lived in his own dark world while Cunningham
spent most of his time seething and complaining. Jack was
different. Never a murmur, never a complaint, even when
the whizz-bangs were flying all around them. Other people
called him brave. Jack couldn't see the point of showing his
emotions, except where Kitty was concerned.

Jack had sat in that cot room and cried for a week. He'd
only emerged when he was certain he could compose himself. He'd gone back down the mines, patting Billy on the
back, all teasing and jostling, the usual jokes and banter
any young man would face from his comrades before his
wedding day. And on the day! Jack had downed a stiff
whisky. He'd played the role of the supportive best man,
the brief speech full of jokes. When Kitty and Billy had
left, he'd fled. Oh, how he'd fled through the night! Out
of Caundon down the country lanes, stumbling and falling.
He had reached Neville's Oak and bayed like a dog at the
moon. He'd cried like he never had before and never had
since. Jack had taken a vow: he'd never marry – and then the
war came.

'Master Jack, am I bothering you?'

He whirled round. Ernst Kurtz the German was standing

behind him; his usual bloodstained apron was missing, trousers one size too big for him fastened with a cord, a flannel shirt open at the neck.

'What is it, Ernst?'

The man looked down towards the back door. Jack pointed to an overturned butt perched against the wall.

'You'd best sit there. Are you in any trouble?'

The German shook his head and sat down, his strange eyes studying Jack. Sometimes the German looked as if he hadn't eaten, dark hair cropped, long pale face, high cheekbones pitted with scars from the pox, slightly slanted, dark-green eyes. Jack secretly considered him a true Prussian. Nevertheless, he felt a kinship with this German who had made it very clear he had no desire to return to his native country. He had worked hard to put down roots here.

'You are well, Jack?' Kurtz spread his feet. He took out a clay pipe from the pocket of his shirt as well as a thick wedge of black tobacco which he sliced with a small knife. He rubbed this between his fingers.

'Do you want some tea?' Jack asked. He made himself comfortable against the wall, sitting on the small raised bank.

The German shook his head. 'You are a very good man, Jack.' Ernst lit his pipe, balancing his flat cap on his knee. He pulled deeply and clouds of pungent smoke drifted upwards. 'I always like a pipe, it helps you think. If you're tempted to say something wrong, by the time you take it out of your mouth, you've thought again.'

Jack laughed. Ernst prided himself on the fact that he could understand what he called 'English humour'.

'Is everyone treating you well?' Jack asked.

'Sometimes the children hum, "Hun, Hun, Hun, go home!"'

'Ah, they're only baiting you. Teasing,' Jack explained. 'The bairns mean no harm. How is the butcher's business?'

'Very good. The farmers see the profit in it now. They bring their livestock in, not much. I can't keep flesh for long: chickens, geese, piglets. One day I'll make a profit and be able to buy cold storage. It's thanks to you, Jack.'

The German offered him a tattered piece of tobacco to chew. Jack shook his head. Kurtz had appeared out of nowhere in the spring following the Armistice. At first he had worked for Father Headon, sleeping in one of the outhouses, and he had worked hard. One night, in the Beaumont Arms, he had opened his heart. He wasn't a member of the Dead Hand Club but the other men felt sorry for him. The Miners' Association had advanced some money, Jack had negotiated with local farmers and an old shop had been found, and Ernst had taken to the butchery business like a duck to water. The farmers had agreed not to demand their money until Kurtz had sold the produce. Everyone had been satisfied, except Grant the grocer.

'What did you do in Germany, Ernst?' Jack asked abruptly.

'I worked for a fiddler.'

'A what?'

'Violins, the strings, you know.' The German demonstrated with his fingers. 'I was an apprentice before the war.'

'So, why the butcher's business?'

'People have to eat, Jack. Everything is going to change, because of the war.' He waggled a finger. 'Trust me. You people will get more pay. No, no.' He took the pipe out of his mouth and pointed it at Jack. 'The gas will come, the water, the electricity. The old ways have gone, Jack. Look at my country. Where is the empire? Where is the Kaiser? And people have to eat. Aren't you discontented? Don't you want more?' he continued. 'You fought the likes of me for four years and came back to what? Low wages, shabby conditions!'

Jack smiled, pleased to be distracted from his own problems. Kurtz was sharp; an outsider, he could sense the growing frustration of the miners, what Cunningham called the 'waiting after the war'. The growing demands for a better life, the increasing refusal to touch the forelock and bow.

'You're not a communist, are you?' Jack teased. 'The ones causing so much trouble in your country?'

'I'm not a communist, I am not a Catholic, I am not a German,' Kurtz replied defiantly. 'I am just a man who wants to put the past behind him and build a future.'

'And that's why you've chosen a Saturday afternoon to come and discuss it with me?'

Kurtz re-lit his pipe and pointed to the wall. 'We'd hear if someone came down the alley, wouldn't we?'

'Why, of course.'

'And Fairfax is not around?'

'Ernst, what is the matter?'

'Fairfax is the matter. He's come to Caundon for me.'

'Don't be stupid! What would the Provost Marshal's Office want with a German? You've told us yourself, Ernst, many Germans and Austrians have stayed in this country and applied for British nationality. You've got your papers; Father Headon helped you. He told me how, in London before the war, there were as many German Jews as there were Irish Catholics.'

'I am not a Jew!' Kurtz declared.

'What are you then, Ernst?'

The German played with the pipe, stubbing at the ash with the tip of his finger.

'Why are you frightened of Fairfax?'

'I have met him before.' Kurtz raised his head. Jack glimpsed the fear in his face.

'You remember, Jack.' He leaned forward. 'In the spring of nineteen eighteen, the Prussians,' that's how Kurtz always referred to his officer class, 'were preparing for their big push. In the prison camps in England, many of our officers believed they should do their duty as well. They encouraged us to escape. Committees were formed. Plans drawn up. Plots devised. I was always chosen because of my knowledge of English. I was captured early in the war . . .'

'Yes, you were!' Jack grinned. 'In fact, I think you were in England before our lot went to France.'

'They didn't know much about me,' Kurtz continued, 'because I always acted a part. We were like you, Jack. Many of the soldiers and officers who crossed into Belgium in the autumn of nineteen fourteen,' he made a rude sound and waved his hand, 'they were dead within six months. Everything was in chaos. Anyway, I came to England with the other prisoners. Oh, I pretended to escape—'

'But always made sure you were captured?'

'Oh yes, I like it here. I always have. Anyway, these Prussians took me at my word. I was always high in their councils.'

'And you betrayed them?'

Kurtz sighed deeply and nodded. 'They were fools. How do you get out of England? And, if you do, where would you go? To Spain? To France? Can you imagine French fishermen or peasants welcoming a German?' He hawked, turned and spat.

'That will do the cabbages a lot of good,' Jack remarked. Kurtz wasn't listening. 'The Prussians caused a lot of trouble. They hoped to distract the British, force them to keep troops in England to guard the camps. That's how I met Fairfax. He and the military police were sent to sort the troublemakers out. I always helped them.'

'In which case you've got nothing to fear.'

'I don't think that Major Fairfax will remember the likes of me. I dealt with his subordinates but two things I learnt about Fairfax. First, he was ruthless. He would have made a good Prussian.'

'And secondly?'

'His superiors think highly of him. His arrival here must be important.'

Jack felt his skin prickle with cold. 'I know what you are telling me, Ernst. Why should this ruthless, high-ranking, trusted officer from the Provost Marshal's Office bother to come to a place like Caundon?'

'That's right. I do wonder if he's here for me.'

'Oh, come off it, Ernst.'

'No, listen. I am going to tell you something, Jack, as if you are a priest. I will tell you two things. First about me and secondly about yourself.'

'Go on,' Jack urged.

'I was born and raised in a small village outside Munich. Very similar to this, though more beautiful. Both the land and the people were softer. I was happy, Jack. I married, she was like a little doll – Elizabeth. I called her Libby. She was beautiful, Jack, hair like the sun, eyes blue and round and innocent. I was an apprentice. The village had a music shop, a good trade under a man called Reinhardt. He was a tall, forbidding man. A widower. He treated me and Libby very well. I would go into Munich for him to buy this or that. Sometimes he even entrusted me with violins. I was happy. I didn't care about the bloody war.'

Jack smiled at how Ernst had picked up English phrases.

'What did I care if the Kaiser saw himself as God incarnate? But, as I said, it was just like here. The drums began to roll, the trumpets blared. Everybody had to go to war or you were a coward, a malingerer. Herr Reinhardt said that he would use his influence, find me a desk job. I joined the colours and soon found myself in the mud of Belgium. Can you suspect what happened, Jack?'

'No.'

'In October, Libby sent me a letter. She told me that she did not love me any more. She and Herr Reinhardt were one, body and soul.' Kurtz's face was now drawn, his eyes hard. 'In fact, they had been so before the war. It all fell into place. The trips to Munich, the encouragement to join the army. Reinhardt had wanted me out of the way. So this is what I did, Jack. After the first great battle, most of my officers were killed, thank God! Good riddance, they were idiots! All they could think of was riding in glory through Paris.'

'You deserted?' Jack asked.

Ernst shook his head. 'I was given leave, a chance to go home, but I didn't tell anybody. I returned home like a thief in the night. I took a pistol I had taken from one of my dead officers. I found Reinhardt and Libby in bed together. They thought they were so safe. I shot both of them, left the pistol and fled. No one knew I was coming home. No one saw me arrive or depart. Provided you had the right papers, travel in Germany was very quick, especially for a war hero. I returned to the front. Within a week I'd shot my own officer, some young Junker who wanted to lead me and the other lads to glory. When a group of Tommies came over the hill, I put my hands up and I was in England by Christmas.'

Jack stared at the German's pallid face. The story didn't shock him. He had heard of similar occurrences in the British Army. Wives and sweethearts who tired of the war and thought their men would never return. On most occasions the men accepted it; they were past caring about anything. Now and again, however, the more foolhardy or hot-headed tried to do something about it.

'And you were never suspected?'

Kurtz shrugged. 'I never tried to find out if I was. I had been cunning. I told my superiors that I was not going home and used the training the army had given me to teach my wife and her lover the true meaning of revenge.'

'And that's why you think Fairfax is here for you?'

Kurtz nodded. 'Why not? The war is over. Reinhardt had influence, powerful friends.'

Jack stared down at the soil. 'Why are you telling me this now?'

'I watch you, Jack. When you are in a camp for four years you always watch people. Fairfax might be here for me.' He sniffed. 'However, there might be a second reason for his visit: Fairfax may be here for you.'

'I don't know what you are talking about, Ernst.' Jack wiped the dirt from his hands. 'We were both soldiers,' he continued. 'We killed people. I have got nothing to hide.'

'I met Bob Daventry, Jack. He was coming from the woods. I asked him how he was. Bob said he had been burying one of his old friends, the usual story.' Kurtz's eyes never left Jack.

'He said he's never visited by Billy Hammond's ghost. He wants to ask you something, about your helmet being found near Billy's body.'

Jack's stomach clenched. To hide his unease he picked up the trowel, stabbing the earth as if it was a bayonet.

'Jack,' Kurtz continued, 'you keep yourself to yourself but the other men say you are a good mate with eyes only for Kitty.' Kurtz scratched at his cheek. 'I am your friend, Jack. Please believe that. I owe you a lot. Fairfax frightens you. He's landed like a great black crow in your village and he struts about, beady-eyed.'

'He's an officer,' Jack replied. 'He's got more time on his hands than he knows what to do with. I don't think you've got anything to worry about, Ernst, and neither have I. The war's over, cenotaphs are being built, plaques put up in churches. Widows have re-married. People like Bob Daventry,' he shrugged, 'they'll become rarer and rarer.'

'But the ghosts, Jack.' Kurtz got to his feet. 'They don't leave us. They never do. You remember that, Jack! In Germany we had a legend, about a man called the Ghost Whistler. They say he could enter a village and whistle up the dead; they'd rise and stand witness against the living so that justice could be done.'

Jack peered up. 'And you think Fairfax is our Ghost Whistler?'

Kurtz crouched before him. 'Yes, Jack, I do.'

'Rubbish!' Jack scoffed. 'Nothing but gossip. The war's over, both here and in Germany.'

Kurtz shook his head. 'It will never be over, Jack. Not as long as you, me, Kitty, Daventry, Cunningham and the rest remain alive. So, why is Fairfax here? Has he come to whistle up a ghost, Jack? If the war's over, why do you and the others meet every Saturday at the Dead Hand Club? The whole village knows about it.' He edged closer. 'And if the war's over, Jack, why do you and the others go out into the woods at night? What do you do there?'

Jack dug the trowel into the earth. 'Ernst, we go and bury our ghosts.'

'Beware of Fairfax!' Kurtz poked his finger in Jack's face. 'I know what he is. I've watched him with Kitty.'

'What are you saying?' Jack knocked his finger away.

'Oh, not that, Jack. Fairfax has studied you closely. He will perch on his branch and study us all before he begins to pick at our past.' Kurtz straightened and walked out through the narrow gate into the alleyway.

Jack watched him go. Then he dug at the earth, following the line he'd cut into the wall. He found the metal box, knocked away the earth, opened it and looked at the watch lying inside. He took it out and grasped it tightly. For a moment he closed his eyes and recalled that terrible night out in no-man's-land: the sky exploding above him, the earth shaking with the battering of shells, the spume of earth and muddy water, the shrieks of men trapped on the wire. Beside him, Billy, pale-faced, pleading and begging with him. Jack put the watch back in the box, placed it in the hole and re-covered it. Fairfax! He looked over his shoulder, up at the window, and saw a shadow move. Had the blind been pulled aside? Had the Ghost Whistler been watching him?

Kitty and her mother sat in the parlour, once the crowning glory of the Beaumont Arms. A former owner had covered the walls with wooden panelling which stretched almost to the ceiling. The huge hearth was empty and cold. A large bay window overlooked the high street. Kitty's mother always prided herself on how well-polished she kept the window. The gold-tasselled red pelmet hung neatly above it and on the mantelpiece stood mementos of her life: a statue bought in Morecambe Bay, framed photographs, two gilt candlesticks (a wedding present), a statue of the Sacred Heart and small vases of dried flowers. The floor was supposed to be polished but the varnish had long since worn off and now most of the floor was covered by carpets Kitty's father had bought from a wholesaler in Sunderland.

They were following the usual Saturday afternoon ritual. The bar and lounge were closed. Jack would be out in the garden or at the football. A moment of quiet from the world of men. Kitty's mother loved to reminisce. She would tell Kitty stories and legends of the past. How her great-grandfather and great-grandmother had come penniless from Sicily.

'Looking for work, they were,' she always declared. 'Not a penny between them, but they were good, decent people.'

And than there was her father's family who fled the famine in Ireland, determined to seek passage to America. Some had travelled on but others had stayed and put roots down in this small Durham village.

This particular afternoon was different. Kitty's mother was agitated; one look at her daughter's face told her that something was very wrong. Kitty had been crying, which was rare for her. Her daughter could become sad but only twice had she really sobbed: when her father, and then Billy, had been killed. Billy's death had been such a shock. They would never forget it: the knock on the door, Father Tom, shamed-faced and self-conscious, stepping through. Kitty had sobbed for days. She had lost weight, didn't eat or drink. Now Kitty's mother glanced at her quickly as she poured the tea: the sheen had gone from her daughter's face, although she had done her best to hide it.

'Did I do wrong, Mother?' Kitty lifted her mother's prized china cups. Usually they would laugh at this ceremony of pretending to be posh. Kitty would imitate the school inspector who held his cup with finger and thumb, the pinkie jutting out. Today was different: Kitty wasn't smiling.

'What do you mean, pet? Do wrong?' Mrs Courtney put the cup on the floor beside her. 'What's happened, Kitty, in one day? Is it Fairfax? It is, isn't it? He's come here to stir up old memories. What did he say?'

Kitty warmed her cold hands against the cup. She had managed to stop crying but this numbing coldness, as if she was going down with an infection, couldn't be shrugged off.

'I don't know.' She shook her head. 'I was talking to Billy's picture this morning.'

Her mother picked up her cup to hide her unease.

'I always thought,' Kitty continued in a rush, 'that everything was as it should be. Me, Billy, Jack, always together.'

'But you always loved Billy. Think,' her mother urged. 'You always did, it was Billy this and Billy that. True, Jack was always there.'

Kitty repressed a shiver. 'We should have talked about this years ago,' she said. 'Yes, I loved Billy, I always did. There was no one else for me. He was different from the rest: gentle, mischievous, he always made me excited. I felt life was good because of Billy. I loved him from . . .' Kitty shook her head. 'I can't remember when I didn't love him. Is that possible, Mother? Did you love Father like that?'

Her mother looked up at one of the faded photographs on the mantelpiece. 'It was different,' she replied. 'But I know what you mean. Once I'd met him and we talked, it was, well, as if all my life I had been waiting for that moment. There could never be any other.' She could have bitten her tongue off.

'So, I did do wrong,' Kitty said. 'I felt deeply about Billy yet I married again. Billy was killed in nineteen seventeen, two years later I married Jack.'

'Do you love him?' her mother asked. She leaned across and gently touched her daughter's face. 'You were always impetuous, full of life, Kitty, but you're also a dreamer. Women like us, we dream of love, a better life, but life's not like that. You and your storybooks and the knights in shining armour. This is Caundon, pet. Our men have been killed, life must go on.'

'You didn't marry again.'

'I might have done. You're different, Kitty. You are only a slip of a girl. You can't lock yourself away like some lady in the tower and grieve over Billy. Life goes on. Go down into the village, people are picking up their lives. Oh, they cry in their beds at night, and sometimes have a quiet weep as they come across memories, but the war's over, Billy's gone. Do you love Jack?' she repeated.

Kitty closed her eyes. 'I'm not too sure if I love Jack because of Billy or Jack because of himself. Did people gossip?' she asked, opening her eyes. 'When I married Jack?'

'No, no, don't start thinking like that.' Her mother shook her head. 'Kitty, you act the lady. You've been to the Evening Institute. You can read, write and teach. Father Headon is talking of getting you more qualified. You do a good job here. People like you. You are Kitty. You are young. You loved Billy and he was killed, like thousands and thousands of other young men. You have a life before you, a good man who loves you. So, don't be stupid! People don't think anything different and, if they did, you wouldn't care.'

Kitty smiled and sipped her tea.

'You know you love Jack,' her mother continued. 'Perhaps differently from Billy but you still love him. You did last night, didn't you? You did this morning? The only difference is Fairfax. What did he say?'

Kitty chewed on her lip. She was tempted to tell her mother about the journal but she felt that was something intimate, secret, almost as if Billy had come back to make love to her out in the fields beneath Neville's Oak. That was something private but her mother was right. Life might never be the same because of Major Fairfax.

'What did he say?' her mother demanded again. 'I'll go up there and give him a piece of my mind, officer or not!'

'It's not Fairfax,' Kitty replied. 'Not really. I keep thinking of the railways.'

'Railways? Kitty, are your wits wandering?'

'No. When we were little, Billy, Jack and I used to go down to the station, remember? Old Thompson used to sit there. Sometimes his own son would join us and we'd play a game. The steam engine would come rushing through. We'd try and count how many carriages or wagons it was pulling. That's what my life has been like. Billy is killed. So I married Jack. I never really reflected; it was one carriage following another.'

'That's the way life is, pet. We have little choice over what we do.' Her mother tried to hide her impatience. Headstrong, she thought, you were always headstrong. 'Look, Kitty.' She put her cup down on the floor again. 'You told me what happened. After the Somme, Billy returned. You went out for walks. You said he was strange and quiet. You even used the word "mournful". Do you remember? He made you promise that, if he was killed and Jack came back, you'd marry Jack. What did you say?'

Kitty stared across at the small wooden sideboard, the knobs missing from two of the drawers. How could she forget? Looking back she realised Billy truly believed he wouldn't return. He had been so insistent. 'Why?' she had asked. 'Why are you saying these things? Who I marry is up to me.'

Sometimes Billy would fall silent so she would tease him: a woman could now vote, even sit in Parliament, so she was not a parcel to be passed around. Billy would joss her back and the conversation would ebb away like water draining through a hole.

'You do remember, don't you?' Her mother broke into her thoughts. 'Billy was ever practical. He was frightened for you. Perhaps he knew you better than you know yourself. He'd know how you'd grieve. He'd also know that you loved Jack and Jack loved you.'

Kitty found she couldn't concentrate. How could she tell her mother how she had slipped, like falling in a dream? And how could she blame Jack? What wrong had he done?

'Come on, Kitty,' her mother urged. 'You didn't do wrong. It's certainly not against God's law for a widow to marry a man she loves. There's no guilt, there's no sin. So why this upset?'

'Nothing is what it appears to be.'

'Well, of course it isn't!' her mother snapped. 'All we have is life, Kitty, with all its sham and trickery, its drudgery, joys and sorrows. Fairfax,' she added grimly, 'is an unwanted interruption!'

Kitty closed her eyes. That was it, she thought. If her life had been carriages trundling by, one after another, Fairfax was the brake – those cold eyes, the way he studied her, hinting that he knew secrets. Was he mocking her grief? Did he see her as a merry widow? Or was it something else? Something about Jack? Kitty put the cup down and got to her feet so quickly her mother exclaimed in surprise.

'Kitty, what's the matter?'

'Nothing, nothing at all. I'm a bit confused. Betty will be here soon. Has Major Fairfax eaten?'

'I gave him his meal,' her mother retorted.

'Good, then I'll see if he wants some of this tea,' Kitty declared. She almost fled from the parlour.

Her mother refilled her cup and sipped, not even noticing she hadn't added milk. She'd tried to persuade Kitty but, somehow, she knew she had lost. Kitty was not convinced. She put her cup down and went and looked at the photograph on the mantelpiece.

'It's all wrong,' she murmured. 'The dead should be allowed to sleep.'

She went to the door and opened it. The Beaumont Arms was quiet. Closing it, she leaned against the door and joined her hands in prayer. She wouldn't tell Kitty what she knew, not now, not yet.

Chapter 5

Kitty took the narrow trackway leading to Nightingale Woods. She hadn't given Fairfax any tea, that was just an excuse to get out. Her mind was all a jumble. She felt sweaty and cold. She'd put an old coat of Billy's on, wrapping the belt round her. She wanted to get away and think. The conversation with her mother had done nothing to improve her state of mind. She wasn't aware of the weather, the fading sunlight, the leaves now forming a thin carpet, the ditches on either side, the towering hedgerows. All she was conscious of was the rap of her shoes on the cobbled track. She heard her name called and looked up. A carter, holding his dray horse by the reins, blocked the path.

'Are you all right, Kitty?'

She couldn't even remember his name. It wasn't important. She stared blankly at the man. He shouldn't really be there. No one should interfere in her thoughts. Kitty felt a stab of guilt at her selfishness. She smiled and raised her hand.

'I'm sorry. I was miles away.'

Kitty slipped by him and continued to walk. She found the stile and climbed it, as she had so many times, and crossed the field. Nightingale Woods, a dark copse of trees, beckoned her. When she had reached it she felt relieved, happy to be there. The gloom was cool and soothing. The sunlight was blocked out. She'd meet no one here.

She walked slowly towards Neville's Oak. The great oak tree, arms stretching up to the sky, always provided a canopy of comfort. Kitty felt as if she was in church. She sat down, her back to the trunk, and stared around. Only then did she notice the white ash and the deep pit beside it. Daventry, she thought; poor Bob's been out here digging his graves.

Kitty stared out through the trees at the fields beyond. Memories of childhood surged back: herself, Jack and Billy, sitting here talking, gossiping, planning what to do. The games they played: Neville's Oak would sometimes be a castle, at others a cave, a tower, a treasure trove. The years had moved on. They had changed but Nightingale Woods and Neville's Oak never did. She loved to mark the seasons by it: watch, during the early days of spring, for the first buds, the first signs of life. As time passed, she came here more often with just Billy. They used to lie here in the grass which fringed the oak. Sometimes they'd picnic on bread, cheese and a little ale, and they'd talk. Oh, they always had so much to talk about! She remembered Billy proposing, her accepting and running home to tell her parents. She'd also told Jack. Kitty recalled Jack's subsequent illness. He'd disappeared from Caundon for a full week. No one had sight or sound of him but then he had rejoined the lads, his 'mates', coming down to the Beaumont Arms, wishing her and Billy every success and happiness. Had he meant it? Of course he did!

Kitty recalled Fairfax's face, his questions, the handing over of the journal. In the space of a few heartbeats Fairfax had dropped a clump of dirt into the clear water of of her life. What had happened? She had no doubts about Billy. She'd loved him and married him. They had made love time and again. They planned a future until the war came. At first she expected him to come back, the same Billy. But stories were soon rife, of how the Germans had dug in and a great slaughter was taking place. When Billy came home, he was still the same Billy yet more quiet, vulnerable, withdrawn. Like the others, he very rarely talked about the war, more concerned about the harvest and what was happening in the village. He kept well away from the other soldiers, even Jack. During his last few days in Caundon Billy talked of death, of not coming home. She had teased him openly but he had been so insistent: what would happen if he didn't come back? Slowly but surely she had been drawn in. Billy had told her in terse, blunt sentences how many men had been killed. How he was lucky to have survived three months, never mind three years. He'd made the proposal. If he was killed, and Jack came back, would she marry Jack? Kitty had accepted eventually. Was it because Jack and Billy had merged into one person? Had she married Jack because she had given her word to Billy? Or because she loved Jack himself? That's what Fairfax had seized on: how can you love two men? Why did you re-marry so quickly?

Kitty stopped her thinking. She cleared her mind and listened to the sounds about her. She was aware of a cold breeze, the sun dipping; the light wasn't so strong, the shadows were lengthening. The wood was lonely. One further problem: Fairfax was a senior officer from the Provost Marshal's Office. He'd come to the Beaumont Arms to search out the truth, whatever that was. So what was he looking for? Why had he chosen the Beaumont Arms and not Caundon's other inn, the Dovecote? Was it something connected with Jack? Kitty suspected it was. If that was true, had Jack done something wrong? Wicked? Evil? Not just the job of a soldier carrying out his duty for King and country but something else? Was that the Jack she had married? The same Jack who'd played and danced with her beneath Neville's Oak?

Kitty was very much aware of Fairfax's presence. Within an hour of his arrival, he had met her and planted seeds. Was the soil fertile? Did she herself have doubts about Jack, her marriage to him? Or was she some vapid, empty-headed girl, quick to fret and worry, unable to bring common sense to bear? But the feeling of danger persisted, of matters not being quite right. She stared around. She heard a man's voice shout, a cry, and realised the football match must be over. Mother would expect her back at the Beaumont Arms.

She got up and dusted the twigs and grass from her coat. She went and looked down at the pit Daventry had dug. Bob had ghosts around him all the time. Perhaps Fairfax was no different. He had arrived in the village and brought ghosts with him, ghosts Kitty knew she should have addressed some time ago.

She was about to walk on when she heard a twig snap and whirled round. A shadow slipped behind the trees.

'Come on out!' she called. She felt no fear. This was Nightingale Woods, her playground. No one would hurt her.

She took a step forward. 'Please come out! Don't hide and skulk!'

The figure stepped out of the trees, tall and gangling with balding pate and long, craggy face. Kitty relaxed. She recognised the moleskin jacket, the old army trousers.

'Come on, Tom!' she smiled, beckoning Tom O'Neill forward. 'You can also bring the sack you've hidden beneath the bush. I'm not Colonel Morrison's gamekeeper.'

Sheepish-faced, the man retrieved a small leather sack, twine tied round its neck.

'You've been out snaring again, Tom.'

O'Neill's deep, melancholic eyes studied Kitty intently. 'You won't tell anyone, will you, Kitty?'

'Tell anyone?' She laughed, welcoming the relief this eccentric character brought. 'Tell anyone, Tom? Everyone knows you poach, including Colonel Morrison, that's why you're never caught. You're not really a very good poacher.'

'I snared two this afternoon.'

'I don't mean that,' Kitty retorted. 'If the gamekeepers wanted to take you, Tom, they would. So, a successful afternoon?'

'Something for the pot tomorrow and the rest of the week.' O'Neill walked to the edge of the freshly dug hole and stared down. 'Daventry! Poor Bob's been digging again, burying his ghosts. And you, Kitty? You are well? What are you doing out here all by yourself? Is Jack behaving himself?'

'Jack always does,' Kitty replied. 'Come on, Tom. I'll walk back into the village with you. You carry the sack but if you are caught you can say I did the poaching.'

Tom fairly danced from foot to foot. He had liked Billy. He had served with him in the Company of Friends and Kitty? Well, she was a lady. Whenever he went to the Beaumont Arms and his pockets were empty, there was always a jug of ale for him. He had been one of the older members of the company. Tom didn't like the dark twisting galleries beneath the pithead and had been only too pleased when the war broke out. A chance to get out of the mines, as he had put it, get away to see the world. He was one of the fortunates, he had survived. He had been a bachelor before the war and vowed he would remain one till he died. 'It's the best way for a man,' he often declared when he had drunk too much in the Beaumont Arms. 'Stay single, stay happy.'

Tom knocked at the loose earth and followed Kitty out of Nightingale Woods.

'Before you say it,' Kitty said, 'we will have to do something about poor Bob. However, I don't want to talk about him. Tom, you were in the war for four years, weren't you?'

The poacher's face became guarded. For the first time since these men had come home, Kitty realised how secretive and close they were.

'Come on!' she urged. 'You're a member of the Dead Hand Club. You meet every Saturday night in the bar. You swap stories. You served with Billy. What was it like?'

'Do you know, Kitty, all I remember is the earth moving, spouting up like a fountain, and the shells falling. The mist cold and clinging, carrying with it faint traces of mustard, cordite and gunpowder. The dead you got used to. There were so many dead, Kitty.'

'Why don't you talk about it?' Kitty insisted. 'Why doesn't Jack and the rest?'

'Oh, we do.'

'You know what I mean. You swap stories but you don't really talk about it.'

'It's the only way.' Tom shifted the sack from one hand to the other. 'You see, when you fought in the war there were two ways of living. One was to worry yourself to death and the other was just to forget it, to live for the minute.'

'You're not doing that now.' Kitty tapped the sack. 'You're filling your larder for the week.'

'No, this is different. In the war you concentrated on what you ate and what you drank, if you could get a good wash, a clean pair of socks, boots that didn't leak. Everything else went out of your mind. It was a habit. You got up, you did your jobs, you advanced, you ran away, you lay in the mud. As long as you didn't think, you were safe.'

'Was that Billy's fault?' she asked. 'Did Billy think too much?'

'You were married to him, pet.' Tom caught at her arm. 'You know what he was like, Kitty. He was brave but, yes, he thought a lot. I think he almost wished his own death.'

Kitty stared in disbelief.

'I don't mean he wanted to be away from you but from the carnage, the bloodshed. It affected Billy more than any of us.'

'Did he do wrong?' Kitty asked.

'We all did wrong.'

'No, you know what I mean.'

'Billy was a good soldier. He ate his food, looked after his mates, carried out orders. He never grumbled.'

'Tell me what he did do.'

Tom bit his tongue. 'Why are you asking me this now, Kitty? Billy's been dead for four years. You've never asked—'

'You know why I'm asking. You know why I didn't ask,' she retorted. 'That's the way it was. Billy was killed. No one wanted to talk about it.'

Tom stood holding the sack, pondering what Kitty had said.

'He wrote a lot,' he smiled. 'Yes, Billy was always writing in his journal. I remember him sitting, tongue half stuck out.'

'Tom.' Kitty turned round to face him squarely. 'Look at me!'

O'Neill lifted his head.

'How did Billy die?'

She watched his eyes, just for a moment she saw a shift as if O'Neill knew the truth but was preparing to say something else.

'How did he die?' she demanded.

'Well, you know how it was, pet. Orders were given, the whistles were blown. It was helmets on, bayonets fixed, ready to go over the top. We were shattered by bullets and shells. I was lucky, Billy was not, that was the end of the matter.'

'No, don't walk away!' Kitty caught his rough, calloused hand. 'Tom O'Neill, stand still and tell me the truth! I'm a big girl. My father was killed. Billy was killed. I want to know how Billy died. Was it in the morning or the evening?'

'It was in the morning, just before dawn.'

You are lying, Kitty thought. You are hiding something; that's why Fairfax is here.

'So,' she continued, feeling like a teacher in front of a group of stubborn boys, 'you were in the trench sheltering from shells and mortars, yes? I've read some of the accounts. I know a little of what happened.'

'We were hit by a hail of metal,' Tom replied. 'Men were dropping and screaming. Billy was one of those. One minute he was there, the next minute he was gone.'

'And so what did Jack do? Surely Jack was worried?'

'Jack was very worried, very upset. Colonel Morrison sent the corpse down to the orderly station.'

'And that's why Billy's watch was never returned home?'

'That's right, pet. We couldn't bring everything home. His body was probably buried with the rest.'

Kitty was about to ask about the journal but no, that was her secret. She decided to change tack.

He made to step round her but she blocked his way.

'No, listen, Tom. When Billy was ready to go over the top, would he take his journal with him? You said he was always writing.'

'Why, of course. Just because you left your trench didn't mean that would be the trench you returned to. That journal was precious to Billy. No one ever read it.' He patted his jacket. 'He always kept it up here. We always kept our valuables about us, just in case we had to run.'

'And Billy's body was never searched?'

'Well, not by us. Daventry never buried him. I suppose he was buried in a mass grave. Or perhaps, and I don't mean to upset you, hinny, that's why we don't talk about it, maybe his body was left at the orderly station and sank beneath the mud. God knows, thousands did.'

Kitty nodded. 'All right, Tom, we'd best get back, otherwise those rabbits will come back to life and wonder what you are doing.'

Kitty walked to the edge of Caundon village with Tom and said she would see him later. Instead of going straight home, Kitty went back up the country lane. Something was wrong. If Billy had that journal on him and his body was never searched, how did Fairfax obtain it?

Kitty walked on and found herself outside the gates to St Bede's Church. The graveyard, on either side of the path leading to the main door, was deserted. No one was there tending flowers or cutting grass. A bee hummed. Lazy butterflies hovered from one flower to another. A sharp contrast to the silence of Neville's Oak.

She walked up the path. The main door was locked but the side entrance was open. She slipped in. She always loved the smell of the church, that mixture of fragrant incense and candle wax, the way the light poured through the windows, creating dappled shadows in the coolness. All the memories it held: first confession, first Communion, confirmation and, of course, her and Billy's wedding day. She stood at the Communion rail and looked up at the high altar: the tabernacle, the three great candlesticks on either side, the sanctuary lamp flickering in its red glass jar. Kitty smiled. When she was little, she thought the candle was red. It took years before she realised it was only a reflection of the glass. She wanted to pray but the words wouldn't come. She stood, allowing her jumbled thoughts to turn and turn again.

'Are you well, Kitty?'

She looked over her shoulder. Father Tom Headon stood in the doorway of the sacristy: black shiny suit, white dog collar, a stole round his neck.

'Is anything wrong?' He came forward. 'I've just heard confessions. Is that what you want?'

She was about to say yes but bit back her reply. 'No, I just went for a walk, Father, then I came here.'

The priest studied her closely. 'You were never very good at lying, Kitty! The years haven't improved you. You're worried, aren't you?'

'Yes, I am, Father. It's Fairfax's arrival, the questions he asks. He made me think about Billy and marrying Jack.'

'Yes, I thought he might do that,' the priest replied quickly. 'I suspect Major Fairfax has a gift for making people think.'

'Do you know why he's here, Father? What would bring a man like that to Caundon?'

Headon breathed in. 'I'm a priest, Kitty. Once I was a chaplain in the army. I did my years of service and when I left I was glad. I visited Colonel Morrison. He told me about Fairfax.'

'And?'

'I think Fairfax was invited here.'

'What?' Kitty took a step forward. 'Invited?'

'That's just a suspicion.' The priest spread his hands.

'What do you mean?' Kitty insisted. 'He was invited here? You didn't invite him, Father. Did Colonel Morrison?'

The priest shook his head.

'Then who?'

'As God is my witness, I don't know. Somebody in Caundon perhaps? I've been thinking about it all day,' the priest hurried on. 'Fairfax must have been told something, given information, that's why he's here. Only time will tell what the truth is.' He looked down the church to make sure it was empty. 'Kitty, I've just heard confessions. When I sit in that confessional, it's a different world: men and women come to confess things. Well, if they were published in a newspaper, they'd die.'

'What things, Father?'

'Memories, guilt, resentments.' The priest paused. 'I can't tell you the secrets of the confessional. Life is like one of those cream cakes I like so much and Dr Martin says I shouldn't eat. You see the icing and, when you cut, other layers lie beneath. It's the same with Caundon. Terrible things happened in France. They are now claiming that a whole generation has been wiped out. Millions of families in this country and throughout Europe were affected. When the war ended, everybody was pleased, happy to come home. They wanted things to be as they once were. They desperately tried to make sure that happened.' The priest took a step closer. 'But that's not the case. Life has changed. It takes time for the other layers to move, to break through the surface. In some cases a few months, in others it might be years. Do you understand that, Kitty?'

She nodded.

The old priest was now impassioned. 'Kitty, I've heard confessions of widows who really believe that their husbands are alive and still living with them.'

'I don't believe that, Father.'

'It's true.' He pointed down the church. 'I sit in that dark little box and my soul is chilled. One widow, I won't tell you her name, confesses every month to quarrelling with her husband, betraying her husband. "Look," I reply. "So and so's dead, he has been for years." "Yes, Father," comes the whispered reply. I give her absolution.' He shook his head. 'A month later she's back, confessing the same sins.'

'Is that what's happening to me, Father? The hidden layers breaking through?'

'It could be, Kitty. Fairfax's arrival is the key to unlock the box of secret guilt and hidden regrets in your soul. You've heard of the story of Pandora, haven't you?'

'It's one of my favourites, Father.'

'That's what's happening now and, before you ask, you have two choices. To slam the lid down and turn the key or to throw the lid back and let whatever lies there come out.'

The priest opened the small gate of the Communion rail.

He walked across the sanctuary and turned, resting one hand against the wooden pulpit.

'I think it's best, Kitty, to open the box. Say your prayers and face whatever comes.'

'What happens if I can't, Father?'

The priest studied this young woman's pale, ivory face, those beautiful eyes, the shock of black hair; even dressed in an old coat she looked as pretty as a picture. The old priest tried to hide his deep sense of sadness. He had held Kitty over the font as a baby and baptised her, helped with her first Communion. He'd quietly chuckled when she had made her first confession and chattered about apples she had stolen. 'The leading member of the Trinity' as he called Kitty, with her two acolytes, Billy and Jack, two good men, always close behind. He recalled both wedding days and sensed what a tortured path Kitty's soul was now following. He had wondered at the time but had kept his own counsel. Now Fairfax had arrived. A man who believed God had been killed on the Somme. No God? No soul?

'What are you staring at, Father?'

'The past, Kitty, the present. If there is anything I can do to help . . .'

'Fairfax?'

'Let him be, Kitty. Let him do his work and go. Do you want to pray?'

She shook her head. 'Not at the moment, Father.'

He went over, took her hand and rubbed it between his. 'I don't want to sound stupid, lass, but that's the best advice I can give.'

She thanked him, genuflected towards the tabernacle and walked down the church, closing the door behind her.

Father Tom sat down on the altar steps and rubbed his face. Mrs Thirkell, his ancient housekeeper, whom he secretly called 'Holy Mother Church', so old and set in her ways, would soon be out banging the lid of the teapot. Father Tom wondered what he could do. Perhaps if he took the train to Hexham sought an interview with the Bishop? Or would Colonel Morrison help? The priest closed his eyes. Colonel Henry Morrison couldn't help himself, locked in the grip of his own past.

'We sow dragon's teeth, Lord,' he whispered. 'They always sprout and bear fruit.'

He recalled his own life and mistakes, the lack of fervour, the indiscretions, the temptations not resisted, the self-pity and lack of compassion, yet he had tried. He was always trying to be a good priest. Fairfax's arrival would mean his people would need him.

'Are you going to sit there all day, Father? Must I work and work to pour cold tea? And scones which have gone hard?'

'Holy Mother Church' stood in the sacristy doorway, battered slippers on her feet, her corpulent body hidden by the largest pinafore the priest had ever seen.

'Do you ever regret things, Ellen?' the priest asked.

'Regret, Father? I regret making your tea! Of scalding myself so you can drink it cold.' Little black currant eyes in the wizened face glared suspiciously at the priest. 'Don't you like my cooking, Father?'

The priest was tempted to reply that it was one of the great penances of his life but bit his tongue.

'You are a good woman, Ellen. By the time you are finished with me, you'll make me a true Christian!'

Holy Mother Church glared at him again, stamped off

through the sacristy and into the priest's house. Father Tom was about to get up when he heard a sound.

'Who is it?' he called.

A figure emerged from the shadowy porch: Len Evans, bicycle clips on, hobnailed boots scraping the flagstones, still puffing and panting after riding his bike.

'Can I have a word, Father?'

'You can have two, Len. Come on.'

The policeman marched up the nave, helmet under his arm. Father Tom half expected him to salute. Evans stopped, genuflected and sat down, unbuttoning the top button of his uniform.

'Finished for the day, Len?'

'Half of it, Father. I'll go home and have some tea. Nice toast coated with dripping. I'll ride round once again—'

'And you'll join the rest of the lads in the Dead Hand Club.'

The policeman grinned sheepishly and ran his fingers through his hair. 'Well, Colonel Morrison is the local magistrate and the lads do no harm. Closing hours may be good for the city but not the Beaumont Arms. They are doing no harm.'

'That's why you are here, isn't it, Len?'

The policeman kept his head down. 'I'm frightened, Father.'

'Of Fairfax?'

'Yes, Father, of Fairfax. You know the reason why. He's more than some Redcap come to hunt out a deserter or a thief who's nicked the regimental silver.'

'I know nothing,' Father Tom declared.

'No, but you suspect.' Len lifted his head. 'I know, Father, and you know, the Provost Marshal's Office has information.

Where it comes from, God only knows. Now, it may be something they've found . . .'

'And?' the priest prompted.

'Or something they knew already, Father, but let wander like a horse. Now they've got a halter and bridle around the horse's neck and want to bring it back to the stables.'

The priest left the sanctuary and crossed to sit beside the policeman.

'Have you done something to be be sorry about, Len? Is that why you've come here, to make your confession?'

'Father, you've heard my confession, you know it's me: my boots, the smell of sweat, I couldn't hide anything. However, I've never confessed anything I've done in the war. Perhaps I should have.' The policeman leaned back against the bench. 'Once we were taking a trench, bayonets fixed, hand-to-hand fighting. I just jumped in with the rest and drove my bayonet into a German. I've killed others, Father, but it was the look of astonishment on the German's face, the way he tried to protect himself. Then I come back here.' He pointed to a painting, depicting Moses carrying the ten commandaments. 'Every time I see that, the words "Thou shalt not kill" leap out at me. I've killed and I've killed again.'

'But that was war, Len.'

'Is that right, Father? Does the Church make exceptions?'

'You know what I mean. Each situation has to be judged by itself. You were a soldier, you thought the cause was right.'

'Yes, I did, Father, until I saw that German's face. Somebody's son, husband or brother.'

'And you did other things?'

'Of course I bloody well did!'

The priest held up a hand.

'Sorry, Father, I didn't mean to swear in church.'

'Oh, don't apologise. I often do it myself.'

'It's Fairfax. A high-ranking officer, he's travelled to the ends of the world, that's what Caundon is to a man like him. He's taken up residence at the Beaumont Arms like an assize judge.' Len ticked the points off on his fingers. 'He must be pretty confident. He must have some evidence about a very serious crime. If they were looking for deserters, it would be a truckload of Redcaps.'

'So, what do you think, Len?'

'It sounds strange, Father, but I think he's here because of a murder. I say strange because for four years I killed on behalf of King and country. I suspect Major Oscar Fairfax doesn't give a damn about that. We are talking about a different type of killing, Father. What's the phrase the lawyers use? Malice aforethought?'

The priest rubbed his hands together. He noticed that the light pouring through the sanctuary windows was beginning to fade. Evans was right. Only a case of grievous murder would bring Fairfax to Caundon. The priest swallowed hard. If that was the case, and Fairfax had his way, an arrest would be made.

'You are thinking the same as me, aren't you, Father? One of us lads committed a murder, with malice aforethought. That's a hanging offence.'

Father Headon slipped to his knees, pressing his thumbs against his forehead.

'But why wait three years?' Evans continued. 'It must be something where evidence exists and fresh proof has been provided.'

Father Headon got to his feet. He stared down at the

policeman. 'You are right, Len. When Fairfax climbs aboard that train and leaves here, Caundon will never be the same again, if he has his way. I attended an execution once in Durham gaol, an Irishman, a Fenian. I have always prayed to God that I never have to attend another. God forbid it should be one of my parishioners!'

Chapter 6

Kitty leaned against the bar. Foam, white and frothy, from spilt beer floated along its polished surface. It reminded her of the sea at Seaton when the waves receded leaving a white lace on the golden sands. She glanced up. Mother had dimmed the oil lights, giving the bar a warm glow. The tobacco smoke from the pipes and the Woodbines curled like forgotten ghosts. Memories of the chatter and laughter. The 'witching hour', as a customer had said, had come and gone. All that was left were stained tables, empty glasses, tin ashtrays full of stubs. Behind her the bottles and tankards gleamed. One bottle caught her eye, a large container containing 'God in a bottle' – it held the fronds from the previous Palm Sunday's celebration.

Kitty felt tired. Her mind teemed with scraps of conversation from different customers about rabbit runs, pigeon crees or the stories of the miners, teasing between the hewers and the fillers. Even here the mines followed them. Black dust from the men's pockets and boots strewed the floor. Yet it had been a good evening. The miners had received their fortnightly pay and were intent on enjoying their Saturday night's drinking and Sunday rest. The Beaumont Arms made a good profit. Kitty's mother even wondered about buying a proper Doulton flush closet or some good-quality chairs carved out of walnut, with intricate balloon backs, the trademark of Newcastle craftsmen who, in their catalogue, proudly proclaimed themselves to be 'purveyors of quality furniture'.

Kitty grasped the wet rag even tighter. The backs of her legs ached from standing so long. In the cellar below, old John was singing to himself as he re-arranged the barrels and furtively finished the tankard he always kept filled. Kitty glanced towards the snug at the far end of the bar. In the great coaching days, that had been the room where the quality travellers could rest and recuperate while the horses were changed. Father had turned it into a small select, what was commonly called the 'snug', with a glass-filled walnut door. This stood ajar, and plumes of cigarette smoke billowed out. The hum of conversation was audible, now and again the faint notes of a song. Every Saturday night the Dead Hand Club met there. Usually Kitty ignored them, now she was full of curiosity. She was still angry with Jack, whom she'd hardly seen all evening. She squeezed the rag and the cold spilt beer seeped out. Was she angry or just frightened? That conversation with Father Headon – she shook her head, it had done no good. She was frightened by Fairfax's arrival and yet angry. But why? At herself for not asking earlier? Or with Jack for keeping secrets to himself? Or was it fear of the unknown?

Major Oscar Fairfax had kept well away. Not once during the evening had he come down. Mother had taken his supper up on a tray: a meat pie, potatoes, a glass of stout, some apple pie and a cup of specially ground coffee with a small brandy. Mother had also been watching her closely.

Kitty finished cleaning the bar, straining her ears to catch any conversation. She bent down and squeezed the rag into a bucket. What was it those men talked about? She'd always thought it was memories, old stories. Not any longer. They had secrets and she wished to be privy to them. She got up and pressed against the bar, staring across at an old stool, its cushioned top frayed and loose. Fairfax also intrigued her. For some strange reason he reminded her of those mysterious characters in novels: the dark knight at the court of Arthur or the mysterious traveller. Did he attract her? There was something about his dark face and eyes, the coolness, the sense of a controlled passion, which reminded her of Billy, and indeed Jack. Was it something common to all men or just to soldiers?

'Are you dreaming?'

Kitty started and looked round.

Fairfax stood in the doorway, cigarette in one hand. He had taken his jacket off but the thick trenchcoat was draped over his shoulders. He looked as if he had been sleeping. He placed the cigarette in the corner of his mouth, watching her all the time. Kitty was relieved that he had made his presence felt, no longer concealing himself. He was dangerous; just the way he stood there so languidly, elegantly, watching her, trying to assess her true worth, unsettled her. She was going to ask about the meal her mother had served but a spurt of anger prevented her. They were past that. They'd crossed a line. What was the point of social pleasantries? She threw the wet rag into the bucket and walked along the bar, trailing her fingers, holding his gaze.

'You slept well, Major Fairfax?'

He gave a slight smile, or was it a smirk? Kitty breathed in.

'You planned all this, didn't you?'

'Planned, Kitty?' He rested against the bar. 'What do you mean, planned? Aren't you going to offer me a drink, a tot of brandy? It always calms the nerves, Kitty. You should drink some yourself.'

'My mother owns a pub,' she retorted. 'I've seen the effect of drink. I'm pleased just to serve it.'

'Why, Kitty, are you a puritan? A teetotaller or a member of the Temperance Society? Do you put your little straw bonnet on and, parasol in one hand, go down to join their meetings?'

'You are making fun of me and, as usual, not answering the question. Why are you really here, Major Fairfax?'

'Call me, Oscar.'

'I'll call you Oscar when you tell me the truth.' Kitty felt her face flush. She turned, grasped a shot glass, took down the precious bottle of brandy and filled it to the brim. She turned, quietly praying that her hand wouldn't tremble, and pushed it across. As he grasped it, his fingers brushed hers. He held the glass up and silently toasted her.

'I am not mocking you, Kitty,' he murmured. 'And if I appear like a fox strutting through the farmyard, then that's the way things are.'

She noticed his eyes were blue. She glimpsed the mischief. You are not being cruel, she thought, you genuinely enjoy teasing me. She caught something else, a deep sadness and hurt. He lifted the glass again, his gaze never faltering.

'I'm an officer and a gentleman, Kitty,' he added. 'I don't flirt. One of the rules of the club is to leave another man's wife alone.'

Kitty made to retort but he held up his fingers.

'Do you know, Kitty, I'm going to give you a confidence. It's from the heart. When a man speaks from the heart, he speaks the truth.'

'And what is the truth?' Kitty interrupted, aware of how silent the snug had become. She relaxed as Evans's strong voice burst into song: 'I am a miner's son, there's darkness in my life. But I know a pretty maid and she is the light . . .'

'You are a pretty maid, Kitty. In the London clubs, the men would gather round you like bees about a honeypot.' He studied her face, the light olive sheen, the large dark eyes, the lips, sometimes thin, sometimes generous. 'Your hair is black,' he murmured. 'Jet black.'

'Why are you here, Major Fairfax?'

'I'm here about life and death, Kitty. The British Army never forgets.'

'You should join us.' Jack stood in the doorway of the snug. He leaned against the lintel. Kitty felt a flush of excitement. Jack reminded her of a boxer about to confront an opponent: shirt open at the neck, braced trousers, feet pushed into his Sunday best shoes. He looked younger, more dangerous than she had ever seen him. Kitty sensed his growing resentment, even hatred for this officer.

'You are drinking our brandy, Major Fairfax?' Jack came forward. 'It is our brandy, isn't it, Kitty? Kitty and her mother run the Beaumont Arms while I hack the coal. What do you hack, Major Fairfax?' He gestured. 'Come on over. Join the boys, our lads. It'll be good to have an officer and a gentleman gracing our presence. You too, Kitty. Bring a glass of lemonade.' And, not waiting for an answer, Jack walked back into the snug.

Fairfax shrugged, tugged his coat closer over his shoulders

and walked across. Kitty removed the cloth and quickly filled a glass – she didn't know whether it was clean or not.

The Dead Hand Club were all there in the snug, sitting on the quilted seats bolted against the wall. The window had been opened so the tobacco smoke could escape yet its fug still hung heavy and thick. Fairfax sat on a stool just within the door. He seemed more interested in the progging mat on the floor than the company. Kitty had made the mat herself out of hessian her father had bought from a hardware shop in Durham. How old had she been? Fourteen, fifteen? At the time she had been ever so proud of it.

Jack took a chair in the centre of the gathering, men with shirt buttons undone, flat caps rolled up beside them, faces flushed, eyes gleaming; they had all drunk deeply that night. There was Len Evans, who should really be riding his bike for one last time around the village. Daventry, Cunningham, Tom O'Neill. Their hostility was tangible. They glared at Fairfax and made no attempt to greet him. Jack was full of devilment. He got up and filled all their glasses from the big earthenware jug. Then he sat down and waited until Fairfax had lit another cigarette.

'Well, Major Oscar Fairfax of the Provost Marshal's Office.' Jack raised his glass mockingly. 'Welcome to the Beaumont Arms and the Dead Hand Club.'

'Do you know why we call it that?' O'Neill slurred.

Fairfax sipped his brandy, did not answer.

'Were you in the trenches?' Evans stared across, rocking slightly backwards and forwards. 'Were you an hofficer?' he scoffed. 'Were you an hofficer with your Sam Browne belt and little revolver in your hand? Did you lead the lads over the top? Or were you one of the staff? Did you keep your little soft arse warm and dry back at headquarters?'

'Len, there's no need for that,' Kitty intervened. She glanced across at Jack; his eyes remained hard.

Kitty realised how little she knew of their world. You are men possessed, she thought, and I have never realised that. You are like haunted houses full of ghosts. You meet here to share those ghosts. Daventry was sitting with a small trowel in his hand. How bizarre you look, she thought. She wanted to leave but stood rooted, fascinated. Every other Saturday she'd come in here. They'd teased and laughed with her, just a group of lads enjoying a drink, but they had been pretending. This was the real Dead Hand Club. They were like actors playing a part and Jack was their troupe leader.

'Well, sir?' Jack put his glass down on the table. 'The officer's been asked a question.'

'I was in the trenches,' Fairfax replied. 'I stood up to my waist in mud, blood and shit. I have seen the whizz-bangs come and the shrapnel scatter like snowflakes. I've seen men trying to push their innards back in their stomachs. I've walked through trenches where the dead carpeted it for yard upon yard. Walking upon the dead, eh?'

His reply blunted the edge of their hostility. Fairfax went to unbutton his shirt.

'Do you want to see my scars?' He tapped his left side. 'A bayonet wound here, took it from a German. We'd entered a copse of trees, I forget the place, not far from the old battle site of Agincourt. They were retreating and we came on too fast.' His hand moved to his right shoulder. 'A bullet wound here.' He tapped his thigh. 'A piece of shrapnel.' He touched the side of his head. 'But the worst wounds are inside, aren't they? Do you want me to match your stories? I'll do so.'

'What stories can you tell us?' Evans challenged.

'What would you like to hear, soldier?'

'About the men who were shot.'

'Many men were shot.'

'You know what I'm talking about.' Evans's face turned ugly. 'Young boys who didn't leave the trenches. The men who'd had enough and tried to desert.'

'Why, soldier, they were cowards, deserters. And, possibly, traitors.'

'They were frightened.'

'Frightened?' Fairfax's voice rose. 'Weren't you frightened? Shall I tell you something, soldier? I was on the Somme when the Germans released mustard gas, yellow and acrid. I watched two of my men choke to death. Do you know why I didn't perish? I was so frightened I wet myself. I peed into my handkerchief and used that to cover my mouth and nostrils while I staggered away. Everyone was frightened. Not everyone fled.'

'A good answer.' Jack lifted his glass. 'But shall I tell you something, sir? I think more of our lads were killed by our officers than by the Germans. You go out and talk to Colonel Morrison about some of the officers sent out to serve under him. Bright-eyed and red-cheeked, waving their pistols: "Come on, lads, over the top!" Over the top for what? The poor bastards were killed as soon as they showed their heads.'

'Aye, you are right there,' O'Neill spoke up, leaning back. 'Mind you,' he scratched his head, 'Morrison's good. He looked after us. Do you know what the colonel told me?'

O'Neill sat forward. 'One day we were sheltering at the bottom of a trench, God knows where the rest of the lads were. The Germans had a machine gun: chatter, chatter, chatter. "Do you think we'll win the war, sir?" I asked. Do you know what the colonel said? One of the few times I ever heard him swear. He said, "I don't give a—"' O'Neill waved towards Kitty. "All I know is that I am taking as many of you lads home with me as possible."'

'He's a good man, Morrison,' Jack agreed. 'Remember the time we were pulled back to that French village? The one where the church steeple was blown off?' Jack closed his eyes, grinning to himself. 'Some of the lads helped themselves to this and that and the French messieurs and their ladies were eager to claim compensation.'

'Ah yes! I remember this,' Evans grinned.

'This French lady came, a farmer's wife,' Jack continued. His eyes glanced at Kitty as if she was a stranger. 'She goes up to old Morrison and claims for three ducks and two pairs of knickers stolen from her farmyard.'

Jack quelled the laughter with his hand. Even Fairfax smiled.

'"Ducks?" Morrison cried. "My lads might steal ducks but if your knickers have gone, it's because you gave them away as a keepsake."'

Kitty found herself smiling.

'"I'll pay for the ducks," Morrison said, "but the knickers are your concern." "Non, non, monsieur!"' Jack put his glass down, imitating the Frenchwoman. '"They didn't take the knickers as a keepsake." "Well, what for then?" Morrison demanded. '"Ah, monsieur, they used them to carry away the ducks."'

There was loud laughter.

'What do you think of that, Major Fairfax?'

'Something similar happened to me,' Fairfax said. 'You recall the great push?'

'How can I forget it?' Jack's voice was sarcastic but Fairfax ignored it.

'Well, the British line was moving faster than our supplies and a great deal of pillaging was taking place. We received orders from headquarters to put a stop to it.'

'Of course,' Jack interrupted.

'It was a village in Alsace,' Fairfax continued. 'We heard a commotion at a farm. A group of the Worcestershire Regiment were billeted there. Anyway, to cut a long story short, I went round the farm building and found this soldier wringing the neck of a chicken.'

'He could have been shot for that!' Evans called out.

'The chicken was dead,' Fairfax continued evenly. 'I said, "Soldier, you know the orders against looting?" "Looting, sir?" the soldier replied. "This is a German chicken, sir. I was crossing the farmyard when it attacked me."'

The laughter grew.

'I am exercising my right of self-defence.'

'And what happened?' Jack asked.

'We shared the chicken,' Fairfax smiled. 'Soft and tender, it was, cooked over a charcoal fire. The soldier was a farmer. He collected some herbs. I haven't eaten finer in any London restaurant.'

'Do you eat finely?' Jack seemed annoyed at the way Fairfax had deftly turned the conversation.

'I eat and I drink. Just like you do,' Fairfax gazed round the room, 'here in the Dead Hand Club. Mind you,' he finished his brandy, 'it's a strange name for a club of war veterans.'

'I'll tell you why,' Bob Daventry spoke up, tapping his trowel against the table. 'We all got marooned.'

'Marooned?' Fairfax asked. 'A strange word for a soldier.'

'It's from *Treasure Island*,' Jack explained. He leaned across and gently prodded Fairfax on the shoulder. 'He took one book to war, our Bob did: *Treasure Island*. He won it in a competition at Sunday School. There's nothing our Bob doesn't know about pirates and being marooned.'

'We were marooned,' Bob continued, eyes half-closed, 'in a sea of mud. We had taken a German trench and were told to hold it. In fact it became our home. The walls were breaking down so we used everything to strengthen it. I don't know if we did it or the Germans. The Boche never really took care of their dead. Anyway, a corpse lay buried in the side of the trench. As the days passed, the walls gave way and the dead hand stuck out. It was really strange,' he mused. 'I don't know what the rest of the corpse was like. There was no smell, Perhaps it was the mud, or the sand. The hand never decomposed, did it, lads? It was soft and full. Anyway, we took it as a sign of good luck. Every time we went over the top, we'd shake it and wish it well. I never discovered who it belonged to.'

'None of us did,' Jack took up the story. 'We were too superstitious to find out. Now and again an hofficer,' again the mockery, 'would come down and tell us to cover it up. Old Morrison didn't object. He was as superstitious as we were. I never knew what happened to that hand or why it didn't decay.' His eyes held Fairfax's. 'But it kept us alive, or some of us. And we weren't ever visited by the Provost Marshal's men.'

Kitty stiffened. She'd heard about the dead hand and always regarded it as just a story; these men viewed it as a precious talisman.

'And every time we gather here,' Evans said, 'we always begin the evening by toasting the owner of that hand be he German, English or French. In the end, Major Fairfax, who gives a damn?' His voice rose. 'Did it really matter? We came home safe. Kaiser Bill has gone and we've done our job for King and country.'

'But he knows all this, doesn't he?' Jack filled his beer glass and pushed the jug towards O'Neill. 'I wager a well-earned pound to one of Major Fairfax's precious guineas that our visitor knows all about the Dead Hand Club. Just like he knows all about me, Len, Tom and Bob.'

'And Billy?' Fairfax added quietly.

Jack's face turned ugly. 'Billy's one of our heroes,' he whispered. 'We toast him too. And all the others who never returned. Do you know something, Major Fairfax? We sometimes talk about why we went through it all. Ever been down a mine, sir? Ever seen the gas roll towards you? Or cough up mouthfuls of coal dust? We had a strike early in the year. Got nothing for it, as I'm sure you know,' he sneered.

The snug had fallen silent.

'I want to know why you are here,' Jack went on. 'I bet my wife asked the same question. You're not going to tell her, are you? What did we do so wrong, apart from kill for God, King and country?'

Cunningham, who had sat slouched in the corner, apparently half asleep, suddenly stirred. 'I didn't kill for God!'

he bawled, smacking his lips. 'But Jack's right, master officer.'

Red spots of anger appeared high on Cunningham's face, his rather slit eyes now gleamed. He was the one Kitty feared the most. Cunningham could be violent; even as a young man before the war, he was free with his fists. Her own father had clashed with him on many occasions. She had always been frightened by this tall, bony man with his pitted cheekbones and simmering violence. Only Billy had been able to calm him. He used to catch him by the wrist, crack a joke and lead him away. Jack would do the same. Cunningham had been raised as an orphan; his parents had died in one of the epidemics which had raged during a wet winter. He was a man full of resentment, which the war had only stoked. Cunningham had played his usual part tonight, pretending to be asleep. He had probably listened to every word, looking for the opportunity to erupt.

Fairfax was studying him intently. 'I know all about you, Jim Cunningham.'

'Do you now? What do you know? That I don't believe in God? That I won't bend the knee, bless myself or let Father Headon hear my confession?'

'I wonder what you would confess.' Fairfax drew on his cigarette. He didn't seem one whit disturbed.

'What does that mean?' Cunningham became defensive.

'Why not invite me round to your house, eh, Jim? We'll have a mug of tea and a chat about it.'

Cunningham faltered, his eyes grew watchful.

Fairfax moved on, ignoring him, intent on Jack. Kitty wanted to leave but she daren't. Fairfax was intent on baiting these men and didn't care about the consequences.

'I do know,' Fairfax confessed, 'a great deal about you all. I am here because of you.' He ignored Kitty's sharp intake of breath. 'We have unfinished business, the army and you. All of you.'

'What business?' Jack asked sharply. 'If you were a civilian police officer, you would have to tell us why you are here. Don't start hinting at secrets. You are not here because Jim Cunningham took a few jam jars, paltry mementos of the war.'

Cunningham sprang to his feet.

'Sit down, soldier,' Jack snarled, his gaze never leaving Fairfax. 'I think our major is a good soldier. I don't think he sat on his fat arse and issued orders. You took men out in the dead of night, didn't you, Fairfax? Hoping to pick up German prisoners.'

'I did my share, Jack. We all did our share. You still go out at night, Jack don't you?' Abruptly he changed tack. 'Kitty, I wonder, could I have another brandy?'

'Get it yourself!' Jack rasped. 'My wife's not a soldier!'

Fairfax shrugged and got to his feet. They heard him walk across to the bar.

Kitty kicked the door closed with her heel. 'Jack, be careful!'

'Why, Kitty, are you concerned?'

'You know he's hunting, Jack. Why don't you tell me why he's here? You must know.' She glanced quickly at Evans and O'Neill but their heads went down.

'It's none of your business!' Jack snapped.

'He's been brought here by someone,' Evans growled. 'It stands to reason. Who? I wonder about that German.'

'Ernst is our friend,' Jack replied. 'No, it's someone else.'

'It could be the priest,' Cunningham declared. 'I wager a pint to a pint that Fairfax would like to know what our priest knows.'

Jack was about to reply but the door opened. Fairfax re-entered.

'Make sure you put that down on my tally, Kitty.' Fairfax made himself comfortable on a stool. 'We were talking about the war, weren't we, Jack? The Dead Hand Club and why you all go out at night.'

Jack glanced up at Kitty. She stared blankly back. The Dead Hand Club went out sometimes, after drinking in the Beaumont Arms, she had always assumed it was a walk in the dark to clear their heads, reminisce, even indulge in a bit of horseplay or poaching.

'Why do we go out?' Jack stared at the ceiling. 'Do you know I was promoted to a corporal?'

'Of course I do, Jack. After the battle of Ypres. They even wanted to make you a sergeant.'

Jack drained his glass, a smile on his lips. 'Platoon!' He got to his feet, hands down by his side. 'Platoon, attention! Let's show the officer what we do!'

'Jack,' Kitty warned.

'Before we do, Corporal,' Cunningham was now into the game, 'let's ask what the major really did. I mean, before we show him. We've got to have guarantees that he won't shoot us.'

'What are you implying?' Kitty asked but Fairfax seized her hand and pressed it quickly. Jack saw the gesture and bit his lip.

'Have you ever shot anyone, Major Fairfax?'

'Private Armitage,' Fairfax replied. 'He came from one of

the southern regiments. His captain thought he'd been killed but he'd deserted. He liked the women, did Private Armitage. He reached one of the Channel ports. We only caught him because he killed a whore. They shot him in the courtyard of a chateau. I was the officer who blindfolded him and stuck the piece of white cloth on his chest. Do you know,' he stared across at Cunningham, 'I never batted an eyelid. Armitage, like the rest, got what he deserved.'

'Then let's show the officer,' said Jack. 'Platoon, attention!'

Kitty watched as every one of them, Daventry included, sprang to their feet, hands by their sides, eyes staring before them.

'Quick march!'

The order seemed so incongruous. Kitty stood aside as the men trooped out of the snug, Jack following behind, marching in single file out into the night. Fairfax finished his brandy. Kitty picked up a stool and sat before him.

'What are you doing?' she whispered. 'Do you realise what you are doing? You are worse than Daventry. He wants to bury his ghosts. You are bringing them all back.'

Fairfax lifted his hand as if to stroke her cheek.

'Kitty, I've hardly known you a day but I can see why Billy and Jack love you.'

'Stop it!'

'I can't stop it, Kitty, because I never started it. What you are seeing here, I've seen before. Go into any church or doctor's surgery up and down the land.' He sighed. 'Any priest, vicar or doctor who's prepared to listen can tell you stories which would chill your blood. I have a friend, Ralph Crosby. He comes from a good family, landed gentry, went to

Eton and Cambridge. Crosby had a great friend, we'll call him John. They used to meet in the Pall Mall Club every Friday night, have dinner together. John was killed at Gallipoli, but Ralph returned, safe and well, to London. Every Friday, at the same time he and John used to book a table in the Pall Mall Club, Crosby orders dinner for two: two glasses, two dinner plates. Two meals are served and Ralph sits and talks as if John sits opposite. Two soups, usually brown Windsor, roast lamb, mint sauce, two puddings, two coffees, two brandies. No one dares stop him. Crosby lives in the land of ghosts, Kitty.' Fairfax got to his feet and put his coat on. 'These men are no different. Come with me and you'll see.'

Kitty grabbed her coat and followed Fairfax out onto the cobbled street. Here and there light glowed from a window. They passed Grant's shop. Kitty saw one of the blinds pulled aside as if the grocer was deeply interested in what was happening. For the rest, the street lay silent. She glimpsed a pinprick of light in the far distance and watched it move. Jack must have taken one of the lamps. Used to moving through the pitch blackness of the mines, this moonlit night, with the stars clear in the sky, would present no difficulty for the Dead Hand Club.

'What are they doing?' she asked.

Fairfax wasn't listening. He was already striding ahead, eager to catch up. Kitty ran behind and, before she knew it or could refuse, Fairfax had taken off his glove and grasped her hand. His touch was warm and soft. Kitty felt a mixture of pleasure and guilt. He followed after Jack and the rest. In the far distance loomed the stone tower of the mine, the great iron wheel black against the starlit sky. The men followed a trackway, the same route she and Billy used to take to

Neville's Oak. They came to a stile and crossed over. Fairfax stopped here.

Jack and the rest were fanning out across the field. The night air was broken by Jack's shouts, ordering the 'platoon' to lie down. She saw the lamp lowered and the five figures fell flat on their faces. It reminded her of a childish game. She stared, tears pricking her eyes, and watched them, grown men, former soldiers, miners and policemen, play out the deadly game of edging across no-man's-land. Every so often a shout would shatter the silence, as if they were protecting themselves from bursts of fire, falling shrapnel or the keen eye of a machine-gunner. They were like children, mimicking the sounds of battle. Fairfax let go of her hand. He stood staring into the darkness.

'Why?' she asked. 'It's a game . . .'

'It's no game, Kitty. You talk to any soldier. Any man who fought in the trenches. What they feared most was a night attack. Crawling through the mud, fearful of being caught on the wire or the Very lights, of getting lost, of being shot by their own kind, of never getting back. It's a game being played up and down the kingdom. No different really from my friend Ralph in his Pall Mall Club.' He stepped closer, staring down at her. 'Do you know what it feels like when you want to scream, Kitty?'

'Like now,' she murmured.

'That's what these men are doing,' he explained. 'They are allowing their souls to scream out the terrors, the nightmares, the hideous scenes.'

'I should stop them!' Kitty's hand was on the stile post.

'Don't do it.' He put his hand over hers. 'They are not in Durham, Kitty. They are hundreds of miles away.'

Kitty let his hand rest there. What do I feel? she asked herself, staring at those darkening figures bobbing up and down in the field. We are all sleep-walkers. Fairfax is like some warlock from a fairy tale. He's come to wake us!

Kitty must have stood for a quarter of an hour. She was aware of Fairfax lighting a cigarette. On one occasion he coughed. The sounds from the field grew distant then became silent. She peered into the darkness. They came trooping back, knocking the dirt and grass from their clothes. Jack led them across the stile. The men looked rather sheepish now, faces ghostly in the lamplight. Jack stood between the major and Kitty.

'Well, sir, have you learnt something? Now we are going back to the Beaumont Arms. Old John and Mother will be wondering what is happening.' He snapped to attention, gave Fairfax a curt salute, kissed Kitty coldly on the cheek and followed the rest back up the trackway.

'Come on, Kitty.' Fairfax saw her shiver. He took off his coat and placed it round her shoulders. 'You'd best go home.' He went to grasp her hand but she pulled it away. She stepped back, tugging his coat about her.

'What do you want from me, Major Fairfax? Do you think I'm some dolly mop or trollop?'

'No, no,' he murmured. 'It's not that, Kitty. I've read Billy's journal. I knew you.' He kicked at the trackway. 'I was fascinated by you before we ever met. You loved Billy, didn't you? He certainly loved you.'

Kitty allowed the tears to come. 'I always loved him. I always did. I always will. He was part of my life.'

'Then why,' Fairfax stepped closer, 'did you marry Jack?'

'Because I loved him too. Because of Billy. Because of the

114

war.' The tears were hot and scalding. 'Because I don't know.'
Kitty kept her voice steady. 'Because I didn't think, not till you
arrived, Major Fairfax, with your questions and your hints.
You gave me Billy's journal deliberately?'

'I gave it because it belonged to you. The army believed it
should be returned.'

'The army took its time.'

Fairfax stretched out his hand. 'Kitty, we should go back.
I am not your enemy.'

'Jack would disagree with that.'

'It's Jack I want to talk about. Please.'

'I'll answer no questions!' Kitty took Fairfax's coat off and
flung it back at him. 'Not till you answer mine.'

'I'll tell you, Kitty, as I will tell Jack, at the appropriate time.' He paused. 'Jack and Billy were close friends,
weren't they?'

Kitty held her breath. In a way she really didn't want the
conversation to go any further. Fairfax stood in the dark like
some avenging angel. Once he answered her questions, her
life, her world might never be the same again.

'Jack and Billy were close friends,' he repeated.

'Yes, you know that.'

'All three of you were raised together?'

'You know that.'

'Billy married you and Jack was his best man?'

Kitty heard an owl hoot, long and mournful from across
the field. Somewhere a dog barked. The sounds of the night
pressed in upon her. She stood rigid.

'Jack and Billy went to war.' Fairfax's tone remained con-
versational. 'A company of friends. Billy was the poet, the
dreamer. Jack was more practical. War does strange things

115

to men, Kitty. It strips away the layers, the pretence, the games.'

'Jack and Billy always remained friends,' she burst out.

'Ah yes, but in the heat of battle, Kitty, when the nerves are red raw and the soul exposed, what about then? Jack told Billy how much he loved you.'

Kitty crossed her arms.

'He told him exactly how much he loved you. How your marriage had cut him to the soul, caught him on the quick.'

Kitty closed her eyes.

'Jack claimed Billy and you never knew his pain. Jack didn't blame you. He blamed Billy, who felt guilty. Billy was one of those men, Kitty, who believed he was never going home, that he wouldn't come out of it alive. He truly believed he had done a terrible wrong.'

'In marrying me?'

'No, not in marrying you, or even in loving you. Perhaps Billy regretted . . .' Fairfax hesitated. 'No, I don't think he regretted anything, except Jack's pain.'

'And the agreement?' Kitty asked.

'I believe it was Billy's way of making reparation. I can only speculate. Billy knew Jack loved you. Perhaps he thought Jack loved you more than he did. He knew that you loved Jack.'

'But not the same as I loved him!'

'It doesn't matter. You'd do anything Billy asked, wouldn't you, Kitty? To an outsider it appears strange, but not to the "Trinity" of Caundon. Billy was killed, you were left vulnerable, grieving. Jack, your closest tie to Billy, comes home and proposes. Why should you object? God knows, Kitty, England has its fill of widows. Life must go on. That's the terrible thing about the war. It happened, then it ended. Yet everyone whose lives were touched by it had to act almost as if it hadn't happened. So people hide, they deceive themselves and each other.' Fairfax had stepped back. Kitty felt as if a disembodied voice was talking to her.

'That's what tonight was about, Kitty: the Dead Hand Club, the pretend attack. Life must go on but they must purge their souls.'

'You're not here about purging, are you, Major Fairfax?'

'No, Kitty, I'm not. Jack and Billy were members of the same company. One night they were sent out on a mission. Something similar to what you have just seen. It happened time and time again. Commanders always wanted to know where the enemy was, their strength. Once darkness fell, each side would try to move, to surprise the other. You were told Billy was killed by sharpnel in a trench. He wasn't. He was killed out in no-man's-land.'

Kitty felt the coldness numb her. This dark trackway, Fairfax's soft tone promising horrors to come.

'Billy was killed, Jack returned. The usual report was filed. Jack claimed that he and Billy became separated so he never really knew what happened to his mate.'

Kitty's mouth turned dry. 'But I was told Billy was killed in a trench – mortar fire, a whizz-bang.'

'So many deaths.' Fairfax sighed, stepping closer. 'Think, Kitty, at the time, did it really matter how Billy died? Weren't you more concerned that he was dead?'

She nodded and dried her tears with the back of her hand. Fairfax offered her a handkerchief, a piece of crisp, white linen smelling faintly of cologne.

'Jack returned to the trench. In the normal course of events Billy's death would be classed like many others: killed out in no-man's-land. Except his corpse was discovered and brought back. Now, at the time . . .' he paused. 'At the time, the cause of his death was given as a wound to the stomach.'

'And is that how he died?' The words came in a croak.

'No. The very brief medical report said that the wound was potentially fatal but was not what killed him. They also dug out a bullet from a second wound which was to the head, the right temple. They were curious as to how a soldier received such diverse wounds. The bullet was English, fired from an officer's pistol. The report was sent through. It caused some comment. Then the War Office began to send us other information.'

'Other information?'

'Letters from someone here in Caundon, written anonymously. These letters claimed that Jack murdered Billy out in no-man's-land so he could marry his wife.'

If Fairfax hadn't caught her, Kitty would have slumped to her knees. He put his arm round her.

'I had no choice,' he told her gently. 'I went through Billy's possessions. I tracked down the journal. The more I read, the more suspicious I became. War is war but murder is still a crime!'

Chapter 7

_____

Kitty felt sick and weak. She was aware of Fairfax helping her along the lane. Her limbs felt loose as if she was ill with a fever.

'Please, please,' she begged. 'Stop for a while.'

Fairfax held her. Kitty drew deep breaths.

'What are you implying?'

'I'm implying nothing, I'm telling you the facts, and they raise a number of questions. Jack and Billy left the trench that night and, according to Jack, they became separated. Billy was not in the trench when he was killed. First, there's the question of the bullet wound in Billy's head. How did he get it? Jack was not carrying a revolver, he wasn't an officer but, in the mêlée of war, soldiers can, and did, grab whatever weapons were to hand. Secondly, Jack returned to the trench without his helmet. According to one report, when Billy was found in the mortar hole, he still wore his helmet. Another one was found beside it, definitely Jack's. So why did Jack lie?

'Thirdly, there's the letters from Caundon. I don't know who wrote them,' Fairfax spoke tersely to hide the lie, 'but

119

the writer believes that both Jack and the members of the Dead Hand Club know a serious crime was committed. Finally, Kitty, we have the motive. There's no doubt that Jack loves you. What I must ask myself is, would he stoop to murder? God forgive me,' he grasped her ice-cold hands 'but I also have to ask myself this – and you'll hate me for it: were you, too, party to what happened?'

Kitty opened her mouth to scream but the sound wouldn't come. Fairfax held her.

'I know that's not true,' he added quickly. 'It's a mockery—'

'It's blasphemy,' Kitty whispered; her mouth was so dry, the muscles in the back of her neck cramped. Never, not even when the heart-breaking news had come from the front, had she felt so much pain. 'David's sin,' she whispered.

Fairfax grasped her hand. 'David's sin?' he queried. 'Ah yes, the biblical king who lusted after Uriah the Hittite's wife Bathsheba and so had him killed in battle. Come. We've got to walk back.'

'Not yet,' Kitty replied. 'I can't return. I don't want Jack coming out to look for me either.'

They had reached the fringe of Caundon village. Kitty found a new strength and almost pulled Fairfax along a lane which led to the old dairy. Off the trackway stood a small byre or cow shed. She opened the door and went in. It was warm, musty but clean and scrubbed. It still had the old bench she, Jack and Billy used to use. She eased herself down, aware of the cramps in her stomach. Fairfax lit a cigarette. He offered her one but she shook her head though she didn't refuse the hip flask he pressed to her lips. She drank the bitter-sweet brandy. She felt the warmth return to her stomach and hands, and became all too conscious of Fairfax's presence, dark and brooding.

'I do not believe you,' she accused.

'I don't believe it myself, Kitty. Hundreds of thousands of men, millions if you count those of the enemy, perished in the most hideous circumstances. Yet, here I am, on a soft, balmy night questioning you about one death which occurred four years ago. That's a singular thing about the army, Kitty.' Fairfax lifted the flask to his lips. 'They train us to kill. They order us to slay our own kind with bayonet, bullet, mustard gas, shrapnel, mine and barbed wire. One thing, however, the army will not permit, one thing it is strict about: it will allow no one to use the uniform, to take the King's shilling and the oath of allegiance, as a pretext for personal vengeance. It's three years since the war ended. This is not the first such case I have investigated.'

'And?' Kitty asked.

Fairfax remained silent. Kitty placed her hands on her knee and dug her nails deep into the skin.

'And?' she insisted.

'Each case differs,' he whispered. 'But, in the end . . .'

'You prove murder?'

'Yes, I prove murder. Two men hanged in Stafford gaol.' Fairfax bit his lip at Kitty's horrified gaze. 'I've said enough,' he stammered. 'I've watched you, Kitty. Believe me, I know a liar when I see one, and you are completely honest. I am breaking my own orders telling you what I know.'

Kitty turned away. The first shock had passed, due, perhaps, to the brandy, or was it something else? A real awakening? A realisation about her life, her loves, a determination to seek the truth? Yes, perhaps that was it. She wanted to know the truth. She found it hard to accept that Jack had told her a lie. Yet, there again, he had not been open with her. Was it really his fault? Did Jack himself know the truth? Was it all hidden by the mud, the killing and the sheer horror of war?

'Why not confront Jack?' she asked.

'In time I will. I need to collect more evidence. I had to tell you. I couldn't sit and watch those eyes of yours beg for the truth.'

'And if I go home now and tell Jack what I know?'

'Then you'll tell Jack what you know. As a policeman, I would be interested in his reaction. He might come and seek me out. Perhaps he'll flee, hide or lie. I don't really care. I have other people to question, Colonel Morrison for one. Then I'll begin my inquiry proper. Morrison's a magistrate, isn't he?'

'Never mind him! What do you want me to do? Come on, Major Fairfax, you haven't just told me this out of compassion. We have a phrase in the north-east, "to tweak the cat's tail". That's what you are doing now. When I embroider, I leave the first thread in each row loose. I later come back and fasten it. I do that because, if I don't like what I am doing, I can unravel it. Am I your loose thread, Major Fairfax?'

'It depends. What do you feel now, Kitty?'

'What do I feel now?' She laughed sharply. 'You have just told me that one man I loved might have murdered another I was married to. How many women are married to their first husband's murderer?' Kitty looked down at the rutted floor. The door was ajar, the pale outline of a hedge was visible on the other side of the trackway. Fairfax was clever; compassionate, yes, but he had not only tweaked the cat's tail, he had truly set the same cat amongst the pigeons! How could

122

she hide this from Jack? How could she lie in bed next to him, kiss, exchange embraces?

'What if it's not true?' she murmured.

'That's a good question.' Fairfax lifted the hip flask and took another drink. 'What if it's not true, Kitty, or only partly true?'

For just a moment she felt a surge of compassion for Jack. 'What are you saying, Oscar?' Kitty emphasised his name sarcastically.

'Some murders,' he replied, 'are the result of carefully plotted malice. The Crown might argue that Jack deliberately led Billy out to his death—'

'Cold-blooded murder?' Kitty interrupted.

'Or an accident of war.' Fairfax seemed eager to fill the silence. 'Battle has its own horrors, Kitty. It changes people in ways they never thought possible. Some men get a taste for killing. We took a trench once. The Germans had mined it. A most horrific ambush occurred, a truly gut-stabbing, ferocious explosion. The trench wall was smashed to pieces, drenched in blood. On the ground lay a man, his face grey and witless; one of his legs hung by a single tendon just beneath the knee. Close by lay three headless corpses, arms and legs missing. We had to pick up the pieces and put them in bags. We didn't know who they were or how many were missing. Just before dawn a corporal reported one of our soldiers was lying about twenty yards from the trench we had taken. The man was unconscious but he came round and spent the rest of that day shouting and screaming for mercy, for someone to help. The man's groans became a terrible music. Four men went out at night. The Germans were waiting. They were like hunters relishing the kill. Two of the rescue party died

123

while the man the two survivors brought back later died of his wounds. When dawn broke I saw one of our men lying near the barbed wire; his arm kept going up and down as if he was gesturing for help. I managed to find a telescope, fix it between two sandbags and took a long look. The man was dead but the Boche had fixed a string to his wrist and kept yanking it up and down. The corpse was fresh bait for another ambush.' Fairfax drew nearer to Kitty. 'I always wondered about that. These weren't soldiers firing guns at each other. What did it matter if another man died? The Germans simply wanted to kill, like a hungry fox loose in a hen run.'

'Are you saying Jack was like that?'

'Perhaps. Did he change? Did the war,' Fairfax stretched out his hand, fingers clenched, 'bring to the surface grievances, grudges, resentments? Did Jack blame Billy for his unhappiness? Did he reach the conclusion that it did not matter if another man died, another corpse was found? Another grave dug in a cemetery which stretched for miles and miles?'

'But Jack loved Billy. We were brought up together. They were like brothers.'

'So were Cain and Abel.'

She got to her feet. 'I must go back.'

'Were they?' Fairfax remained seated.

'Were they what?'

'Were they really like brothers? Was there any real bond between them? Or were you the bond, Kitty? And when Billy married you, there was nothing left for Jack except a great gaping hole in his soul, which filled with angry resentment.'

Kitty turned away, shaking her head. 'You don't know Jack.'

Images of him came through her mind: Jack sitting in the

kitchen mending a pot or repairing leather; his sharp, dry sense of humour; the way he gently teased her mother or laughed at himself. His bravery and leadership down the mines. The way he had won a reputation for looking after others. Oh, he could be moody and temperamental but he was the first to admit it. A hard man but gentle, caring and soft in their love-making. And yet Kitty did sometimes find his sheer passion, his possessiveness, disconcerting. Strange, Kitty thought as she stepped out of the shed onto the trackway, how neither of us rarely refer to Billy. Never once had Jack complained about the way she studied Billy's picture or talked to it in her bedroom. He knew it happened but never made any reference to it. Why was that? Guilt? Or simply a husband indulging his wife?

Fairfax came up behind her. 'What will you do, Kitty?'

She spun round. Fairfax's face seemed leaner, smoother, his eyes larger. She smelt the brandy and tobacco smoke.

'What will I do, Major Oscar Fairfax? What can I do? I'll watch and I'll wait like you do. Perhaps I'll go and see Father Headon. I'll pray.'

'Do you think Jack killed Billy?'

'No, Major Fairfax, I'm not thinking of that. Like most human beings I tend to be selfish. Perhaps I'll begin to wonder whether I killed Billy. Unaware of the pain I've caused. Perhaps my mood will change. Now I feel sad and numb. But I can't . . .'

'You can't what?'

'I'm thirty years of age, Major Fairfax. All my life I've known Jack and Billy. Hand in hand we went. I can't believe that all those years, all the happiness, the bonds which bound us together, can be cut like a piece of thread. Nor am I a

Judas. I will not do your job for you, Major Fairfax. If you are going to prove that my dream is a nightmare then do it but, for God's sake, don't ask for my help! Did you read fairy stories, Major Fairfax, about the hero who had to face ogres and giants, dragons and monsters? Well, I've got to slay mine and you've got to confront yours.'

Kitty stared at this harsh-faced, self-composed officer who threatened to inflict ruin and hardship on so many she loved.

'You are a good scholar, aren't you, Major Fairfax? I am sure you know more about us than we do about each other. Do you enjoy it?'

'I beg your pardon?'

'You heard the question. Why are you taking time to reply? Do you enjoy it, Major Fairfax? Is it the power? The fear you can provoke? Or are you waging your own private war for justice?'

And, not waiting for an answer, Kitty walked quickly down the trackway. She heard Fairfax call her name but Kitty couldn't face any more. She broke into a run, allowing the tears to fall freely. The quick patter of her shoes seemed to echo along the street. She was sure the sound must disturb those in the houses on either side but she was past caring.

She reached the Beaumont Arms. She didn't go in but stood for a while, drying her tears. She stood at the entrance to the bar. Jack and the rest were back in the snug. She could see they were on the point of breaking up. Evans already stood in the doorway, helmet on his head, loudly demanding if the others remembered where he had left his push-bike. She heard the muffled laughter as she fled down the passageway and up the stairs.

Kitty was relieved to get into her room and light the oil

lamps. She stared around. Everything was clean, neat and precise. Her mother had even laid out her best dress and brown laced boots for Mass the following morning. Linen underwear and a pair of stockings were piled neatly on a chair. Kitty sat on the edge of the bed. She felt tempted to pull out Billy's photograph but a picture on the wall caught her attention, one of her favourites: a painting by a local artist of Neville's Oak, her place of dreams. The full horror of what Fairfax had said dawned on her. She began to shiver as if a cold draught seeped through the window. No tears, just a soul-wrenching terror. She couldn't believe. She couldn't accept. What would happen if it was the truth? If Fairfax was correct? Kitty clutched the eiderdown. Sounds on the stairs startled her. She hurriedly pulled open the drawer and took out the oilskin pouch bearing Billy's journal, unbuttoned the front of her dress and slipped it inside. Even as she did this, she realised she was accepting, or acknowledging, the possibility of Fairfax's allegations. She watched the handle press down. The door opened. She felt a sob in her throat. She wanted it to be anybody but Jack, even Fairfax, but of course it was Jack. He stepped sheepishly inside. He wore his cloth flat cap, jacket in one hand, boots in the other.

'I should have left these downstairs in the kitchen but John's there waiting to lock up.'

Kitty stared at him. She was aware of Jack's strength, his rather long, harsh face, deep eyes, bushy brows, the lock of hair falling over his forehead, the ruddy brown of his skin, strong arms and hands.

'I am sorry about what happened,' he stammered. Any other time he would have come and sat beside her on the bed. He was watching her curiously. He took a deep breath. 'You took your time coming back.'

'Why did you do that?' Kitty demanded.

'Do what?'

'Go out into a field and run around like madmen?'

Jack let the boots fall to the floor, leaned against the door and sighed. 'Because we are madmen, Kitty. During the day we work in the mines, we hew the coal.'

'I know what you do during the day.' Her voice rose. 'Don't lecture me as if I am a child!'

'We all have fears, Kitty.' Jack refused to be provoked. He knew something dire had happened. He could read Kitty like a book; her face seemed thinner, paler, her eyes dark and round. She sat tense on the bed as if shrinking from him.

'Do you remember when we were children?' He tried to keep his voice level. 'And we'd sit in class all day with Miss Martindale? When the bell rang after the end of school, we'd run and run?'

'I remember those days, Jack. You, me and Billy.'

He took a step closer. 'What did Fairfax tell you?' he demanded.

'Let Fairfax be.'

'Oh, influenced by the officer, are we? Does he come between husband and wife?'

'Don't say that, Jack. The only people who can come between you and me . . .' She got to her feet. 'Are you and me.'

He went to grasp her hand. 'What did that arrogant bastard say?'

'How did Billy die, Jack?' Her heart skipped a beat. Jack

128

just seemed to crumple as if someone had punched him hard beneath the heart.

'What's the matter, hinny? Why do you ask questions like that?'

'Fairfax is here because of you, Jack! Do you know that?'

'Because of me?'

Any other time Kitty would have taken his astonishment as innocence but there was a guarded look in his eyes. She felt that cloying, heart-draining weakness return. Whatever she asked Jack, she'd never know the truth, not now.

'Do you love me, Jack?'

'Of course. Don't be stupid!'

'How much do you love me, Jack?'

'I don't know. I can't weigh it. It's not a sack of coal or a bag of sweets.'

'Did you resent me when I married Billy?' She didn't wait for an answer. 'Why didn't you say?'

'What could I say?' He put his hand out. 'Kitty, I loved you then and I love you now.'

She stepped round him. She was glad he was no longer between her and the door. Jack stood nonplussed.

'Kitty, what's the matter? What is all this?'

'I don't know you, Jack. Shall I tell you what Fairfax brought? Billy kept a journal.'

The colour drained from Jack's face. 'Billy's journal?'

'Yes, Jack, Billy's journal.' Kitty took a step closer. He made no attempt to touch or caress this fierce angry woman. 'I'm going to read Billy's journal. I am going to look into Billy's soul. Until Farifax goes, I do not want to share this bed with you. I don't want to talk to you until you are prepared to talk to me. I don't want to be pushed aside as a woman who shouldn't be told what she wants to know.' She placed her hand on the door handle. 'When you are ready to tell me the truth, about everything, Jack, I'll be prepared to listen.' Kitty opened the door, pulled it close and started in surprise. Fairfax stood in the stairs.

'Were you listening?' she accused.

He moved his coat from one arm to the other and shook his head. 'Can I help you?'

'Oh no, Major Fairfax, I believe you've helped enough.'

Kitty went further up the stairs, past his room, to the small attic on the top floor. Despite the dark, Kitty fumbled and found the key still in the lock. She turned it and stepped inside. She knew where the box of matches were and lit a capped candle as well as the small oil lamp on the table. The room was kept for visitors, people who simply wanted a bed as they passed through, or her cousins from Bishop Auckland. Mother always kept it ready. Kitty was grateful to be alone at last, away from Jack and Fairfax. She lay down on the bed.

'What happens if it's true?' she whispered into the darkness.

She became abruptly aware of Billy's presence and sat up. Was it her imagination? She didn't believe in ghosts but memories from the past flooded in: how Billy would slip into a room, his black, tousled hair, smiling eyes, the way he stood with hands in his pockets, body slightly crooked like a little boy. She became acutely aware of the differences between Billy and Jack. Billy was as open as a summer sky. She remembered the phrase from the Gospels: 'There was no guile in him.' Tears stung her eyes. She stretched out her hands.

'Oh Billy!' she whispered.

If only he was here to comfort her, to say that all was well, that Fairfax was wrong. She could almost hear his voice: 'You know how it is with Jack, Kitty. He's strong and broods too much. Do you remember the first day down the mine? He kept wondering why the roof didn't fall down and for the first two weeks he'd always check the cage.'

Kitty recalled their last sombre time out at Neville's Oak. Billy in uniform, sitting, legs crossed beneath the great oak, staring out across the fields as if memorising every detail.

'I mightn't come home, Kitty,' Billy declared. 'What if I don't? I'll still always love you. If Father Headon's right, and we live for ever, then I shall live for you. I'll never be far away. Heaven won't be complete without you.' He had grinned impishly. 'And Jack!'

Kitty clutched her chest. That's where it had all begun, those strange conversations. Had Jack put Billy up to it? Or was it just Billy? She felt the journal, undid the buttons of her dress and drew it out. Despite the hurly-burly of the evening, the brandy and the shock Fairfax had given her, Kitty couldn't sleep. She lit more oil lamps and, re-arranging them on the small table, opened the journal and began to read.

Kitty wouldn't be able to imagine the dirt and the wretched surroundings in which I am writing this. The attack's over. I am sitting in the bottom of a German dugout about three yards under the earth. Jack, Daventry and Cunningham are with me. There's an old table littered with food, equipment, candle grease and all sorts of odds and ends. The floor is covered with German clothing. Outside, the trench is blown to pieces and full of corpses. The ground is ploughed up by enormous shell holes, all the trees have gone, only a few gaunt sticks remain. The stench is horrific. It seems to be everywhere and affects everything. So different from Neville's Oak! I close my eyes and pretend I'm there. I can smell the bluebells, the fresh mown hay, the breeze from the river.

The Germans have buried some of their dead beneath the floor of the trench. You have to be wary where you tread. If the mud is disturbed, thousands of white maggots come wriggling out. In one place a hand, blue and bloated; close by, a man buried to his waist, arms bound to his side, glassy eyes wide open, face stained a livid yellow. There's no rest from such gruesome sights. Yet we are all growing used to it. True, some men can't bear the pain. Sometimes it's not only the enemy we kill. We heard a story from another battalion. Two soldiers disliked their sergeant who always gave them the most dirty and dangerous jobs; even when they were in billets, he picked on them, so they decided to kill him. Four days ago, according to the story, they asked to see their adjutant.

'Well?' the officer demanded. 'What is it you want?'

'We've come to report, sir. We are very sorry but we've shot our company sergeant major.'

'Good heavens!' the officer replied. 'How did that happen?'

'It was an accident, sir.'

'What do you mean, you damned fools? Did you mistake him for a spy?'

'No, sir, we mistook him for our platoon sergeant.'

Jack roared with laughter when he heard the story but

I think it's true. Both men were shot by a firing squad against the wall of a nearby convent. Others will do anything. Some of the Lancashires sheltered with us. One rifleman disobeyed the orders of his officer. He mounted the fire step and bellowed across: 'Hey, Fritzie, here I am!' The words were hardly out of his mouth when we heard the crack. A sniper's bullet knocked off his helmet, scoring a wound to the scalp. Despite the injury, he picked himself up, gathered his souvenirs and addressed his startled mates. 'Cheerio, boys, I've got my Blighty but don't tell the colonel it was self-inflicted.'

One of our lads tried the same game. He wasn't from our village but further north. He waved his hand above the parapet to catch the Boche's attention. Nothing happened. He waved his arms. Nothing happened. He put his elbows on the fire step, hoisted his body up and down. 'Bloody hell!' he shouted. 'I think we are in luck, lads, the Germans have gone home!' He peered over the top – crack, a bullet struck him straight through the head. Jack's told me about a Scotsman who did the same. He stuck his hand over the top and got it in the fingers. He was sent back to the orderly station, forgot to stoop low and, crack, got it right in his head. The killing goes on all the time: snipers, rifle grenades, mines, sometimes great shells.

Daventry's not well. He fires his gun as if he's a machine. Colonel Morrison shouldn't let him bury the dead. Bob's more concerned with the corpses than he is with the living. Cunningham, too, is growing worse. He had a pair of rosary beads and a prayer book. He burnt these and threw the hot ash in the

133

direction of the Germans. Since then he refuses to say a prayer. Jack's worried about him. Says Cunningham has become strange ever since he brought him back after being cut off. I think something happened but neither he nor Jack will talk.

Nobody thinks of going missing except Grocer Grant's son. They still say he's on the loose. Others can't take it any more. Colonel Morrison and I went down to examine a trench. A man was lying on his face. I flashed my torch and saw one of his feet was bare.

'Get up!' Morrison yelled.

'It's no good talking to him, sir,' a soldier shouted.

'Why, what's wrong?' Morrison demanded. 'Why has he taken his boot and sock off?'

'Find out yourself, sir.'

Morrison gestured at me. I shook the man by the arm. Only then did I notice the hole in the back of his head. He had taken off his boot and sock to pull the trigger of his rifle with one toe; the muzzle was in his mouth. A terrible way to go! The colonel says it's not really suicide.

There's no reason out here. I insist on keeping this journal. Jack and the lads want to know what I write but I can't show them. Through it, I can escape from here. I huddle down and think of Kitty. She is in our bedroom on our wedding night and all her clothes have fallen away like veils. She has the devil in her. All naked, standing in those shoes with rosettes on, unpinning her hair. Such memories become too much. I stare at the mud and pretend we are under Neville's Oak. Or go back in time: summer days, leafy lanes, and always

Kitty. I keep myself alive for her and her alone. Jack's different. I wish he wouldn't take chances. We have enough to fight, not only the Germans but the mud and the dirt.

Morrison keeps us busy. He's organised a routine for the day: breakfast at eight, clean the trench, inspect rifles, lunch, stand to at dusk. We do two-hour sentry spells, work two hours, sleep two hours. Sometimes I stare out through the periscope at the German trenches, distant streaks of sandbags, some of coloured cloth. There's nothing else. A village once stood nearby. Somewhere in the distance, Morrison claims, is a famous chateau. When we get bored we hunt for lice: two dangers we have constantly to look out for, the sniper and the shrapnel.

Last night was cloudless. The stars hung low and the Germans opened a terrible bombardment. It went on all night. The air vibrated with the din. Colonel Morrison said they were throwing everything at us: machine guns tapping, bullets whistling with the great German sausage mortars exploding all around us. We hadn't a minute's sleep. Jack and I huddled close. He began to talk. For the first time ever I realised how Jack was cut up by my marriage to Kitty. At first I tried teasing.

'What could I do, Jack lad? Both of us couldn't have married her. If we had,' I joked, 'Father Headon would have had words.'

'It's not that,' he replied. 'It came so unexpected.'

'What do you mean? Unexpected?'

Do you know something, I've never seen Jack's face turn so ugly.

'Unexpected,' he repeated. 'We never talked about it.'

'Jack,' I joked. 'I was marrying Kitty not you.'

'Did you love her?'

'Did?' I asked. 'Do, Jack, and shall. Kitty also had some choice in it.'

Jack turned away at that but he made me wonder. Just the look in his eyes. The other men say he's grown sullen and harsh. A good soldier, better than all of us! Jack will go home but I'm not too sure about myself. The list of dead grows longer. They are even saying whole villages will be empty, not a man returning.

Morning came, the sun rose, strong and golden, a great light in the sky. Its light seemed to have changed but a gunner told me that's the effect of the cordite. Morrison kept us busy cleaning the trenches. Daventry was out with his damned shovel. Cunningham has gone missing. Jack thinks he's plundering the dead. Evans sits like a ghost, claims he wants to see the padre. Jack came up with my mess tin, he'd found some beef stew.

'I don't know how old it is,' he said, pushing it into my hand. 'But it tastes fine.' He sat in a corner of the trench and chewed it. Jack was more relaxed than the night before.

'I am sorry,' he began. 'Sorry about talking about Kitty and you. I had no right. I just miss her, Billy. There's not a day or night goes by when I don't think of her.' He finished his stew and threw the tin beside him. 'If I catch one, Billy—'

'Don't talk like that,' I said. 'If anyone is going home, Jack, it will be you.'

'No, listen.' Jack edged closer. 'If I catch one, and you go home, you'll tell Kitty, won't you, how much I loved her?' His face, all dirty, broke into a smile. 'You'll tell her how much I missed her and, if it hadn't been for Billy boy, I would have won her hand.' His face became all fierce. 'You will tell her that, won't you?'

'I think she knows already.'

'No, I want your promise. Tell her what I've said.' He pointed to a cut on his wrist. 'We've got some Australians further down the line, they are of Italian descent. They talked to me about a blood oath. Do you know what that is, Billy?'

He grasped my hand, also cut, God knows where, and pressed his bloody cut against mine until the blood mingled.

'There was no need for that,' I protested. 'We are as one, Jack. No need for strange oaths and promises.'

Jack shook his head. 'When this is all over, Billy boy, and we all go back to the Beaumont Arms for a pint, those of us who are left, it will never be the same. You know that, don't you? We just can't go through this, Billy, wipe our lips and walk away. It will never be the same. Look at Daventry. Morrison believes he's a lunatic. And Cunningham? These are the ones who are left. Even old Morrison's taken to sitting and brooding all the time. 'Perhaps none of us will go home.'

A cloud crossed the sun. I saw the shadow racing down the trench and couldn't prevent a shiver.

'If I don't go home, Jack, you're the one who will have to speak to Kitty.'

'Come on, Billy, with a love like Kitty's you'll survive, you'll pull through.'

I jumped as a distant shell landed and the sound came billowing towards us. I remembered Kitty, the last time I was on leave, in her pinafore and laced-up boots, flowers in her hair. She was talking about the school and teaching.

This journal is meant for you, Kitty, but this morning, sitting in the bottom of that muddy trench, I knew, as God made Neville's Oak, that I wouldn't be going home. I didn't feel sad, just a realisation, a certainty. My real fear is not so much death as never seeing you again. I can understand now why Grant the Grocer's lad went for a walk. Nevertheless, he shouldn't have done it, he shouldn't have left his mates, for there are worse terrors than death. Not seeing you is perhaps the greatest.

I grasped Jack's hand.

'What's the matter, lad?'

'Jack, you talked about not going home. What happens if I don't?'

I paused. I wasn't aware of the cordite, the foul smells from the cesspit, the distant crunching of the guns or the clouds of white smoke billowing across the sky.

'You've got to promise me, Jack, if I go down and you go back, you'll look after Kitty.'

'Don't be stupid.' Jack pulled his hand away. 'It's you she loves, Billy.'

'No, no,' I insisted. 'Jack, you must promise me!' I

recalled sitting under Neveille's Oak and the conversation I'd had with Kitty. 'I have this feeling, Jack, deep in my heart. I'll never go home. My mining days are over.'

Jack grew very angry. He jumped to his feet, hastily remembered and crouched back down again. He had tears in his eyes and was shouting at me. In the end I calmed him down. I made him promise; this evening, before I go to sleep, I am going to recite that promise to myself.'

Kitty let the journal fall into her lap. She stared at the glow of light from the oil lamps. It was as if she had been there sitting between the two men. She could imagine that trench, Jack and Billy, faces dirty, sharing their food. Was Jack so consumed with passion that he realised that only a bullet separated him from what he wanted? But that could not be, surely. Jack wouldn't turn heaven to hell on earth.

Kitty blew the candle out and, grasping the journal, lay down on the bed. She hugged it to her, her fingers still caught between the pages. There was little more left to read and she dreaded the anguish its conclusion would provoke. She recalled the words etched in stone on the side altar of the church: 'Sufficient for the day is the evil thereof.' She closed her eyes; there'd been enough pain for one day.

Chapter 8

Kitty was up early the following morning. She went down and found their bedroom empty. She changed, washed and put on her Sunday best. Jack was waiting for her in the parlour, dressed in his Sunday suit, brown polished boots laced up.

'Is that collar too starched?' she asked.

Jack ran his finger round his neck. 'I've had tighter.'

They looked at each other.

'I'm sorry,' Jack began.

'Not now.'

Kitty went and looked out of the window, drawn by the sound of a pram, its wheel loose, clattering and squeaking along the street.

'The Murphys are off to Mass,' she remarked.

'So should we be.' Her mother stood in the doorway, an old-fashioned bonnet clamped firmly on her head. She glanced quickly at both of them.

'Old John said there was some commotion last night. He was moaning about everything being left to him.' She looked at Kitty from head to toe. 'Pretty as a picture! Did you sleep well, lass? I mean,' she added warningly, 'that bed in the attic.'

'It's nothing, Mother.'

Kitty was about to go to the door when she heard a clatter on the stairs – Fairfax deliberately making a noise. He reached the bottom and stood in the doorway. He was dressed in a grey, three-piece suit. A white scarf round his neck concealed most of the knotted, blue tie. Kitty thought how handsome he looked. She wondered if Major Fairfax had a life of his own or did he spend most of his time probing into those of others?

'Are you going to church, Major Fairfax? I didn't think you believed.'

'The same could be said of many of those who attend.'

Kitty smiled at the retort. 'I think you had best go on, Major Fairfax. We'll be making our own way.'

Fairfax gave a mock salute, opened the door and left.

'I don't like him.' Kitty's mother spoke up. 'I never did like the officers. Think they are a breed apart, they do. We must be going.'

Kitty picked up her handbag and, feeling rather self-conscious in her high-heeled boots, left the Beaumont Arms. She half hoped Jack would come up beside her, link his arm through hers as he always did, but when she looked back he was intent on helping her mother. The rest of the village, or those who claimed to fear God, were also making their way up to church. The morning was gorgeous, a cloud-free sky and strengthening sun though the breeze was cool and fresh. The more she walked, the more self-conscious Kitty became. She nodded at acquaintances but wondered if they knew what had gone on the night before. Don't get hysterical, she thought, they don't and probably wouldn't care, at least not yet.

'Good morning, Mrs Allerton!'

It was Edmund Grant the grocer, a podgy, thickset man, his hair plastered firmly back. Kitty forced a smile. Grant had button-like eyes, a snub nose, a wispy moustache and beard which he was always scratching with stubby fingers. The suit he wore was of good quality, as was the shirt. A prosperous, self-made man, Grant was unpopular with the villagers because of the prices he charged, especially during the war. There had been public rejoicing when the Co-operative moved in to challenge his trade.

'Good morning, Mr Grant.'

The grocer sidled up alongside her. Kitty smelt the eau de cologne he must splash all over himself. Even though Jack was only a few paces behind, Grant had the temerity to grasp her by the wrist as if eager to take her hand. She moved her arm.

'What's the matter, Mr Grant? Unsteady on your feet?'

His lips parted in a yellow-toothed smile. 'I'm just curious, Mrs Allerton, about the young officer you've got staying.'

'He's not so young,' Kitty smiled back. 'And where else should he stay, Mr Grant?'

'Of course, of course!' Grant beamed back.

Kitty glared at him. She hated this man, she always had. Even as a young lass, Grant had tried to paw her, entice her with sweets. Kitty had always been courteous but resolute in her refusal. She had heard the stories about Mr Grant and the young he liked to lure into the back room of his shop. Old Foster, the village policeman before Evans, had once warned him. Grant didn't care. He was very wealthy and had friends in high places. The older he got, the worse he grew. During the war Grant had renewed his interest in Kitty. On one occasion he had tried to block her leaving his shop, hand snaking out to touch her breasts. She had kicked him in the shins.

'If Billy was here!' she'd warned.

'But your man isn't here, is he?' Grant had sneered.

Now he was all sweet and squirmy. Kitty fell back, hoping that Jack would catch up with her.

'And how is Mrs Grant?' she asked. 'Still ill with the vapours?'

'It's not the vapours,' he retorted. 'Different ailments.'

Aye, Kitty thought, with a man like you, the poor woman's probably sick in mind as well as body.

'And a very good morning to you all.'

Kitty jumped as Ernst Kurtz came out of a narrow alleyway. Kitty sighed with relief. The German seemed to know what was going on. He quickly looked back at Jack pretending to be interested in his mother-in-law's chatter whilst Kitty walked so stiffly beside Grant. He forced his way between them and raised his bowler hat.

'I always like to see you, Kitty, on a Sunday morning. I then believe there is a God in heaven!'

Kitty smiled at the genuine compliment. Kurtz was always friendly, quite protective; he had as little time for Edmund Grant as she did. The German almost shouldered the grocer aside.

'Why do you bother coming?' Grant, his fat face now puce with anger, demanded. 'I thought you were a Lutheran!'

'I am of no faith,' Kurtz replied. 'But Father Headon is a good pastor and I like to hear him preach. Jack, how are you?' He turned. 'And you, ma'am?'

They were now on the trackway leading out of the village towards the parish church. Others joined them, exchanging pleasantries, commenting on the weather. Kitty glimpsed Evans and O'Neill. They looked tired and haggard-faced. Both had probably continued their drinking elsewhere last night.

'Oh, there's our atheist!' someone called.

They went under the lych gate. Kitty glimpsed Cunningham standing outside the church door. He was handing out bills from the Atheist Society and, all the time, issuing his usual challenge to the Almighty.

'If there is a God,' he bawled, 'then why the war? If there is a God who loves, then why do the poor starve?'

Now and again he'd break off to say good morning to this person or that. Father Headon, dressed in a white alb and green vestments, stood on the other side of the door smiling at his parishioners. Kitty always found this scene amusing. The priest could have had Cunningham removed, even arrested, but never once had he interfered. 'It's good,' Father Headon had declared to his congregation, 'for you to hear the other side and Jim Cunningham is as welcome to his views as anyone.'

This morning the priest studied Kitty's face and raised his hand. She nodded and went by him into the church. It smelt sweetly of incense and candle wax. The altar had been specially prepared for this High Mass of the week. The three candelabra on either side of the tabernacle had been lit, the oil lamp placed on its hook above the pulpit. Altar servers were scurrying around with the offertory cruets and old Thompson, the stationmaster, was already climbing up to the old organ loft. Kitty, Jack and Mrs Courtney went to their usual pew to the left of the altar just before the Lady Chapel. Kitty knelt on the hard wood and realised how tired

144

she was. Everything had so abruptly changed. On a Sunday her usual routine was to walk to church with Jack and her mother, they would avoid Grant, say hello to Kurtz and have a quiet laugh at Cunningham's strange antics. This Sunday was different. She stole a glance to her right. Jack, too, was not concentrating on where he was.

'Jack!' she hissed. 'You're still wearing your cap!'

He quickly doffed it and smiled. Kitty would have reciprocated but she caught a movement in the far aisle where Fairfax had taken his seat. Like a shadow in the sunlight, she thought, or a wolf amongst the lambs. She stared up at the high altar. The green cloth covering the tabernacle door, the red sanctuary lamp, the plaque the villagers had put up listing the names of those killed in the Great War. Billy's name was there, along with the sixty or seventy others. For the first time in her life, Kitty wondered if Cunningham's atheism was correct. Was there a God? And, if he existed, did he love? Did he care? Why couldn't Billy have come back? She closed her eyes and felt guilty. If she thought that then she shouldn't have married Jack. Why did I? she asked herself. Because I loved him. But do I love him now? She opened her eyes and stared at her husband. If Jack had killed Billy, surely he couldn't kneel here in the presence of Christ. Perhaps Fairfax was right. War changed everything and the commandments of God were suspended.

The sanctuary bell tinkled. Father Headon, six altar boys trotting before him, swept into the sanctuary.

'*In nomine patris et filii et spiritus sancti . . .*'

Mass began, following its set routine. After the Gospel, Father Headon climbed into the pulpit. Kitty sat back on the bench and stared up. The priest seemed rather nervous.

He laid out a piece of paper on the wooden ledge and gazed round the church. Kitty was sure he was searching for Fairfax. She followed his gaze. The major sat, arms crossed, staring boldly back at the priest.

'I should preach on today's Gospel,' Father Headon began. 'Instead,' he glanced down quickly and caught Kitty's eye, 'I want to talk about the war.'

A low murmur echoed round the church.

'War is condemned by God. The killing of one's brother is strictly forbidden. However, there are times when a nation must take up arms to defend itself. I shall not comment on the Great War but I can comment on its effects here in Caundon. Everyone in this church, myself included, for I lost a younger brother, was touched by the war. In some cases lives were shattered. In others twisted and wrenched. Nothing is the same. So, what advice can I, as a priest, offer you? There is little comfort I can provide except to urge you to live for the day, serve God, try to forget and try to forgive. Get on with your lives . . .'

The priest warmed to his theme. Kitty listened attentively to Father Headon's plea for compassion and understanding. She felt as if he was speaking to her. But how could she turn away from what Fairfax had told her? The war had come to live with her and, unless resolved, would haunt every minute of every day for the rest of her life. She became distracted. The poise she had assumed when leaving the house and walking to Mass began to slip. Her agitation at one point grew so intense, she almost got up and walked out of the church. At last the priest ended his sermon. At Communion Kitty took the consecrated wafer, her mouth so dry she found it hard to swallow. She returned to her bench and knelt, head down, certain that Fairfax was study-ing her.

After Mass the congregation filed out and stood, as they always did, in the cemetery, gossiping and talking. The chil-dren stamped about on the gravestones, playing hide and seek or hopscotch on the pavement which ran along the far side of the church. Kitty stood with Jack and her mother, half listening to the chatter of old Thompson. Occasionally, she caught Jack's gaze. He indicated with his head that they should walk off by themselves but she ignored him.

Fairfax had strolled down to stand beneath the lych gate. He'd turned, not so much watching her but the villagers, as if learning and memorising friendship groups. He had left before the final blessing, his way of telling Father Headon that he did not wish to have words with him. The villagers chose to ignore Fairfax but Kitty could sense how the major's influence was spreading, making itself felt. Some of the men looked nervous, agitated, as if the presence of an officer brought back bad memories of the war, and this one was a Redcap, hunting for deserters and absconders. Kitty looked back over her shoulder. Father Headon and his housekeeper, Holy Mother Church, were making their final farewells to the parishioners. Kitty caught up with the priest as he walked back up the nave, ignoring her mother's exclamation of surprise as she quickly left their group.

'Father, can I have a word?'

'Was it about my sermon?' The priest turned and walked back.

'It's not fair!' Holy Mother Church trumpeted. 'I've got Father's dinner ready!'

'No, it's not fair, is it, Father?'

'Do you want to speak to me now, Kitty?'

'I want to speak to you, Father, but not here. Can I walk back with you, at least into the sacristy?'

The priest looked surprised but nodded and, once they were there, he closed the door on Holy Mother Church's grumbles.

'The altar boys have escaped,' he commented, gesturing at the offertory cruets stacked on a stool. 'You want to speak to me about Fairfax don't you, Kitty?'

Kitty ran her tongue round her lips and blinked back her tears. 'He's going to start something, Father, which will affect all our lives, mine in particular.'

Father Headon began to divest. 'I know.' He turned away slightly. 'I heard about last night. Some of our parishioners, well, you know what Caundon's like. Very few things remain secret for long. The Dead Hand Club, a young miner's wife walking back with that strange officer.' He smiled at Kitty. 'You don't have to be a detective, Kitty. I watched you and Jack come into church, more like strangers than husband and wife.' He sighed. 'I am just waiting for the good major to approach me. I am sure he'll want to know what I have learnt.'

'And what is that, Father?'

'Kitty, Kitty.' He came towards her. 'If I told you what I knew, that would be a great sin, a breach of trust. How can you guarantee that what you say to me now is not told to someone else?'

'Then hear my confession, Father.'

'What do you have to confess, Kitty? When I was slimmer and more handsome,' he tapped his balding head, 'and well thatched up here, I baptised you. I heard your first confession and tried hard not to laugh at your funny little sins. What can Kitty Allerton have done to need confession on a bright Sunday morning? You didn't follow me here for that, did you?'

Kitty smiled. 'So, you can read minds, Father?'

The priest walked to a small door which led out to the back of the church. 'Once upon a time,' he drew back the bolts, 'there were two little people. Jack and Billy. I called them "the two knights", Kitty was their princess. Both these lads used to serve on the altar, and after Mass Kitty would steal in here.' He opened the door. 'To escape their parents, as well as a long list of jobs waiting for them, they'd slip through here, straight across the cemetery to their hideout at Neville's Oak.'

Kitty grinned and walked towards him. The priest caught her wrist.

'I'll never refuse a confession, Kitty. What you have got to do is think about what you have to confess. Pray about it.' He held her gaze.

'You know more than you are telling me,' Kitty murmured.

'Kitty, in time we will all know.'

'Are you worried, Father?'

'Of course I am.' The reply came in a whisper. 'And if it wasn't for Holy Mother Church waiting in the presbytery with her rolling-pin, I'd go back into my church, fall on my knees and beg for God's help. So you go, Kitty. Walk to Neville's Oak. Try not to brood! Brooding is bad for the soul.'

Kitty went out into the cemetery. This old, disused part was now full of wild flowers and their scent hung heavy in the air. The path they used to take was overgrown but she followed it out, through the old gate, which had never been repaired, and into the field. She paused. On the breeze she heard slight murmurs, the odd shout of a child still playing in the cemetery. She recalled the priest's words, and how she, Jack and Billy used to fly like birds under the sky to their favourite meeting place. She walked quickly and wondered if Jack or Fairfax would realise where she had gone and follow her. The small glade round the oak was deserted. Kitty chose her favourite spot, took off her coat, spread it out and sat down. Above her a jay chattered noisily in the branches as its mate skimmed over the fields.

Kitty was determined not to go back in time, to brood on bitter-sweet memories. She loosened her boots and eased them off. She tried to recall every word she'd heard and read the previous evening. One thing she and Billy had under-estimated was Jack's sadness, which he'd hidden so well, at their marriage. Perhaps that was understandable. She was more concerned about what Billy had written in his journal: Jack's intensity, the story of murders by soldiers on the front line. Had the war affected Jack so much that he'd begun to brood? Had the deaths of others sown the idea that Billy must not return? She went cold at such a thought. Was Jack so calculating? So vengeful? So passionate in his desire for her? Kitty chewed her lip. She must answer these questions. Was it Billy's doing, or Jack's or hers? Or was it like everything they did, the result of three lives closely enmeshed? And what of Fairfax? She remembered the officer walking beside her, holding her hand: a dark, brooding presence both new and strange. Kitty had received admiring glances, the good-natured whistles of appreciation, even the greedy lust of Edmund Grant but, apart from her father, there had really only been two men in her life, Jack and Billy. Fairfax had changed all this. Whether she liked it or not, there was a bond between them: not only Billy's death but his journal. Fairfax had read it as intently as she had. She blushed slightly at what Billy had written. Was the major's interest in her purely official or was there something else? Kitty lay back, staring up at the sky, and before she could stop herself drifted into a light sleep.

Kitty woke with a start and got hurriedly to her feet. She hadn't meant to stay so long, she had just wanted time to be by herself, to master her thoughts. The Beaumont Arms would be busy. Mother would need her help and she wanted to speak to Jack to arrange some form of truce, a way of living until this was all over.

Major Oscar Fairfax had decided to busy himself this Sunday morning. He waited under the lych gate watching the parishioners, particularly Jim Cunningham who was sunning himself against one of the gravestones. Fairfax watched as the tall, gangly miner got to his feet and drifted over to talk to the others. Cunningham now acted the faithful parishioner, his handbills rolled up and pushed into his jacket pocket. At last the group broke up. People walked out of the graveyard; some nodded to Fairfax, others ignored him.

'What are you going to do now, Jim?'

Cunningham stopped and glanced sideways at Fairfax. 'You've been waiting for me, haven't you? You are not going to let go, Major Fairfax. Just like the other bastards I served under during the war.' Cunningham forced a smile, his voice had fallen to a hush; those who passed by didn't realise something was wrong.

Fairfax studied the man's unshaven face. 'I find you interesting, Jim. I thought it was impossible to find an atheist in the trenches.'

'Well, you've found one!'

'Come.' Fairfax gestured with his head. 'There's another pub in Caundon. Let me take you for a pint. What's the name of it?'

'The Dovecote, some way out of the village.'

Cunningham agreed to accompany him. He had expected Fairfax to approach him and had wondered how long it would be before this sharp-eyed officer began his interrogation. Ah well, Cunningham thought, there were worse places to be interrogated in than the Dovecote Arms.

'Jim!'

Cunningham turned. Ernst Kurtz came loping down the trackway after them, jacket over one arm, the detachable collar of his shirt stuffed into a trouser pocket. The German stopped, panting for breath, hands on his knees.

'What is it?'

'Ernst gestured at Fairfax. 'It's him I wanted a word with. Typical English, eh?' He beamed at Fairfax. 'Do you always do things in such a civilised manner, Major, like take your victim for a walk?'

'You should know, Ernst.' Fairfax tapped the German on the chest. 'That's why you are here, isn't it? What can't you control, your fear or your curiosity? Well, this time, Herr Kurtz, I have no business with you.'

Kurtz tapped him back on the chest. 'Well I, Major Fairfax, might have business with you.'

Cunningham was pleased at the reaction in the major's eyes.

Ernst stepped back and saluted. 'Now I'm off to the Beaumont Arms.' He nodded at Cunningham. 'Jim, if I don't see you there, at least I'll have the consolation of seeing the major again.'

He loped back towards the church. Fairfax watched him go.

'Strange, isn't it, Jim? I can call you Jim?'

'You can call me what you like.'

'The men of Caundon,' Fairfax continued conversationally, 'fought Ernst and his ilk for four years. Now he comes and lives amongst you.'

'He's just a working man, Major Fairfax. I am sure the village of Caundon can be found in France, Germany or Russia, full of men and women who grub for a living and spend most of their time bowing and kneeling to an altar or a throne.'

'Or answering questions from interfering officers?'

'Yes, yes.' Cunningham watched a hawk skim across the sky. 'What questions do you have for me?'

'None really.'

'So I can go back to the Beaumont Arms?'

'I haven't come to question you but to ask for your help.'

'Help? How can I help an officer?'

'You were there the night Billy was killed.'

'Ah, no.' Cunningham stopped and made as if to turn back. 'Major Fairfax, I don't talk about my mates. Billy was a friend, so is Jack. I have nothing to tell.'

'Don't you think it's strange, Jim? Jack, Billy and Kitty? Billy and Kitty get married. Jack was angry about it, I know he was angry. I have heard the word "seething" used to describe him. Then one cold night Jack and Billy are sent out on a reconnaissance patrol. Jack comes back lively as a robin but his mate, his friend, is later found in a bombed crater, a wound to his stomach and an English bullet in his head. Jack comes home and marries Kitty.'

Cunningham's face turned ugly. He raised a fist but Fairfax didn't flinch.

'Hitting me is no solution. Tell me, Cunningham, have you ever loved a woman?'

Cunningham dropped his fist. 'Once.'

'Tell me about her.'

'Her name was Bernadette, Bernadette O'Connor.' Cunningham stood, eyes half closed, rocking backwards and forwards. 'She lived in Stanley, a small village not far from Ushaw Moor.'

'I know where it is.'

Cunningham opened his eyes. 'I am sure you do, Major Fairfax. I wouldn't be surprised if you knew all about Bernadette O'Connor.'

'No, you tell me, Jim.'

'I used to go through there on weekends. We met at a football match, one between the mining villages. She was in service. I really loved her, Major. Like a little doll, she was, red curly hair, pale-faced, delicate as ivory. She took pneumonia. Fought it for a month.' Cunningham gestured back towards the church. 'I lit so many candles I'd hardly money left for ale. Waste of bloody time! The church took my money and death took Bernadette.'

'And that's when you really lost your faith?'

'No, Major, I didn't lose it, I hadn't any to begin with.'

Fairfax studied the gangly miner with his narrow, lined face, glistening eyes and thin lips twisted into a bitter smile. His hands now hung by his side, heavy, grained with coal dust. The boots were scuffed, the trousers frayed and patched. The collar of the shirt was none too clean. Fairfax hid his own sadness. Men like Cunningham haunted every village and town in England. Victims spat out by the war: lonely, frustrated, growing more bitter with the passing of each year. Yet, if the records were to be believed, this man was also a murderer.

'You still haven't answered my question.' Fairfax walked on. Cunningham followed.

'Which question is that, sir? You have asked so many I'm beginning to lose count.'

'One in particular: if Jack and Billy were your mates, Jack surely should have looked after Billy, brought him back?'

'Funny things, the trenches, sir.'

They were now clear of Caundon, out in the country-side. Fairfax stopped to light a cigarette. He offered one to Cunningham.

'Go on, they are Capstan, better than Woodbine though not as good as the Sweet Afton you can buy in Dublin.'

Cunningham took one. 'So, you've been across the water, have you, Major? I suppose there's plenty of business for you in Dublin.' He lowered his head to take the light. Fairfax drew on his own cigarette and squinted at the sky.

'Jim, I don't flatter people. I made a rule. I never offer a cigarette to any man who didn't fight for King and country. You and me, Jim, we're the same. We are soldiers. I don't believe in God but I believe in my King, my regiment and the law. I do unpleasant things, be it in London or Dublin. Sometimes I feel as if I am the only sane one in an insane world or an insane man in a world I cannot understand.'

Cunningham stared back, puzzled.

'Let me give you an example.' Fairfax sighed. 'I won't tell you its name, but imagine a small village outside Dublin. The Black and Tans had been there, the usual brutalities. A passing British officer had intervened and was shot dead for his pains. Some people claimed it was the Fenians. Other witnesses said it was the Black and Tans themselves. I was sent to investigate.' He flicked the cigarette ash. 'Can you imagine it, Jim? I'm in this little rundown village, the church has been sacked, houses are burning, corpses litter the street but only one death concerns me.' He lifted a gloved finger. 'One death, Jim, that of a British officer. Can't you see the madness of it? Why one death amongst so many? Why not the poor farmer who had his head blown off? Or his wife who had been beaten and raped trying to protect him? So it is now. On the night Billy Hammond died, thousands of soldiers died across Europe. I am investigating Hammond's death four years later because of the reasons I have mentioned: the King, the army and the law. You and I were paid to kill Germans, the more the better. We even got medals for it. If we had lived hundreds of years ago, we might have brought their heads back as trophies. Now, what keeps me sane, Jim, is knowing the difference between murder and a soldier's duty. If Billy Hammond was killed by Germans then he's another casualty of war. If he was murdered, with malice aforethought, his killer should hang.'

'I'll not do it!' Cunningham threw the cigarette down and stubbed it under his steel-capped boot. 'I'll not do it, do you hear?' He turned away.

'Bapaume!' Fairfax shouted.

Cunningham stopped dead in his tracks.

'Bapaume!' Fairfax repeated like a preacher quoting a favourite text.

Cunningham looked round. Fairfax walked back towards him.

'We are going to miss that pint, Jim.' He opened his cigarette case. 'Have another cigarette.'

Cunningham took it and the proffered light mechanically.

'Strange people, the French,' Fairfax murmured. 'I can't see why they don't just take a man out, stand him against a wall and let a firing squad take care of him. Instead, they lash him to a board and let the guillotine take his head off. Ever seen a man decapitated, Jim? The French want you, you know. I mean, they don't know your name or where you live but they have a corpse, that of a priest, found dead, bayoneted in his own church during the battle of Bapaume. They know it wasn't the Germans. According to the record, the church and the orchards around it were filled with northern lads. You know the way of the world.' Fairfax sniffed. 'I have asked the survivors this and I have asked the survivors that – it's like sifting shale from coal. Eventually you reach the truth. Now, Jim, are you going to tell me about Bapaume or shall I tell you? Or, if you don't want to help me, well, I can have you on a train to Darlington tomorrow morning. You'll be in London by Tuesday. Who knows, this time next week in a French prison in Calais.'

'You absolute bastard!' Cunningham breathed. 'You devil's shit!'

'Don't get like that, Jim. I am not interested in priests, the French law or their corpses. I am only interested in your story and any help you can provide. Come on.' He grasped

Cunningham by the arm. 'I didn't want to threaten, I mean about the guillotine.'

'Yes you did,' Cunningham breathed. 'You are going to get the truth, Major Fairfax, aren't you, one way or the other?'

'Tell me about Bapaume.' Fairfax walked a little brisker. 'Let's get that story out of the way before we reach the Dovecote Arms.'

Cunningham sucked at his teeth and hid his terrors. If he had his way he would have run back to Caundon and sought out the rest. Warn them that this man was more dangerous than he appeared. After all, every one of them had secrets to hide.

'Tell me about Bapaume,' Fairfax repeated. 'If you want, we can forget about the Dovecote Arms and go back to your house. We could have some tea, Jim. You could show me all the plunder you took from the corpses: cigarette cases, the fob watches, the pens, the leather wallets. We might even find something from Bapaume Church. Quite the little magpie, aren't we? Anything that glitters.'

Cunningham paled and Fairfax watched with satisfaction the beads of sweat course down the unshaven cheeks.

'You see, Jim, how knowledgeable I am. Bapaume?'

'It was snowing,' Cunningham began, 'so we could move more freely without being observed by the enemy machine-gunners and snipers. We entered Bapaume. Orchards stretched between the church and the chateau farm. It was a place of horror. We had been attacking since dawn, the place was full of dead and wounded. On every side the injured were shouting or blowing whistles to attract attention. Others just lay quiet under hummocks of snow. Our regiment had mixed with others, companies had broken up. I remember one of

these hummocks moving. It was a Highlander, his bare thigh
a mere blackened stump, yet he was brave and gratefully took
the cigarette we offered. We could do nothing for him or the
others. All the wounded later died.

'The Germans opened up again and we hid amongst
the trees. Night fell. We had moved beyond the orchard.'
Cunningham paused and narrowed his eyes. 'So different from
a day like this. The snow turned to sleet and the Germans just
kept shelling. We tried to sleep but, every minute it seemed, the
shout would go up: "Sound to, they are coming! Sound to!"
The Germans poured down whizz-bangs. The night became
bright with bursting shells then the gas, smelling like rotten
eggs tinged with almonds: pungent, sickly, heavy. More gas
canisters fell, followed by high-velocity shells, boiling the mud.
We were fighting in goggles and masks. Eventually we broke.
We just scattered. It was every man for himself. Earlier that day
I had made the acquaintance of a Lancashire lad. He claimed
to be eighteen, really no more than seventeen. Somersby, that
was his name.'

'Ah yes, Somersby,' Fairfax interrupted. 'His corpse was
found in the church.'

'Somersby was all a-panic, crying, screaming, hysterical. I
managed to quieten him down. I confess we ran faster than
the rest. We reached the orchard. The wounded were now
quiet. The main door of the church was locked but a side
one was open. I went in, it was warm and clean. We made
ourselves comfortable. It reminded me a bit of Caundon
Church. Suddenly the sacristy door opened and this fat priest
came out. He was really fat, white-haired, red greasy cheeks.
In one hand he had the biggest glass of wine I have ever seen
and in the other a chunk of cheese. Most of the priests I met

were good chaps and I've nothing but praise for our padres, whatever they believe in, whatever they do.'

'But the French priest?' Fairfax prompted.

'He came waddling down that church like a toad, big fat mouth full of cheese and wine. Somersby was grievously wounded. I didn't realise that until we got in there – neither did he, due to shock or fear. He had taken a piece of shrapnel low in his back and, as the pain made itself felt, he began to scream. I turned to the priest. I knew a little French. After all, we had been with the mademoiselles, hadn't we? *"Aidez moi!"* I said. *"S'il vous plait. Nous sommes Anglais. Aidez moi!"* The priest just stared at us with those goggly eyes of his. "Help me!" I demanded.'

They had now rounded the bend. The Dovecote Arms was in sight.

'We can sit in the garden,' Cunningham murmured. 'I like the smell of apple blossom.'

'Go on with your story,' said Fairfax.

'I repeated my request for help. Do you know what he did? He bit into the cheese and took a slurp of wine and answered me in fluent English. He explained he was a priest and could not take the side of combatants.' Cunningham laughed. 'Can you imagine that? Somersby was bleeding to death. I hadn't eaten or drunk for days and that fat bastard, in his own church, in a country I was fighting for, was telling me he couldn't bloody help!' Cunningham wetted his lips. 'He turned his back on me and quoted: "Those who live by the sword shall die by the sword." I called him a misbegotten bastard. I told him what I thought: about the wounded lying outside, men dying of their wounds, of thirst, freezing cold, while he stuffed his belly. Somersby was now deep in shock.

He had fallen quiet. I grasped my rifle. We had been expecting hand-to-hand fighting so the bayonet was still fixed. I just charged at that priest. I knocked him to the floor. He was crying for mercy. I gave him a bayonet thrust straight to the heart. I didn't give a damn then and I don't now. I couldn't give a sod! I went to his house. I took red wine, cheese and meat, and brought them back to Somersby but he was unconscious. So I sat, got drunk as a lord and helped myself to what I wanted.

'Then I fell asleep. I expected to be woken by the Redcaps. As long as it wasn't the French, I didn't care. I even toyed with the idea of surrendering. It was Jack who woke me. He had been sent out to scout. He'd come into the church and realised immediately what had happened. He dragged the priest's body away and hid it in a cellar. He used a bucket of water to clear the blood and then checked on poor Somersby. He had died during the night.' Cunningham paused. ' "Come on, lad," Jack murmured to me. "You've done enough damage here for one night." He grabbed my rifle and knapsack then dragged me out. Later that day we rejoined our unit.'

'And he never told anyone?'

'That was our Jack. He didn't even ask me why. Now and again he'd look at me sadly. Perhaps he told Billy but I knew Billy would keep his mouth shut. Anyway, he was killed a week later.'

They had now reached the gate leading into a small garden adjoining the Dovecote. The tables were already full of farm hands and others drifting in for their ale or cider before rejoining their families for Sunday dinner. A few recognised Cunningham and greeted him; Fairfax they ignored.

He led Cunningham to a seat beneath a large sycamore tree.

'It's going to get hot,' Fairfax observed.

He went into the pub and came back with two brimming jugs of Newcastle ale.

'If you are not used to it,' Cunningham remarked, 'drink it slowly.'

'I drank poteen in Ireland and survived.' Fairfax toasted him with the jug. 'The French can go hang. If I had been in your shoes I would have done the same. So, after that, there was no God?'

'Yes, I thought I had closed the door for good.'

'But Jack and Billy they had problems of their own, hadn't they? They quarrelled?'

Cunningham sipped his ale. 'Yes,' he admitted. 'They quarrelled. We all knew it was about Kitty.'

Chapter 9

The Beaumont Arms was busy, customers thronged into the bar and snug. Kitty's mother was cooking dinner in the kitchen: vegetable soup, roast ham, potatoes, vegetables and steamed apple pudding. As usual, they had visitors – the Ashcroft children and their widowed mother. Evans the policeman would drop by, as well as others Kitty or her mother thought should be invited. The customers were mostly men, their children played hoops and quoits outside on the pavement. The men would drink until mid-afternoon before going home to their Sunday dinner when the village would fall quiet.

Kitty had barely put her foot in the door before Mother was asking her to do this and that. Kitty felt slightly guilty at not coming home immediately. Her mother, in her printed pinafore, Betty, John, and young Timothy Ashcroft who served as a pot boy were charging around like wild horses. Kitty fled upstairs and changed quickly.

'Now is not the time,' she murmured to herself, 'for reflection and dreams but for hard work.'

She changed her shoes, clattered downstairs and took a pinafore out of a small closet.

'Where's Jack?' she asked.

'Out in the stable, attending to his lamp – well, that's his excuse.'

'And the major?'

Her mother just raised her eyes heavenwards and almost pushed Kitty into the bar where her arrival was greeted with roars of approval from a line of waiting but patient customers.

In the small outhouse which also stored his miner's equipment, Jack sat on an overturned box and dressed the lamp. He did this every Sunday. He usually found it soothing, today he half wished he could knock the lamp aside, stride into the Beaumont Arms and confront his wife. But that wouldn't do. Public interest was quickening. Last night's escapade was all round the village, and down the mine tomorrow there would be interminable questions.

'Aren't you going to have a pint, Jack?' Evans, dressed in his Sunday best, stood in the doorway, looking rather incongruous in a pair of old riding boots he'd bought for what he called his 'Sunday constitutional'.

'I wanted to be by myself,' Jack grinned. 'But come in, Len. Pull up a bench. Give us both the benefit of your wisdom. You've come to talk haven't you?'

Evans sat down on an upturned barrel, making sure he closed the door behind him. 'I was up early this morning. Cycled out to see my inspector. He owes me a favour or two.'

Jack put down the greasy rag. 'And?'

'His name is Graham Phillips. He was a major in one of the Border regiments; he also served in the Provost Marshal's Office.'

Jack nodded. 'Go on.'

'He knows all about Fairfax. He called him a "human ferret", a man obsessed with bringing others to justice. Most of Fairfax's friends were killed in the war, including a younger, much-beloved brother, a pilot in the Royal Air Corps. Fairfax's wife died later, a victim of the Spanish influenza.'

'So, we now know more about Fairfax.'

'According to my inspector, Fairfax has a reputation for having no heart or soul.'

'I could have told you that, Len.'

'Jack, listen.' Evans pulled the barrel closer. 'I know and you know that we've all got things to hide. Four years out in the poppy fields! We all did things we are ashamed of. Sometimes I didn't leave the trench and, if I did, I sheltered in the nearest crater or bomb hole.'

'As did the rest of the world.' Jack laughed sourly. 'What else did you do, Len?'

'Another group I was with, well, they shot their officer.'

'Some of them deserved to be shot! You know that. If their men hadn't shot them, they would have been court-martialled. Even the army recognises that absolute, bloody stupidity can be a crime!' Jack leaned down to clean his lamp.

'True, most of our crimes were crimes of passion,' Evans replied evenly, 'born of fear, terror but . . .'

'But my possible crime wasn't, eh, Len? Is that what you are saying?'

'Jack, Jack, I am only trying to help. You and Billy were great friends. Everyone knows that you both loved Kitty. In the week before you married—'

'That's my business, Len.'

'We all know about the argument,' Evans went on. 'We all remember the night you went out with Billy, just the two of you, sliding across the cold mud. You had your rifles, helmets and all the other baggage we carried. You later said you'd become separated yet Bob Daventry told us how your helmet was found next to Billy. Bob also told us about the two wounds, one in Billy's belly, the other to his head. You didn't become separated, did you? You must have been with him.'

Jack blew his cheeks out. 'I told you what happened, Len. I don't remember about my helmet. Billy and I became separated. I crawled back to the trench, Billy was later found dead.'

Evans got to his feet. 'I don't think Fairfax believes that.'

'I couldn't give a shit what Fairfax believes!'

'Can't you see what Fairfax is planning?' Evans leaned down. 'He's going to take you before the Durham assizes, Jack. He's going to talk to the Crown prosecutors. They'll say that you planned to kill Billy from the start. You actually joined the same regiment, the same company to be near him. You seized the opportunity—'

'Opportunity!' Jack scoffed back. 'Opportunity! Ah, don't be stupid, Len! Billy and I had served three of a four-year war. Why didn't I kill him immediately? God knows, half of Germany was trying to do the same.'

Evans shook his head. 'You don't know those lawyers, Jack. They'll argue that you might have tried before, or that you were waiting for the right opportunity or that as the war dragged on, your resentment and hatred grew until you couldn't control it any longer.'

'They can say what they like, Len. They won't have either the truth or the proof.'

'There's something else as well. How was this reported, Jack? Somebody here in Caundon must have written to the War Office or the army, laying allegations. Someone pretty insistent, who's either found evidence,' he saw the look on Jack's face, 'or made it up. Somebody with influence, Jack.'

'Influence?' Jack got to his feet. 'This is a Durham village, Len, not a great palace.'

'There's Morrison and we mustn't forget either our beloved MP, Macclesfield.'

'Macclesfield knows nothing about me!'

'He's a Tory, financed by local businessmen. Jack, you've got to start thinking and planning. You can't sit in a darkened shed cleaning an oil lamp. Fairfax isn't a piece of coal you can chip away.' Evans got up. 'I wish you'd come for a pint.'

Jack shook his head and opened the door. 'Have your drink, Len.'

'Won't you tell me what you're—'

'Have your drink,' Jack repeated. 'It's Sunday.'

Evans sighed and walked away. Jack closed the door behind him and returned to his task. Only when he was sure Evans was across the yard did he look at his hands and notice how they were trembling. He closed his eyes. He was back in no-man's-land. Him and Billy, squirming through the mud. They had come across the corpse of a German, glassy-eyed, spread-eagled, staring up at the sky. Billy had cracked a joke about how the poor bugger was now in a better place than either of them. They had crawled on. Above them the whizz-bangs and the Very lights. Now and again a machine gun would chatter. They lost their way and they squirmed around like tadpoles in dirty water until they found their bearings. They were drenched in mud, pushing their rifles before them, when the firing started—

'Fairfax is talking to Cunningham.'

Jack glanced up. Ernst Kurtz had slipped through the door. He was leaning against it, staring down at him.

'So, Fairfax is talking to Cunningham. I'm relieved.'

Kurtz tugged at his shirt and passed his rolled flat cap from one hand to the other. 'I thought they were here after me.'

'Will you ever go back to Germany, Ernst?'

'No, lad. Give me ten years and I'll be a prosperous Durham businessman with a fine house and a bonny wife,' he joked.

Jack smiled at Kurtz's attempts to imitate the Durham accent.

'He's here because of you, Jack. So I've come to make you an offer.'

'Oh, aye, what's that? You want to be my lawyer?'

'No, Jack, I'll kill him.'

Jack dropped the rag, his jaw sagged. Kurtz laughed deep in his throat.

'Ernst, you would hang!'

'I should have hanged years ago, Jack. It can be done.' The German sat down on the barrel Evans had used. 'Caundon has many lonely lanes, I have a Luger pistol. A swift bullet in the back of the head. It would take them years to find his grave.'

Jack stared down at the ground. He was repelled by Kurtz's offer but what really chilled him was how Fairfax's presence was making itself felt. Evans riding across to see his inspector. Kurtz offering to repay years of favours with one dreadful act. Cunningham walking with Fairfax, who'd leave none of them alone. Jack closed his eyes. They had all been in that trench. When he got back, without Billy, they had given him strange glances but they knew, or he thought they did, that mates never harmed each other. Not lads who had sat side by side on the same school bench, clasped hands ever since they could walk!

'I could do it, you know.'

'Don't be stupid!' Jack snapped. 'Don't lift a finger, Ernst, do you understand? Let's say you did. The army would come here, they'd search and they wouldn't go away until both you and I were in handcuffs.'

Kurtz's eyes filled with tears. Jack was astonished. The German sat there staring at him.

'What's the matter, Ernst? If the lads from the bar could see us, they'd think we were a couple of nancy boys.'

'Don't you realise what you've just said, or haven't said, Jack? Fairfax is your enemy. I offered to kill him and you refused.'

'And?' Jack asked.

'Never once did you say that you were innocent or let justice take its course or that you had nothing to fear.'

'Ernst, we are all guilty of something. I know what happened out there in no-man's-Land but that's a matter between me, Billy and God. I am not going to jump up and down like a Jack-in-the-box and protest about events. I want it left well alone.'

'And Kitty?'

'Kitty must ask herself three questions. Do I love her? Does she love me? And does she believe me?'

'Then why not tell her the truth? There is a truth, isn't there, Jack?'

'Why all this fascination with the truth?' Jack took a piece of string he used as a wick and ran it through his fingers. 'What is the truth, Ernst? Some people say we should never have been in France in the first place. Others claim we should never shoot at each other. I don't know what the truth is, Ernst. Perhaps it's like a plant. You just can't see it all, the roots, the bulb. Sometimes,' Jack threw the string onto the floor, 'the truth can hurt. It can give rise to fresh doubts. I don't believe truth is the great healer, certainly not in this matter.'

Kurtz was about to leave when a thought occurred to him. He turned round to make sure the door was closed.

'Jack, you are a member of the Dead Hand Club.'

'Well, yes, of course I am.'

'And you know I am German.'

'I can see you're not the Duchess of Portsmouth!'

Kurtz laughed. 'Every so often, Jack,' he lowered his voice, 'I go through to Durham . . .'

'Yes, so I gather.'

'There are quite a few Germans in England. Men like myself who either don't or can't return home. You'll find us in many trades. We call ourselves the Frei Korps because we are free, no Prussian Junkers to tell us what to do! We look after each other. We don't meet in a pub, that would be too dangerous. So we hire an assembly room and drink beer, eat ham and sausage. Some of us pretend we are back in the beer halls of Munich or elsewhere.'

'What has this got to do with Fairfax?'

'All in good time, Jack. Let me tell you about the Frei Korps. Most of us are working men, ordinary soldiers, just relieved to be out of the killing. A few are officers. Some of high breeding. After the war most officers returned to Germany full of threats, saying how the army was stabbed in the back. The men who stayed have more sense. They are not your typical Junkers; most of them were trained at university, either at home or abroad. One of these is a young man, Anton Riffleman. We were on no more than nodding acquaintance. However, the last time the Frei Korps met, Anton singled me out. We have a rule. We never talk about our past lives in Germany. Anton was full of questions about what I was doing what I would like to do, where I lived. I told him about Caundon. About my good friend Jack and his lovely young wife Kitty. Anton became very interested. He then left me alone. Later in the evening, when I had drunk deeply and was wondering whether to chance my stomach on one of your buses or sleep in a friend's room, Riffleman came back with a bottle of Schnapps and two glasses. Now, Jack, I drink Schnapps like a baby does milk. Riffleman seemed very interested in Caundon. I mentioned the Dead Hand Club. He asked me about its members. What they did how they talked. Did the English, like us, have secrets? Of course I told him nothing. By the time the evening was over he was as drunk as, what do you call it?'

'A newt?'

'I would have said a duck.' Kurtz laughed. 'The way he walked. By now it was almost midnight and our time in the hall was up. My friend, Otto, was insistent that I stayed with him the night. He took me back to his lodgings. I remember the landlady was fat and very, very welcoming. She said I looked flushed and brought me a jug of water and a big mug of black, steaming coffee. It was the best I'd drunk since leaving Germany. Otto was very friendly with her.'

'Ernst,' Jack intervened. 'What has this to do with Fairfax?'

'A great deal, you'll see. I later discussed the evening with my friend Otto. He was very impressed by the way Riffleman seemed fascinated by me. He told me how Riffleman had been a member of, what do you call it?' Ernst tapped his head. 'The understanding, the understanding corps?'

'Intelligence Corps,' Jack smiled.

'That's it, the Intelligence Corps. Anyway, he had been captured, come to England and stayed because he fell in love – well, that's his story. Otto also informed me that Riffleman is a big friend of your local MP, Macclesfield.'

'Why?' Jack asked.

'Apparently Macclesfield serves on a committee in the House of Commons dealing with German affairs. Due to the demand for war reparations and the unrest in Berlin following the Spartacus rebellion, Macclesfield uses Riffleman as an adviser. At the time I thought nothing of it. This morning, however, it struck me that if Riffleman is advising your MP, why is he so interested in a small community of ex-soldiers in a small mining village in Durham? I mean, Caundon is not your Whitehall, is it, Jack?'

'No, it isn't.' Jack felt the hairs on the nape of his neck prickle with a cold sweat. Fairfax was dangerous. He was not just an army clerk from the Provost Marshal's Office looking over old records. Someone with influence was making their presence felt. Someone with access to the local Member of Parliament who, in turn, used his own connections amongst German ex-patriates to find out about him and others in the village. Fairfax must be well primed but who had set the ball in motion? Who could hate him so much?

'Have you met Riffleman recently?'

Kurtz shook his head.

'And what did you tell him?' Jack demanded. 'That first night in Durham?'

'I couldn't tell him what I didn't know,' Kurtz declared. 'Time and again Riffleman came back to you and Billy. He acted as if he was fascinated by what he called a dramatic love story. Of course, I now realise what he was after.'

Kurtz was about to continue when there was a knock on the door. Kitty entered with a tankard full of frothy ale.

'Kitty, you look as beautiful as ever,' the German exclaimed. 'I'd like to think you were bringing that for me. But . . .' Kurtz shrugged, got to his feet, stepped hastily through the doorway and was gone.

Jack was grateful for the tankard. Kitty kept her eyes averted.

'Kitty, I love you.'

She pressed the tankard into his hand.

'Kitty, I love you. What I want to know . . .' Jack hesitated. 'What I want to ask is, do you love me?'

Kitty was about to walk away but changed her mind.

'Jack, I have always loved you but love depends on knowledge. I always believed I knew you.' She crouched down. 'If you told me the truth, Jack, then it would make it easier. Why don't you tell me the truth, Jack? You always boasted there were no secrets between me, you and Billy. Why don't you tell me what really happened? How Billy really died. I'll believe you.'

Jack sipped from the tankard. 'Would you, Kitty?'

Kitty got to her feet and moved away. 'That's where we are, Jack,' she said over her shoulder. 'If you can't talk to me, if you can't tell me the truth . . .'

And she was gone.

Jack gripped the tankard fiercely. He felt like throwing it at the wall and running after her. He recalled Billy's face, pale and sweat-soaked, eyes pleading with him, his own sense of shame and disgust. He closed his eyes and drank. Kitty had left the door half-open. Jack gazed at an upstairs window. One of the Ashcroft children had pulled the blinds aside and was staring down into the yard. Jack went cold as his memory was jogged, of digging in the vegetable patch the day before and Fairfax spying on him from a window. At the time he had dismissed it but Fairfax was a cunning opponent, sharp, incisive. Had he glimpsed what had been uncovered? Jack threw the rag on the floor and left the outhouse. Fairfax was absent, no one else would be watching. Jack went to the vegetable patch and began digging. The more he dug, the greater his panic. The metal box had been removed, Fairfax had struck first.

Fairfax sat under the spreading branches of the shady chestnut and watched Cunningham leave. The miner had proved a valuable source of information. Fairfax hid a flicker of pleasure. A pot boy came over and took his jug.

'Do you want more, sir?'

Fairfax stared at the boy's pale face, the spots round the mouth and high on the cheeks.

'How old are you, lad?'

'Just gone eighteen, sir.'

Fairfax tapped the table. 'Not for the moment. I am expecting someone else, a Mr Charles Hargreaves.'

'Oh yes, sir, he is lodging at the Dovecote. He arrived late last night. The landlord had to send the trap down to the station to collect him. I think he's gone for a walk, sir.'

Fairfax nodded absent-mindedly and dismissed him. Hargreaves was to meet him here later this afternoon. From what Fairfax could gather, friendly rivalry meant the mining community of Caundon stayed away from the Dovecote and patronised the Beaumont Arms, so this was a safe place to meet.

Fairfax leaned back on the hard wooden bench and stared around. It was still summer. Only a few golden leaves strewn on the flower beds and grass showed autumn was thinking of coming. He wondered how long this investigation would last. Although he tried to concentrate on the case, Fairfax could not get Kitty's face out of his mind: the way she walked and talked, how she had sat beside him in the darkness last night. What was it about her? Fairfax had attended dinners and soirees in London, official banquets. He had met a host of beautiful women society debutantes, daughters of the landed gentry. Yet he always felt distant, as if there was an invisible curtain between himself and them. No quickening of interest. Oh, he could flirt and be gallant. Wasn't that part of his job? But Kitty Allerton was different: her smooth, ivory colouring, her jet-black hair, eyes full of life and expression. The way she kept herself, what was it, contained? Yet it was done so elegantly. She was sharp as well. A girl raised to do her duty yet one who, behind the façade of a humdrum existence, thought deeply about life.

Fairfax quietly conceded he had never met her like before or the close, intense relationship between herself and those two men. It touched a chord deep in Fairfax's heart, echoes perhaps of his relationship with Maurice, his own brother. Now that was a name and a memory that pricked his heart and stirred his soul. He and Maurice had been so close.

They had shared the same bed, toys, schooling and friends. They discussed everything, then Maurice was gone, followed afterwards by the death of Eleanora. A harsh coldness had enveloped Fairfax's life which the war had only strengthened. Fairfax could empathise with the Dead Hand Club, men who had been through the great blooding and survived. But those men regarded the war as over and wanted to be left alone; for Fairfax, the war would never be finished. He wanted to hunt those who had not played their part, be it the businessman he'd met on the train to Caundon or the likes of Jack Allerton who had used the war for his own nefarious purposes.

Surprisingly enough, Fairfax's superiors in London had been very encouraging, insisting that he take full charge of the case. 'You've got to go to Caundon personally, Fairfax,' his colonel had said. 'And I want to see results.'

'I or we, sir?' Fairfax had replied.

The colonel smiled coldly. 'Sharp as a razor, Fairfax! One of these days you'll cut yourself. Yes, you are right, "we". This is not just a matter for the Provost Marshal. The Secretary of State himself has expressed an interest.' The colonel's popping blue eyes had stared at him soullessly.

Fairfax fully understood what the colonel was saying. If the Secretary of State was interested, that meant an MP, with some influence, was also interested. Yet it had not gone according to plan. Fairfax had done his homework well. He had studied maps of Caundon, listened to briefings, gone through army records until he felt as if he knew the members of the Dead Hand Club as well as he knew the men from his own company. One thing he had not counted on was Kitty Allerton! True, Billy's journal had stirred his interest, but there was something else—

'Sir?'

Fairfax looked up. 'Lieutenant, you are hiding the sun. For God's sake, man, don't salute, just sit down!'

Lieutenant Hargreaves sat on the wooden chair vacated by Cunningham. Red-haired with a white, freckly face, Charles Hargreaves did not look like a lieutenant from the Provost Marshal's Office. With smiling green eyes, a well-clipped moustache and long sideburns, wearing a tweed suit and stiff white collar, Hargreaves looked the proper young squire.

'You can certainly act the part,' Fairfax murmured.

Hargreaves loosened his leather watch strap as if it was too tight.

'How is your room?'

'Pleasant enough. Small, no bigger than a dugout, but the sheets are clean, the water's fresh and the landlord's wife is the best cook I have met for many a day.'

'Strange that, isn't it?' Fairfax replied. 'I've never yet met any soldier who fought and survived the Great War who doesn't like his food.'

'It's a part of the legacy, sir, isn't it? I mean, look at today.' Hargreaves leaned back and stared up at the sky. 'Sunshine and cool breezes, the country lanes full of the perfume of hawthorn and wild flowers. To crown it all, a jug of ale and beef stew pie. Why, sir, it's the next best thing to heaven!'

'Is it now?'

'And how are you finding Caundon, sir?'

Fairfax described his arrival in the village, those whom he had met and questioned. Certain things he kept to himself, like digging up what Jack had hidden in the vegetable patch. Hargreaves heard him out and sat staring at a bee which had landed on the table.

'Do you understand all that, Charles?' Fairfax asked curiously.

Fairfax called across to the pot boy and ordered ale for both of them. 'Bring it in pewter jugs!' he called after the lad. 'I always believe,' he remarked, 'that ale tastes better out of pewter. Do you want me to go through what I've said again, Charles?'

Hargreaves nodded. Fairfax sighed and repeated his main findings in Caundon.

'So, sir, we have the remnants of a Company of Friends attached to the Durham Regiment. They stuck together and went through the same hell we did. Their leader appears to be this Jack Allerton who happens to be our quarry. Correct, sir?'

Fairfax nodded.

'Jack Allerton loved, was possibly infatuated with, his best friend's wife,' Hargreaves continued. 'Indeed, he seemed more concerned about her than he was with the army or the war. He and Billy fought together for three years. Now we come to Billy Hammond's death. According to popular report around the village, Billy was killed in a trench by shell burst. We know that's not true.'

'But that's not really important, is it?' Fairfax intervened as the pot boy returned with the ale. 'Many men were killed and their family and relatives spared the gruesome details. What does it really matter, if a soldier died in the course of his duty, how he met his death?'

Hargreaves waited for the pot boy to leave. He sipped the ale and wiped the foam from his neatly clipped moustache.

'If I understand you correctly, sir, the facts of this case are

178

quite different. Jack and Billy left the trench on a reconnaissance patrol, a normal occurrence. They became lost. Jack claims he was separated from Billy who was later found dead in one of the many craters which peppered no-man's-land. Now that should have been the end of the matter except that Jack's helmet was found next to Billy, and Billy suffered two wounds. One was to the belly, and the other, the fatal injury, was caused by a bullet in the head from an English revolver.'

'There's something else.' Fairfax picked up his coat, felt in the inside pocket and handed over the dirt-grained tin. 'This was Billy's. From the little I can gather, the watch it contains was Kitty's wedding present to him – Billy always wore it. Before Billy's corpse was buried, all his personal effects were removed and sent back to the family. His watch was not found. Jack had it all the time, he brought it back and hid it.'

Hargreaves opened the tin and whistled under his breath. 'This could send our man to the scaffold,' he murmured.

'Yes it could, Charles. So let's construct our case. Two men leave the English trenches and go out across no-man's-land. The Germans open up with their machine guns, whizz-bangs, grenades, whatever. Our two lads decide to take shelter, which is exactly what you and I would do. This is where the mystery begins. Jack is unhurt. Billy, however, receives a wound to the stomach. Was that due to enemy fire? Or Jack?'

'But I thought it was caused by a shell, sir.'

Fairfax made a wry grimace. 'What kind of shell, Charles? A German grenade? An English grenade? Did Jack first try to kill Billy that way and fail so he decided to finish the job with a bullet? Jack murders his friend, takes the love token and flees the crater. He gets back to his trench, tells a story and thinks that's the end of the matter.'

'Except for Daventry.'

'Yes, Charles, except for Daventry. Daventry was a soldier whose mind was unhinged. He believed, as the war went on, that he wasn't there to fight for King and country but to bury the dead. If the truth be known, he should have been sent home, he was suffering from shell shock, but somehow he remained. In the course of the war Daventry buried many of his friends. Billy was his friend so Daventry goes looking for his corpse. He brings it back, Jack's helmet with him. If it hadn't been for that, Billy's corpse would have sunk into the mud. Colonel Morrison sends the corpse down for proper burial. A busy medical orderly notices the wound to the stomach and the bullet to the head fired at close range. He finds this curious. Well, any soldier would. Why should a man with a stomach wound inflicted by a shell, fired from some distance away, also have a wound inflicted at very close range? The bullet is taken out and recognised as English.' Fairfax sipped his ale. 'Let's face it, Charles, by the end of the war, our doctors, nurses and medical orderlies knew more about weapons and gunfire than many of our superiors.' He lit a cigarette. 'But war is war, Billy's dead. His corpse is wrapped in a canvas cloth and taken out for burial. The medical orderly's report, together with Billy's journal, are filed. Some interest is shown but then quietly forgotten.'

'Until influence made itself felt.'

'Yes, I wonder about that.' Fairfax scratched his chin.

'The evidence is quite damning,' Hargreaves declared. 'But . . .'

'But what?'

'If Jack really hated Billy, why wait three years?'

'How do we know he did? There could have been other attempts? Or Jack Allerton could just have been waiting for the opportunity.'

'There is one drawback.' Hargreaves took the proffered cigarette. He fumbled in his pocket to find a box of matches and lit it carefully. 'I know everything falls into place, sir. Jack's infatuation with Kitty, his quarrel with Billy, the circumstances of Billy's death. But think, sir, we are two soldiers out in no-man's-land. We are carrying grenades, a rifle, rounds of ammunition and a bayonet.'

'I know what you are saying, Charles. Jack did not carry a revolver. He wasn't an officer. So how did Jack, who probably never handled a revolver in his life, get one to kill his friend? Why didn't he just use his rifle, even his bayonet?'

'More importantly, sir, here is Jack who has been wanting to kill his friend for years. He now wants to go back to claim his reward. Why didn't he bury Billy's corpse? The reports claim that there had been heavy rain, the soil was soft. If I had a pound for every corpse not discovered, I'd be a millionaire.' Hargreaves scratched his head. 'Why not bury the corpse? Why take the watch but not the journal? Why keep the watch? Hide it away? Its discovery would certainly cause Jack hideous problems.'

Fairfax drew on his cigarette. The same questions had troubled him. He had investigated many a murder, many a suspicious death. Murderers not only hid their corpses but as much of their handiwork as possible. Jack Allerton had done neither.

'And what have you found, Charles?'

'Well, as you know, sir, I've been to Aldershot to check

through documents. I have a file for you in my room. According to it, that particular sector of no-man's-land on that particular evening was very, very busy. Our line was manned by both the Durham Regiment and the Berkshires. Now the Germans had been dropping shells constantly, using the barrage as cover to move troops up into their forward trenches. From what I can gather, Morrison and his opposite number further down the line became very agitated so reconnaissance patrols were sent out. The Berkshires were led by a Major Redmond who, so far, I have been unable to trace. I have some evidence that he comes from Skipton in Yorkshire.'

'A Yorkshireman in a Berkshire regiment?'

'Sir, by the time the war was finished the names Berkshire and Durham meant nothing. Units were re-formed and amalgamated. Officers drafted to this regiment or that. Now Redmond claims in his report, written in pencil on a piece of scrap paper, that he was out in no-man's-land that evening and encountered other English patrols. He also claims his losses were heavy. At one time they met a group of Germans and savage hand-to-hand fighting took place.'

'I wonder if Redmond met our Jack and Billy?' Fairfax murmured. 'That could answer some of our questions. Did Jack kill Billy and have to flee because of the presence of other English soldiers? If it hadn't been for them, would Jack have buried Billy's corpse?'

'Did Jack Allerton ever file a report on what happened?'

'No, Charles, he didn't. He reported verbally to Morrison and that was the end of the matter.'

'Did Morrison suspect anything?'

'I have yet to question him. Cunningham gave me valuable information. He claims when Jack returned, he didn't

seem all that concerned about Billy. Cunningham thought
it was shock. What's more interesting is that our Company
of Friends, the Dead Hand Club, are very, very close. Billy
was killed in the spring of nineteen seventeen. The war went
on for another eighteen months. Jack very rarely mentioned
Billy's death. He seemed most reluctant to discuss it. If we
could only find Redmond,' Fairfax added. 'I'd like to know
if he or any of his officers lost their revolvers. If they could
throw any light on that particular night. Once I've collected
more evidence I'll have Allerton arrested.'

'And his wife?' Hargreaves slipped the question in so quickly
it took Fairfax by surprise.

The lieutenant lifted his jug and toasted his superior.
Fairfax felt himself colour with embarrassment.

'What's the matter?' he snapped.

Hargreaves was grinning like a Cheshire cat. 'Do you know
what they call you, sir, in the Provost Marshal's Office?'

'I couldn't give a damn!' Fairfax pulled on his cigarette.
'I think you've told me this before, Charles. Cold as a fish,
isn't it?'

'This Kitty Allerton seems to have made a difference, sir.'

Fairfax closed his eyes.

'She's touched you, hasn't she?' Hargreaves' surprise was
now evident.

'Do you know something, Charles,' Fairfax replied slowly,
'I loved Eleanora, I really did. I just liked being in the same
room with her. One of the real horrors of war is not the
fighting but being separated from those you love, the risk
of never seeing them again. Eleanora was like that for me.
I could sit in a garden and watch her from sunrise to sunset.
I never tired of her. Everything she did, everything she said

mattered. If she was in a temper or a sulk, I'd become agitated. Oh yes,' Fairfax smiled thinly, 'I did have a heart, Charles, and I called it Eleanora. I never wanted anyone else. When Maurice was killed she was a tower of strength. I remember us talking, how we'd have a son and we'd call him Maurice. Eleanora promised that she'd tell him all about his dashing Uncle Maurice, brave as a lion, courageous as any warrior.' Fairfax found it hard to control his feeling of desperation. He hadn't expected this. But Hargreaves' words had jogged memories, made him realise truths he had ignored.

'In a way Eleanora became part of me and Maurice. I thought I would never meet her like again – until I got off the train at Caundon and walked into the Beaumont Arms.' He stretched across and gripped Hargreaves' arm. The lieutenant remained impassive. He deeply liked and respected Fairfax. They had worked together on many a case but Oscar Fairfax always kept himself aloof and passive.

'I am speaking to you, Charles, as a brother officer and what I say is sacred between us. Oh, don't worry, I'll do my duty for God and the King. But Kitty Allerton? Yes, there's something about her, Charles. Just something in her eyes.' He gestured with his free hand. 'A look, a smile, the way she acts.'

'Eleanora's ghost?'

'No, no, more than that. Anyway,' Fairfax released his grip, 'thank God our dear colonel can't hear me talk. So, what I've said, Charles . . .'

'What have you said, sir?'

'Good man.' Fairfax got to his feet. 'I think I've drunk too much Newcastle ale.'

'Sir?'
Fairfax looked at him.
'Who's behind all this, sir?'
'I'll be meeting him tomorrow.'

Chapter 10

Kitty stared out of the attic window. The sky was streaked with light, turning the clouds a reddish-gold. It promised to be a fine day. 'Even for a Monday,' Kitty whispered.

Already the street below echoed to the sound of hobnailed boots, the dull clatter of miners making their way towards another week's work. The hewers, the fillers, the putters and the boys who manned the pit ponies. A dark, sombre procession of trudging men heading towards the tall, stone tower which housed the great jack engine which lowered the cages.

'I'll be leaving, Kitty.' Jack stood, a shadowy outline in the doorway.

'I'll come down.'

They went along the passageway, down the stairs. The Beaumont Arms was quiet as a church. They crossed to the outhouse where Jack kept his lamp and boots. Kitty had prepared his bait the night before. Jack sat down on a stool.

'Do you love me, Kitty?'

'Jack, my answer is the same as yesterday.'

He grunted and sighed as he pulled the boots on and did

up the laces. He picked up his knapsack, helmet and lamp and came up close to her.

'You know I love you, Kitty. I always have, I always will. Fairfax is a liar.'

'In which case prove to me he is a liar, Jack. Share your nightmares with me.'

'I can't, not yet.'

Then he left her, trudging out through the gateway to join the rest. Kitty heard the shouted greetings and bursts of laughter as someone cracked a joke. The noise of their boots echoed, raising memories from the war, of the soldiers marching down to the station, the children running alongside with bunting and flags.

Kitty went back along the passageway and into the kitchen. Sunday had passed in a haze, cooking, serving and cleaning. By the time the evening had come she had been exhausted. Fairfax had slipped quietly back into the Beaumont Arms – 'Smelling strongly of ale,' her mother had commented. 'He must have been well fed elsewhere because he didn't ask for a meal.'

Fairfax had kept to his chamber. Jack had been like a ghost, in and out for his food, murmuring excuses. He seemed to want to be anywhere but close to her. Kitty noticed how agitated and defensive he had become.

She lifted the kettle off the hook above the fire, grasping the cooling cloth carefully, and took it across to the waiting teapot. She warmed it and afterwards opened the caddy, absent-mindedly throwing in the spoonfuls of tea. She let the pot brew on the tabletop.

'I can't let this go on,' she whispered.

But, there again, she had no control over events. It was like a dance. Fairfax would strike up the beat but how, when? She went across and poured out a mug of tea. She checked the milk in the metal jug in the pantry – it still smelt sweet and wholesome. She wondered what to do. Confide in her mother? Go and see Father Headon? She looked through the half-open kitchen door and glimpsed a bundle of washing.

'No,' she murmured. 'Monday is washday.' To get on with life, to do what she had to do, that was perhaps the safest and sanest thing to do.

She finished her tea and went back to her bedroom. Jack had left it neat and tidy, almost as if he had never been there. Kitty emptied the washbowl, poured fresh water, washed and changed: dark fustian stockings, a green smock, a light-blue pinafore. She stared at the drawer and thought of Billy. She had promised herself that she would finish reading the journal but even that would have to wait. She remembered Billy's mother, sick and housebound on the corner of Fleet Alley where she lived with her sister and brother-in-law. Kitty had never been close to her. 'A woman who keeps to herself, is my mum,' Billy had described her. 'Lives in her own dreams and fantasies. Never been the same,' he'd tapped the side of his head, 'since Dad was killed in the mine.'

Kitty looked in the mirror. 'I wonder if Billy's mother knows something.'

She put on her boots, took her coat from the peg on the back of the door and hurriedly left the Beaumont Arms. The sun had now risen, bathing the streets in a false glow of gold. The village lay quiet, only the sounds of the mine, the rattle of the great wheel and the metallic crash of the coal tubs, echoed on the morning breeze. No one was about. It was still the summer holidays, but the children wouldn't be released onto the streets until they had done their chores, had their breakfast and their mothers wanted them out of the way. The same old routine, Kitty thought as she hastened along. But how many of the people she had grown up with recognised the threat Fairfax now posed? Did they wonder? Did they care?

She reached Mrs Hammond's house and knocked on the door. It swung open almost immediately. Billy's mother stood there, grey-faced, grey-haired, a long nightgown under a not so clean dressing gown. Kitty thought she looked pale and wan, her eyes tired and fretful.

'Oh, Kitty, it's you. Come in. I was just going to take a breath of fresh air. Dr Martin said I should and the streets are always quiet in the morning. You don't have children shouting at you. But it will wait, it will wait. Come in.'

Kitty closed the door behind her and followed Billy's mother into the kitchen. The fire had already been lit. The floor and table were scrubbed. Kitty flinched at the sour smell of boiled ham.

'The rest have gone out,' Mrs Hammond explained. 'My sister's got a job at Colonel Morrison's, a part-time cook, she has to be there before dawn. And, of course, her husband's off to the . . .' Her voice trailed away. Billy's mother had never liked the mine. She found it difficult even to speak of it.

She gestured Kitty towards the table. 'Come on, sit down. You look well. Why have you come so early?' She glanced at the old clock on the mantelpiece. 'Good Lord, nothing's the matter, is it? How's Jack?'

Kitty watched her eyes. Billy's mother showed no sign of knowing what was going on.

'It's Billy I've come about.'

Mrs Hammond's eyes filled with tears. 'I always think of my Billy. Why, what's the matter, pet?'

'Was he happy?'

Mrs Hammond slumped in the great chair at the top of the table. 'Well, of course, pet, he always was. You know how much he loved you.'

'And did he tell you about what he planned? What he said to me about Jack? About if he didn't come home?'

Mrs Hammond scratched her chin, a faraway look in her eyes. 'He did love you, Kitty.' She smiled thinly. 'I admit there were times I was jealous. I mean, after his dad was killed, Billy was all I had. He was so happy in his marriage but then he went to war, didn't he? When he was home on leave he came round here, you know, to see his old mam.' Her voice took on a tinge of self-pity. 'Oh, he acted all brave but I'd heard the stories. He went out to look at his rabbit hutch, where he kept Marston the old buck. I found him staring through the rusting mesh as if his pet was still alive. "Billy," I said, "what on earth are you doing?" He tried to hide it but I could see the tears in his eyes. He got to his feet and told me how much he loved me. If he didn't come back, I must always remember that he'd tried to be a good son.' She wiped the tears from her eyes. 'I told him not to be a stupid hinny. I put my arms round him. I asked if he had been like that to you and then he told me. If he didn't come back, like many others hadn't returned, he hoped Jack would marry you. That was it.'

'Did he tell you anything else? Were he and Jack still good friends?'

'He did say Jack had surprised him. Had more of a temper than he had thought. But Billy put that down to the trenches and what was happening over there.'

'But he put nothing in writing?'

'Ah, no.' Ethel Hammond shook her head. 'Do you want some tea?'

'Yes, thank you.'

'You know Billy,' Mrs Hammond continued. 'He did like to write but his letters were always the same: he was in good health, he was in no danger, the war would soon be over and he would come home. Only there out in the yard did I ever get the truth – that and the other thing.'

'What other thing?' Kitty asked.

'Stephen Grant.'

'The grocer's son?'

'Yes, the grocer's son. On the last day of his leave Billy came to say goodbye. I had been down to Grant's shop to buy some tea. I didn't have enough money. Billy lost his temper. He went down to pay the balance and gave Grant a piece of his mind about high prices, the war and didn't he have any pity.' Mrs Hammond shrugged. 'Well, you know Edmund Grant, don't you, Kitty? He's got shops in Caundon and the other villages. A prosperous man. Look, I'll make you that tea.'

She bustled out of the kitchen and came back a few minutes later with a steaming mug. Kitty hid her smile at the tea leaves floating on the top.

'I know. I know.' She tapped Kitty on the shoulder. 'I always forget to use the strainer but the tea leaves are good for you. They cleanse the stomach.'

Kitty sipped. The tea had no sugar and tasted rather strong. 'You were talking about Billy and the tea you bought from Grant's.'

'Yes, when the lad returned he was in a bit of a temper. Billy didn't like the Grants, both father and son. Said he didn't like

191

the way the father looked at you, and the son was no better. "Hush, Billy," I said. "That's no way to talk of a man killed fighting for God, King and country." "Killed?" Billy replied. "He wasn't killed, he was shot as a deserter."'

Kitty froze. She hadn't known this. 'I thought Grant's son was killed in action like the rest.'

'Not according to our Billy, he wasn't. Grant left the trenches, tried to disguise himself. Thought he could hide out in the woods till the war was over but a French farmer caught him. He was court-martialled and shot.'

Kitty sipped her tea, trying to stop her hand from trembling. Never once had she heard this story, but she understood why. Many of the companies and platoons formed at the beginning of the war were made up of friends, colleagues, members of the same family; closely-knit units with a tremendous sense of pride. Of course, such companies had vanished after the Somme and the other great battles. The survivors always sang the same song: Everyone fought well, those who died were heroes. It was a matter of village pride.

'There is so little I know,' Kitty murmured.

'About the war?' Mrs Hammond hugged the dressing gown closer round her shoulders and stared longingly at the fire. 'Don't be surprised, Kitty. Did you ever ask Jack what he and the men discuss when they are in the mines?'

Kitty smiled and shook her head.

'Well, that's the way of men. They live in their own world. They don't share things with us. Why do you think they keep us out of the bars? A woman can drink as much as a man! And if they're like that about the Beaumont Arms and down the pit, they're hardly going to tell you what happened in France. It will be years before the likes of us find out what really occurred there.' She leaned across and gently pressed Kitty's hand. 'What's the matter, pet? I can see you're worried. Is Jack behaving himself?'

'Oh, yes, yes.'

'And the rest? I get so few visitors. Just that silly bugger Daventry. Every so often, about once a month, he comes and knocks on my door. Same story. Someone really should take him to the doctor's. The poor man should be committed.'

'Why, what does he say to you?'

'He's always sorry about Billy. As if it was his fault. I don't pay much attention to him now.'

'No, please, tell me.' Kitty gripped Mrs Hammond's hand. A week ago she would have dismissed this as a piece of nonsense, the rantings of a poor, half-crazed man. Now everything was precious, everything connected with the war or Billy.

'Well.' Mrs Hammond sighed. 'Daventry apparently buried many of the lads who were killed. According to him, he took Billy's body down to the makeshift morgue. He now says it was a mistake, he should have buried Billy himself. At first this used to upset me but I've got used to it.'

'Why should he apologise?' Kitty asked.

'I don't know. I asked him the same myself once. "Oh," he replied, "the lads tell me that."' Mrs Hammond compressed her lips and blinked hard. 'It's not his fault,' she added. 'It's not any of our faults.' She was silent for a moment. 'Why all this now?' She asked. 'What's your interest?'

'Nothing. Nothing.' Kitty got to her feet and picked up her coat from the end of the table. She put it on and slowly began to do up the buttons. 'I must go,' she said. 'I've got washing to do and Mum will be complaining.' She went across and

193

kissed Mrs Hammond on the forehead. 'Stay in the warmth,' she murmured. 'I'll see myself out.'

Kitty was down the hallway when Billy's mother called her back.

'What is it?'

Mrs Hammond stood in the doorway of the kitchen, shoulders hunched. In the poor light she looked even more frail.

'You'll stay away from Grant, won't you?'

'Why?' Kitty came back.

'I shouldn't really tell you this.'

Kitty glimpsed the fear in Mrs Hammond's eyes. 'What's the matter?' Kitty took her back into the kitchen and made her stand before the fire. 'Why are you so frightened of that fat tub of lard? He's threatened you, hasn't he?'

'Yes, yes, he did.'

Billy's mother was now trembling. Kitty brought her a stool, made her sit in front of the fire and crouched before her.

'What happened? Come on, tell me.'

'It was after Billy was killed. I was here by myself like I am now. I heard a knock on the door. Now, I was shaken up by Billy's death. You were good, Kitty, you forgot your own grief and came and looked after me, did what you could. I thought it was you! When I opened the door it was Edmund Grant in a three-piece suit, his fob watch dangling across that fat stomach. "Can I come in, Mrs Hammond?" He was through the door like a whippet, almost pushing me back here into the kitchen. No, it wasn't during the war.' Mrs Hammond lifted her head and blinked. 'It was just after the Armistice. Anyway, Grant had brought me some coffee and biscuits, said it was a present. There was something about his face and eyes which frightened me, hard and cold. More like a policeman than a grocer. He came quickly to the point and asked if Billy had ever spoken about how his own son Stephen had been killed. I said he hadn't. I was too canny to tell the truth. Grant stood glaring down at me. "Are you sure, Mrs Hammond? And what about pretty Kitty? Did he tell her?" "Oh no, not that I know of," I said.'

Mrs Hammond chewed the corner of her lip.

Kitty recalled those dark wintry days when she had come round here. 'Of course!' she breathed. 'I remember you asking me what I knew about Stephen Grant. I said nothing and forgot all about it.'

Mrs Hammond pressed a finger against Kitty's lips. 'Now you do know, pet. If I were you I'd keep it to myself.'

'I've never heard Jack or the others talk about Grant's son. I know he was disliked.'

'Oh, he was disliked all right, with a father like that, and the son was really no better.' Mrs Hammond licked her lips, glanced sideways then leaned forward like a conspirator.

'Do you know what I think?' she whispered. 'I think the only person that knew about this was Colonel Morrison.'

'And he wouldn't want to tell the rest,' said Kitty. 'It might lower morale and it was nothing to be proud of.'

'Ah yes,' Mrs, Hammond nodded, 'but I suspect Colonel Morrison confided in Billy. After the war Morrison came home early, he was wounded in the knee. I suspect our Mr Grant went out to see the Colonel. You know what Grant's like. He's rich with some powerful friends. I bet he warned Morrison to keep his mouth shut. Probably told him off for letting Billy know. He wields considerable influence does our Mr Grant. He came round here to warn me off. He probably thinks I am the only person in the village who knows.' She smiled. 'But I don't like being threatened, Kitty. I'm glad I told you. I've got a feeling, deep in my water, there's trouble brewing. There is, isn't there? That's why you're here.'

Kitty got to her feet, her mind racing. Her hands felt icy-cold. She stretched them out to the fire. 'I'd like to ask you a question, Ethel.'

'It must be important.' Billy's mother smiled. 'You don't often call me Ethel.'

'I asked it just before I married Jack.'

'Ah yes, I remember. Did I think you were doing right? Come here, pet.' Mrs Hammond took Kitty's hand between hers. 'You did right, pet. Billy was dead, there were always the three of you. If Billy had come back, I don't know what would have happened but I have a feeling that, well, Jack would have married and you'd have all continued to live in each other's pockets. You do love Jack?' She narrowed her eyes. 'Or you did love him. In the end, that's all that really matters. You know that's what Billy wanted.' Mrs Hammond's chin trembled. 'You didn't do wrong, Kitty. The war's like the mine, it sucks people in, mangles their lives. Are we to blame because we try to put things right? There's nothing wrong with love, pet. It's the absence of it that causes the problems.'

Kitty kissed her on the forehead and whispered goodbye.

'And don't forget, Kitty, stay away from Grant. I never did like the way he called you "pretty Kitty". It chilled the blood.'

And, with this warning ringing in her ears, Kitty opened the door and went out into the street.

She stood on the pavement for a while. The breeze now

smelt of coal dust and that pervasive petrol smell which always wafted in from the mine. She walked down the street to the smart glass front of Grant's the Grocers. The lettering on the shop window was elegantly painted. Peering through, Kitty could see the sweet counter: this had always attracted her as a child with its pastilles, sugared almonds, mints, jars of cinnamon, toffee and black bullets. To the right was the hardware: polish, paints, pots and pans, hessian or harn for mat-making. She squinted and glimpsed the great clock on the wall. It was seven thirty. Kitty could see a light at the back of the shop but decided now was not the time to approach Edmund Grant.

She walked along the street and round the corner, trying to recall the number of Daventry's house. Poor Bob always left between seven thirty and seven forty-five. Sometimes he'd go to the pithead and talk to his mates or wander the countryside. Kitty felt slightly embarrassed. She always walked around Caundon but never dilly-dallied. Looking across the street she glimpsed the odd curtain blind twitch. She walked on. She was just past Daventry's house when the door opened. Unkempt and more wild-looking than ever, Bob stepped out, an old pit shovel in one hand.

'Good morning, Bob.'

Daventry paused and stared shiftily down the street. His eyes were watery. The collar of his shirt was dirty and frayed beneath the shiny black jacket, his trousers were hog-tied, one boot had a toecap missing.

'You haven't shaved,' Kitty said kindly. 'Do you want me to do it for you? And you really should change.'

Daventry made to refuse.

'Come on!' Kitty grasped him by the elbow. She sniffed.

'You don't smell too clean, Bob, and the lads down the mine don't like that.'

Daventry's fingers went to his lips. He was about to refuse, his agitation more intense than usual.

'Come on,' Kitty urged. 'Come back and have a good bath. I'll shave you. It's time you had some new clothes.'

Bob's trousers were stained and buttons were missing; they were held up by a pair of battered braces and a piece of frayed string.

'You can also have some bread, dripping, bacon and a mug of tea.'

Daventry needed no further urging – he was always hungry. He followed Kitty back to the Beaumont Arms like a faithful dog. John and Betty were already busy.

'Why have you brought him here?' Betty demanded, half-way across the yard, a jug of water in her hand. 'He smells!'

'That's because I've been digging!' Daventry shouted back.

'You are a madcap, Bob Daventry. You always were.'

'Mad but not bad, Betty,' came the sharp reply.

Kitty waved a finger and gently pushed Bob into the outhouse. Betty and John came up to help. The water tub was filled. Kitty's mother found some clean underwear, shirts, old boots and socks. Bob had no qualms about stripping down. Kitty felt a pang of compassion. Daventry's body was scarred with old wounds, red-blue lines and blotches.

'More the mine than the war,' Daventry explained, stepping into the tin bath. His body was dirty. The soapy water had soon turned black. Kitty offered to shave him but her mother pushed her aside.

'It's a long time since I've done this, Bob.' She picked up the lathering mug and brush and began to carefully coat

Daventry's face in a thick white foam. Kitty stood fascinated: her mother was as gentle as if Daventry was a baby.

'I did this before, you know, Bob Daventry.'

'Ouch!' Daventry cried as he turned.

'Keep still!' she warned. 'Don't you remember? My husband invited you and some of the lads for a party. You drank cider out in the yard there. You became so drunk you spent the rest of the next day sleeping it off. The least I could do was give you all a good meal. You hadn't shaved, remember? You were so drunk your hand kept shaking. So I did it for you whilst all the other lads laughed!'

Daventry splashed the water like a child. 'Eeh, lass, I remember.' His face became sad. 'Golden days, weren't they? The sun was always hot and strong. I remember that cider. The first time I'd ever drunk the stuff. Felt as if I was floating on air like a balloon.' He blinked and scratched a bony knee in the water. 'All those lads have gone now.' Daventry pushed away the razor and turned his head quickly. 'Do you realise that, lass? Your man and all those boys. Salt of the earth, weren't they? Now buried deep in the mud of France.' His face and body became tense as he began to shake. 'It's not fair!' he sobbed. 'It's simply not fair!'

Kitty's mother was becoming upset. She cleaned the razor. 'Well, we've still got our memories, Bob, and that dulls the pain somewhat.'

Kitty stared across the yard. 'Is Major Fairfax up yet?' she asked.

Daventry jumped up, splashing the water over Kitty and her mother. He stood like a tall, gangly boy.

'Bob, what's the matter?'

He grasped the rope towel and wrapped it round himself.

'I don't like Fairfax.' He was still gaping at the doorway as if he expected the dreaded major to step inside. 'I really don't like him at all. I wish he'd stay away from us.'

Kitty was tempted to question him there and then but her mother insisted on finishing shaving him. Then Daventry dried himself and dressed quickly. Kitty, taking him by the hand, led him into the kitchen. She sat him by the fire, brought across a tin plate with bread, dripping and cold bacon and a mug of strong tea. Daventry gulped these, licked his lips and stared at Kitty.

'Are you still hungry, Bob?'

Kitty went into the pantry. She cut a piece from the shoulder of ham her mother had cooked yesterday. She gave this to Daventry, sat down and quietly prayed Fairfax would have breakfast in his own room. Her mother, Betty and John bustled in and out but, as the morning wore on, they became engrossed in other matters. Kitty seized her chance. She moved the stool and sat opposite Daventry. He'd now finished the ham and drained his cup. He glared round.

'Where's my shovel?'

'It's outside in the yard, Bob.' Kitty leaned across and took his hand. It was surprisingly soft and warm, like that of a child. 'Bob, why do you carry that shovel?'

Daventry looked at the door. Kitty got up, went across and closed it.

'It's because of the ghosts,' he replied. 'All those lads I've buried. They come back and ask me to finish the job.' Daventry rolled his eyes. 'I don't mean to frighten you, Kitty. Sometimes it doesn't happen. Other times I see them as clearly as I see you now. They are not frightening, they just

look tired, dressed in their dirty uniforms. I have conversations
with them.'

'Does my father come back?'

'He wasn't in my company.'

'No, no, he wasn't.' Kitty recalled her father going to Bishop
Auckland to enlist. 'And do you ever see Billy?'

Daventry's eyes took on a guarded look. 'I liked Billy,' he
replied. 'Always kind to me, was Billy. Always shared a tin
of tea or his bully beef. He saw Colonel Morrison once and
said I should be sent to a doctor. Morrison said that we'd
lost too many men.' Daventry's dark-brown eyes shifted
backwards and forwards.

Kitty could never really make her mind up about Bob.
Sometimes he acted like a half-wit, at others sane and collected.

'Do you mind me asking this, Bob?' Her words came out
in a rush. 'I didn't invite you back here just for a bath, a shave
and some food. I want to question you about Billy's death.'

Daventry hunched his shoulder. 'I . . . I . . .'

'Please!' Kitty urged.

'I don't remember much, lass. Jack and Billy were sent out
on a patrol. It was well after midnight. All hell had broken
loose. The Boche were raining down shells, mortars. We knew
there was some movement in their trenches. Colonel Morrison
was all agitated. He and the other officers wanted to know
what exactly was happening.' Daventry closed his eyes. 'On
our right were the Berkshires, on our left, I forget now, I think
they were Australians. Anyway, Jack and Billy went out.'

'Were they friends?'

'Oh, don't be daft.' Daventry opened his eyes and grinned.
'Of course they were.'

'They didn't quarrel?'

Daventry's face became secretive. 'Oh, we were always quarrelling but . . .' His lips moved. 'I must remember, I must remember what Cunningham told me.'

'What did Cunningham tell you?'

'Nothing, I've forgotten.'

'Bob,' Kitty said in exasperation. 'You brought Billy's body back. Why?'

'Well, I remember that, Colonel Morrison had given us a tot of rum because we were ready to go over the top. Jack came back covered in mud, his face pale like a ghost. He said Billy was dead, killed out in no-man's-land, and he couldn't bring his body back. I was very upset, I liked Billy. I went to see Colonel Morrison, I asked him permission to go but he told me not to be daft. Anyway, we'd attacked but then retreated. It was a really misty morning so I seized my opportunity. I went wandering across no-man's-land. Kitty, it was like a butcher's yard, bodies everywhere. I couldn't find Billy's until I came to a crater. He was just lying inside.' Daventry blinked. 'I can't remember now if we were attacking or not, but I do remember finding Billy.'

'What was he like?' Kitty asked.

Daventry shook his head. 'You don't want me to tell you.'

'Tell her what you found.' Fairfax stood in the doorway. He was dressed in a sporty tweed jacket, trousers, gaiters, smart black shoes. The waistcoat was also a dark-green. A fob watch hung elegantly down. He had a flat cap in one hand and his walking stick in the other. Daventry made to rise but Kitty, eyes bright with anger, pressed him back onto the stool.

'This is my house, Major Fairfax, my kitchen, and Bob

Daventry is my guest.' She pointed to the door. 'In future I'll make sure that's not so well oiled. You should knock.'

'I am sorry. I was going out but I heard Daventry's voice and thought I'd listen. If you want, I can leave. But Bob,' he smiled at the ex-soldier who stared back like a frightened rabbit, 'you can either answer Kitty's questions or mine.'

'Don't be so cruel!' Kitty snapped. 'Can't you see he's frightened?'

Fairfax walked across, sat on the bench which ran alongside the kitchen table, positioning himself between Kitty and Bob.

'What's it to be, Bob?'

Kitty felt a surge of temper. Daventry was petrified.

'Go on,' Fairfax urged. He fished into his trouser pocket and brought out a shilling which he pressed into Daventry's hand. 'I mean you no harm.'

'Tell me, Bob,' Kitty intervened. 'Go on, you're safe here.'

'Billy was good to me.'

'I know that.'

'Billy was good to me. I couldn't leave his body out there.'

'Didn't Jack offer to go with you?'

Bob shook his head. 'No one went out into no-man's-land.'

'Not even for the corpse of his best friend?' Fairfax asked softly, ignoring Kitty's glare.

'You know what it was like.' Daventry's voice rose. 'Nobody went out there, not unless they had to.'

'Just tell your story,' Kitty insisted.

'It was early morning. The mist was very thick. I found Billy in a crater. He was lying there, a terrible wound to his stomach.'

'And the head?' Fairfax asked.

'Yes, the side of his face was all covered in blood. There was a wound to his temple. I grabbed him by the collar and pulled him back.'

'And what else did you bring?' Fairfax leaned closer. 'His rifle? His knapsack?'

'His rifle and knapsack were gone.'

'Did you see a revolver in the trench?'

'All I saw was the helmet lying beside Billy so I took that back with me. Colonel Morrison was angry but he understood. He told me not to be such a bloody fool. Billy's corpse was taken down to an orderly station.'

'And the helmet?'

'Now that was strange.'

Kitty watched Daventry closely. He was trying to tell the truth but he was also being sparing with it.

'Whose helmet was it?'

'Why, Jack's,' Daventry replied. 'And that's all I know.' He drummed his boots on the kitchen floor. 'I've spoken the truth. I can only tell you what I saw.' He sprang to his feet. 'Miss Kitty, I thank you.' And, before they could stop him, he was across the kitchen and through the door.

'If he had no knapsack,' Kitty spoke as if she had not noticed Daventry's departure, 'how did you find the journal?'

Fairfax tapped his jacket. 'Apparently it was inside, only discovered when they . . .'

'Go on, say it!' Kitty snapped.

'When they stripped the body at the orderly station.'

'Why wasn't it sent to me direct?'

'Because it got caught up in the bureaucracy of war. The army are still returning personal effects.'

'And the helmet?'

'The helmet Daventry took back was Jack's.'

'So?' Kitty shrugged. 'Evans once joked that he had worn a German helmet for two months. In the chaos such things could happen. Billy probably lost his knapsack and rifle.'

'Perhaps, perhaps.' Fairfax tapped his foot. 'But, there again, Jack claims that he and Billy became separated when they left the trench.'

'They may have been wearing each other's helmet.'

'And the revolver?' Fairfax asked. 'Your husband suffered two wounds. One to the stomach, probably a shell, grenade or shrapnel but, from what I can gather, that didn't kill him. His death wound was a pistol shot close to the head.'

Kitty repressed a shiver.

'It wasn't German: the Luger is quite distinctive. It was an English officer's pistol.'

Kitty stared at the skillets hanging from a hook above the fireplace.

'Jack didn't have a revolver.'

'No one said he did but how did Billy receive that head wound?' Fairfax breathed in deeply and dug into his jacket pocket. He drew out a small leather bag and cradled it in his hand. Kitty watched fascinated.

'I am going out today,' Fairfax continued. 'There are other people I have to question. Colonel Morrison for one. I'll tell you what I am also going to do. By the powers given to me as a provost marshal, I am going to gather the Company of Friends together. I will hold a formal inquiry. Colonel Morrison is a local magistrate. He will have the right to chair such an inquiry.'

Kitty tried to stop her hands trembling.

'And the purpose of this inquiry?'

'To establish once and for all the true circumstances surrounding the death of Billy Hammond near the village of Betancourt on the twenty-third of March nineteen seventeen.' Fairfax chose his words carefully. 'I must inform you, Kitty, that there is an allegation, a strong suspicion that Jack Allerton seized the opportunity of that night patrol to murder Billy Hammond and the motive for that murder was yourself.'

Kitty sat rigid, shaking her head.

'That's not true!' she whispered. 'That's simply not true!'

'Kitty, I want to tell you what I am doing. I don't have to but I want to. I am searching for proof and the more I discover, the more suspicious I become. One member of the Dead Hand Club has already told me about the conspiracy of silence around Billy's death. Those men seem to know more than they admit. There is another officer from the Provost Marshal's Office in the area. He is helping in my inquiries. He is searching for a Major Redmond who lives either in Durham or North Yorkshire. Redmond was attached to a Berkshire regiment; he was also in no-man's-land that night.'

'I don't believe it! I just don't believe it!' Kitty glared fiercely at him. 'Hasn't the army got better things to do than concentrate on this?'

'We have evidence,' Fairfax replied.

'And what else?'

Fairfax was concerned at the change in Kitty's appearance. She sat rigid, hands in her lap, the skin of her face drawn pale and tight.

'There's something else, isn't there?' she said. 'Has someone laid a complaint? Made allegations?'

'I don't need gossip and allegations.' Fairfax blinked at the lie. 'Do you recognise this?' He opened the leather bag and lifted out the dirt-stained watch. Kitty stared in disbelief. Her hand went out then she let it drop.

'It's my wedding gift to Billy. Please, please, can I see it?'

Fairfax handed it over. Kitty opened the clasp and stared at the cracked glass. She touched the initials carved on the inside. "B.H." Fairfax took it gently from her fingers.

'I know from witnesses that Billy carried this everywhere and had it on him the night he died. So why did Jack keep it hidden all these years, buried in a secret place in his garden?'

Pale as a ghost, Kitty got to her feet and quietly left the kitchen.

Chapter 11

_____

Kitty lay on her bed, a tear-soaked handkerchief in one hand. She turned on her side and stared at the wall. She couldn't believe or accept what had happened in the kitchen. Billy had loved that watch, treasured it. 'Whenever I touch it, Kitty, I'll think of you. It will measure my life. Every second of that life will be my love for you.'

In his short letters home Billy had called it his good luck charm; despite the mud and the bloody chaos and the marching, the watch had come through safely. How could Jack have taken it? Billy wouldn't have given it to him, surely? If he had, why hadn't Jack handed it over? Why hide it for years in some dirty hole in the garden? Kitty dried her eyes. In that second she recalled how, when she was a child and upset by some harsh words, she'd do as she was doing now, lie on her side and stare at the wall.

'But what else can I do?' Kitty whispered.

Different emotions warred within her. To go down and demand Fairfax return the watch? Snatch it from his hand and march up to the pithead? She could go down the mine. She had done before. She wasn't frightened! Yet, beneath all this, lurking like a sharp-edged rock in a pool, was the real danger: was Jack a murderer? A sick-minded thief? A man she had grown up with but hardly knew? Kitty felt her throat constrict. She couldn't believe that. She didn't want to confront Jack, to condemn him, perhaps discover the awful truth. She cursed his taciturn, pig-headed nature, lashing out with her leg, but all she kicked was the bedpost, bruising her toe. She winced and sat up. There must be something she could do. She got up and went to her dresser, took out Billy's picture and placed it on top.

'Help me?' she murmured.

Kitty abruptly realised the foolishness of her plea. All that stared back was a sepia photograph of a man she had once loved. Billy was dead, Jack was her husband. Jack was the danger. Jack was the problem. She tried to concentrate by going up to the attic and taking from her hiding place Billy's journal. When she hurried back down, her mother was standing on the stairs, staring strangely at her. Kitty forced a smile and almost threw herself into the bedroom, slamming the door behind her. She tried to read the journal but the words seemed to move and she couldn't concentrate. She lost her place. She closed the journal and put it under the mattress.

'It's not the past,' Kitty told herself. 'It's the present, that's the problem.'

She heard a knock but ignored it. The door opened and her mother came in. She didn't stand over Kitty but sat beside her on the bed.

'Kitty, what is the matter? Tell me now. I want to know. I heard Fairfax with you in the kitchen and then you fled. Good Lord, look at your face, it's wet with tears.'

Kitty made to turn away.

'Don't do that!' Her mother's voice rose to a shout. 'Don't do that, Kitty!' She grasped her daughter's hand. 'I'll sit here and you'll sit here until you tell me the truth. It's to do with Jack, isn't it? Look, my darling daughter. I try to run a pub, make ends meet and forget the great hole in my life. You've been fortunate, Kitty, more than any woman I know. You've been loved by two good men. So, if you want to sit like a child, weep and tell me nothing, fine. But what happens to you and Jack affects me too!'

Kitty smiled. 'You are turning into a schoolmarm, Mother, or a sergeant major.'

'Your dad said I was better than the latter, that I could put the fear of God into more men than any officer did. Now, come on, Kitty, tell me.'

In halting phrases, Kitty told her everything that had happened since Fairfax's arrival. Her mother, as customary, never interrupted. Kitty told her everything: about the journal, the watch, Fairfax's suspicions.

'I don't know what to do,' she concluded. 'I don't know where to begin.'

'Let's start with what's important and what's pressing, Kitty. Did you love Billy?'

'Of course.'

'And do you love Jack?'

'Of course but—'

'No buts. Did you love Jack until Major Fairfax stepped into this hotel?'

'Yes, I did, but what he said—'

'Do you believe him?'

'I don't want to but the proof—'

210

'Proof!' her mother scoffed. 'A lawyer can make proof as good as I can make a pudding. Do you believe your husband Jack is a murderer? That he deliberately and maliciously slew Billy so as, to quote your phrase, to commit David's sin and take another man's wife?'

Kitty shook her head. 'No I don't.'

'Neither do I.'

'But there is a shadow between us.'

'There are always shadows between husband and wife. Some are just a bit deeper than others.' Her mother let go of Kitty's hand. 'My father once owned a lurcher, a hideous dog, Kitty. No creature was safe from it in the hunt. My father also owned chickens. I used to watch the lurcher in the farmyard. It would stand, head lowered, eyes concentrating on these fat fowl. If it wasn't for my father's hobnailed boot that dog would have taken all their throats. Fairfax is like that. He's walked into this chicken run and he intends to taste blood.'

Kitty tapped her mother lightly on the shoulder. 'You should have written plays.'

'I don't like Fairfax or what he's doing. He may be right, I may be wrong. Jack might be the greatest assassin since Bluebeard. I remember seeing that story at a lantern show down at the village hall. I'd love to go to one of those films they are now showing in London,' she added wistfully. 'Life is changing so fast, Kitty. Betty was telling me we'll have gas within two years, electricity shortly afterwards. The United Bus Company are going to plan a route through Caundon. It will bring good trade to the pub.'

'What's that got to do with Jack and Fairfax?'

'Oh, everything, Kitty. I lost my father in a mining accident, my husband in the war, a half-brother at sea, two cousins down the mine. One thing I have learnt, Kitty.' Her tone grew fierce. 'Life goes on or it leaves you behind. You visited Billy's mother, yes? Do you want to become like that, Kitty? To give up your life, to become a shadow? If you believe Jack's innocent then fight back.'

'He won't help.'

'Kitty, you've never whined. Don't start now! Jack is taciturn, bull-headed, stubborn. In a previous life he must have been a donkey. Fairfax is here because of suspicions but someone else has got more than one finger in this pie: our sweat-faced grocer, Master Edmund Grant for a start.'

'Grant! You are sure?'

'Of course I am and so are you. Grant's a miser. He owns shops in Caundon and elsewhere but he lives above one rather than spend his money. A man with airs and graces, is old Edmund Grant. He once boasted he would make a fortune and go out and buy one of those old places in the country. He's always had an eye for you, Kitty. Him and his bloody sweets! That's not the only thing he gives out!'

'What do you mean?'

'Your father and I, Kitty, were socialists born and bred. Colonel Morrison is a landowner, a Tory, yet a man with a deep sense of responsibility to the community. You couldn't find a kinder gent. Grant's different. He wants to escape from what he is, from what he was. He's not a socialist or a Tory, he's a snob, of the worst kind. He believes everything is up for sale. To cut a long story short, Grant's a very generous benefactor of the local Tory party, particularly Macclesfield, our redoubtable MP – two nostrils in the same dirty nose. They richly deserve each other. Macclesfield's fought his way high in the party. I'd bet my life that Grant and Macclesfield have more than a hand in this mischief.'

'But how?' Kitty asked.

Kitty's mother dabbed at her neck and loosened the buttons of her chemise. 'If I understand you correctly, there are unanswered questions about Billy's death, enough for the Provost Marshal's Office to send a lurcher like Fairfax scurrying north. Grant must have done something to help it along.'

'But he wouldn't be held in high regard. I told you what Billy's mother said – Grant's son was shot as a coward for desertion.'

'Perhaps the two are linked. I am sure if Grant had known his son had deserted and been caught, he might have saved him. From the little I know, army justice at the front was summary, quick and ruthless.'

'Should I see Grant?'

'You've got to be careful, Kitty. Betty went walking last night with her young man. He's a pot boy at the Dovecote. Fairfax has a helper, a Lieutenant Charles Hargreaves, who is staying there. According to him, Fairfax and Hargreaves are looking for someone . . .'

'How does he know all this?'

'The pot boy's a good listener and Hargreaves is rather careless with his papers. So,' her mother turned to face her, 'what are you going to do? Sit here and grow maudlin or plot?'

Kitty smiled. Her mother pushed away a lock of hair from Kitty's forehead.

'You'll make a good teacher, Kitty. Colonel Morrison says that he'd pay the fees for you to go away to college, evening classes or whatever. You've got a good mind and a strong will. Think, Kitty.' Her mother kissed her on the forehead.

She left. Kitty lay back on the bed and stared up at the ceiling. She couldn't forget Grant's fat, smiling face. He was always free with his fingers! Even when she was newly married she'd catch him looking at her in church, wet-eyed and fleshy-mouthed. The very thought made her skin crawl! His son Stephen was no better. A young man noted for his drinking as well as his aggressive, sly ways. During their childhood both Jack and Billy had clashed with him, a great talker and boaster. Yet he had been shot. She could understand Grant's grief but also recognised his rage and jealousy. Perhaps he hated her, Jack and Billy more than she ever knew. Grant was most likely the key to all this.

Kitty got up and pulled out the journal from beneath the mattress. She turned to the back page where the writing suddenly broke off. Billy had drawn a German helmet and, underneath, written the words: 'Not as fierce as they seem, they are men just like us.' Billy seemed to be speaking to her. She could feel his presence, the way he would stand in a room and watch her. She got to her feet and went to the window. Her mother, as always, talked sense but who could she turn to? Father Headon? Daventry, that poor, feckless idiot? Cunningham? Evans? But they were all members of the Dead Hand Club. She looked back at the journal lying on the bed and smiled. Of course, Ernst Kurtz the German! He had always liked her in a frank, admiring way and he was close to Jack. Kitty stared down the street. A woman passed, her basket full of groceries. An idea began to form. She would have to get to Grant!

She heard a knock on the door.

'Come in, Mother!'

When Kitty looked round, it was Fairfax. He had his coat on, he was staring at her strangely.

'I am sorry,' he apologised. 'I didn't mean to upset you in the kitchen. Kitty, look, if this goes wrong, if Caundon becomes . . .'

Kitty folded her arms and leaned against the windowsill. 'You are not sorry, Major Fairfax. To feel sorry you've got to have a heart.'

His eyes flinched.

'You've got to have a soul to experience compassion. Do you know what compassion is, Major Fairfax? Father Headon told me it comes from the Latin, the ability to suffer, to feel for someone.'

'I feel for you.'

'Do you really? In which case why did you show me that watch?'

'I wanted to prove that this was not some wild goose chase.'

'Oh, I think it is, Major Fairfax.' She tightened her arms. 'You've been a soldier. You've seen the blood and muck, the terror. Isn't it true some men's hair went white overnight? Lying terrified in the trenches as the nightmare broke out all about them?'

Fairfax nodded.

'I've read Billy's journal. So have you. Soldiers even committed sucide. I never knew, until the last few days, what real horrors men like my Jack and Billy, Daventry and the others went through. God knows what horrors Jack and Billy experienced that night out in no-man's-land. Did Jack's mind become unhinged? Has that ever occurred to you?'

'That's what I am trying to find out.'

'I don't think so, Major Fairfax. I think you are judge, jury and executioner. You showed me that watch to shake my faith. You and your helper out at the Dovecote, Hargreaves. Oh, yes.' She smiled. 'I know more than you think. You're like two lurchers and you think my Jack's the rabbit. You showed me that watch to shake my faith. Now you come up here as Job's comforter. This is my bedroom. This is Jack's bedroom.' She turned her back. 'Now get out!'

'Kitty!'

'Major Fairfax, you pride yourself on being a gentleman and an officer. Please go!'

Kitty sighed and relaxed as the door closed then hurried over and threw it open. He stood on the top stair.

'Major Fairfax?' she said sweetly.

'Kitty, what is it?'

'If you want to help, tell me, what has Edmund Grant said to you?'

Fairfax's mouth opened and closed.

'Good Lord, Major, it's the first time I've seen you surprised.'

And, stepping back into the bedroom, Kitty slammed the door behind her. She waited until his footsteps faded on the stairs before opening the door again and asking Betty to bring up some hot water. When she had brought it, Kitty stripped, washed herself carefully and, opening her wardrobe, laid out her very best attire. Black stockings, white petticoat, a frilly bodice, the plum-coloured, tight-waisted dress which fell down to her ankles, black, silver-buckled boots. She must have spent an hour preparing herself carefully, combing her hair and piling it up with gilded combs. Earrings and necklace followed. She finished dressing and checked herself in the mirror.

Good Lord, woman, she thought, thank God Jack can't see you now! She put on her best coat, with its silver-embossed buttons and silken collar, then took a small reticule from a chest beneath the bed. She checked herself once more in the mirror and then carefully made her way downstairs. Mother was waiting at the bottom. She stared open-mouthed.

'Kitty, it's Monday and it's washday! Where on earth are you going? What are you doing? But you do look beautiful! You are not going to see Fairfax, are you?' she added warningly.

'I've seen him off, Mother. I'm doing what you advised. I'm using my brain. I'm sorry about the washing but, unlike Major Fairfax, this can't wait.' And Kitty was through the door and out in the street before her mother could reply.

It was just before noon. Most of the neighbours' doors were open. Kitty drew curious glances, not to mention a few wolf whistles from young lads playing hopscotch on the pavements. Kitty coloured slightly. She was glad to see Grant standing in the doorway of the shop. He gaped.

'Why, Miss Kitty!'

'Edmund.' She smiled. 'I want to see you later. About one?'

'But that's when I close for lunch.'

'Precisely' Kitty replied sweetly.

The look in Grant's eyes was confirmation enough. She smiled again and walked on.

Kurtz was busy in his butcher's shop, gutting a line of chickens. He was washing them in a bowl of hot water before tying their legs and hanging them up on a hook. Kitty walked in warily, glad of the sawdust on the slippery, blood-soaked floor.

'Ah, Kitty, good morning. You look beautiful. Why are you here?'

'Can I speak to you, Ernst?'

The German stared hard at the little boy who acted as his assistant. 'Charlie, watch the shop! I don't expect further trade till this afternoon. Kitty, as you English say, step into my parlour.'

He led her into an ill-furnished back room, small but clean-swept. A table stood against the wall, there were stools and chairs, a half-open cupboard, a small washstand. Kurtz closed the door and leaned against it.

'Kitty, should you be walking the streets of Caundon dressed like that?'

'Like what, Ernst?' She smiled. 'I've come for your help.'

'So you dress like Mata Hari?' Ernst pushed over a chair. 'You know who Mata Hari was?'

'I do.' Kitty sat down on the chair. She still felt slightly ridiculous, rather embarrassed, a little wary of Ernst's reaction.

He pulled up a stool and sat opposite her. 'There's no need to dress like that, Kitty, when you ask for my help. I always regard Jack as my friend and you as his lady. I know there's trouble. I wish . . .' He pressed his lips.

'What do you wish, Ernst?'

'There's only one thing I'd like, Kitty, just one. I wish Jack would invite me to sit with the Dead Hand Club on a Saturday evening.'

'It's about that I've come. Ernst, I am going to trust you.

I am going to tell you what has happened. What I know and what I plan.'

Kitty spoke for about half an hour. Ernst sat listening attentively. Only twice did he get up, to deal with a customer and to bring Kitty a cup of tea. After she had finished, he sat drumming his fingers on his knees.

'You are a Mata Hari, Kitty. What you propose is quite dangerous. If Jack got to know—'

'If I don't do anything, it will be even more dangerous for Jack.'

Kurtz nodded solemnly. Kitty looked up at the old clock fixed to the wall. A gift from Father Headon, it once hung in the village hall.

'It's now twelve forty, Ernst. I'll finish my tea and walk along to Grant's. He'll clear the shop. I'll try and leave the front door off the latch. The rest is up to you.'

'Does this grocer have so much influence?' Kurtz asked but then he laughed. 'I should know better, Kitty. A similar man in Germany made sure that I joined the army so he could sleep with my wife. I am glad I live in England.' He got up. 'In the end, there's really no such people as Germans, English or French. There's just people. The real difference between them is not some border but those who have power and wealth and those who don't.' He led her back into the shop. 'Take your time. I'll be there after one.'

Kitty left the makeshift butcher's shop and walked slowly back to Grant's. More people were out on the streets; they eyed her curiously but Kitty was determined to carry her plan through. She dallied awhile, spoke to this person or that, and arrived at Grant's just as the clock showed a few minutes to one.

She walked in. The tangy odours evoked memories of childhood. She had always thought this was an Aladdin's cave with its steep, glass cases, bottles, shiny equipment, the gleaming oak and mahogany, the well-polished brass lamps, the cloying, mouth-watering smells. There were customers in the shop, being served by Grant and his two assistants dressed in white aprons. As soon as he saw her, the grocer scurried forward.

'Kitty, it's good to see you! What do you want? Oh, you do look splendid!'

'Why, Edmund, I have come to see you.' Kitty lowered her head. 'I need your help.' She touched him lightly on the chest.

The grocer's face became even more plum-coloured. He wetted his lips and looked over his shoulder.

'Perhaps you'd like to wait in the back room. You won't be disturbed.' He raised his eyes to the ceiling. 'My wife is slightly indisposed and I must see to my customers until we close for lunch.' Grant waved Kitty forward, lifted the counter flap and ushered her into the comfortable rear room.

It was well furnished: a long couch, tables, chairs, a small oaken cabinet with brass clasps. Kitty noticed that the doors to the house and the rooms above, as well as the one leading to the shop, had at least two bolts. She'd heard stories about the grocer's back room and some of the ladies who visited him. She sat down on the edge of the couch, half listening to the sounds from the shop. She breathed in deeply. She would have to remain calm. She only hoped that she'd be successful. At last she heard Grant ushering the customers out.

'It's time for lunch! It's time for lunch!' he declared. 'Even a grocer must eat!'

Sounds of laughter. The chatter of the young boys as they took their aprons off. Grant's final instructions that they take an extra quarter of an hour and be back at 2.15 p.m. prompt. Both assistants needed no second bidding and left the shop like whippets. Kitty heard a door bell jangle, the sound of bolts being pulled across and the blinds being drawn. Grant's footsteps.

He came in. He immediately reminded Kitty of a little ball of grease with his fat, sweaty hands. He doffed his apron to reveal pinstriped trousers and waistcoat, and silver armbands which kept the cuffs of his sleeves back.

'Well, well, Miss Kitty.' He rubbed his hands together. She was sure he was going to add: 'At last I have you here.'

'It's such a surprise,' he gushed. 'And you look so fetching.' Grant closed the door but didn't draw the bolts. 'Perhaps a little sherry?' He took a key from his waistcoat pocket, went across to the mahogany dresser, unlocked it and took out a silver-gilt tray, two small glasses and a squat, dark bottle. He filled both glasses to the brim, gave one to her and sat close to her on the couch. The smell of his eau de cologne made Kitty wrinkle her nose but she kept smiling as she clinked her glass against his. The sherry tasted smooth, rich and sweet. She coughed.

'Just sip it,' Grant remarked patronisingly. 'Do you want some more?'

Kitty answered with her eyes. Grant jumped up like a grasshopper and refilled her glass.

'Well, we have the full hour.'

'Won't someone come in?' she asked, eyes widening. 'Surely your wife will be expecting you to visit her during the lunch hour?'

'She takes her laudanum and I take my sherry.' Grant smiled. 'Right, Kitty, why come and see me now? Most of the time you haven't a kind word for me.'

Kitty sipped the sherry. 'Times change, Edmund. I have been a widow once and now this business . . .'

'What business?' Grant stared at her owl-eyed.

'Major Fairfax,' she whispered, dropping her head. 'He's not here to inquire after my health, Edmund. More the doings of Jack and the others during the Great War.'

'Oh that.' Grant sighed. 'You know my poor boy.' He glanced sideways. 'I lost him, a hero's death.'

'Just like my Billy. Edmund,' she moved her hand, brushing his knee, 'I wish now I hadn't married Jack. I made a mistake.' She breathed in. 'You know, Edmund, I don't think things are going too well for Jack. If anything awful happens,' she continued in a rush, 'I am going to have to leave Caundon.'

'Leave?' he echoed.

'I don't know.' Kitty took a lace handkerchief from the sleeve of her dress and dabbed at her eyes. She no longer felt nervous. Grant was a reprobate, a liar, a scheming, nasty-minded man. She had no qualms about what she was doing. The rage began to boil within her. She only hoped Grant would take this as fear.

'Yes, I may have to leave Caundon. Perhaps go to Bishop Auckland, Durham or even Newcastle, find lodgings, continue my studies as a teacher.'

Grant narrowed his eyes. He sipped his sherry. Kitty noticed how thick and wet his lips were. You stand at the entrance to the trap, Kitty thought, you can smell the lure but will you walk in? She moved away slightly.

'I haven't told anyone about this, Edmund.' She dropped

her head and, as if irritated, took off the small hat she wore, releasing the pins, shaking her hair loose. 'But they don't send an officer like Fairfax all the way from London because someone has stolen a silver spoon from the officers' mess.'

'And you think Fairfax is investigating Jack?'

'I know it's Jack. He refuses to talk to me. He won't tell me anything. Did you know, Edmund . . .' In halting sentences Kitty told him about the watch Fairfax had found. She dabbed her eyes and glanced up quickly.

Grant was hooked, his hand was quivering slightly. 'But how can I help, Kitty?' He edged a little closer, almost pushing her up against the hard arm of the couch. 'I have little influence.'

Liar, Kitty thought. The lie steeled her nerve. She turned, putting the sherry glass on the floor, placing both hands on his knee.

'I think Fairfax is going to tear our community apart, Edmund. Most of the members of the Dead Hand Club are terrified of him. I wouldn't be surprised if Jack fled.'

'That would be a foolish thing to do.' Grant's plump hand found hers.

'Mother's struggling to manage the Beaumont Arms,' Kitty continued, moving her hand gently within his. 'I am going to need help, Edmund. References. I want to move away.'

'But I won't ever see you again, clipping across the cobbles every Sunday morning.' Grant licked his lips. 'Head held high.'

She lowered her eyes. 'But you will be able to visit me.'

Grant's hand went out, slightly shaking. He began to undo the top buttons of her dress.

'Why, Edmund, what are you doing?' She leaned closer.

'It's rather warm in here,' he gasped. 'And you are agitated.'

'Yes, yes, I am.'

Edmund Grant couldn't believe his luck. Here was this very pretty young thing offering herself, begging for his help. He wished now he had told his assistants to keep away the entire afternoon. His hands went down. He undid more buttons. The sight of the lacy bodice beneath, Kitty's relaxed posture, the brocade choker round her throat only fired his imagination further. He put his arm round her shoulder and drew her towards him.

'Kitty,' he murmured. 'I can give you all the help you need. But I need help too.' His eyes took on a pleading look. 'My wife is ill . . .'

Kitty allowed herself to relax, falling against the back of the couch. She almost bit through her lower lip. Grant's hand travelled down, plucking at the hem of her dress. He pushed it over her knees and, becoming rough, got up and pulled Kitty onto his lap. She gazed at him from under half-closed lids. Grant was already lost in his pleasure. He quickly undid the top stud of his collar. He pushed back her dress. He glimpsed the petticoats beneath, the black stockings, the tight-laced boots of what he had called this arrogant, high-stepping young lady. Kitty struggled in token resistance. Grant's hand went higher, pulling up the dress so urgently the buttons popped. She pushed him away.

'No, no!' she gasped. 'You'll ruin my dress, Edmund.' She got up, loosened the belt and stared towards the door. 'Are we safe?' she whispered.

Grant was red-faced, sweaty with excitement. 'Of course we are! Of course we are!' he replied urgently.

'I must make sure.'

'The doors are bolted, you—' Grant bit back the curse.

'No, no, let me make sure.'

Kitty went round him, through the door and into the shop. Grant had been so confident he'd pulled down the blind to both the windows and the street door. Kitty glimpsed the waiting shadow and closed her eyes.

'Thank God!' she whispered. Ernst had arrived. 'I'll just check the bolts, Edmund.'

She pulled back both the bolts, top and bottom, and hurried back to Grant. He was now standing up. As soon as Kitty came in through the door, he slammed it shut, drawing across the bolts, then he was on her, yanking her dress up, feverishly ordering her to strip. Kitty made her body go slack. Grant was so intent on his pleasure he didn't hear the soft footfall. Kitty's dress, her petticoats were summarily stripped off her. Grant embraced her, pulling her body up against his. His hands seemed to be everywhere. Kitty threw her head back, arching her body, as Grant burrowed his face between her breasts, his nails scoring her back.

'Stop it!' she whispered. 'Edmund, stop it!'

'I like a bit of reluctance.'

Kitty began to scream. 'Help! For God's sake, Edmund!'

Grant would have continued but there was a pounding on the door. Mouth open, eyes popping, he stood breathing heavily but Kitty didn't give him a second chance. She grabbed her dress from the floor and quickly pulled back both bolts. The door swung open. Kurtz stood there, walking stick in one hand, a butcher's knife in the other.

The grocer stumbled back, sitting down on the couch.

'Well, Mr Grant, I've heard of personal service . . .' Kurtz closed the door and leaned against it. He looked quickly at Kitty. 'I think you'd best get dressed. And you, Mr Grant, perhaps you could put your trousers on.'

Grant, fingers shaking, obeyed. Kitty quickly dressed and put on her coat to cover the damage to her dress that Grant had inflicted.

Kitty went to a far corner and sat on a stool. 'He tried to rape me.'

Grant's face turned ugly. 'You lying, tricky bitch!'

'Now, now, Mr Grant,' Kurtz replied soothingly. 'That's no way to talk to a lady.'

Grant threw his hand out, pointing accusingly at Kitty. 'She came in here. She offered herself!'

'That's a lie!' Kitty replied with a half-smile. 'Isn't it, Ernst?'

'Yes, it is.' Kurtz crossed his arms. 'You tried to rape her, Mr Grant. You lured her into your back room and, in your haste or your lust, forgot to bolt the front door. I came here,' he held the knife up, 'to see if you had any more of these. I heard Kitty scream.'

'What?' Grant sprang to his feet. 'That's not true!'

'It is,' Kitty declared.

'But why are you dressed up like that?'

'Because I am depressed, Mr Grant. Because I wanted to ask Ernst a favour.'

'To trap me?'

'No,' Kitty quickly replied. 'To help Jack. I was hoping to go and see Colonel Morrison,' she added as an afterthought. 'And Father Headon. I went to see Ernst this morning. I told him I was trying to get his help and yours in this

226

business with Major Fairfax. I came here and you offered to help.'

'But—'

'Your two assistants know that. I suspected something was going to happen. When I heard you tell them to take a quarter of an hour extra. You are not usually noted for your open-handed generosity.' Kitty blinked quickly. 'Nevertheless, I thought I was safe. After all, your own wife lies sick upstairs.'

'I told you, she's on laudanum.'

'You can tell that to the magistrate.' Ernst was now enjoying himself. 'That's before you are committed for trial at the assizes in Durham. I'll take an oath on what I saw and heard. Kitty struggling against you. It was just by chance I came in.' Kurtz put the walking stick on the floor and juggled the knife from one hand to the other. 'I was so glad I was able to help.'

'They won't believe you!' Grant spluttered. 'Not her and a German!'

'Won't they?' Kitty interjected. 'Ernst is well liked and respected in this community, which is more than I can say for you, Edmund. I am the widow of a war hero, the wife of another. Your son, Mr Grant, God forgive us all, was shot for cowardice.'

'No, no!' Grant, all fight drained out of him, slumped down on the couch.

'Other things will come out in court,' Kitty continued remorselessly. 'How you gave money to your good friend, the Tory MP Mr Macclesfield, to have a false allegation laid against my Jack.'

'You'll go to prison,' Kurtz warned. 'You will, Mr Grant.

How long do you get for rape? Five, six years? Kitty is well thought of in this village. She teaches young children. She is well known in the Beaumont Arms for keeping herself to herself. How would it look, Mr Grant? Your wife doped on laudanum upstairs while you assaulted and tried to rape a pretty young woman? What do you English say? The papers will have a field day? What will happen to your shops then, Mr Grant, and their profits?'

Grant had turned a pasty white. Kitty even felt sorry for him as she saw the sweat beads on his forehead.

'You are in this together, aren't you?' Grant's voice turned to a slur. 'You've tricked and trapped me.'

'No more than you've done to me,' Kitty taunted. 'You are responsible for Major Fairfax's presence here! Or partly so. He's been here, hasn't he? Meeting you in this back room?'

Grant sat, hands hanging between his legs.

'It's true what Kitty says, isn't it?'

Grant's face came up, his eyes filled with hate. 'Yes, I am partly responsible. But there's more to it than just me, Miss Kitty.' His words came out in a spit of hate. 'Even if I tried to stop it, I couldn't!'

'Stop what?' Kitty asked.

Grant smiled coldly. 'I'll take my chances.' He leaned back on the couch. 'Go and complain all you want. I may go to prison but so will your Jack. He'll be lucky not to hang.'

'You have a shrivelled soul and a dirty heart!' Kitty exclaimed.

'Have I?' Grant turned to face her squarely; his face had a leering look.

Kitty's heart sank. She tried to hide her consternation. She had underestimated Grant. He had lusted after her more than she thought. Something about her, Billy and Jack had provoked real hatred, a deep-rooted malice.

'You are forgetting one thing, Mr Grant,' Kurtz snarled. 'Your son! Only Colonel Morrison, Billy's mother – a sick, frightened woman – Kitty and myself know what happened. We are not here to stop Fairfax. We are here to find out what he knows.'

'What do you mean?'

'A bargain,' said Kurtz. 'You tell us what Fairfax knows and you have my oath, and Kitty's, that your son's fate as well as what happened today will be forgotten.'

Grant sat rocking backwards and forwards on the edge of the couch. 'Is that all?'

'That's all,' Kitty spoke up. 'We are not fools, Mr Grant. Fairfax is like a runaway horse. He has the bit between his teeth. Even if you withdrew your allegations, he'd still press on.'

'They shot my son Stephen.' Grant pointed a finger at Kitty. 'If his so-called company of friends had looked after him, he wouldn't have deserted.'

'They did look after him,' Kitty replied, 'even though Stephen was never one of them.'

Grant's gaze fell. 'If only I had known.' His voice rose in a wail. 'I could have intervened. I do have friends in high places.'

'I am sure you have,' said Kurtz drily.

'He shouldn't have been shot.'

Kurtz looked up at the clock. 'You've got under an hour, Edmund. So, let's hear your story. Let's discover why Fairfax is here and what you've told him.'

Grant got up and refilled his sherry glass. He drank it quickly and filled it again.

'I am sure you'll understand if I don't offer you one.' He stared at Kurtz, ignoring Kitty. 'I accept your deal and, when I have finished,' he forced a smile, 'you'll see that you've gained nothing.'

Chapter 12

'Stephen never really wanted to join up,' Grant began, 'but we knew it was only a matter of time before he was called up.' The grocer rubbed his podgy hands together. He refused to look at Kitty or Kurtz but sat staring at the floor.

Kitty suspected that even now she would not have all the facts. It's true, she reflected, I have lived my life and not been aware of what is happening around me. Grant she had always dismissed as an old lecher but the feelings he had for her ran deep, tinged with more than just spite and envy.

'I tried to get my son a desk job but that was at the beginning of the war. Men were volunteering and being drafted into the Company of Friends. We all thought it would be over by Christmas and Stephen would have to come back here to live. I knew he wasn't at ease with the other men. From what he told me when he was on leave, people like Jack and Billy,' his face turned ugly, 'did little to help him. He fought for three years and when the company was pulled back for rest and relaxation, my son, the stupid fool, decided to desert. He really thought he could hide out in the forests. He made matters worse by robbing a farmhouse. He was caught by the French, handed over for trial and shot within the week.'

'But what has that got to do with Jack and Billy? They weren't responsible,' Kitty insisted. 'I've read Billy's journal, I've nearly finished it. He makes no reference to your son.'

'Oh!' Grant scoffed and gestured with his hand. 'Kitty, you and your two husbands,' the phrase came out as an insult, 'went to school with my son Stephen. You knew him and he knew you. Be honest, there was no liking between you.'

'We did try,' Kitty protested. 'Stephen was . . . Oh, never mind.' She shook her head. 'I will not speak ill of the dead.'

'Aye, but the dead speak ill of the living, don't they?' Grant accused.

'What did your son tell you?'

'When he came home in the early months of the war he described a growing tension between Jack and Billy. How Jack would sometimes voice his anger.'

'But this is tittle-tattle, gossip,' Kitty declared. 'What else?'

Grant looked as if he was going to protest. Kurtz intervened.

'What else is there? We are going to find out anyway.'

Grant sighed and got to his feet. He drew the bolts on the door leading to the stairs. They heard him go slowly up. A short while later he returned with a battered leather briefcase. He undid the clasps and handed a typed page to Kitty.

'This is not the original,' he smirked. 'I received it from Stephen a month before he deserted, two months before your Billy was killed.'

Kitty took the piece of paper. It was of good quality and the copyist had typed out the letter neatly. There was no address but that was standard.

7th January 1917

Dear Father,

We have now been pulled back for a short respite but soon we will return to the fighting. I see no point in it: the constant trudging, the mud, the corpses. The food is filthy and, as you know, my companions are scarcely welcoming. I have tried my best but Billy Hammond keeps to himself and Jack is the leader of the rest, Cunningham, Evans, O'Neill and, of course, Daventry who should be confined to an asylum.

Kitty looked up and narrowed her eyes. 'I didn't think your son was so literate.'

The grocer coloured. 'He was good with words. He was an intelligent boy.'

Kitty returned to her reading.

Jack is full of resentment. He moans continually about Kitty, whom he believes should be his wife. He's called Billy a liar and a thief. Recently Jack managed to find some brandy and offered to share it with me. We sat in a dugout, the whizz-bangs and shells falling all around us. Jack was in a right rage. He complained how Billy had deceived him, that Kitty was betrothed to him and their wedding shouldn't have taken place. I tried to joke him out of it but he wouldn't listen. The more he drank the worse he became.

'I will have my revenge,' Jack muttered. 'And if the Germans don't take care of Billy Hammond, I will!'

I tried to reason with him but Jack wouldn't listen.

'We go out on patrol,' he declared. 'One night we must have it out. And only one of us will return.'

He went on and on about how he would do it, before finishing the brandy and falling into a drunken stupor. The next morning he couldn't remember what he had said. He looked at me sourly but never raised the matter again. I thought of warning Billy, even informing Colonel Morrison but what good would that do? The rest don't like me. I won't be believed.

I look forward to coming home. Give my love to Mum. Your affectionate son, Stephen.

Kitty weighed the letter in her hands, before passing it on to Kurtz.

'And you sent this to the War Office?'

'Naturally.'

'Why did you wait so long?'

'I didn't. I sent it in the summer of nineteen nineteen, just after you were married to Jack. I made observations, the little gossip I had heard.'

'Who from?' Kitty demanded.

'Oh, Daventry for one. When he first came home, our hole-digger was often in here for sweets, bread, whatever he could cadge. He used to chatter about Stephen. How he didn't know what had happened to him.'

'And, of course,' Kurtz handed the letter back, 'you spoke to him about Billy Hammond.'

Grant re-folded the letter and put it back in the briefcase. 'Of course I did. Daventry was more lucid then, he could remember more. He told me about Jack's helmet being found near Billy's body.'

'You knew all this?' Kitty interrupted. 'And didn't tell me?'

'Why should I?' Grant sneered. 'He also told me that he brought your husband's corpse in, about the two wounds: one to the stomach and the bullet hole to the head. He's probably forgotten all this. Daventry was also concerned about your husband's watch. Apparently Billy saw it as a good luck charm but it had gone missing.'

Kitty kept her face impassive.

'And then there was other chatter. It's wonderful what men will do when they have some beer or ale down them. Cunningham told me a strange story. How Jack refused to describe how your Billy died. The other lads, as Cunningham called them, tried to find out but Jack wouldn't tell. I thought that strange.'

'And so you went to your MP.'

Kitty, despite the warmth of the room and her earlier struggle with Grant, felt cold at how this little toad of a man had collected and taken all this information to his MP.

'Yes, I went to Macclesfield. I wanted my own son's execution investigated. When I met him I also told him about Billy Hammond's death.'

'Of course you would!' Kitty retorted. 'You'd claim it was unfair that your son was shot for desertion whilst a man you regarded as a murderer used his uniform and the pretext of a war to kill his friend so as to marry his wife.' Kitty fought to keep her voice level.

'Why shouldn't I?' Grant looked at the clock and started re-fastening his waistcoat. 'You may not like me, Miss Kitty, but that doesn't change the facts.'

'Oh, I'll change the facts all right.' Kitty also prepared to leave. An idea had sparked in her mind. She felt a small glow of joy. 'Can I see the original of that letter?'

'You can see but not touch,' Grant retorted. 'Even if you try to destroy it, Fairfax has copies.' He opened the briefcase again and took out a manila envelope. He pulled out a long piece of paper, the ink black and faded, the paper stained.

'I think you're lying, Mr Grant.' Kitty kept her eyes on that damning letter.

'What do you mean, lying?'

'I suppose you've lost the envelope this letter came in?'

'I threw it away. What do you mean, lying?'

Kitty looked at him sharply. 'I am a teacher.'

'Not yet fully trained.'

'No, but I do teach in the village hall. Its cupboards are full of old slates, exercise books, papers. I used to go through them after Billy died, and read what he had written. Those cupboards also contain copies of your son's writing.'

'What are you saying, that this is a forgery?'

'May I look at the typed copy again? If it's the truth you have nothing to fear.'

Grant handed it over. 'My son could read and write,' he declared proudly. 'If you look at the school register, you'll find he won prizes for a speech on Children of the New Forest.'

'Oh, he could read all right.' Kitty got to her feet. 'But is this an accurate copy? Word for word, letter for letter?'

Grant stared guardedly at her. Kitty leaned down, her face only a few inches from his.

'I want you to think, Edmund Grant, about your son's schooling. I am going to prove your letter's a forgery. You are a grocer, you sell paper, you know where to buy it. The shops in Durham, particularly with the shortages caused by the war, have stocked old lined paper. I am sure that there, or in Bishop Auckland or somewhere, someone forged this letter.'

'But that's my son's handwriting!'

'Is it?' Kitty demanded. 'If I remember rightly,' she bit her lip in temper, 'Stephen was an intelligent boy. He could read but didn't he have some trouble with punctuation and spelling?'

Kitty buttoned up her coat. What she had said was more bluff than truth. However, if she returned to the old schoolroom, she might find something. Stephen Grant's letter was too lucid, too clear.

'I think I've said enough.' She went to the door and opened it. 'We'll let ourselves out of your shop. Mr Grant, I am going to prove that you are a liar and a forger! If necessary I will search out handwriting specialists.'

Grant sprang to his feet. 'Why won't you just accept it?'

'First, Mr Grant, there's something wrong with that letter. Secondly, I've known Jack Allerton since he was knee high to a daisy. Never once have I known him to drink brandy, never mind get drunk on it. Thirdly, why should Jack confide in your son? Stephen and Billy never got on but it's a well known fact here in Caundon that Jack and Stephen detested the sight of each other.'

Kitty walked over, her hands clenched in fury. She was pleased to see Grant step hastily back.

'Do you think this fight's over? Believe me, Mr Grant, it's only just begun!'

She left that detestable back room, flung the shop door open and walked quickly down the street, not even heeding Kurtz's call. Kitty was so enraged, she wasn't aware of the people she passed, women and children sitting on doorsteps. She reached the Beaumont Arms but didn't stop her furious walk until she was down the country lane as far as the stile which the Dead Hand Club had crossed the previous Saturday evening. Once there, she sat down, put her face in her hands and let the tears fall. She became aware of Kurtz standing beside her. He touched her gently on the head. She realised she had left her small hat in Grant's shop. She stared up.

'It can stay there!'

'What?' Kurtz asked.

'My hat. I left it in Grant's.'

Kurtz dug into his jacket pocket and pulled it out.

'Thank you.' Kitty took it. 'I've got to get back to the Beaumont Arms without Mother seeing me like this. I feel like a tart or a streetwalker.'

Ernst sat down, squeezing himself between her and the hedge, his back to the stile.

'You are neither,' he reassured her. 'You are very brave, a daring young woman, Kitty.'

'But have I done any good?' She sighed. 'I can't really prove what I said. But, believe me, Ernst, that letter is a forgery. Jack would never drink brandy. He would never confide in someone like Stephen Grant. I think our grocer is guilty of a clever forgery.' She drew a deep breath. 'I am not giving up. It's only early afternoon. Ernst, would you come with me?'

'I have left the boy in charge of the shop.' Ernst got to his feet. 'And, as Father Headon would say, once you have put your hand to the plough . . .'

Kitty didn't stop to help him with the quotation but sprang to her feet. With Kurtz striding beside her, she made her way back along the lane to the church. Only then was she aware of how warm the day had grown. The lane was full of the sweet smell of honeysuckle. She stopped under the shade of a tree, dabbing at the sweat on her neck.

'Ernst, I think I'm going mad. I'm aware of nothing but Jack, Fairfax, Grant and the hideous shadow which now stretches across all our lives. What day of the week is it?'

'Monday,' Kurtz replied. 'A shrill whistle echoed from the mine shaft. He took a step closer, his eyes full of laughter. 'You are like a woman possessed, Kitty. I'll always remember this. I'll never try to cross you. However, much as I want to help, why are we going to the church? What are you looking for?'

'Well, as my father would say, I've started the hare running and I've got to follow it. I want to check Stephen's handwriting while that forgery is fresh in my mind.'

The schoolroom was really part of the church hall which lay about an acre's distance. It was closed for the summer. Kitty didn't have her key so she had to stop at the presbytery. Holy Mother Church, the housekeeper, opened the door and glared fiercely at her.

'Father Headon's out,' she trumpeted. 'He should have come back for his lunch but the poor man is wandering. So, what do you want?' She narrowed her eyes. 'Why, it's Kitty. What are you dressed like that for?' She pointed suspiciously at the German. 'And why are the Boche here?'

Kurtz bellowed with laughter.

'Don't laugh at me, you Hun!'

'Please,' said Kitty, 'I need to get into the church hall. I want to visit the school. It's very important. I left my key at home. Father Headon keeps a spare.'

'You'll bring it back, won't you?' Holy Mother Church said distrustfully.

'Cross my heart and hope to die!'

The housekeeper waddled off, returned and thrust the rusting key into Kitty's hand. 'The main door is locked but you'll find the rest open.'

Kitty thanked her and left Holy Mother Church on the step shouting warnings about the company she kept and to never turn her back on the Boche!

The village hall was surrounded by a small orchard, a place full of sweet memories. Kitty was determined not to linger. She opened the main door. The place smelt musty. She went up the stairs to the small office which lay between the two classrooms. Everything was in order as she had left it at the end of term: the long row of desks, the high teacher's table, the slate boards neatly stacked, a tray of inkwells and pens. The room was warm, the windows being closed and shuttered. Kitty asked Kurtz to open some of them and went to a cupboard at the far end of the senior classroom. Inside, the tattered exercise books were neatly stacked. She took them down.

'Stephen Grant left school early,' Kurtz pointed out. 'There will be a vast difference between a child's writing and that of a man.'

'No, no.' Kitty shook her head. 'You know the life of Caundon, Ernst. We had Saturday school and Sunday school. Stephen Grant was intelligent and did read the books his father had bought him. He also liked to win prizes.'

Helped by Kurtz, Kitty searched both the cupboard and the office until she found what she wanted: an exercise book covered in brown wrapping paper with the name Stephen Grant written proudly on the cover. She took it to the teacher's desk. Despite the nostalgia and poignancy the writing provoked, she went through the exercise book carefully. Kurtz stood looking over her shoulder.

'There is a similarity,' he murmured. 'And any changes, well, Grant would argue that Stephen was older and writing clumsily from a trench.'

'Look.' Kitty handed the exercise book to him.

'Don't forget I'm a German.' Kurtz took the exercise book and began to read it. He smiled. 'He doesn't use, what do you call it?'

'Punctuation,' said Kitty. 'Stephen was always in a rush. That letter Grant showed us had short, punctuated sentences.'

The German handed it back. 'A good lawyer could still argue a case. Do you really believe that letter is a forgery?'

'Yes, I do. I am going to prove that it is.'

'That will be hard. Look, Kitty, I must get back to my shop. You'll be safe here?'

Kitty turned and put her arms round his waist and pressed her head against his chest.

'Kitty, there's no need.'

'There's every need, Ernst.' She stepped back and, standing on tiptoe, kissed him on each cheek. 'What you did I'll never forget.'

Kurtz blushed and walked to the door. 'And I haven't finished yet, Kitty.'

Before she could reply, he went thundering down the stairs. Kitty heard him close the door, his footsteps on the path. She leaned against the teacher's desk and gazed round the deserted schoolroom. So many memories! She stared at the bench where she, Jack and Billy used to sit. She went over. Jack's name was still carved there. She remembered watching him do it, whispering at him to stop. Of course, her whispering attracted the attention of Miss Martindale who descended on Jack with her wooden ferrule like a wolf on a lamb. Jack was always the adventurous one, Billy the dreamer.

Kitty squeezed herself in, sat on the narrow wooden seat and put her face in her hands.

'Lord, what is happening?' she prayed. 'A week ago everything was normal.'

Kitty tried to forget Fairfax. Last Monday, what did she think of Jack? She recalled her wistfulness, the sadness which memories of Billy evoked but Jack she loved as she always had. So why had Fairfax's visit shaken her? She took her hands away from her face and stared at the teacher's desk.

'Did Fairfax shake me?' she exclaimed loudly. She shook her head. 'No, no!' she murmured. 'I love Jack. So what?'

She got up from the desk, moved over to the window and stood staring down into the orchard. The apples were tinged with a flush of red. Fairfax had stirred guilt buried deep within her. Guilt at Billy's death and marrying Jack. But the war had shattered so many lives. She had simply done what she could. She honoured Billy's memory but the class she came from, the people she worked with, they didn't have the luxury to sit and reflect, to play emotional games. Oh, she could stand here dreaming, she could plot against Edmund Grant but at the Beaumont Arms Mother would be waiting. Life was waiting, and, more importantly, so was her husband. Fairfax's investigation was based on a lie. She was sure of that but could she prove it?

Kitty hastily pulled across the shutter and let the bar fall. She looked round the school room. She closed the door, went downstairs, locked the church hall and hurried back to the presbytery. She was halfway up the path when she heard her name called. Father Headon came striding up behind her, black hat in one hand, small Gladstone bag in the other.

'Kitty, did you want to see me?'

'Not really, Father. I have just been down to the schoolroom. I had to borrow the key.'

The priest looked at her from head to toe.

'Oh, don't say it, Father. Please don't ask why I am dressed like this! There is a good reason.'

The priest smiled. 'I am sure there is, Kitty. You are not preparing for school, are you? I really must talk about your training. But that's not on your mind now, is it?'

'No, it isn't.' Kitty looked over her shoulder at the presbytery. Holy Mother Church apparently hadn't spotted her so the door to the presbytery remained firmly closed.

'You've been busy about Major Fairfax, haven't you?'

'Father, I have and I think his suspicions are all based on a lie. I can't tell you everything but our grocer Edmund Grant has a finger in this pie. In fact, more than a finger, I think he's baked it himself.'

Father Headon's smile vanished and his face paled. 'Edmund Grant?' He stepped closer, his tired old eyes wrinkled up in concern. 'Are you sure about that, Kitty? Grant's a very dangerous man.'

'I think Jack's innocent,' Kitty declared. She studied the priest carefully. 'And so do you, don't you, Father? Jack's been to see you. You've heard his confession.'

The priest closed his eyes and breathed in.

'Please, Father!'

'Kitty.' Father Headon opened his eyes. 'I am a priest. I hear confessions. Yes, I've heard Jack's.'

'And?'

The priest's agitation grew. 'You know I cannot tell you. For me that would be a most grievous sin.' He grasped Kitty's hand and squeezed it. 'All I can say is this, Kitty. You are married to a good and a brave man. War does terrible things. That is all I shall say on the matter.'

'But you know Fairfax is going to hold an inquiry. He'll probably ask Colonel Morrison to chair it. Father, would you act for Jack?'

'I am not a solicitor, Kitty. I know little about the law but I know a great deal about what is going to be said. Can't you hire a solicitor?'

Kitty shook her head. 'We haven't the time, Father. There's old Mr Lambert in Bishop Auckland. He looks after Mother's affairs but he can hardly find his way to his chair, never mind to Caundon. Fairfax would dance rings round him.'

'In which case, Kitty, why not ask your friend?' The priest smiled. 'I met someone at the Beaumont Arms this afternoon. They saw you walking out here with Ernst Kurtz. The German is a good man.' The priest's grin widened. 'Even though he's not a Catholic and doesn't support Newcastle football team! Kurtz will be good.'

Kitty nodded in agreement. What Father Headon said made sense. Kurtz had proved to be a great ally and a good friend. She leaned forward and kissed the priest on the brow.

'What's that for, Kitty? If Holy Mother Church saw it!'

'Just a thank you, Father, and say a prayer for me. Oh.' She pushed the hall key into his hands. 'Would you do me the favour, Father, of returning it?'

The priest agreed. Kitty, aware of how time was passing,

ran back down the path and out into the lane. She hurried into Caundon. She glimpsed Ernst Kurtz and raised her hand. He waved back but walked on and she wondered why he hadn't returned immediately to his shop. Keeping her head down, Kitty hastened on. She entered the Beaumont Arms by the back yard. Thankfully, her mother, John and Betty were busy in the bar and she fled gratefully upstairs.

At Caundon mine Major Fairfax was also the subject of discussion. Jack had no doubt how dangerous the situation was turning. Ernst Kurtz's warning still rang like a bell through his mind. Cunningham had only increased his anxiety. To a certain extent Jack could understand Kitty's reaction. He had shielded her from the worst, never really discussing the war. Now, like a dam breaking, the past had burst into their lives. Yet he was sure of Kitty; she was strong, resourceful. In the dark of the mine, where the only light came from his lamp and those of his mates, Jack had decided something must be done.

'Did you get the message out?' he asked Cunningham who was standing next to him in the shaft.

'I've told Evans to bring Daventry. We'll all meet at the pithead.' Cunningham coughed at a swirl of dust caused by the draught of a door being opened at the far end. Like Jack he was stripped to the waist, wearing nothing but a pair of old trousers tied by a cord, and steel-tapped boots. His face and chest were grimed with sweat and coal dust.

'I have asked the foreman for an afternoon break. We can take it up at the pithead.' Jack heard the distant blast of a whistle. 'And there it is!' He turned and shouted, 'Right, lads!'

The galleries rang to the clash of boots as the miners from

that particular shift made their way to the pit bottom platform. Jack was aware of the dripping of water, the glare of lights on the whitewashed roof. He glanced around. O'Neill was there, Cunningham too. They got into the steel cage. The branksman closed the doors. There was a crash and rattle as the steel rope began to pull them up. Gusts of cold air cooled their sweat. Slimy walls raced by. Up the shaft they went until they reached the top. The cage doors were pulled open. The miners took off their hats, giving their numbers to the waiting officials. Jack was aware of the noise of the mine, the pound and throb, the steel rope, tinkling bells, and everywhere the grime of coal dust, the smell of sweat tinged with fear, petrol and oil. They went into the washroom and cleaned hands and faces under the running tap. Then they were out in the fresh air.

Jack stared up at the sky. It was rare for them to take a break above ground but today they had to. He, Cunningham and O'Neill walked out across the grimy yards to a small hut near the cooling tower. Evans and Daventry were already there. The policeman had moved his bike behind the shed; helmet off, uniform undone, he was sitting on a pile of timber.

'You should have stayed down the mine.' Jack punched him playfully on the shoulder. 'You're getting fat, Len. And how are you, Bob? By, you do look clean. I recognise those trousers . . .'

'Miss Kitty looked after me. She was very kind. But then that Major Fairfax came and started questioning me. He knows about the watch, Jack. He showed it to Kitty.'

Jack swore and beat his fist against his thigh.

'What's this?' Cunningham asked. 'What watch?'

'Billy's watch,' Jack sighed.

Cunningham hadn't washed his face very well but even Jack noticed how he paled.

'For God's sake, Jack, you had Billy's watch? I thought it was lost.'

O'Neill rubbed his face with the wet rag he had brought from the shed. 'Jack, what's the matter?' he asked. 'Why have you called this meeting?'

'It's about Billy,' Jack replied.

He sat down on the ground and crossed his legs. He peered up at the rest. He was aware of the rattle of the great wheel and the clatter from the engine shed.

'No one can hear us here.' Jack squinted against the sunshine. 'Do you remember when we were lads and we used to pretend to be Red Indians? Sit down, for God's sake, or I'll go back to work with a crick in my neck.'

They all obeyed, sitting in a semi-circle. Jack quickly studied Daventry. Poor Bob looked more agitated than ever. He could hardly sit still. Jack now realised he had made a mistake. Perhaps he should have confided in these men years ago. Yet he had taken an oath, a solemn promise. If he couldn't tell Kitty, why should he tell these?

'Well?' Cunningham demanded. 'What are we going to do? Talk or look at each other? Jack, you are in real trouble, you know.'

'So you tell me.' Jack smiled. 'And I bet Fairfax really squeezed your neck, Jim.'

'I had no bloody choice but to tell him,' Cunningham retorted. 'He's a wicked bastard, Jack, and he means to have you. I only told him the truth and that's bad enough.'

'Which is?'

'You and Billy went out on reconnaisance patrol at night.

247

Billy never came back but poor Bob here brought Billy's corpse in and your helmet. How Colonel Morrison sent the body back to an orderly station. How you never talked about Billy's death. How old were you then, Jack? Twenty? Twenty-one? You'd played with Billy when you were in nappies but you never once informed your mates how Billy really died. You kept all quiet: told us to tell everyone how he'd been killed in a trench by shrapnel.' Cunningham turned, hawked and spat. 'Fairfax made great play of that.' He continued. 'We never questioned you, Jack, and you never told us. You never really explained the helmet, and now we find you had Billy's watch. You were with him all the time, weren't you?' Cunningham leaned forward. 'He must have been dead when you left, otherwise you wouldn't have that watch. Why didn't you show it to us? Why didn't you give it to Kitty?'

Jack gazed round the group. Daventry's eyes had a pleading look. Jack half smiled.

'It's my fault, isn't it?' Daventry blurted out. 'If I hadn't been so bloody stupid and gone for Billy's corpse no one would have known. Now Major Fairfax is after me.'

'You know what Fairfax is going to say,' Evans cut in. 'Let's grasp the nettle, Jack: there were words between you and Billy over his marrying Kitty. You were out there in no-man's-land by yourselves.' Evans stared round. 'He's going to say that you murdered Billy. Do you realise what could happen then, Jack? If you are arrested and go on trial, you won't be the first miner to be hanged on Durham gallows.'

Daventry began to sob quietly.

'You've got to tell us, Jack,' O'Neill broke in. 'You really have.' He licked his dry, chapped lips. 'I don't want Fairfax coming after me.'

His words were greeted by a murmur of approval.

'He'll do that,' Evans agreed. 'He'll start saying that we are your accomplices.'

'Accomplices!' Jack scoffed. 'I was by myself with Billy.'

'No, there's a legal term.' Evans pulled his handkerchief out of his pocket and dabbing at the sweat above his thick serge collar. 'Something about being accessory after the fact.'

'Well, I for one knew bugger all.' O'Neill poked Cunningham with his elbow. 'And if our God-fearing atheist here is correct, Fairfax has been really rooting in our past. We've all got a lot to hide. We all did things out there we were ashamed of and I suspect everyone here has a secret. What's worrying us, Jack, is what's yours?'

'Ernst came to see me yesterday,' Jack replied slowly. 'He says Fairfax is probably here because someone important has an interest in the case.'

'Bugger that!' Evans replied. 'Aren't you going to tell us, Jack?'

They all sat in silence.

'If I do,' Jack chewed the corner of his lip, 'I want you all to take an oath, a miner's oath, that you'll never tell anyone else.'

'About time,' Cunningham declared. 'Why didn't you tell us before, Jack?'

'Because I, too, took an oath,' Jack replied. 'An oath to Billy. I swore I'd never tell anybody what happened that night out in no-man's-land. Do you remember that night, Evans? The sodding Germans raining shells down on us, the sea of mud beyond our trench, the flash of light, the clatter of the machine guns. The shrapnel falling thick and heavy as snow. Colonel Morrison was beside himself.'

'Aye, I remember!'

'None of us thought we'd live to see daybreak,' Jack continued. 'Billy and I went out that night but, let me put the record straight, I loved Billy, more than a brother, more than a mate. Of course I was cut up when he married Kitty. But the longer Billy was in the trenches, the more he believed he'd never be going home. Apart from arguing about this, Billy insisted that, if anything happened to him, I'd look after Kitty. The last time he was on leave he said the same to her.'

'Oh no! Oh no!'

Jack looked up quickly. Daventry had risen to a half-crouch.

'If we take the oath, Jack, does that mean we can't tell anybody?'

'You can't tell anybody, Bob.' Jack looked at Daventry's stricken face and deeply regretted inviting him here. 'You can't tell anyone until I say.'

'But Fairfax' Daventry wailed. 'He's got eyes everywhere, Jack. He'll know I've met you here. He'll come hunting me.'

'What can he threaten you with?' Evans scoffed.

'He could have me taken away and put in a house for imbeciles. I know about those places.' Daventry sprang to his feet, fists clenched. 'Oh, I've left my shovel somewhere. Jack, I don't want to hear this. I don't want to take any oath. What I don't know won't hurt me.'

'Oh, Bob, sit down, for heaven's sake!' O'Neill grasped him by the arm but Daventry shook him off.

'You are the only family I've got, Jack. And Miss Kitty. She was so kind. But Fairfax will come, he's an officer! He'll press his swagger stick into my chest. I'll become frightened and I'll tell him.' Daventry backed out of the circle, ignoring their protests. Jack could see he was terrified out of his wits and quietly cursed Fairfax. He got to his feet and made to go forward but Daventry waved his hand.

'I've lost my shovel! I . . .'

And, before they could stop him, Bob Daventry was running across the yard. He ignored the shouts, curses and exclamations. He shouldered aside miners and officials, racing like a whippet to the main gate. He slipped and slithered on some wet coal dust. He looked round pitifully for his shovel but couldn't find it. Footsteps sounded behind him. He stared around at the watching faces. Were these Fairfax's spies? he wondered wildly. They would all know he was here. And who was that, crouched by the gate, smoking his pipe? Wasn't that old Millsey? And there, beyond the gates, wasn't that Ashcroft?

'I buried you all!' Daventry screamed. 'Why don't you leave me alone!'

He felt a hand on his shoulder but shook it off. He sped through the gate, running as fast as he could along the cobbled track. Then the stitch in his side made him pause. He collapsed in a sweat-soaked panic. He stared around. He was away from the mine now. Out in the fields. The sun wasn't so strong. He gazed at the top of the hill. Sheep browsing there. Or were they ghosts? A line advancing against him, helmets on, bayonets fixed? Daventry closed his eyes. He could hear the shells falling, the screams of men hiding in holes in the ground. He saw grey liverish corpses. The roar of the guns drew nearer. Daventry staggered to his feet. He glimpsed puffs of smoke and, unaware of where he was, went towards it.

'I'll find the colonel,' he murmured.

Daventry reached the railway line. Scrambling up the gravel-sided bank, he stood on the metal rail watching a cloud of black smoke hover against the sky, totally unaware of the train thundering towards him in a clatter of pistons and wheels. Daventry spread his hands. He'd go back to the trenches. He'd finish the business he should have done. He'd be safe from Major Fairfax and the threats.

Daventry was still standing, arms extended, when the train from Durham hit him, sending him spinning into the air.

Chapter 13

Fairfax made himself comfortable on the soft chair. He glanced across at Charles Hargreaves; the lieutenant seemed composed enough. Fairfax had met him in the Dovecote and they had walked up the country lanes to Colonel Morrison's mansion, a Jacobean hall surrounded by copses of trees and the wide open fields of his estate.

Morrison, dressed in a dark suit, white shirt and regimental tie, sat behind his great oaken desk. He was fiddling with a meerschaum pipe which he emptied and cleaned with a penknife. Morrison was tall, sandy-haired, slightly thinning on top. He had a youthful, clean-shaven face though with all the telltale scars of a man who had experienced the horrors of four years in the trenches. Fairfax always recognised the type. In fact, as he'd confided to Hargreaves, such characteristics were more visible than any uniform or medal: a wariness in the eyes, a tendency to pause before speaking, a slight restlessness as well as a cold detachment from what was going on around him. At the moment Morrison seemed more intent on his pipe than he was on them. Fairfax stared appreciatively around the walnut-panelled room with its bookcases stretching from floor to ceiling, the great black and white marble fireplace. The pictures on the wall, each framed in gold, caught the gleam of the lamp, a sharp contrast to the dark-red carpet and heavy curtains.

'This is my study,' Morrison declared. He stared sourly at Fairfax. 'I like to come here, I like to think . . .'

Brood more like it, Fairfax thought.

'How is your wife?' the major asked quickly.

'It's kind of you to ask. She's in good health but visiting friends in Durham. She'll be away for the week.'

To escape you, Fairfax thought. He had carefully studied Morrison's file. A very good soldier, a first-class officer. In fact, a true rarity, an infantry officer who had survived the war from September 1914 to the Armistice of November 1918. The price had been heavy. Morrison was still visiting specialists in Durham and Newcastle. Nothing specific but Fairfax recognised the deep need for psychiatric help. Morrison was moody, withdrawn, complaining of impotence, perpetual fatigue. His wife ran the estate while Morrison became more and more of a recluse.

'I know of you, Fairfax.' Morrison filled his pipe, pushing the tobacco as he would a bullet into a revolver. 'My colleagues in the regiment jokingly refer to me as the "hermit of Caundon". However, I have friends and contacts in the War Office as well as amongst ministers of the Crown.' He lifted a hand. 'I am not threatening you, I am just telling you what, I am sure, Mr Macclesfield and his good friend Mr Edmund Grant have said: how important they are and what a serious matter this is. You've done your homework, haven't you?' He smiled at Hargreaves. 'Major Fairfax, Witch-finder General.' Morrison gently moved his head. 'Have you been called that before, Fairfax?'

'I have, sir, by the local priest.'

'So you know who Matthew Hopkins was? During the Civil War he travelled the villages of Essex, hunting down and burning witches.'

Fairfax refused to be provoked. 'I am an officer of the Crown, sir, a provost marshal. Old women and men don't concern me. Deserters, murderers, cowards, they are my business.'

Morrison struck a match and lit his pipe. He became almost hidden behind the billowing grey smoke. 'You can smoke if you want. Would you like something to drink?' His hand went to the bell rope.

'No, sir, perhaps later,' said Fairfax.

Morrison's hand fell away. 'Why don't you let it all be?' he sighed. 'Let the dead bury the dead. Forget the war. What does it really matter? You were there, weren't you, Fairfax? Trenches full of dead. Row upon row of corpses.' Morrison sucked at his pipe. 'I have one stark memory: burying some of the lads after the Somme. It was nothing like the ceremony you now see before the Cenotaph. About a dozen of the company, in the dead of night, following a lantern, slipping in the mud, stumbling over graves already dug. We stopped at a long ditch. White crosses stood piled against the wall. The men arranged the planks, lifted the ropes and lowered the corpses one after another.' He glanced up. 'There's a real knack to it, Fairfax, burying corpses in a sea of mud in the dead of night. Rain beating down. A padre was present, coughing and spluttering: he was dying of consumption. After he'd finished, we threw the earth in, planted some of the white crosses and went back to the trenches. We were hardly there an hour when a shell fell, scattering us with fragments of metal. The wounded lay

255

sprawled, shrouded in acrid smoke. They had only been struck by splinters but they were new recruits.' Morrison re-lit the pipe. 'Most of them died of shock.' He leaned across the table. 'Can you appreciate that, Fairfax? We buried corpses at ten o'clock; by eleven thirty most of the burial party were dead as well. Did you know of the original strength of my company, a few men out of hundreds came back to Caundon and the surrounding area.'

Fairfax lit a cigarette and studied the colonel.

'You know what I ask myself, Fairfax? Why did I survive I went through the entire war and received only slight wounds, that's all. People say I am lucky,' he clenched his fist, 'that I should enjoy every single day of my life. I'd love to but, even here, sitting in this study, I am aware of the ghosts around me.' He pointed to the window. 'I have fanciful thoughts.' Morrison coughed. 'If I laid every corpse I've seen, every man I lost, head to toe, I could reach the far horizon.' He fished amongst his papers. 'What, I ask myself when the War Office wrote to me recently, the sodding hell? I don't know what happened between Jack Allerton and Billy Hammond. They were both good soldiers. Billy particularly I liked: gentle, kind, never moaned. A good listener, he often gave good advice. I had men like you, Hargreaves, blown away, sergeants and corporals disappeared. Jack Allerton and the rest survived. If I had my way I would have made them officers. These mining lads are the salt of the earth. Whatever hell we faced, they just laughed, demanded mugs of beef tea and their bully meat.'

'I appreciate what you say.' Fairfax thanked Morrison as the colonel handed across an ashtray. Fairfax stubbed out his cigarette. 'But I am here because of the thousands who died. Men like your brother and mine. They sacrificed their lives for

God, King and country. They did their duty. They never came home.' Fairfax found himself getting angry. This topic always stirred him. Why should I, he thought, have to defend myself? Witch-Finder General indeed! He took another cigarette out of the silver case and lit it quickly. He glimpsed Morrison's faint smile and recognised that the colonel knew he had, at last, provoked his visitor.

'I think it is disgraceful, sir, as does the War Office and the army, that men who shirked their duty can now live in a nation which is reaping the rewards of victory.'

'Rewards?' Morrison broke in. 'Go and tell that to the miners!'

'They are alive!' Fairfax snapped. 'Many of their former colleagues aren't!'

'Those who returned,' Morrison's eyes gleamed at the prospect of debate, 'have lost any sense of enjoyment, of being alive.'

'With all due respect, sir, you are alive, so are countless others. I rejoice at that. But what about those who shirked their duty? Or, in the case of Allerton, used the army for private murder and profit?'

Hargreaves shifted back on the chair. He tapped his foot on the floor, his usual warning to Fairfax not to be provoked.

'Nonsense!' Morrison sat back in his chair, cradling the pipe. 'Allerton's no murderer!'

'Well, tell us in your own words what happened that night.'

Morrison shrugged. 'You read it in my report. The two lads went out, Jack came back, Daventry, against my orders, later brought Billy's corpse back. I noticed Billy had a wound to his stomach and a gunshot to the head. I sent the body down

257

to an orderly station for burial. After Daventry's self-sacrifice that was the least I could do.'

'And you didn't think that was strange? A gunshot wound to the head?'

'I never examined the poor lad. Fairfax, you must remember what it was like. The Germans were raining shells down, their machine-gunners were busy. I thought they were going to launch a major attack. I sent a runner to what's his name, Major Redmond of the Berkshires. Are you still searching for him? We agreed to send out scouts. The Germans did the same. All hell broke out in no-man's-land. Some of our lads were taken prisoner. We took some Germans. There was shouting and screaming, hand-to-hand fighting. It wasn't a bloody picnic!' He laughed. 'Shall I tell you how we caught one German? The poor bastard lost his way and threw himself into our trench thinking he was home.'

'OK,' Fairfax intervened. 'Billy Hammond's corpse is brought back. He had lost his helmet but Jack Allerton's helmet is found nearby.'

Morrison just shrugged. 'Such confusion was common!'

'And what else had Billy lost?' Fairfax demanded.

'His rifle, backpack and, I understand, his watch. It was chaos.' Morrison replied. 'Billy's body was brought back. He was very popular with the men. I considered it important to get his corpse away as soon as possible.'

'And did you search the corpse for personal effects?'

'I told you: I wanted the corpse away as soon as possible. I don't have to repeat myself. My task was with the living and the wounded. There was nothing I could do for Billy Hammond.'

'And Jack's reaction?'

Morrison closed his eyes. 'I can't remember it.'

'Oh, come, Colonel.'

'Oh, come nothing, Fairfax! Jack busied himself elsewhere. Daventry, God bless him, brought the corpse in. I took one look at it and sent it down on a stretcher.'

'You know Billy had his journal on him?'

Morrison pulled a face.

'What did Jack report to you?' Hargreaves intervened.

Morrison re-lit his pipe. 'Jack said they had become separated. He'd gone round and round before finding his way back to the trench.'

'But that story's not true, is it?' Hargreaves insisted. 'How did the fictitious tale of Billy being killed by a shellburst in the trench become the accepted story?'

'That's the way the lads wanted it. It not only applies to Billy's death but to countless others. I didn't want to tell his young widow, and neither did his mates, that Billy had spent a night out in no-man's-land in absolute hell.'

'The same reason,' Fairfax spoke up, 'Stephen Grant's death was kept a secret – to preserve morale.'

Morrison's face turned ugly.

'Stephen had his qualities but he was a bad soldier, a malingerer, a coward and a deserter. He left his platoon, his company. He became a thief. He was captured and shot. This happened well away from our headquarters so I kept it quiet. The only person I told was Billy Hammond.'

'Why?' Hargreaves asked.

'Because I bloody well wanted to! Billy asked me so I told him.' Morrison wagged a finger at Fairfax. 'And Grant Senior is not much better. He's been out here threatening me, telling me to keep my mouth shut about what happened to his son. I told him I was more interested in the pride of my company, that he had nothing to fear, and I sent him packing. I know who is behind this, him and that toady Macclesfield. I can't stand that man. If he ever comes onto my property I'll set my dogs on him.'

'So, you don't like your Member of Parliament.'

'Don't be sarcastic, Fairfax. He's a nasty piece of work with little love for me, my regiment or my men.'

'Let's go back to Jack Allerton.' Fairfax chewed the corner of his lip. 'He was angry that Billy had married Kitty?'

'Well, of course he was, he loved her. And the war jangled his nerves.'

'To the best of your knowledge, did Jack threaten Billy?'

'No.' Morrison picked up a box of matches and tossed them to and fro in his hands. 'There were some scraps but they were the best of mates. Billy told me that if anything happened to him, Jack would look after Kitty.'

'And you don't think that's a motive for murder?'

Morrison let the matches fall onto the desk.

'Do you know Jack had Billy's watch?' Fairfax pressed his attack.

Morrison tensed, blinking quickly.

'You didn't, did you? Yes, Jack has had it since Billy's death! Kept it hidden in his garden. You do realise that Billy's head wound was caused by a bullet fired close to the temple?'

Morrison's agitation grew.

'An English bullet from an English revolver, Colonel Morrison. Was Jack Allerton carrying a revolver?'

Morrison shook his head.

'Did you lend him yours?'

Again he shook his head.

'And did Daventry report seeing a revolver anywhere near the corpse?'

Morrison refused to meet Fairfax's gaze. 'No, no, he didn't. He would have brought it back, wouldn't he?'

'And isn't it strange' Hargreaves added, 'that Jack never went looking for Billy or showed any surprise when Daventry brought his body back? He avoided it. Why did he tell you, Colonel, that he was separated from Billy? Yet the very morning he returned to the trench, he was carrying Billy's watch?'

Morrison was silent.

'Isn't it true' Fairfax pressed, 'that the story about Billy being killed in the trench rather than out in no-man's-land originated with Jack? We know from another source that, after the war, when the men were coming home, Jack insisted that this be the story given to Kitty. Didn't he also claim that Billy's watch and journal were probably lost in the mud? We can produce witnesses that this conversation took place on a troop train heading into Calais. Has Allerton ever, in the years since Billy's death, offered to explain what happened out there?' Fairfax lit another cigarette.

'What are you saying, Fairfax?'

'I am no witch-finder, Colonel Morrison. I am a policeman investigating the possible malicious murder of one of His Majesty's soldiers by another: Jack Allerton took Billy out on that reconnaissance and they sheltered in a crater. Jack, in his scrambling around no-man's-land, found a revolver, or maybe he had one even before he left the trench.'

'Nonsense! Nonsense!' Morrison shook his head.

'No, it's not, Colonel. Do you remember Lieutenant Skelton, a young man from Teesdale? His father owns land around Catterick.'

'Yes, of course, a good officer.'

'He was until a sniper killed him, the day before Billy Hammond died.'

'I remember that. Skelton was carrying messages between the trenches. He showed himself for an instant, that was enough.'

'And you had his body sent back to the orderly station.'

'Of course, that was routine.'

Fairfax kicked the leather briefcase beside him. 'And, according to routine, Colonel Morrison, Skelton's personal effects were listed. Do you know his revolver was missing as well as some bullets? A revolver of the same calibre which, I understand, gave Billy Hammond his death wound. The official who listed Skelton's personal belongings actually wrote: "Revolver case empty, pouch of bullets gone."'

'But that doesn't mean anything,' Morrison scoffed.

'Who took Skelton's body down?'

'Why, it was always Daventry and . . .' Morrison leaned his elbow on the arm of his chair.

'And Jack Allerton?'

'Yes, it was Jack Allerton. I often sent him with Daventry. Jack was level-headed, careful. He could control Daventry, the poor madman!'

'Do you know what I think happened?' Fairfax declared. 'Allerton stole that revolver and kept the bullets with him. That night, out in no-man's-land, he shot Billy Hammond in the head and threw both the revolver and the bullets away. The crater they were sheltering in came under attack. I suspect that's where Billy got the belly wound, but he was already dead. Jack panicked and fled into the darkness, leaving his helmet behind. There may have been a struggle, during which

Billy lost both his helmet and his rifle. Perhaps Jack disarmed him. Jack scrambled back to the trench. He's taken the watch because it's a symbol of Billy's love for Kitty. Jack has settled his grievance, he is free to return home the conquering hero and win Kitty's heart.'

'That's a bloody lie!' Morrison sat back in his chair and stared at the books on his library shelf.

No, it's not, Fairfax thought. The colonel was clearly agitated.

'The evidence against Jack Allerton is mounting,' Fairfax continued. 'The revolver, the bullets, the helmet, the quarrel or bad words with Billy. Allerton's reaction to Billy's death. The way he concocted a story for the good people of Caundon.' Fairfax picked up his briefcase and rested it on his knee. 'You know, Colonel, and so do I, that he has a case to answer. As for Major Redmond, who was in the same sector with Jack and Billy that night, we've found him near Skipton. He'll be with us in a couple of days.'

'You have other evidence?' Morrison asked.

'Oh yes.'

'And what do you want me to do?'

'You are Jack's commander, you are also a local magistrate. You have the power to summon Jack Allerton, and the rest, so I can question them in your presence. At that preliminary hearing I will produce further evidence as well as Major Redmond.'

'Why him?' Morrison demanded. 'Redmond reported nothing untoward.'

'As you say, Colonel, it was all confusion out there. Like many an old soldier, Redmond later wrote his memoirs. He sent them to the War Office for clearance. He recalls that night quite vividly. Redmond obliquely refers to meeting two Durham lads out in no-man's-land. He said the same in a report filed just after the incident.'

'When will this inquiry take place?'

Fairfax glanced at Hargreaves. 'Thursday or Friday of this week.'

'And then what?'

'If Allerton's answers are not satisfactory, and I suspect they won't be, I'll arrest him. He'll be committed for trial in either Durham or London.'

Morrison was ill at ease. He fumbled with his pipe and matches got up and walked to the window.

'I don't believe all this,' he declared. He was about to continue when there was a knock on the door. 'What is it? I told you I didn't want to be disturbed!'

He'd expected a maid but Father Headon stepped into the room.

'I can't see you now, Father.' Morrison gestured at Fairfax and Hargreaves, who also rose. 'As you can see, I'm busy.'

'It's about these two gentlemen I've come.'

'I see. Hargreaves, a chair for the padre.'

The lieutenant obeyed, putting a chair between his and Fairfax's. Father Headon sighed and sat down, cradling his hat. He politely refused Morrison's offer of a drink.

'I met Kitty Allerton today,' he began. 'She was in a strange state, dressed in all her finery. She asked if I could help her over this business with Jack. Major Fairfax, that's why you are here, isn't it? Like dirt in a pool, the news is beginning to spread.'

Fairfax stared back.

'I said I couldn't help her, the poor bairn. I baptised her, I felt a coward . . .'

'And can you help?' Morrison asked eagerly.

'Let me say this.' The priest paused, searching for words. 'Major Fairfax, you are here about the night Billy Hammond died out in no-man's-land, yes?'

'Has Allerton spoken to you? I mean, outside the confessional?'

'He has spoken to me in confession, Major Fairfax. He has confessed a sin but not the one you think.'

'And what do I think, Father?'

'That Jack Allerton murdered Billy Hammond so as to marry Kitty.'

'Father, if he has committed a sin, he answers to God. If he has committed a crime, he'll answer to the law and army justice,' Fairfax replied. 'What I want to know is, can you produce any evidence which would clear Jack Allerton's name?'

'No.' The priest shook his head wearily. 'No, I cannot do that. I was right.' He smiled weakly at Morrison. 'There is little I can do to help.'

Kitty sat on the edge of the bed. Through the window she could see the sun beginning to set. The evening breeze carried the sounds from the mine, the shrill whistle blast marking the end of the shift. Jack will soon be home, she thought. And what could she say?

She had returned to the Beaumont Arms, changed quickly and scurried about helping her mother with this and that: the bar, the cellar, the kitchen, the hard, grinding work of the wash house. She'd barely reflected on what she and Kurtz had done.

She felt ashamed, slightly embarrassed but at least she had learnt something. Grant was the source of all the venom and poison. But how could he be stopped? And, even if he was, what other so-called evidence did Fairfax possess?

She took out Billy's journal from beneath the mattress and opened it. Only a few pages remained. His scrawl had got worse. This time he had used a thick black pencil. Kitty began to read.

'Colonel Morrison says the Germans are massing for another attack. I have had long chats with him.'

Kitty smiled. Billy and Morrison had always got on. Before the war the colonel had even offered to help Billy in his education and never objected when Billy wandered onto his estate. She read on.

> Morrison is in a strange mood. Very sad and dejected. He told me his brother has been killed out in the Far East, fighting with the Arabs. He also confessed he had news about Stephen Grant. God forgive me, I never liked the lad and he was no mate of mine. We thought he had been wounded or been cut off. Companies have now merged with each other. We've lost so many officers, Morrison even approached Jack and myself. Kitty would laugh at that! Me and Jack marching through Caundon with our officer's epaulettes and posh, shiny boots! Anyway, Morrison told me that Grant had deserted. Gone quite a distance before the French caught him. He had been involved in some thievery, faced summary court martial and was shot. Poor man! His dad will be stricken to the heart! I never liked either of them. I always thought Grant the grocer

was a lecher, hot-eyed for my Kitty. Morrison, I think, regretted telling me and asked me not to say anything to the others. Not that they would listen.

Poor Daventry's in a dreadful state. The only consolation is that I don't think he has any nerves left to shatter. The poor fellow seems more attached to his shovel than he does to his rifle. Cunningham too. He's beginning to protest more and more about the padres. He refuses to attend any service and keeps to himself. I've seen him talking to Jack, heads together. I think old Jack helped him through some scrape during that great retreat in the snow last winter. Evans, too, was cut off. Said he took up with some Australians. We don't talk much now. One day merges into another. No-man's-land is a sea of mud. There used to be a wood, now there's only black charred trees. A visiting French officer said he used to hunt here as a boy. Jack and I found a farmhouse. Not much different from the cottages at home. We went up into the attic. I found a pair of children's clogs, very pathetic. Someone's house, someone's home!

During the day we have to keep an eye on the Boche, especially their shells. They dealt a direct hit to some of the Berkshires and we had to go down and clean the mess: that horrid stench of cordite and burning flesh! Now and again their machine guns open up, the bullets scything the air. I agree with Jack. We are doing nothing out here except clamber over barbed wire, keep our helmets on and make sure we don't get foot rot. At least the Germans have stopped sending gas. I think they have run out. I don't know which is worse, the stench of the gas or the flannel masks we have to wear. Cunningham pisses into his: he claims it helps and offered to do the same for me. I just laughed. Jack seems in better humour. He apologised for the things he said. When he talks about Kitty, it's like being back in the past when the three of us used to go to school and run like hares through the field. Such a different world! It's almost as if I had two lives: before the war and now. I wonder if I'll ever finish this journal. Each day I lie down. I pray that God will take us out of this, that I'll see Kitty again. A little voice deep inside me says I won't. I made Jack promise again that he will look after her.

I wonder what Kitty's doing now. I used to love watching her cook or sew, particularly when she gets cross – her tongue comes out and she narrows those lovely eyes. At night I close my mind to what is happening around me. I feel Kitty comes to me. I can smell the soap she uses, sweet and fragrant, and the fresh smell of her hair. I used to wake up before her and just lie and look, that beautiful hair fanned out over the pillow, that lovely face lost in sleep. I know Jack misses her but what will be will be.

Morrison's becoming more and more nervous about what the enemy are planning. He sent me down to the Berkshires to get some supplies. I met their Major Redmond, a good chap. He said he wanted the colonel and himself to plan a reconnaissance. God save us from that! It's like swimming through a sea of mud at the dead of night. You can't tell friends from foe and there are whizz-bangs and shells dropping all around you. I have Kitty's watch safe and I keep this journal pushed down into my jerkin, the best place to hide it!

Everything decays here. Nothing lasts except my love for Kitty.

That was the last page. Some of the other pages were stained. There was a drawing of a German inside the back cover and a sketch of a ruined tree.

'Did you learn anything?'

Jack stood in the doorway. He had stripped off everything except his flannel underpants. His body was black and sweat-grimed. Kitty put the journal down. She came over and kissed him gently on the lips.

'I'll come down with you,' she offered. 'We can talk in the outhouse.'

They went downstairs, out across the yard. John, busy getting the bar ready, whistled mockingly at Jack who made a lewd sign back. Kitty filled buckets of water from the pump and filled the bath while Jack lit the two gas lamps on a ledge. It was late evening though the sun hadn't yet set. Once the door was closed, the outhouse was dark. Jack stripped off and stood in the bath.

'You seem different, Kitty.'

'What do you mean?'

'Well, more composed. I met Stationmaster Thompson as I was coming back from work, he said he had seen you out in all your finery.'

'Oh, I went to see Ernst.'

Jack stopped mopping his body with a wet rag. 'And?' he demanded. 'How can the German help?'

'Oh, finish washing.' Kitty smiled. 'You look slightly ridiculous standing there naked, half-clean, half-dirty.'

Jack obeyed and stepped out. He took the flannel towel

from a peg and vigorously dried himself. Kitty's mother had already laid out what he called his 'evening clothes': flannel underwear, open-necked, striped shirt, fustian trousers with its broad belt and heavy braces, woollen army socks and a pair of old soft shoes which had once belonged to Kitty's father. Jack dressed hurriedly.

'Kurtz?' he demanded as he tied the laces.

'Jack, don't let's beat round the bush. I know why Fairfax is here. He thinks, the army thinks, helped by that greedy lecher Grant, that you killed Billy out in no-man's-land.' Kitty breathed in.

Jack went to embrace her.

'No, no, Jack, not now! What I have to say is important. I love you, Jack, and I loved Billy. I can't explain it. Other people might think it strange. I don't. Nor do you, nor did Billy. In a way I am glad Fairfax came. I suppose I always felt guilty at marrying after Billy's death.' She swallowed hard. 'At least Fairfax brought that guilt to the surface but it's only guilt, Jack. I don't believe you murdered anyone, certainly not Billy. What I can't understand is why you've never told me what truly happened out there. Why can't you trust me? Fairfax is going to hold an inquiry,' she continued in a rush. 'Kurtz has agreed to help us.'

'What can he do?'

'More importantly, Jack, what can you do? Why can't you just tell the truth?'

He came over and grasped her hand. 'Do you really love me, Kitty?' He put his arms round her waist and pulled her close.

'You know I do, Jack.' Her eyes filled with tears. 'Why couldn't you tell me about the watch?'

Jack's hand fell away. 'I couldn't, Kitty.' He opened the door, looked across the yard, then closed it sharply. When he looked back at her, his face was hard.

'I went to Durham once,' he declared. 'I met two brothers and a sister. They were triplets.' He smiled. 'You wouldn't think it to look at them but they were! Coming back on the train I thought, that's what Billy, Kitty and I are, triplets! So much together, we think like one, you'd think we came from the same womb. We lived in our own little world, Kitty; that's why people like Stephen Grant hated us. We didn't need anyone else, brother, sister, mum or dad. We used to get up in the morning, when we weren't sleeping round each other's houses, dress, have breakfast and, come hail or shine, we'd meet on the corner and go to school. We sat together, we learnt together, we played together. On Saturdays and Sundays it was the same. We used to talk about everything. As we got older nothing changed. People came to accept this. We went to the lantern shows, the dances, the galas and the festivals. The first time I travelled on a bus, you and Billy came with me. I used to kiss you goodnight and so did Billy. In many ways we were innocents. I loved Billy. I always thought he was a finer man than me . . .'

'Don't, Jack!'

He shook his head. 'You and Billy had it wrong. When you became engaged and got married, it wasn't that I envied Billy or resented him. In a way I knew that would happen. Don't you realise, Kitty, our lives changed? It would never be the same again. Oh, I could come round to your house, like any brother, be uncle to your kids, but it was the end, Kitty. Once there were three then it became two and one.' He picked up the towel and began to fold it carefully. 'I suppose I showed my resentment. You know Billy. Kind, more hurt than angry. I tell you this, Kitty, when Billy died, he and I were still the best of friends. Before it happened I was worried for him.'

'You mean about dying?' she asked.

'Yes.' Jack pushed his hair from his forehead; he glared fiercely at her. 'Kitty, right from the start of that carnage I promised myself I was going to go home, I was going to survive. I tried to make Billy think the same.' He paused. 'At first he did but he couldn't hold on to the belief, it seeped away like water dripping through a crack, to be replaced by a certainty that he never would come home. He talked to you about it when he was on leave and he began to make me promise. Oh, the story was well known in the company.'

'And Billy's death?' Kitty held herself tense.

'Billy was killed and I married you.' He stepped closer and kissed her on the forehead. 'Deep in my heart I felt guilty as well. Guilty of taking Billy's place, his woman, and the certainty grew in me that one day I would pay for all this. I always thought someone like Fairfax would turn up. That's why I kept silent.' He stared at her. 'Don't you think that the thought must have crossed Fairfax's cunning mind that you might be my accomplice?'

Kitty swallowed hard.

'I've seen the likes of Fairfax,' Jack continued, throwing the towel down on a stool. 'I wouldn't put it past him to accuse both of us of plotting Billy's death. That's why, right from the start, I told Cunningham, Evans and the rest to say Billy was killed in the trench. Colonel Morrison also agreed.'

'Then how did he die?' Kitty demanded.

'I am not telling you, Kitty, not now.' He put his hands on her shoulders and squeezed. 'You are not going to know,

Kitty. I took an oath and, I won't break that oath until Fairfax, if he wants, takes me to court.'

Kitty made to protest but he kissed her harshly on the lips.

'What you don't know can't hurt you. Don't you think that smelly little grocer Grant has kept his eyes and ears open? The slightest hint from you, Kitty—'

'I wouldn't have told him,' she said.

'No, you wouldn't, Kitty. But sooner or later you would have told your mother or someone else, and Grant collects gossip.'

Jack was about to continue when they heard the sound of raised voices and hurried footsteps.

'Jack! Jack Allerton!'

He opened the outhouse door. Evans, red-faced and sweaty, stood there.

'For God's sake, Jack, you've got to come! It's poor Bob Daventry!'

Kitty went cold.

'He's been killed!'

'How?' Jack demanded.

'Went onto the railway track. He must have been sent spinning like a top. Jack, I'll need help to bring his body back.'

Jack was about to reply when Fairfax, swinging his walking cane, walked through the gate.

'Have you heard the news, Major Fairfax?' Jack shouted.

Fairfax stopped and raised his eyebrows. 'News, Jack?'

'Daventry's dead.' Jack strode across. Fairfax shifted the cane from his left hand to his right. 'Are you satisfied, Major Fairfax? Now you have the scent of blood in your nostrils?'

Fairfax stood his ground and stared coldly back. 'I treated Daventry with gentleness, didn't I, Kitty?'

'You did.' Kitty rushed across and grabbed Jack's arm, pulling him away. Fairfax stood flicking some cigarette ash from the lapel of his coat.

'I think you'd best go in,' Kitty said to him.

Fairfax was about to agree but then turned back.

'Evans, you'll need help with the corpse. Let me assist.' And, spinning on his heel, Fairfax walked back through the gate.

Chapter 14

The news of Bob Daventry's death soon spread all over Caundon. Evans, helped by Fairfax, Jack and others, brought the battered corpse from the railway line to his small, shabby house. Father Headon came down to give him the last rites. Afterwards some of the women prepared the body for burial. Kurtz fashioned a makeshift coffin and Father Headon announced the funeral would take place the following Thursday morning at eleven o'clock.

People couldn't decide whether Daventry had simply wandered onto the track. Many commented on his agitated state and believed the poor man finally lost all his wits and committed suicide. Feelings ran high against Fairfax. If Kitty hadn't intervened, a shouting match between the major and members of the Dead Hand Club could have spilled over into violence. Fairfax, however, was unbowed and Kitty secretly admired his courage. He strode into the bar later in the evening and ordered a whisky and soda which he sipped slowly before picking up his coat and stick and loudly announcing he was going for an evening walk. Some of the men wanted to follow him.

'Don't be daft,' Jack intervened. 'We can't blame Fairfax for Bob's death. We're all at fault. Perhaps we should have taken better care of him.'

People accepted this. They had their own feelings of guilt. Many secretly regarded Daventry's death as a blessing, whispering how the poor man had scarcely had a life since he returned from the war.

Daventry's death and imminent funeral led to the closure of the pit on Wednesday afternoon. Most of the villagers flocked to the church where the body was received later that day. Father Headon, dressed in black and gold vestments, blessed the corpse at the church door. Members of the Dead Hand Club then carried the coffin, draped in a purple coverlet, to lie on trestles before the sanctuary.

Afterwards, tea, sandwiches and cake were served in the village hall. Colonel Morrison was present. He scowled when Fairfax, accompanied by Hargreaves, sauntered in. Morrison took them aside.

'Do you think this is the best place for you? I mean, in the circumstances?'

Fairfax, who had now reverted to his army uniform, took off his cap and placed it under his arm.

'I couldn't think of a more appropriate place, sir. The Requiem Mass, I understand, is at eleven o'clock tomorrow. Around the same time, Major Redmond will be arriving at Caundon station. I also understand the pit will be closed tomorrow as well as a sign of respect. I suggest we hold the inquiry at one o'clock in your house.'

Morrison was taken aback. 'Couldn't you wait a little longer?'

'Sir, look around you,' Fairfax replied. 'We are not welcome here. What we are doing is unpleasant. However, I have a task to do and I must finish it one way or the other.' He gestured at Hargreaves. 'The lieutenant has the summons. I intend to demand the presence of Jack Allerton, Len Evans, O'Neill and Cunningham.' His eyes shifted and he glimpsed Kitty at the far corner of the hall. She seemed busy serving tea but he knew she was watching him. 'Major Redmond will be present as will Edmund Grant the grocer.'

'For God's sake, you surely don't trust that little gutter-snipe.'

'He has vital evidence,' Fairfax replied, gazing round the hall. 'But I'm damned if I can find him.' He tapped Hargreaves on the shoulder. 'You'd best serve the summons, Charles, and then we'll be gone.'

Hargreaves quickly went round the hall. To Jack and the others he gave a brown manila envelope. When he had finished, he and Fairfax left. The contents of the envelopes were soon known to all. Kitty opened Jack's. It was on official notepaper and, citing certain statutes and regulations, summoned Jack Allerton to a preliminary hearing of the provost marshal at Caundon Hall at one o'clock the following day. She thrust it into Jack's hand and hastened over to Morrison.

'Can he do this?' she asked, grasping the colonel's arm.

Morrison patted her hand affectionately. He had always had a soft spot for Kitty, bright, vivacious, honest and direct.

'I could refuse.' He smiled down at her. 'But, to give Fairfax his due, he's doing the best he can. If he wanted to, he could summon Jack to Durham or even London for such a hearing. I think it's best if I told everyone that.'

Kitty agreed and Morrison went to the far and of the hall where he stood on a small platform and demanded silence.

'I hope those concerned,' he began, 'don't object but what is happening in Caundon is now becoming common knowledge. The Provost Marshal's Office has sent two representatives, Major Fairfax and Lieutenant Charles Hargreaves, to investigate a certain incident which occurred during the war. Major Fairfax regrets the death of Bob Daventry—'

He was interrupted by murmurs and shouts of protest.

'But Major Fairfax has to do his job. I must do mine. I am sure this incident will be cleared up. Notices have been served of a preliminary hearing at Caundon Hall tomorrow at one o'clock, after the funeral. I expect, and I know I speak for the families of the men concerned and for Father Headon here, that we will all act in a proper manner.'

His words were greeted by a murmur of agreement.

'Proper manner!' Cunningham hissed from where he stood behind Kitty and Jack. 'I'd love to string the bastards up! Apart from Colonel Morrison, I have never yet met an officer I've liked. Are you going to obey the summons, Jack?'

'I've got no choice and neither have you.' Jack looped his arm through Kitty's. 'Let's go home, pet. At least it will be a day away from the pits.'

They left the hall and walked back through the warm dusk. Kitty felt at peace. She had done what she could and believed Jack was telling the truth, though she still felt a twinge of fear about what might happen tomorrow.

'You are not going to tell me?'

Jack grasped her by the arms, pulled her close and kissed her full on the lips.

'Tomorrow, Kitty, Fairfax will put us all on oath and then I shall have to speak. Morrison says you can be there. Now,' he smiled at her through the darkness, 'are you going to stand there like a sergeant major or take me back to the Beaumont Arms and ply me with demon drink? The other lads will be joining us. We want to toast Bob's memory.'

They walked on. Behind them rose the voices of others leaving the hall, making their way back to the village.

'Do you know something, Kitty.' Jack paused and stared up at the sky. 'I have always loved you, I always will. Despite what you might hear tomorrow, I loved Billy and did my best, both as a mate and a soldier. I am glad it's come to this,' he continued. 'Once it's out in the open, it will be finished. Life can go on.'

They reached the Beaumont Arms. Kitty, helped by John and Betty, opened the bar. Jack and his companions took over the snug. The other villagers came in. Colonel Morrison joined them. He told Kitty that, for an hour, he would pay for all drinks. The news soon spread and the bar became packed. Jack came from the snug to help Kitty behind the bar. Toasts were made to Colonel Morrison and Bob Daventry. The evening turned into a wake, memories were stirred and names of others killed in the Great War were mentioned and saluted.

After Morrison left, the party broke up, people drifting back to their homes. Fairfax came down, accompanied by Hargreaves. They both stood at the far end of the bar, ignoring the scowls and muttered curses.

'Could my lieutenant hire a room?' Fairfax asked.

'I think it can be arranged.' Kitty placed two glasses of whisky on the counter before him. 'Why, Major, are you frightened?'

For the first time since he had arrived in Caundon, Fairfax smiled with genuine amusement. It gave his face a fresh, boyish look.

'Do you find that funny, Major?'

'What do you think, Charles?' Fairfax lifted his glass, toasted Kitty and stared at his lieutenant.

'We are used to it, ma'am. It's not the first time people have turned ugly. Officers are not liked, provost marshals particularly.' He drained the glass. 'I'll move my baggage, sir.'

Kitty asked John to help the lieutenant. When they'd left, Fairfax asked for his glass to be refilled.

'To the top, Kitty. Oh, and make sure you prepare my bill right. I want to make sure I pay for everything I've eaten and drunk.'

Kitty filled the glass and handed it across. 'And what about the rest, Major Fairfax?'

The major stared blankly.

'The chaos and anguish you have caused?'

Fairfax's face became harsh and impassive.

'What makes you do a job like this?'

'Justice, the law.'

'I don't think so.' Kitty leaned against the bar. 'Why are you called Oscar? It's a strange name.'

'My grandfather was German. I'm named after him and, to answer your question bluntly, Kitty, as I have told you and others, it's wrong for a man to escape justice.'

'If that was the case,' Kitty replied fiercely, 'we should all be swinging by our necks, Major Fairfax.'

He seemed to ignore her, more interested in taking a cigarette out of his case. He closed it with a snap and beat the end of the cigarette on the bar.

'Not you, Kitty.' He looked at her wistfully. 'You are innocent of everything except loving and caring.'

'What is it you really want?' she insisted. 'Why don't you

answer my question? It's not really justice, is it, Major Fairfax? There's something else.'

His head came back, eyes watchful.

'Do you feel anything for anybody?' Kitty continued. 'No, it's not that.' She held his gaze as if trying to find the soul behind his eyes. 'You don't believe in anything, do you? You consider us all creatures of the dark. You are here to impose order and justice. You don't believe in the good, so you don't see any good. Isn't that true, Major Fairfax? Has it ever crossed your mind that people aren't bad or wicked? They are just weak and frightened.'

Fairfax dropped his gaze and, picking up the whisky, drank it quickly.

'I can't say I know you, Major Fairfax, but I don't think you appreciate what it is to be frightened, to be weak, to be hunted. You came through the Great War and survived. You lost your brother, your wife, but that only hardened you.' She put four glasses on the counter and filled them.

'I can't drink those, Kitty.' Fairfax nodded to where the snug door was open. Jack stood, staring across at them. 'They'll think you are trying to bribe me.'

'Those glasses aren't for you, Major. One is for your brother Maurice, one for your wife, one for my Billy, one for poor Bob Daventry.'

Fairfax drained the glass in his hand. Then he picked up the first of the whiskies Kitty had just poured.

'I wonder what they'd say to you, Oscar, if they were here.' Would they talk about the law? About justice? About vengeance and retribution?' She shook her head. 'Is that why your brother died, or my Billy? No, I believe they'd talk about compassion, kindness and looking for the good.'

Fairfax didn't seem to listen. He finished the glass of whisky meant for his brother and picked up the one Kitty had poured for his wife. She noticed his hand shook slightly, his face had paled. He finished that glass and placed it on the bar.

'Goodnight, Kitty.' Without a further word, Fairfax turned on his heel and walked out.

'What are you doing?' Jack called out.

Kitty lifted the glass meant for Billy and toasted him. 'I was trying to talk to the major.' She smiled thinly. 'But I don't think he was listening.'

The whisky burnt her throat. Jack went back into the snug. Kitty stared down at the half-empty glass. She was tired, drained by the day. And tomorrow?

'Ah well,' she murmured. She'd said her piece and that was important.

She took off the heavy white linen apron and slowly climbed the stairs to her bedroom where she opened the drawer and took out Billy's picture.

'Will you be there tomorrow, Billy?' she whispered. 'Will we be three again? You, Jack and me?'

Kitty heard her mother call her name. She kissed the picture, placed it back in the drawer and went downstairs.

The following morning Kitty and Jack were up early. Despite the agitation, both had slept well. Jack insisted on shaving and dressing in his Sunday best. Accompanied by Kitty and her mother, he left the Beaumont Arms and they made their way up to the church. The Requiem Mass began. Father Headon delivered a short homily touching on Bob Daventry's life. Kitty gazed round. At the back of the church she glimpsed Fairfax and Hargreaves attired in full uniform. Kurtz smiled at her. When she glanced over to where Edmund Grant usually sat, the bench was empty.

The day seemed to suit the occasion. Dark clouds blocked out the sun and, as the final clods of earth were tossed down onto Daventry's coffin, a slight drizzle began to fall.

When the others went to the village hall after the funeral, Kitty, Jack and the rest made their way along the trackway to Caundon Hall. Colonel Morrison had everything prepared. Fairfax and Hargreaves must have left as soon as the Mass finished: they were already seated at the top of the table in Morrison's library, a beautiful oak-panelled room. The fire had been lit and the heavy curtains pulled. Candelabra along the table winked and glowed.

'We won't stand on ceremony,' Morrison began, taking his seat and indicating that Jack, Kitty and Kurtz do the same – the German had attached himself to them as they left the church.

'I think he should be with us,' Kitty had insisted. 'Ernst is sharp, Jack. He can do no harm and, perhaps, a lot of good.'

Kurtz seemed eager to help. He, too, was dressed in his Sunday best and beamed across at Fairfax and Hargreaves. Cunningham, Evans and O'Neill sat further down the table.

Morrison picked up a small Bible, a piece of paper on top. 'I won't make a meal of this. I am going to act more as a commissioner for oaths than a magistrate. Jack, you and the rest must swear that you will tell the truth. Major Fairfax and Lieutenant Hargreaves here will also take an oath, as will any witnesses who are called.' He glanced at Fairfax. 'Major Redmond and the grocer Edmund Grant are waiting in my study. They'll join us as necessary.'

Fairfax, refusing to meet Kitty's eyes, grunted his approval and lifted his heavy briefcase. He put it on the table before him and took out two thick files. He handed one to Hargreaves. Morrison got up and began to administer the oath. Jack took it, followed by the other three who all sat nervously plucking at collars, shuffling their feet, staring longingly at the door.

'I regret the circumstances,' Morrison said, re-taking his seat, 'but the procedures are quite simple. Major?'

Fairfax cleared his throat and opened his file. Kurtz tapped the tablecloth.

'Er, Colonel Morrison, sir.' Kurtz's voice was harsh. 'Major Fairfax and Lieutenant Hargreaves have not taken the oath.'

Morrison, flustered, quickly administered this. Both officers recited the words swiftly, one hand raised, the other on the Bible.

You don't really believe what you are saying, Kitty thought, both of you are eager to get on. She was chilled by the demeanour of the two: Fairfax was businesslike; Hargreaves, despite his youthful appearance, acted the able shadow. Kitty leaned back in her chair and studied both men. In your minds, she concluded, the result of this inquiry is a foregone conclusion.

'Jack Allerton,' Fairfax began. 'You were born in Caundon in September eighteen ninety-six? You are a miner by trade and you volunteered for the Durham Regiment at the outbreak of the war. True?'

'Yes,' Jack replied.

'And you served with what is now called a Company of Friends which included Evans, O'Neill and Cunningham.'

'There were a lot more!' Cunningham shouted down the table. 'But they gave their lives as heroes!'

'Hush now,' Morrison ordered. 'Let the major have his say.'

'Your close friend Billy Hammond joined at the same time. You were members of the same company. Your commanding officer was Colonel Henry Morrison.'

'Who is now the presiding magistrate,' Kurtz broke in.

'I am only here as an official,' Morrison explained. 'I will make no judgements. That is a matter for Major Fairfax.'

'Both of you served with distinction.' Fairfax kept his eyes on the file. 'You earned a reputation as,' he looked up, 'brave soldiers. No mention of any dishonour. Your own colonel thought you were officer material but you refused. Why?'

'Apart from our commanding officer,' Jack replied tartly, 'we didn't like officers. It's remarkable how many of them were fools, more intent on getting themselves and their men killed than the enemy.'

His words were greeted by a burst of laughter from his companions. Morrison clicked his tongue. Hargreaves glared angrily across. Jack smiled sweetly back.

Hargreaves took up the questioning. 'Now, in the summer of nineteen thirteen,' he glanced quickly at Kitty, 'Billy Hammond married Kitty. We understand from common report that you, Kitty and Billy had virtually grown up together. Father Headon, your local priest, called you the "Trinity". You were hardly ever alone, always together. You—'

'We were the best of friends,' Jack interrupted. 'Do you know what a friend is, Hargreaves?' He tapped his hands gently on the tablecloth.

'But,' said Fairfax, 'you were not happy that Billy Hammond married Kitty. At first you hid your resentment.' He pointed down the table. 'But, if I question your companions, and they are on oath, they would say this resentment surfaced and, while you and Billy were in France, it led to harsh words. Isn't that true?'

'You don't have to question them!' Jack snapped. 'Of course I felt resentment. I, too, loved Kitty but, above all,' Jack turned and glanced at his wife, 'I realised that Billy and Kitty's marriage brought to an end a lifelong friendship among the three of us. Matters would never be the same again. My wife knows this. Can I point out that, whatever the circumstances, if Kitty had been free, I would have asked for her hand. However, it was Billy, not myself or Kitty, who insisted that if he didn't return home and I did, I would look after her.'

'But we only have your word for that,' Hargreaves interrupted.

'No, you don't!' Kitty snapped. 'You have mine and Billy's. It's in his journal. He spoke to me about it. I remember the occasion well, the heartache it caused.'

'You are not on oath,' Hargreaves pointed out.

'It's still the truth.'

Fairfax nodded. He glanced across at her. 'You are not on trial, Kitty.'

'And neither is Jack,' Kurtz spoke up.

He was about to continue when there was the sound of footsteps outside, someone shouting. They heard the front door opening and shutting. Morrison sat for a while and shrugged.

'You'd best continue, Major.'

'Very well. I would like to take you, Mr Allerton, to the evening of the twenty-third of March nineteen seventeen.

You and your company were in the Vervins sector. The Durhams held one line, Australians on your left and the Berkshires on your right. The reports of all commanding officers agree that the Germans were massing for a possible attack. The weather was poor, the clouds low. Aircraft reconnaissance was impossible so night patrols went out.'

'That's correct.'

'And you offered to go with Billy Hammond?'

'Colonel Morrison asked for volunteers. Billy offered, so I went with him.'

'And how did you go?'

'On our bellies, over the top, swimming through mud whilst the Germans – well, you've read the reports. They were throwing everything at us. Billy and I, we had our helmets, rifles, our backpacks and masks in case of a gas attack.' He shrugged. 'I believe that's all.'

Morrison nodded in agreement. The room was completely silent. Kitty tensed.

'Can I remind you, Mr Allerton,' said Hargreaves, 'that you are on oath?'

'Aye, and I'm also on oath to Billy Hammond.'

Kitty closed her eyes and quietly prayed.

'Billy and I,' Jack continued, 'reached some barbed wire. It wasn't the German lines; they had put it up as a trap. We got through. Shells and whizz-bangs were falling, and I got separated from Billy. Suddenly I heard a scream. Terrible! I crawled back. Billy had lost his helmet and I couldn't find his rifle. He was lying twitching on the mud with a hideous stomach wound. A piece of shrapnel had cut deep and ripped him open.'

Kitty's mouth went dry. Now she was being told the truth, did she really want to hear it?

'Ask any doctor,' Jack continued in a matter-of-fact voice. 'There's nothing worse than a belly wound. It was really deep. Billy said he could feel every throb. His cries attracted the attention of the German machine-gunners. They opened up. Every time I moved Billy, his screams were hideous. I got him into a crater. We just lay there. I wanted to take him back but even when I tugged at his shirt collar he convulsed in pain. I struck a match – his face was white and sweat-soaked.'

Kitty grabbed the edge of the table to steady herself.

Fairfax, alarmed, leaned over. 'Are you all right, Kitty? Do you want to hear this?'

She ignored him and looked at Morrison. 'I am fine.' She glanced to her right: Evans, O'Neill and Cunningham sat, elbows on the table, hands to their mouths.

'The shelling continued.' Jack cleared his throat. 'Billy was a horrible mess. If I went for help, I might never make it. If I waited till morning, Billy's agonies would continue. I tried to move him once again. I offered to pull him through the mud on his back. Billy shook his head. Said he couldn't bear it. I'd fought for three years, I'd seen wounds of every description. I knew Billy could live perhaps a day, two days, in absolute agony but then he was going to die.'

'Did you have a revolver with you?' Hargreaves asked. 'A few hours before your reconnaissance, one of your lieutenants, Skelton, was killed. You and Daventry took his body down to the orderly station. They couldn't find his revolver.'

'I know nothing about Skelton's revolver,' Jack retorted. 'I didn't plunder the dead. I remember Skelton, young and bumptious. He wouldn't take advice. He was killed by a sniper because he disobeyed orders.'

Fairfax glanced at Morrison who'd closed his eyes as he tried to recall events.

'Yes, that's right,' the colonel agreed.

'Can you explain, sir?' Fairfax demanded.

'Yes, yes, I can, now Jack's reminded me. Skelton did disobey orders. He did something very stupid. He went out over the top in the afternoon. We were all anxious to know what the Boche were doing.'

'He thought he'd be a hero,' said Evans.

'How do you know?' Fairfax demanded.

'Skelton climbed on the platform,' Evans explained. 'He had his revolver out, standing like a hero from a *Boy's Own* paper. I was with him. I told him to be careful. He climbed the ladder. He must have been one foot from the trench when the German sniper got him. I pulled the lieutenant's body back and, as far as I remember, he was carrying no gun. It probably still lies out in the mud if some farmer hasn't dug it up!'

'You are on oath,' Hargreaves reminded him.

'Aye and so am I,' Cunningham declared. 'I was with Len. He needed help with the corpse – it got jammed on the ladder.'

Fairfax pursed his lips and made a note. 'Very well, Mr Allerton, let's return to you and Billy Hammond in that crater.'

'Billy drifted in and out of consciousness. He tried to control his sobs but the pain was intense.'

'And how did Billy Hammond, who was dying of a stomach wound, come to have a bullet from an English revolver in his head?' asked Hargreaves.

289

'He put it there himself.'

Kitty closed her eyes.

'That's a lie!' barked Hargreaves.

'No, it isn't,' Jack countered. 'The Germans were firing their machine guns. We could hear shouts and cries out in the darkness. An officer and two men from the Berkshires joined us. They were all agitated. One of the men had a slight leg wound. The officer, I think he was a major, had gashed his foot, more of an accident than a wound. I asked them if they could help with Billy. The officer agreed. We tried to lift him. Billy begged us not to. We had him almost out of the crater but, what with the wound and the Germans opening up again, we let him slide back. The officer said he had done his best, he wasn't going to wait any longer. They left. Billy was now just clutching his stomach, staring at me.'

Kitty fought back her tears.

'"Jack," Billy whispered. "You've done what you can. You really have. Just leave me here." I told him not to be a fool. Billy smiled back. "I doubt if I'll be seeing Caundon again. You know that, Jack, and so do I." He fumbled in his coat and handed me the watch. "Give that to Kitty. Tell her I love her, that I always will. Remember your promise to me, Jack." I was alarmed. I told him to stop talking like that. Billy wouldn't accept it. He forced the watch on me. I said I was going back to get help from the other lads. I didn't like the way Billy was talking so I took my rifle and threw it as far as I could. I left him my helmet and said I would be back. Billy grasped me by the hand. I could see a trickle of blood beginning to bubble between his lips. "Jack, one last thing." "What is it, Billy?" I asked. "Swear that you'll tell nobody about what happened tonight."' Jack put his face in his hands. 'I didn't know what he meant but I made him as comfortable as I could. He had no bayonet or rifle. I couldn't see any other weapon so I went out into the dark. Corpses lay about. It was black as hell. I could hear voices. I heard a pistol shot behind me. I crawled back, and as I did so I met the major from the Berkshires. He'd got himself lost. He had no weapons. He asked me if I had seen his revolver as he'd certainly had it in the crater. I just cursed. I knew what had happened. The officer, who'd also lost his two companions, came with me. I got into the crater. Billy was dead; lying nearby was a revolver. It was really dark. The officer thought Billy had died of his belly wound. He picked up his revolver.'

'You mean this officer didn't comment?'

'Comment!' Jack placed his hands on the table and leaned across. 'Lieutenant Hargreaves, you've fought in the war. We were out in no-man's-land, the Boche not too far away. Mortars, whizz-bangs and shells were exploding all around us. My best friend was dead. The officer had lost God knows how many men and was in a right panic. He couldn't comment!'

'Continue,' Fairfax said harshly, nudging Hargreaves.

'The officer from the Berkshires believed the Germans were on the move. He wanted to get out of the crater. Why should he be concerned with Billy? In his eyes he was just another corpse. What could I do? I had Billy's watch in my pocket. A shell landed nearby. Puffs of smoke rolled towards us. The officer thought it was a gas shell. That convinced both of us. We left the crater on our bellies. We parted in the dark. I don't know what happened to the officer. Just before dawn, I reached our lines and made my way back to Colonel Morrison's trench. The rest you know.' Jack turned and put his hand over Kitty's; it was ice-cold. Her face was pale as she sucked on her lips.

'I am not going to cry,' she whispered. 'I promise you.' Her voice grew stronger.

'Why didn't you tell me this?' Morrison demanded.

'I had made an oath to Billy. What could I say? Tell everyone that Billy Hammond had shot himself?' Jack squeezed Kitty's hand gently. 'You know what people think, those who weren't out there – oh, Billy took the easy way out, the coward's way. They'd forget about the wound, the hideous conditions, the certainty that he was going to die anyway. I kept my mouth shut and the watch hidden, to protect Billy, to protect Kitty and because of the oath I had taken.'

'And to protect yourself?' Hargreaves asked.

'Why should I want to protect myself? True, I felt guilty. Every time I think of it I wonder if I could have brought Billy back, but I did what I could and that's the truth of it.'

'So, you believe that Billy,' Fairfax balanced a pencil between two fingers, 'whilst being moved by Major Redmond – oh yes,' he saw the surprise on Jack's face, 'the same Major Redmond who is outside waiting – that Billy took Redmond's revolver, hid it on his person and, when you went out for help, shot himself?'

'Yes. He shot himself because of the wound and the pain he was in. Billy was a brave man,' Jack continued. 'He shot himself not only because of the pain. He knew I'd come back when I heard the shot. He didn't want me and his mates sacrificing ourselves for him.'

Morrison whistled beneath his breath. 'The story is logical enough, Major Fairfax. It fits with what I know both of Billy and of Jack.'

'Well, let's see what Major Redmond makes of all this.' Fairfax looked across at Jack.

'Ah!' Kurtz rapped the tabletop with his fingers. 'This Redmond has already been questioned by you?'

'Of course not,' Hargreaves scoffed.

'That is good.' Kurtz smiled grimly. 'Otherwise I'd say he was a tainted witness.'

'He has not been questioned,' Fairfax confirmed. 'Major Redmond wrote an account of that night's events which is similar to Jack Allerton's story. Redmond did go out to no-man's-land. He lost all but two of his men. He talked of finding two Durham lads in a crater, one of them badly wounded.'

'But,' Hargreaves interjected, 'he has no proof that Billy's belly wound was the result of enemy fire.'

'What are you saying?' Kitty leaned across, her face furious. 'That Jack caused that? Where's the proof?'

'Let me continue,' Fairfax said. 'Major Redmond was contacted by the Provost Marshal's Office. He is still on the reserve. I have never met him or spoken to him, and neither has Lieutenant Hargreaves. We will ask him questions. For all I know he may be the wrong man; he may have met two other people.

'We were the only Durham men in the area,' commented Morrison.

'In which case,' Fairfax gestured towards the door, 'perhaps we should see him now.'

Morrison picked up a small hand bell and rang it. The door opened and a black-suited butler stepped in.

'Ah, Stainesly. Ask Major Redmond to be kind enough to join us here.'

'Ah, yes, sir. But Mr Edmund Grant—'

'Never mind about him,' Morrison interrupted. 'Bring Major Redmond in.'

The butler shrugged and left.

A short while later Major Redmond was ushered into the room.

Chapter 15

Redmond was dressed in a double-breasted jacket, trousers, gaiters and smart, shiny black boots. He was a tall, balding man, harsh-faced with a drooping moustache. He sat down at the far end of the table. He took the oath Morrison administered and composed himself, hands clasped before him as if in prayer. At Fairfax's insistence he gave his full name, army rank and a short summary of his military service.

'Before you proceed, Major Redmond,' Ernst Kurtz intervened, 'do you know why you are here?'

'I do not.'

'And have you been briefed or given any information about a soldier in the Durham Regiment called Jack Allerton?'

'I have not.'

'And you are here of your own free accord?'

'I am but I would like to know why.'

Morrison lit his pipe and sat back, almost hidden by plumes of smoke. He wafted it away. 'Very good, Major Redmond. The reason you are here is as follows.'

Morrison gave a succinct description of Fairfax's case. Kitty watched this severe-faced officer lose his composure and begin to tug at his tightly starched collar.

'Major Redmond,' Fairfax pointed round the table, 'is there anyone here you recognise from your war days? Do get up and walk around.'

Redmond pushed back his chair. 'Well, I recognise Colonel Morrison. I met you, Major Fairfax and Lieutenant Hargreaves when I came in this morning.'

'And the others?'

Redmond walked slowly round the room. He stopped beside Kitty and smiled. 'I wish I had met someone as bonny as you in the trenches,' he laughed. 'No offence meant, ma'am.'

'None taken.'

Redmond studied Evans, Cunningham, O'Neill and stopped at Jack.

'Would you stand up, please?'

Jack got to his feet.

'Yes, I know you, a little older, not so pale, and a damned sight cleaner and better dressed.'

'You are sure?' asked Morrison.

'I was frightened as a rabbit that night,' Redmond confessed, 'but I would remember your accent.'

'Well, go on, man!' Morrison barked at Jack. 'Say something!'

'I recognise you too, sir. You're better looking now.'

Redmond snorted with laughter.

'Return to your chair,' Morrison said. He gestured at Fairfax to be quiet. 'I want you, Major, to tell me exactly, in your own words, what happened that night.'

Redmond obeyed. He spoke softly and to the point. Kitty

sighed with relief because his story agreed in almost every detail with Jack's. Hargreaves looked openly discomfited. Fairfax looked worried.

'This man,' Redmond pointed at Jack, 'was with another who was very badly wounded in the stomach from a piece of shrapnel.'

'Could that wound have been inflicted by Allerton?' Hargreaves asked quickly before Fairfax could stop him.

'Oh, don't be stupid!' Redmond snapped. 'It certainly wasn't a bullet wound. I picked up the man's body. If Mr Allerton had thrown a grenade at such close quarters he would not only have injured himself but blown his friend to smithereens.' Redmond shook his head. 'This is all a nonsense. Hammond – was that the other man's name?' He didn't wait for an answer. 'He was in terrible agony. Allerton was eager to pull him back to his own trench. We tried to help but it was impossible. So we left him there.'

'And you had your revolver in its pouch when you entered the crater?'

'I did. I knew it was there.'

'And when you left?'

'It was gone. I thought I had dropped it. I've told you what happened. I got separated from two of my men and found myself back in the crater. Again, Allerton was there. I also found my gun. It was near the dead man's body. I was in a hurry. I didn't know about the bullet wound to the head, it was dark. After a while, one corpse looks like another. God knows, there were so many out there that night. I took my revolver and left.'

'But Allerton had been there all the time you were gone, hadn't he?' Hargreaves asked

'Lieutenant Hargreaves!' Morrison snapped. 'You are leading this witness!'

'I have no way of knowing positively,' Redmond replied coldly. He had apparently taken a dislike to Hargreaves. 'I can only report what I saw that night. In my view Allerton was doing all he could to comfort and save his companion.'

Kitty looked down and tried to stop herself trembling.

'He was desperate for help,' Redmond continued. 'That's why we tried to assist. When I got back to my trench, I noticed my pistol had been fired, just once. I thought it was curious; that's why I can remember the details so well.'

'And you do not know whether or not Allerton stayed in the crater while you were gone?' Fairfax demanded.

'If I remember correctly, Allerton told me he had left the crater but had come back. He didn't tell me the reason why.'

'So, he said he left while you were gone,' Morrison insisted.

'Yes, sir, he did.'

'And you believed him?' Hargreaves challenged.

'Yes, I did. We used to become caked in mud. Our bodies were hot so it used to harden very quickly on our uniforms. When I met Allerton again, he was soaking wet.'

'So he had just returned?' Morrison asked.

'I believe so. In the confusion I didn't ask about it. I picked up my revolver and fled. I didn't want to be captured by the Germans.'

'And if you were on oath in court,' said Morrison, 'and you were asked to swear to the truth of this matter before a jury?'

'I would say that from what I saw, sir, Jack Allerton tried to save his friend Billy Hammond.' Redmond paused and glanced at Kitty, who fought back a sob. 'He seemed more intent on saving Hammond than he did himself. Kipling wrote, "Save the last bullet for yourself and go to your God like a soldier." I believe that's what Billy Hammond did. He wouldn't have been the first, or the last, man to do such a thing in that hideous, blood-spattered place!'

Kitty stared across at Fairfax. He had lost his cool poise. She glimpsed a look of regret. Was it for starting this business, she wondered, or for failing in it?

'Will that be all?' Redmond asked.

Morrison looked at Fairfax who shrugged. Redmond pushed back his chair and got to his feet. He saluted Morrison, turned and did the same to Jack.

At the door he stopped and asked, 'Am I the only witness?'

'No,' Hargreaves answered. 'There's Mr Edmund Grant.'

Redmond shook his head. 'I was with Mr Edmund Grant in the study. He became very agitated. He asked the butler for a sheet of writing paper and envelope, wrote something and fled. Didn't you hear him leave?' Redmond opened the door and quietly closed it behind him.

Hargreaves sat, lips compressed, staring at a point above Kitty's head. Fairfax drummed the tabletop with a pencil. Morrison looked severe but Kitty could see his eyes were dancing with merriment.

'Well, well, well,' the colonel murmured. 'Now this is a turn-up for the books. I wonder what happened to our grocer.' He picked up the handbell and rang it vigorously. Stainesly the butler came in, carrying a buff-coloured envelope on a silver platter.

'I didn't know Mr Grant had left,' said Morrison.

'I tried to tell you, sir,' the butler answered. 'He was very agitated, sir, pacing up and down, rubbing his hands together. I could see that he was most uncomfortable with Major Redmond. He wrote you a short note and left immediately.' Morrison took the envelope. 'Thank you, Stainesly. I think we'll have tea in the drawing room. These matters are now drawing to a close.'

The butler withdrew and Morrison, using a paperknife, opened the envelope. He read the note.

'Mr Grant no longer wishes to give evidence,' he declared.

Fairfax put his hand to his mouth.

'You'd best read it out, Colonel,' Hargreaves murmured.

'Dear Colonel Morrison, I would like to inform you that I feel no longer able to give evidence or assist you and Major Fairfax's inquiries over a certain incident which may have happened, during the war, involving the death of Billy Hammond. I have thought deeply about this matter and I have re-examined my son's letter. Only now, on reflection, do I realise this letter may not have been written by him but perhaps by some mischievous troublemaker. I would therefore like to withdraw any evidence or information I gave on this matter. I apologise for the inconvenience caused. Yours sincerely, Edmund Grant.'

Hargreaves threw his pencil down on the table. 'He should be arrested for wasting time!' he shouted.

'I don't think so,' Morrison replied sweetly. 'Edmund Grant supplied information which, at the time, he thought genuine. He has now had time to reflect before he went on oath. He has committed no crime and had the sense to both think and act prudently.'

'He was put under pressure,' Hargreaves retorted.

'What pressure?' Morrison bellowed, clutching the arms of the chair. 'I wouldn't entertain the man!'

'And I haven't spoken to him,' Jack declared.

Hargreaves was going to turn on the others but Fairfax tapped him lightly on the wrist.

'Leave it, Charles, this matter is at an end. Colonel Morrison, I would like to thank you. Mr Allerton, please accept my apologies and that of the Provost Marshal's Office for any inconvenience and distress caused.'

'You'll put that in writing?' Kurtz intervened.

'I'll put that in writing,' Fairfax confirmed.

'Well.' Morrison rubbed his hands together. 'That's concluded this business. I would like to see a copy of your report, Major Fairfax. As far as I am concerned,' he stared up at the ceiling, 'and I, too, have friends in parliament, this matter is closed.'

The meeting broke up. Morrison led them out of the library, down the gallery to the drawing room where the butler and maid had laid out a small buffet and the best china cups.

Morrison moved to his drinks cabinet, nodding to Redmond who was sitting on a chair just inside the door. 'I think we'll celebrate with something stronger.'

Kity refused but all the men took a tumbler of whisky.

'I want to propose a toast.' Morrison was now very much in charge. 'To brave soldiers, living and dead; in particular, Billy Hammond and Bob Daventry.' His eyes grew misty. 'It was a privilege and an honour to serve with those two as well as with those present!'

His words were greeted with shouts of approval. Hargreaves looked uncomfortable but Fairfax remained as calm and collected as ever. The maid came in and began to serve tea. Kitty wanted to thank Ernst Kurtz but, when she looked round, the German had gone. She, Jack and the rest gathered in the centre of the room. Fairfax and Hargreaves kept to themselves whilst Colonel Morrison took Redmond by the arm and led him to the window to show him the gardens.

'I wonder why Grant scuttled off like a rabbit?' said Evans.

'I don't know,' Jack replied. 'But I don't think he'll be staying long in Caundon. You can't do what he did and still serve tea and coffee the next morning. He has shops elsewhere. He should be told to move on.'

Kitty sipped her tea. She felt both elated and tired, as well as deeply sorry for what Jack had been through, the chaos and heartache Fairfax and Grant had caused in all their lives. She wanted to be away, absorb the details of Billy's death and be alone with Jack.

'Kitty, are you all right?'

She seized Jack's hand. 'I'm champion. Don't you worry about me, Jack.' She chewed her lip. 'I'm sorry Billy was in so much pain. I can see now,' she didn't care if the rest knew, 'why you didn't tell or give me the watch. I want to be alone for a while. No,' she smiled, 'not to grieve.'

Kitty finished her tea, went across and thanked Morrison. At the doorway she stopped, blew a kiss in Jack's direction and left.

Kitty stood outside on the path, staring up at the sky. She really should go back and thank Major Redmond but she knew Jack, he would be inviting him down to the Beaumont Arms. She wondered if she should visit Grant but decided not to, that would be dangerous. She gazed around. The trees were turning, some of the leaves were edged with gold; summer would be over soon and school would begin again.

She was angry but, to be truthful, she also felt cleansed and purged by Fairfax's visit. The guilt, the nostalgia, the petty recriminations had all disappeared. She had loved Billy and he'd been killed. She was now with Jack, her man, her husband. They could face anything life threw at them.

She heard the door open behind her but didn't turn. 'Major Fairfax. I hope you are leaving soon.'

'The evening train, Kitty. Will you be so pleased to see the back of me?'

'No, Oscar, more what you represent.'

'Can we speak?'

She turned. 'I will say goodbye to you, Major Fairfax, at the Beaumont Arms and, God forgive me, I don't want to see you again. Jack's a good man, he was a very brave soldier.' She walked towards Fairfax. 'People like my Billy and your brother died, I suppose, so we could live better lives.' The anger she had felt in the library now returned. 'I object, to the very depths of my soul, to men like Edmund Grant being able to pollute the waters of our life. Daventry's dead. Jack fell under suspicion. You moved so quickly, even I—'

'I don't think you were convinced,' Fairfax broke in. 'Not you, Kitty.' He dug his hands into his pockets. 'I keep thinking about what you said last night in the bar, about compassion. Perhaps you are right. I am going to write a report for the War Office and my superiors. I'll recommend that anything Edmund Grant says now or in the future be dismissed as a lie. I am sure ministers will let Mr Macclesfield know not to waste their time and that of the Provost Marshal's Office.'

'And Jack?' Kitty asked.

'That's the reason I came out. I want you to witness my apology. I pride myself on being an officer and a gentleman,

Kitty. I am going to speak to him directly in the presence of his commanding officer. Not because my inquiry has collapsed due to lack of evidence,' a muscle twitched high in his cheek, 'but because I now believe the allegations were downright lies. I will apologise for the grief and pain I have caused. Believe me, Kitty, I will make sure that grief and pain is known in other quarters. Will you come?'

Kitty shook her head. 'I know what you are saying is the truth. There is no need for me to witness it. It's a soldier's thing and every man in that room is a soldier. Let them hear it; that will be enough for me.'

Fairfax smiled. 'And Edmund Grant, Kitty? Did you have anything to do with changing his mind?'

'In a way, yes. I could have proved, Major Fairfax, that the so-called letter from his son was a forgery.'

Fairfax gave a half-smile. 'I heard about your visit to the village hall. The schoolroom lies above, doesn't it?' He threw his head back and laughed. 'Do you know, Kitty, I'll say this for you, and I don't want your husband to hear, otherwise he'll think I'm paying court to you. I did wonder why two men could love you so much but, like everything, I complicated it. You are a remarkable woman, Kitty Allerton, and quite a formidable opponent.' He put his hand in his jacket pocket and took out the silver cigarette case. 'Take this, Kitty. It belonged to my brother. He would have liked it to be in the hands of a woman like yourself. If I apologise it will only sound hollow; this is the best I can do.'

Kitty was about to refuse. Fairfax looked at her pleadingly.

'Do take it,' he urged. 'Keep it. It's something close to me, Kitty, and, when you touch it, think kindly of me.'

And, before she could reply, he was gone through the

half-open door. Kitty looked down at the silver cigarette case, stroking it with her fingers. She placed it carefully in her pocket.

I wonder why Edmund Grant changed his mind she mused. What frightened him so much? Redmond's evidence had certainly finished the case but Grant wouldn't have known that.

The door opened.

'Are you coming back in, Kitty?' Evans called.

'No, I'm not. Tell Jack I'll meet him at the gates.'

Edmund Grant, eyes glistening with tears of rage, fed the fire in the great iron bucket in his back yard. He tore the papers up and pushed them into the leaping flames. He was in a sweat, a mixture of anger and fear. He dreaded Fairfax coming to challenge his flight from the inquiry. Grant now bitterly conceded, at least to himself, that he had not thought this matter out. Resentment over the treatment of his son, his deep abiding lust for Kitty Allerton as well as his anger at the way Jack Allerton had supported both Kurtz and the Co-operative had driven him to act.

He heard a sound behind him and turned fearfully. He expected Fairfax but his frightened shop assistant opened the door for Kurtz.

'You have no right to come here again!' Grant shooed the boy away.

'I have every right, Edmund.' Kurtz closed the back door and leaned against it. He gestured at the bin. 'Destroying the evidence, are we? Your son wrote no such letter.'

'You've already told me that.'

'Aye.' Kurtz grinned. 'And Kitty Allerton would have proved it. What were you going to say, Edmund? May I call you Edmund? How would you have blustered it out in court?'

'I am not frightened of court. I still have friends,' Grant mumbled. 'I'll just tell Macclesfield I made a mistake.'

'But I am not your friend, am I, Edmund? And, last Monday, you did attack young Kitty in your back room.'

'I didn't attack her.'

'Oh, I'll say otherwise.'

'I am not frightened of Kitty Allerton.'

'No, Edmund.' Kurtz came to face him squarely. 'But you are frightened of me! I meant what I said when I came back on Monday, after I'd left Kitty in the schoolroom. I told you Jack would prove his innocence but you suspected that, didn't you?'

'Your threats mean nothing to me now.'

Kurtz poked his finger into Grant's plump stomach. 'My promise that Monday still holds. If you ever hurt, or try to hurt, my good friend Jack Allerton or his sweet wife Kitty, I'll come for you, Edmund Grant! In the dead of night I'll settle with you!'

'You'd hang for murder,' Grant blustered.

'Would I, Edmund? Even if I did, I'd die a happy man. But there'd be so many suspects! You don't think this is all going to drain away like water down a hole? Poor Daventry's death, Fairfax's investigation. Colonel Morrison, Evans, Cunningham, O'Neill – they all know what you tried to do.'

Grant blanched as he wiped the sweat from his forehead.

'Bit by bit, drop by drop,' Kurtz grinned, 'the story will come out and spread. I mean, Edmund, you are not popular, are you? Quite a few ladies in Caundon have good reason to dislike you. So, if anything happened to you, the list of suspects would be very long.' Kurtz turned and looked up at the house. 'Edmund, you have shops in other villages. Now, if I was your friend, I would strongly advise you to move away. You have done enough damage in this little community and I could think of a number of people, including myself, who would like to buy this shop. If you moved away, Edmund, then we really would be friends.' He pressed a forefinger against Grant's mouth. 'Think about what I have said, Edmund. I am sure you'll see I am being both truthful and reasonable.' Kurtz opened the back gate and left.

Grant stared at the iron bucket and watched the paper turn to ash. He closed his eyes, breathed in and coughed on the smoke. Kurtz was right, he was frightened of him. Last Monday the German had made matters very clear, with his quiet menaces and promises of bloody retribution. Grant had tried to brazen it out. He had gone to Caundon Hall to give evidence but the presence of that hard-faced Major Redmond had shaken him. Was he there to speak for Jack Allerton? Grant's nerve had finally failed and he'd fled. Perhaps it was time he moved on. He angrily kicked at a stone and, going back into the shop, vented his anger. He shouted at his assistants that they were to go home as he was closing the shop for the day.

In the Beaumont Arms Kitty sat on the bed and carefully put Billy's journal and photograph, as well as the silver cigarette case Fairfax had given her, into a square silk bag, a gift from her grandmother. She would keep them here as treasures. She felt a chapter in her life was closing. Billy was gone. She would never forget him. She would treasure the memories but Jack was her husband. In a way they would make Billy's death meaningful. One day they would have children. If it was a boy – she smiled and rubbed her stomach. No, there'd be two boys; and they'd called them Billy and Jack. She carefully put the silk bag away in the bottom drawer. She stood and listened to the faint sound of laughter from the bar below. The Dead Hand Club were meeting.

Kitty heard footsteps on the stairs, the sound of a case being carried, John's voice. Fairfax was leaving. He had told Kitty's mother that Hargreaves had returned to the Dovecote and that he intended to catch the late train to Darlington and from there proceed to London. Kitty felt tempted to open the door, go down and say goodbye. Yet what more could she say? She heard old John wheezing, mumbling at the weight of the bag, his shuffling footsteps followed by the sharp footfall of Fairfax. Kitty held her breath. Fairfax had stopped outside her door. Was he going to knock? She clasped her hands, closed her eyes but the footsteps continued downstairs.

'Thank God!' she sighed.

Her mother called but Kitty ignored her. She wouldn't leave this bedroom until she was sure Fairfax had left the Beaumont Arms. She sat down on the small stool before the mirror. Tonight she and Jack would have a party.

She heard a knock, a slight tap, and the door opened. Jack, his collar undone, grinned in at her.

'For God's sake, woman, aren't you coming downstairs? Major Redmond is entertaining all of us. He's not as dour as he looks.'

'Come in, Jack.'

He closed the door behind him. She went to him, put her arms round his waist and stared up at him.

'I love you, Jack Allerton, and I always will.' She embraced him and kissed him on the forehead. 'I am sorry,' she whispered. 'But so much happened, so quickly.'

'Oh Lord, lass, worse things happen down the pit.'

'We owe Ernst a lot.'

Jack pulled away and grinned. 'I'm beginning to suspect that. It's to do with Grant, isn't it?'

'He's just a liar and wished us ill.'

'Well, our officer friends have gone.' Jack playfully nudged her towards the bed. 'Now or later?' he teased.

'Definitely later.' She pushed him away. 'Is Ernst downstairs?'

'Of course he is. The Dead Hand Club have decided to widen its membership to include him. Germans are now welcome but not officers.' He opened the door and mockingly waved her forward. 'If the lady would like to join us?'

Major Fairfax strode up Caundon High Street. He stopped at Grant's shop, opened the door and went in. The grocer, all fearful, came bustling towards him. Grant took a packet of cigarettes down from a shelf. 'They are a gift,' he mumbled.

Fairfax knocked the cigarettes away, gripped him by the shoulder and squeezed hard. 'I do not want to hear from you again, Mr Grant. You are a liar. You always have been a liar and you will remain a liar. If I didn't want this matter closed and Jack and Kitty Allerton protected, I'd drag you down to London to face the wrath of my masters. I have just come to ask you one question, one that's never been answered. You seem to know a lot about what happened with that Company of Friends out in the trenches. I just want to confirm a suspicion. It was Daventry, wasn't it?

You got all your evidence, your facts from that poor man, didn't you? Before his mind really turned, you learnt all you could.'

Grant just blinked.

'Do you know what really upsets me, Mr Grant? It is being used by a man so full of hate and bile like yourself. I am resolved it will never happen again.' He shoved Grant away and walked out of the shop.

When Fairfax reached Caundon station, old Thompson told him he would have to wait for another twenty minutes. Had the officer enjoyed Caundon? he asked. Would he be coming back? Fairfax smiled and shook his head.

He went back outside, sat on a bench and stared down the cobbled street. The village was quiet now. Daventry's funeral and the party at the Beaumont Arms, which he had glimpsed but not joined, had drawn everyone in. Fairfax lit a cigarette. He leaned back and closed his eyes. He didn't feel too angry about Edmund Grant. Fairfax knew that the village of Caundon would soon take care of him. Hargreaves had been disappointed but, there again, he was a young, ambitious officer who resented the time spent to achieve so little. Fairfax was just pleased he had come here. Kitty Allerton had been worth it. He thought of her sweet face and jet-black hair; the way her cheeks would become flushed when she lost her temper; her courage and determination. Fairfax took his brandy flask out and undid the stopper.

'To you, Kitty! It'll be a long time before I meet your like again!'

He drank, put the stopper back and sat cradling the flask. He heard a sound and turned. The Ashcroft children were there. They'd heard all about this officer and recalled the way he had greeted them when he had first arrived. He stared at them, their thin arms, bare feet and dirt-stained faces.

'Does Kitty Allerton teach you?'

The elder one nodded.

'And is she a good teacher?'

Again the nod.

'Are you looking forward to going back to school?'

'Yes, we are.' The eldest one found her voice. 'Mrs Allerton is very kind. In autumn, before the weather turns, she always takes us out to Neville's Oak and tells us the most marvellous stories.'

'What's your name?'

'Mary, my name's Mary. Do you have a penny, mister?'

Fairfax turned away and drew on his cigarette. Mary Ashcroft looked at the harsh outline of his face. There were stories about this man. Some people claimed he was the cause of Bob Daventry's death. Mary remembered that he had given them nothing last time. She grabbed the dirty hands of her two companions and they returned to their usual listening post round the corner.

Fairfax heard the whistle of the incoming train. He got to his feet and felt in his pocket. He took out three half-crowns and placed them carefully along the bench.

'Mary Ashcroft!' he called.

The girl's head popped round the corner.

'I've left you a present.'

Mary gazed suspiciously back. Fairfax picked up his bag and walked into the station. The train pulled up in clouds of puffing steam. Behind him he heard Mary Ashcroft's screams of delight at the coins he'd left.

Fairfax stepped into the first-class carriage, carefully stowing

311

his baggage. He sat down. Once again he thought of Kitty Allerton and the events of the last few days. He leaned back, sighed and began to compose the letter of resignation he intended to submit on his return to London.

If you enjoyed this book here is a selection of other bestselling titles from Headline

THE TIES THAT BIND	Lyn Andrews	£5.99 ☐
WITH A LITTLE LUCK	Anne Baker	£5.99 ☐
LOVE ME TENDER	Anne Bennett	£5.99 ☐
WHEN THE PEDLAR CALLED	Harry Bowling	£5.99 ☐
REACH FOR TOMORROW	Rita Bradshaw	£5.99 ☐
WHEN THE LIGHTS COME ON AGAIN	Maggie Craig	£5.99 ☐
STAY AS SWEET AS YOU ARE	Joan Jonker	£5.99 ☐
CHASING THE DREAM	Janet MacLeod Trotter	£5.99 ☐
WHEN THE DAY IS DONE	Elizabeth Murphy	£5.99 ☐
MY SISTER SARAH	Victor Pemberton	£5.99 ☐
NO ONE PROMISED ME TOMORROW	June Tate	£5.99 ☐
THE SOUND OF HER LAUGHTER	Margaret Thornton	£5.99 ☐

Headline books are available at your local bookshop or newsagent. Alternatively, books can be ordered direct from the publisher. Just tick the titles you want and fill in the form below. Prices and availability subject to change without notice.

Buy four books from the selection above and get free postage and packaging and delivery within 48 hours. Just send a cheque or postal order made payable to Bookpoint Ltd to the value of the total cover price of the four books. Alternatively, if you wish to buy fewer than four books the following postage and packaging applies:

UK and BFPO £4.30 for one book; £6.30 for two books; £8.30 for three books.

Overseas and Eire: £4.80 for one book; £7.10 for 2 or 3 books (surface mail).

Please enclose a cheque or postal order made payable to *Bookpoint Limited*, and send to: Headline Publishing Ltd, 39 Milton Park, Abingdon, OXON OX14 4TD, UK.
Email Address: orders@bookpoint.co.uk

If you would prefer to pay by credit card, our call team would be delighted to take your order by telephone. Our direct line is 01235 400 414 (lines open 9.00 am–6.00 pm Monday to Saturday 24 hour message answering service). Alternatively you can send a fax on 01235 400 454.

Name ....

Address ....

....

....

If you would prefer to pay by credit card, please complete:
Please debit my Visa/Access/Diner's Card/American Express (delete as applicable) card number:

Signature .... Expiry Date ....